P9-BZR-351

The
Night
the
Lights
Went
Out

ALSO BY KAREN WHITE

The Color of Light

Learning to Breathe

Pieces of the Heart

The Memory of Water

The Lost Hours

On Folly Beach

Falling Home

The Beach Trees

Sea Change

After the Rain

The Time Between

A Long Time Gone

The Sound of Glass

The Forgotten Room
(cowritten with Beatriz Williams and Lauren Willig)

Flight Patterns

Spinning the Moon

The Tradd Street Series

The House on Tradd Street

The Girl on Legare Street

The Strangers on Montagu Street

Return to Tradd Street

The Guests on South Battery

The
Night
the
Lights
Went
Out

KAREN WHITE

BERKLEY
NEW YORK

BERKLEY
An imprint of Penguin Random House LLC
375 Hudson Street, New York, New York 10014

Copyright © 2017 by Harley House Books, LLC
Penguin Random House supports copyright. Copyright fuels creativity, encourages diverse
voices, promotes free speech, and creates a vibrant culture. Thank you for buying an authorized
edition of this book and for complying with copyright laws by not reproducing, scanning, or
distributing any part of it in any form without permission. You are supporting writers and
allowing Penguin Random House to continue to publish books for every reader.

BERKLEY is a registered trademark and the B colophon is a trademark of
Penguin Random House LLC.

Library of Congress Cataloging-in-Publication Data

Names: White, Karen (Karen S.), author.
Title: The night the lights went out / Karen White.
Description: First edition. | New York: Berkley, 2017.
Identifiers: LCCN 2016053299 (print) | LCCN 2017001224 (ebook) |
ISBN 9780451488381 (hardcover) | ISBN 9780451488398 (ebook)
Subjects: LCSH: Interpersonal relations—Fiction. | Divorced women—Fiction.
| Suburban life—Fiction. | BISAC: FICTION/Contemporary Women. |
FICTION/Family Life. | FICTION/Suspense.
Classification: LCC PS3623.H5776 N54 2017 (print) |
LCC PS3623.H5776 (ebook) | DDC 813/.6—dc23
LC record available at https://lccn.loc.gov/2016053299

First Edition: April 2017

Printed in the United States of America
1   3   5   7   9   10   8   6   4   2

Jacket photos: woman by Johner Images /
Getty Images; background by Karen White
Jacket design by Rita Frangie
Book design by Kelly Lipovich

This is a work of fiction. Names, characters, places, and incidents either are the product of the
author's imagination or are used fictitiously, and any resemblance to actual persons, living or
dead, business establishments, events, or locales is entirely coincidental.

To Connor, Georgia born and raised

Acknowledgments

Having lived in the real "Sweet Apple," Georgia, for more than twenty-four years, I have far too many people to thank here for inspiring this book. Just know that I appreciate your friendship, and love living here alongside all of you in this beautiful Atlanta suburb.

There are a few people, however, who helped me considerably with my research. Thank you to Joe, Sam, and George Ivey of Little River Farms for sharing their gift of time to tell me the wonderful stories of their family who have called Georgia home for generations, and who remembered what our corner of the world was like before subdivisions.

Thanks to FAO Tim Farnell of the City of Milton Fire Department for his insight into what happens in emergencies (and who has convinced me that I will need to put a fire in my next book to use all his research tips). And a huge thanks to Detective Scott Harrell of the City of Milton Police Department, whose patience in answering all my questions about police procedures was not only deeply appreciated but immeasurably helpful in the writing of this book.

Last but not least, a huge thanks to the usual suspects: my long-suffering husband, Tim White, who has forgotten what it's like to eat a home-cooked meal unless he's at someone else's house, and to Susan Crandall and Wendy Wax, talented authors who have gifted me with their friendship and critical eyes for longer than we would care to admit.

The
Night
the
Lights
Went
Out

THE PLAYING FIELDS BLOG

Observations of Suburban Life from Sweet Apple, Georgia
Written by: Your Neighbor

Installment #1: A Plague of Bulldozers and White Escalades

A woman at my hair salon today asked me where I'd learned to put on makeup. I considered this a compliment, having always taken good care of my skin for the sole purpose of making it a smooth palette on which to put makeup. I could tell she was a transplant to our north Atlanta suburb of Sweet Apple by her accent. And by her question. Every true Southern mama teaches her daughter about makeup. I think in some parts of the Deep South (like the Mississippi Delta), girls are born with makeup brushes clutched in their tiny hands. This might be hearsay, but have you ever noticed how many Miss Americas are from Mississippi?

She asked me to say a few words for her, like "honey" and "fiddledeedee" and "damn," to hear my accent, and then actually asked if I'd ever heard of the hanging of an innocent man around these parts. I had the sudden and horrible thought that those who aren't from around here might think that *Gone with the Wind* or that song about the night the lights went out in Georgia were true compasses showing what they might discover here in Sweet Apple.

That's when I decided I needed to write a blog, a sort of tutorial or map for the newcomers here. A way for them to educate themselves on the ways of the South and its natives before they do something heinous like wear white pants after Labor Day or show up at a funeral without a chafing dish full of Southern comfort food.

Just like all polite Southern conversations, this one, I thought, should start with the weather. For those newcomers who haven't yet experienced what we locals refer to as the furnace, the heat of a Georgia summer arrives suddenly. The cicadas begin their whirring song in the trees as a sort of advance warning, and by the time the tree frogs begin burping in unison, summer is here.

But if you live in one of our new neighborhoods, you won't be able to hear the cicadas or the frogs because of the incessant thumping of your neighbors' HVAC systems, rumbling all day long like an endless shouting match.

I'd like to suggest turning off the air-conditioning in the evenings when it's cooler, to hear yourselves think for a change. Hear the voices of your neighbors, even. It's easy to think we all live in our own air-conditioned bubbles, but we don't. We have to share our breathing space with our neighbors. And don't forget we're all supposed to love our neighbors no matter how difficult they sometimes make it. Like when they vote to bulldoze another farm, or park in the fire lane at Kroger, or tailgate me in their white Escalade (sometimes it's a Mercedes or BMW SUV and even the occasional Honda—but it's always white) even when I'm going the speed limit. Being late for a chemical peel does not give you the right to tailgate, no matter how uneven your skin tone. It's not very neighborly.

Yes, we're supposed to love our neighbors. Yet I still can't shake my daydreams where I come up with a thousand different ways in which I can make some of them disappear. Permanently. Thank heavens they're just daydreams.

One

MERILEE

Sweet Apple, Georgia
2016

I f there was one thing that Merilee Talbot Dunlap had learned in eleven years of marriage, it was the simple fact that you could live with a person for a long time and never really know him. That it was easy to accept the mask he wore as the real thing, happy in your oblivion, until one day the mask slipped. Or, as in Merilee's case, when it fell off completely and you were forced to face your own complicity in the masquerade.

No, she knew she hadn't made Michael have an affair with their daughter's third-grade math teacher. But she had allowed herself never to question any discrepancies in her marriage, content in her role as suburban wife and mother, until the props and scenery were pulled away and she was asked to exit stage right.

"Mommy?"

Merilee turned toward her ten-year-old daughter, Lily, blond and fine boned like her father but with a perpetually worried expression that was all her mother's. It seemed Lily already had a permanent furrow between her brows from the worry she'd been born with. The last months since the divorce and the stress from the upcoming move hadn't helped.

"Yes?"

"What if I don't meet any friends in my new school? And what if I don't have anybody to sit with at lunchtime? And I'm thinking I shouldn't be in the accelerated English class, because what if I'm not smart enough?"

Merilee carefully snapped down the lid of the plastic container she'd been filling with her collection of old maps. She'd been collecting them since she was a little girl, when she'd been in an antiquarian bookstore with her grandfather and he'd shown her an ink-drawn map. It had sketches of horses and cows and fences, and a cozy log cabin with smoke curling from its lone chimney.

"That's where you live," he'd said, pointing to the cabin.

It looked nothing like the white-columned brick house in Sandersville, Georgia, she'd lived in all her life and she had told him so, only to be made to understand that the cabin and everything around it had been plowed under to make room for her house and their neighbors' houses in the twenties, when he and Grandma weren't even born yet.

For a long time it had given her nightmares, thinking she could hear the cries of the people from the cabin, not completely sure they'd been removed before the demolition. It scared her to think of how temporary things could be, how your life, your house, your family, could be erased like a sand castle at the beach. And when her little brother had died, she'd known for sure.

Her grandfather had bought her the map, unaware he was fostering what would become a lifelong obsession. Merilee wasn't sure whether her love for old maps was because they reminded her of the grandfather she'd loved more than her own parents or because she'd needed proof that things changed. That no matter how good or bad things were, they were never permanent.

Merilee knelt down in front of Lily, silently cursing her ex-husband one more time. As if making her feel extraneous and unwanted weren't bad enough, his inability to keep his pants zipped and his eyes from wandering had added an extra layer of vulnerability to their daughter.

Gently holding her bony shoulders, she looked into Lily's pale blue eyes. "You've never had problems making friends. You're a nice person,

Lily, and that's why other girls like to include you. Remember that, okay? It's who you are, and if you stick with that, you'll be fine. And Windwood Academy is much smaller than your old school, which is a nice thing when you're the new kid. You'll know everybody in all of your classes pretty quickly."

"And if they don't like me?"

A little bit of the old spark lit her eyes, making Merilee inwardly sigh with relief. "I'm going to make them an offer they can't refuse."

Lily laughed her sweet laugh, a sound that evoked champagne bubbles popping, almost eradicating the guilt Merilee felt over having left *The Godfather* in the DVD player one night. It had been right after she'd learned of Michael's affair, when she'd felt the need to watch violent movies with lots of blood and bad language after the kids had been tucked into bed. Lily had flipped it on the next day thinking it was *The Princess Bride*, and in the five minutes it had taken for Merilee to realize what was happening, Lily had been exposed to more violence than she had seen in her entire ten years. After much apologizing and lectures about the difference between movies and real life, it had become a secret joke between them. For weeks Merilee had watched her daughter for any signs that she might need counseling, glad for once that her daughter had always had the maturity of a forty-year-old rather than that of the young girl she was.

Merilee stood, her right knee popping, yet another reminder of why her husband had wanted to trade her in for a younger model. "As for the accelerated English class, they put you in there for a reason. You'll do great. And if you find you don't like it, we'll move you—just give it a try. That's all I ask, all right?"

Lily's small chest rose and fell with an exaggerated sigh. "All right. Should I tell Colin to finish packing his suitcase?"

"I asked him to do that three hours ago. Where is he?"

Lily twisted her mouth, unsure of her role. She wasn't a tattletale, but she also liked to keep to a schedule. "He found a hole in the backyard and has been sitting in front of it waiting to see what might crawl out."

Merilee swallowed a groan of frustration. Her eight-year-old son had always moved to his own clock, content to study his world at its own pace. Merilee found it endearing and frustrating at the same time, especially on school mornings when Colin wanted to study how long it took for toothpaste to fall from the tube without his having to squeeze it.

"Would you please run out and remind him that I told Mrs. Prescott we'd meet her at three o'clock and it's almost two thirty? She's ninety-three and I really don't want to keep her waiting in this heat."

"Yes, ma'am." Lily ran from the room, blond hair flying, calling her brother's name with the harsh, authoritative tone Merilee recognized as her own. She bit her lip to prevent herself from calling out to remind Lily that Colin already had a mother.

She picked up the stack of plastic containers and moved to the garage, empty now except for the used Honda Odyssey minivan she'd bought with her own money. She'd let Michael keep the Mercedes SUV and his Audi, wanting the excision of him from her life to be a clean cut, even if it meant not having heated seats or a state-of-the-art stereo system. It was the principle of the matter. And at the moment, the only thing she had in abundance were principles.

Through the open rear door, Merilee spotted the jewelry roll she'd tucked into a back corner of the minivan. It was her brother's Lego figures. She'd taken them from his room without asking, knowing her mother would never have let her have anything that had belonged to David. Deanne had wanted to claim the grief as her own, dismissing anyone else's as not big enough to count. So Merilee had taken them and wrapped them in her Barbie jewelry roll and kept them hidden, taking them out only on the anniversary of David's death, as if somehow that might bring a part of him back. It had been a while since she'd done that, but still she kept them, hidden in her sock drawer as if afraid her mother might find them and ask for them back. As if David were still the precocious boy of seven instead of the twenty-nine-year-old young man he should be.

After tucking the last of the smaller boxes and their suitcases into the back of the Odyssey, Merilee made one final pass through the rooms of the now-empty home she'd lived in for less than two years. The rental house was already furnished, so it had almost been a relief to let Michael have all the furniture they'd accumulated over the past eleven years, and she'd felt a pang of regret only when their four-poster bed had been hauled into the moving van. It had been the bed where both of their children had been conceived. She imagined that if she ever had to see Tammy Garvey again, after the woman had been sleeping on that bed with Merilee's husband for a while, she'd mention that to her.

Having gone back inside, she listened to her footsteps echo against the bare walls as she moved from room to room. The house had never really felt like home to her, just as none of their previous four houses had. Michael thought they needed to upgrade every couple of years to keep up with his job success. They had moved into a bigger house in a nicer neighborhood each time, staying within the same school district to make it easier on the kids. And easier for Michael's affair, Merilee had realized much later.

Merilee thought she should be thankful for the frequent moves, knowing that leaving a beloved home would be almost as painful as leaving an eleven-year marriage. Or burying a favorite dog. Instead, this parting was as easy as pulling off a Band-Aid—it would sting a little but be forgotten as soon as they'd unpacked the first box in the new house.

The kids strapped themselves into the backseat of the minivan as Merilee headed down the driveway one last time and drove down the street without looking back. No neighbors came out to wave good-bye. She didn't know them well, having always worked and not had the time to build relationships in each of the neighborhoods they'd lived in, and hadn't expected any more fanfare when they left than when they'd arrived.

She waved good-bye to the guard at the front gate just as the first drops of rain began to pelt the dry asphalt and her dirty windshield, already splattered with the remains of dozens of insects. The rain and bugs were, Merilee thought, a fitting tribute to her old life, the one she couldn't quite let go of yet had no interest in holding on to, either. She thought of the boxes of old maps shifting around in the back of the minivan, reminding her again of the impermanence of things and how nothing stayed the same no matter how much you wanted it to.

SUGAR

Sugar Prescott sat at her dining room table in the front room of the old farmhouse, tapping out a letter to her best friend, Willa Faye Mackenzie Cox, on her 1949 Smith-Corona typewriter, her bottle of Wite-Out sitting nearby. She rarely had to use it but always wanted to make sure it was close by just in case. At ninety-three, she didn't have a lot of time to waste. And Willa Faye had all the time in the world to sit and wait for a letter. Her daughter had recently moved her to a senior living facility with the improbable name of the Manors. If there was one good thing about not having children, Sugar decided, it was being spared the indignity of being moved into such a place, like a box of old toys that a child has outgrown but doesn't want to get rid of completely.

She glanced outside, not wanting to miss the approach of her new renters. She hadn't met Merilee Dunlap or her children before, but the Realtor, Robin Henderson, who'd been handling the rental of the Craftsman cottage behind Sugar's farmhouse, had only good things to say about all three of them. Robin's children had attended Prescott Elementary with the Dunlap children, making Robin privy to the unsavory gossip surrounding the Dunlap divorce. Not one to gossip, but a good listener, Sugar had suggested the cottage as a good spot for the family to land while they decided what to do next. It wasn't as if she had any desire to befriend anyone, but Sugar had the feeling that Merilee Dunlap, whoever she was, was suddenly and unexpectedly on her own and in need of help. And Sugar was in a position to understand that need more than most. She suspected, but would deny if anyone asked, that she was getting soft in her old age.

She typed one last word, then drew the carriage back before standing and approaching the front window. The rain had tapered off, leaving a smoking, dripping landscape, her climbing roses on the front porch supports waterlogged, with petals opened as if gasping for breath. The small lake that sat in the front of the property, separated from the road by the white ranch rail fence, was thick like syrup, as brown as molasses because of the rain. She had a sudden image of her brother Jimmy sitting on the muddy bank, fishing for turtles, his feet bare and his freckled nose red and blistered. Although all four brothers were long gone, Sugar now found herself seeing them more and more, as if old age were nothing more than the past and present squeezing together like an accordion until no air was left.

She watched as a white minivan turned off the paved road onto the long drive leading around the lake to the farmhouse, winding between the stately oak trees that had been planted by her great-grandfather before the Civil War, their roots as wide as the trees were tall. The road was a ribbon of red Georgia clay, soft and muddy with rain, the minivan hugging the side, where grass gave the wheels some traction. Sugar smiled to herself, thinking that Merilee Dunlap knew something about driving in wet Georgia clay.

She moved to the front porch and waited for the minivan to pull to a stop. It wasn't ideal, sharing a driveway, seeing the comings and goings of her renters, but if there was one thing she wouldn't do, it was have one more strip of her property bulldozed for another driveway. Her brothers had done a good enough job of plowing under all the farmland the Prescott family had once owned, and she would not continue their legacy, no matter how inconvenient it was for her.

The woman who carefully stepped from the minivan wasn't what Sugar had expected. She was younger—mid-thirties, Sugar thought—and much prettier. As if men didn't divorce pretty women. She was surprised to find that she'd thought she'd be able to spot a flaw in her new tenant, something that would explain how she'd ended up in the predicament she was in. As if Sugar didn't know better.

"Hello," the woman said, stepping carefully onto the flagstone walkway before sliding open the side door of the minivan and waiting for two children to emerge. The children were as blond as the woman was dark. She had straight, no-nonsense brown hair, parted at the side, and hazel eyes that looked almost green. Her only makeup was a flick of mascara, a touch of nose powder, and a sheer gloss of exhaustion.

"I'm Merilee Dunlap," she said, extending her hand.

Sugar grasped the tips of her fingers, still unused to the way women shook hands these days, but didn't return the smile. She didn't want Merilee to think of her as anything more than her landlady. "And these must be your children, Lily and Colin."

"They are. Children, this is Mrs. Prescott, whose house we'll be renting." Both children extended hands as they were introduced, confirming to Sugar that their mother, despite other issues, had done a good job in teaching manners.

"Our old neighborhood was called Prescott Farms," said Lily, her eyes wide and earnest, her forehead creased as if she spent a lot of time trying to make sense of the world around her.

Sugar's mother had barely been cold in her grave before her oldest brother, Harry, sold the property for no other reason than somebody wanted to buy it. The memory still hurt. "Yes, well, that was part of my family's farm back when I was a little girl. Most everything around the county with the Prescott name on it used to belong to my family. But that was a while ago, when there were lots of Prescotts around these parts. Now there's only me."

Facing Merilee, she said, "Please call me Sugar. Everybody does. My real name's Alice Prescott Bates, but I've been known as Sugar Prescott my whole life and I see no need to change it now. I was married just a short time before I became a widow, so my married name really never stuck. And the children can call me Miss Sugar."

"I smell cookies," the boy said, looking up at her with a hopeful expression. His light blue eyes were the same shade as those of her youngest brother, Jimmy, making her forget, just for a moment, that he'd been gone more than seventy years. And in that moment of weakness, she stepped back to open the door wider. "Come on inside," she said. "They had sugar on sale at Kroger, so I had to bake a batch of chocolate chip cookies. If you don't want them, I'll have to give them to my friend at the nursing home, because I don't eat them."

"We really don't mean to intrude," Merilee said, a hand on each child's shoulder.

"Yes, well, the cookies won't eat themselves, so somebody has to."

The little girl's eyebrows knitted together. "Are they gluten free? I keep having tummy aches and my friend Beth says I probably have a gluten allergy."

Merilee put her arm around Lily and sent a pained look at Sugar. "She's never been allergic to chocolate chip cookies before. I think the upheaval of the last few months has just given us all a bit of a stomach upset."

"My tummy's fine," Colin announced. "I can eat Lily's if she doesn't want them."

Sugar began leading the way back to the kitchen, then stopped as Colin paused at the threshold to the dining room and pointed at the typewriter. "What's that?"

Sugar took a deep breath, more concerned about future generations now than she'd been ten minutes before. "That's a typewriter. It's what people used to use before computers. I used to have a good-housekeeping column in the *Atlanta Journal* back in the day, and they gave me this typewriter when they retired both me and the column in 1982."

His eyes widened as if he were being presented with the key to Disney World. "Wow. That was way before I was born." With a quizzical expression on his face, he turned his head to look up at Sugar. "So you must be very old."

"Colin . . . ," Merilee began.

Sugar waved her hand in the air, stopping her. "You are correct, Colin. I am very old. Ninety-four in December, as a matter of fact. Thank you kindly for pointing that out."

Lily was frowning again, or maybe she hadn't stopped. Pointing at the typewriter, she said, "Does that mean we don't have Wi-Fi in the new house?"

All three new tenants looked at her with panicked faces.

"The young man I hired to update the house said he'd make sure it had all the modern conveniences. His name is Wade Kimball. I've got his card in the kitchen, which I'll give you so you can call him directly with any questions, as I do not involve myself with modern technology if I can help it."

"I've got to have Wi-Fi," Lily said, still frowning. "I need to access the school portal to check on assignments. I learned all about it in orientation last week."

Merilee's voice sounded weary. "I'm sure Mr. Kimball can get us set up right away if it's not there already."

"That's right," Sugar said matter-of-factly, taking the plastic wrap off the cookies and putting the plate in the middle of the large kitchen table. "No use borrowing worries."

Merilee smiled, her face relaxed for the first time. "My grandfather used to say that."

"Wise man," Sugar said.

"That he was." Merilee's face became strained again as she turned to her children and made sure they took only two cookies and placed their napkins in their laps. She didn't ask for her own cookie, and Sugar didn't offer her one. They'd already been there longer than Sugar had anticipated.

"Don't get any crumbs on the floor, children," Merilee said, hovering near the table, seemingly as eager to leave as Sugar was for them to go.

While Sugar poured two glasses of milk, Merilee moved to the large picture window behind the sink, a real farmhouse sink that had been installed in the house before they'd become popular as a decorating focal point.

"You can see our house from here," Merilee said.

Well. "Don't worry. I won't be snooping in your business."

Merilee's cheeks pinkened. "No, that's not what I meant. It's just, well, I guess I'm just used to living in a neighborhood with people on all sides. When Robin showed me the house I almost said no because it seemed too isolated."

The younger woman looked so young, so vulnerable, that for the second time that day Sugar forgot that she didn't want a relationship with her tenants. "What made you change your mind?"

Merilee didn't pause. "It's close to the children's activities and their new school and the right price. I didn't have a lot of options. And the house and all this land are lovely. Perfect, really."

After a moment's hesitation, Sugar put the glasses on the table and moved to stand by the window next to Merilee. The clouds wore streaks of pink as the late-afternoon sun shredded them like cotton candy, and she saw all four brothers again as they'd been as children, bare chested and barefoot, running across the pasture toward the woods, hollering like stuck pigs. "I think your children will like living there. I grew up here in this house with my four brothers—I was the youngest child. My daddy built the house you'll be living in when I got married. Didn't live there long on account of my Tom getting killed in the war. But the house is good, solid construction—not like what they build nowadays. And there's a cellar for when there's a tornado. Make sure you know how to get in and out and how to latch it. Nearest tornado siren's about three miles away and you might not hear it."

"Thank you," Merilee said quietly, peering closely at the line of trees behind her new house. "Do those woods belong to you?"

Sugar kept her breathing even. "Yes, they do. But I wouldn't encourage you or the children to explore. There's a barn on the far side that might be a temptation, but that's also off-limits, mostly because kids will think the woods are a good shortcut. They're not. They're very dark and deep if you don't know where you're going. And we still have black bears and more poisonous snakes than I can shake a stick at. It's just better if you and the children stay away from the woods."

She felt the young woman's eyes on her but didn't turn.

"Look, Mommy—a rainbow!" Colin sprayed crumbs from his full mouth.

Before Merilee could say anything to him, his sister joined them at the window. "If I had an iPhone, I could take a picture."

Merilee's sigh was almost imperceptible. "Yes, well, you're ten. You don't need an iPhone. Where's the small camera I bought you for Christmas?"

"It's so inconvenient." Lily paused for a moment, as if to make sure everyone had heard her big word, which she'd probably picked up from her mother. "If I had an iPhone, my camera would already be in my purse."

"You don't have a purse," her mother pointed out.

Lily frowned as Colin shoved another cookie into his mouth, undoubtedly hoping that the conversation with his sister had distracted their mother.

"I saw that, Colin," said Merilee without even turning her head. "Which means you're not leaving the supper table until you eat all your vegetables, regardless of how long it takes."

Colin swallowed thickly. "Yes, ma'am."

Merilee looked up at the sky, pale pink now, the clouds bruised with shadows. "Thank you for the cookies and milk for the children. The rain's completely stopped, so we should get going. I'd like to get our clothes hung and our suitcases unpacked before bedtime." She stared out the window for a long moment without stepping away. "How perfectly quiet and still those woods must be. Like time's being held back or something, you know?"

Without responding, Sugar turned back to the kitchen table and placed two paper plates and a box of plastic wrap in front of the children, with instructions to divide the cookies evenly. She'd never had children, but she'd had siblings, so she understood the importance of equal measure. Then she pulled out Wade's business card from a drawer and handed it to Merilee.

"Call him anytime. If there are any repairs, he'll give me a fair estimate and will actually show up when he's supposed to."

Merilee studied the card. "So he's like a handyman? I'm looking for someone to build me more bookshelves for a collection I have."

"Just call him directly—I don't like to be . . . involved with any tenant issues. He's very handy because he's a builder, but he does work for me because his grandma is my best friend and I've known him since he was in diapers. Just let him know who you are and he won't say no."

"Thank you," Merilee said, taking the card.

Sugar gave Merilee the keys to the cottage before walking them to the door. "I had my housekeeper put clean sheets on all the beds. There are clean towels in the linen closet in the hallway and in both bathrooms. You'll be responsible for keeping it clean from here on out."

"Thank you, Mrs. Prescott . . . Sugar. You've been more than kind."

"I didn't do it to be kind. I did it because it's my job. And because I don't want a phone call in the middle of my shows asking where all the sheets and towels are."

Merilee's smile faltered as Sugar held the door open to let them pass, noticing the frown on Lily's face.

"Can you call Mr. Kimball now, Mom? I need to make sure we have Wi-Fi."

"Please stop worrying, Lily. I'll call him in just a minute." There was an edge to Merilee's voice that hadn't been there before. As if her last nerve had already snapped and she was grabbing at its threads.

Sugar turned to Merilee. "Just remember what I told you about the woods. They're fine to admire from a distance, but they're not safe."

"Got it," she said, sliding open the back door of the minivan. "With school starting and all their activities, I doubt we'll have much time for exploring anyway."

They said good-bye, then pulled away, Sugar watching all three heads strain forward in their seats as they waited for the sight of their new home to loom into view from under the canopy of the oak trees, baby birds looking for sustenance.

She listened to the drip of water trickling off the porch roof and onto the old wood steps. Looking up at the sky, she stepped off the porch and into the drive, aware of the hum of the Honda's engine in front of her, just out of sight behind the oaks. Like so much in her life now, Sugar didn't need to see things to know they were there.

She allowed her eyes to follow the rainbow, noticing its colorful arches ending in the middle of her woods. She didn't need to go there to know there was no bag of gold or anything else a person would want to find. Her lips turned up in an unfamiliar grimace as she headed back inside, feeling the breeze from the opened windows teasing her with the scent of rain and old memories that seemed as permanent as the red clay that lay beneath her feet and under the tall pines of the dark woods.

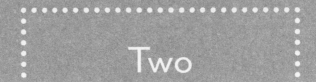

Two

MERILEE

A cluster of moms surrounded by high-end SUVs stood in the parking lot following first-day drop-off at Windwood Academy. The women appeared to be listening with rapt attention to the tall blond woman in the center of their semicircle, her hair arranged perfectly beneath her white tennis visor, her long and lean limbs brown and glowy. Merilee noticed this last part only because her ex-mother-in-law had given her a bottle of glowy lotion for her last birthday and Lily had told her it made her look sparkly like Katy Perry in one of her videos. Merilee had thrown out the remainder of the bottle, realizing she wasn't the type anymore to look glowy, much less sparkly.

But the blonde definitely was. Her whole body glowed. Her face glowed. Even the hair visible beneath the visor appeared to be lit from within. The woman looked vaguely familiar, and Merilee realized she'd probably been one of the mothers she'd met at the open house the previous week. She'd only been to the one "let's get acquainted" event, her work schedule precluding her attendance at any of the various parties that were held almost exclusively on weekdays.

Merilee was terrible with names, had been ever since she started dating Michael. He was so good at it, always reminding her who everyone was when they were at a party, that she'd simply stopped trying. She hoped she was only out of practice instead of permanently disabled. Her children's futures probably depended on it, since Michael wouldn't be there to make sure Merilee remembered the names of Lily's friends who were or were not speaking to each other. And which of Colin's teachers appreciated his dreamy attitude and which didn't. It had always been a game with them, her recalling every detail about a friend or teacher—details always overlooked by Michael—and then he'd fill in the missing part, the name. But now she had to do it all on her own.

She smiled vaguely in the direction of the blond woman and her entourage and had almost made it to her minivan when she heard her name being called.

"Merilee? Merilee Dunlap?"

Great. The woman remembered not only her first name but her last as well. Forcing a warm smile on her face, Merilee turned. "Oh, hello. It's good to see you again."

The other women parted like the Red Sea as the tall blonde walked toward Merilee, and she remembered that the woman had been wearing a Lilly Pulitzer sundress and two-carat diamond stud earrings when they'd met before. But she didn't remember her name. "I thought that was you. I looked for you in Mrs. Marshall's homeroom. I'm the room mother and wanted to welcome Lily myself."

Merilee remembered the voice. It was very Southern, heavily laced with dropped consonants and elongated vowels. The most memorable part about it was that it sounded exactly like Merilee's mother did.

"We were running a bit late this morning." Feeling suddenly short and frumpy in her dark skirt and blazer, Merilee had the strong urge to explain. "My son couldn't find his new uniform shoes. They somehow managed to find their way back into the box they came in and then got shoved so far under his bed that it took nearly twenty minutes to locate them. And then Lily spilled her bowl of cereal and milk down the front of her skirt, and I had to quickly iron one of her other ones so she could wear it."

The woman gave her a warm smile from behind dark Chanel sunglasses as if she knew exactly what it was like to be a frazzled single mother. "Bless your heart. And on the first day at a new school. You'll get used to the routine—I promise. It took me a whole month to realize that I should have a skirt and blouse for every school day plus one, and have Patricia have them cleaned and ironed as soon as my girls dropped them on the floor."

Not exactly sure how to respond, Merilee picked out the first confusing part of the sentence. "Patricia?"

"My house manager. I couldn't live without her. You know how crazy busy it is with all the kids' schedules." She reached into her large handbag, which was more briefcase than purse, with a designer's logo sprouting over its surface like kudzu. "I was going to stick this in the mail to you, but since you're here I'll give it to you now. It's a sign-up sheet for parties and field trips—it lists everything for the year. Just let me know your availabilities and ask Lily to bring it in to school and give it to Bailey as soon as you can. Bailey is very responsible and will make sure it gets to me." The woman smiled, her teeth perfect. "Only sign up for four—every mother wants to be at every single event, but then it just gets crowded—plus there won't be room on the bus for the kids."

"Only four . . ." Merilee took the list and looked at it, almost letting out an audible sigh when she saw the woman's name at the top of the page, *Heather Blackford, Class Mother,* followed by three different phone numbers. Now she remembered. Heather had a daughter in Colin's class, too, both girls' names starting with "B."

"Yes. And if you could turn it back in tomorrow, that would be terrific. I'll have Claire put it all in a spreadsheet and I'll e-mail it to all the mothers. Please write neatly—Claire has a way of butchering your name if she can't read it."

"Claire?"

"My personal assistant. She's only part-time, but I would simply *die* of exhaustion without her."

The ladies behind her all nodded in understanding.

"Yes, well, I'll take a look at it and get it back to you tomorrow." Merilee was already wondering how she was going to approach her boss to ask him for more time off. The divorce and move had already eaten up most of her vacation time, and although Max was kind and understanding, everyone had their limits.

"And don't forget the 'I survived my first week of fourth grade' party at my lake house this Saturday. I'll be handing out disposable cameras to all the moms and dads to take pictures throughout the year at our various events—I like to do little photo albums for all the kids and the teachers at the end of the year." She beamed, like it was just a small thing. "Oh, and I took the liberty of signing you up for a dessert because we're overrun with vegetables and dip and pimento cheese. I figured you'd know how to make something sweet."

"Oh . . ." Merilee simply blinked her eyes for a moment, wondering whether Heather had meant to be insulting by implying Merilee's lack of a perfect figure meant she ate a lot of sweets.

"Because you're from south Georgia. You mentioned that when we met. You said I had the same accent as your mother."

Feeing oddly relieved, Merilee said, "Yes, of course. Where did you say you were from?"

"Here and there—but mostly Georgia. I can always tell a native Georgian. Hard to hide it, isn't it? It's almost like no matter how far you go in life, all you have to do is open your mouth and somebody knows exactly where you're from."

There was something in the way Heather said it that made Merilee pause. "Yes, well, I'll call my mother today and ask her what she might recommend."

"Wonderful." Heather beamed. She pointed a key fob toward a black Porsche SUV with vanity plates that read YERSERV, and the rear door slowly raised. As the other mothers oohed and aahed appropriately, Merilee stared into the trunk, where fourteen metallic gift bags with blue or pink tissue paper expertly pleated at the top were arranged in neat rows.

Heather moved toward the car. "A little lagniappe—that's Cajun for 'a little extra' for all my Yankee friends—for the first day of school. My treat. I thought we could each give our children a bag at pickup today and then head over to Scoops for ice cream afterward. I've already reserved the party room at the back of the store. Claire is picking up the helium balloons this morning and will have it all decorated in Windwood colors."

"You are just too much," one of the mothers said as the other women eagerly stepped toward the car and took a bag.

There was something in the tone of voice that made Merilee glance over at the woman who'd spoken. She wore a floral dress, not particularly stylish or flattering, along with pantyhose and pumps, and was, Merilee noticed, the only other mother besides herself who wasn't dressed in tennis garb. And, like Merilee, was the only other mother not smiling. The woman caught her gaze and raised her eyebrows before grabbing two pink bags and bringing one back to Merilee.

"I'm Lindi Matthews, Jenna's mom." Merilee took the outstretched hand and shook it, amazed at the strength of the grip considering how very thin Lindi was. She looked like a runner, very long and lean, with no fat in her cheeks or neck. When Merilee had suggested to Michael that she start running to lose the weight that had crept up on her since giving birth to their two children, he had said he didn't like the idea, that he didn't want her to look all chicken necked. Apparently, he didn't like her looking slightly plump, either.

Lindi smiled, and Merilee thought she was pretty in a natural, no-makeup way, a distinct contrast to the other mothers, who appeared to be wearing full makeup to play tennis. Assuming they actually participated in the sport and didn't just wear the cute skirts—like yoga pants, which weren't actually an indicator of whether you practiced yoga. "I didn't get to meet you at the open house because I had to leave early for a work thing. I take it you're new," Lindi said.

"New to Windwood Academy, but we've lived in Sweet Apple for six years. We've been at the public school since the beginning, but my in-laws thought the kids needed a change."

Lindi regarded her with light brown eyes. "Your in-laws?"

"I'm recently divorced, and, well, it got uncomfortable at their school because of certain . . . people, and my in-laws thought it best we move the children. They're paying for it, so I couldn't argue. Besides, they're in Dallas and this is the only way they could probably think of to help me out long-distance. They're on my side, if there's such a thing."

"Wow. Well, that's a story for after we know each other better. I have a feeling we have a lot in common."

Her accent was definitely not Southern, so Merilee guessed at the next obvious thing. "Are you divorced?"

Lindi shook her head. "No. But I don't play tennis. Or golf. And I work outside the home." She indicated Merilee's outfit. "We're like unicorns here at Windwood."

It was such a relief to hear somebody put it into words that Merilee laughed out loud, making the other mothers look over at them.

"It's easy to be intimidated by this crowd, but they're a good bunch. Just a little . . . intense. Especially Heather." Lindi pressed a business card in her hand. "Call me. We should have coffee. I can fill you in on some of the stuff that doesn't get covered in the new-parent orientation. I'm on the school board, so I've got insider information." She winked. "Seriously, though, call me with any questions you might have. From one unicorn to another."

Merilee smiled. "Thanks. I will. Actually, I do have a question. I'm looking for a carpool partner. Any idea where I can go to find someone who lives near me? My kids have always taken the school bus, so this is completely new to me."

"I can probably help you. Where do you live?"

"Near the intersection of Prescott Bend and Prescott Road."

Lindi tilted her head. "That's the Prescott farm, isn't it?"

"Almost. I'm renting the old cottage behind the house."

"You're renting from Sugar Prescott?" Heather approached, her smile still wide and pleasant but her voice strident.

"For the next six months, at least. It's a beautiful little cottage, and so peaceful with the small lake and the woods. It's like a place out of time. The children and I really like it."

Heather's expression turned to one of concern. "I hope you don't have to deal too much with Sugar. She's two years older than dirt and just as mean. I had a little run-in with her at the drugstore—remember, Liz?" She turned to a petite brunette whose face was barely visible beneath her tennis visor as she nodded vigorously. "It was when Brooke was having those horrible spring allergies and I needed to get her medicine—and we were so late for her tennis lesson. Sugar was very unpleasant about giving up her spot in line; I'll tell you that much."

"How horrible for you," Lindi said, her face serious. "Well, I've got to go," she said to Merilee. "I'll think about potential carpool partners and let you know."

"Thanks," Merilee said, waving the business card. "I'll text you so you have my number."

"Bye, ladies," Lindi said with a quick wave. "I'll see you at the lake party on Saturday."

Merilee watched as Lindi slid into a white Prius, then looked down at the business card. LINDI F. MATTHEWS. MATTHEWS AND MATTHEWS, FAMILY LAW.

Heather touched Merilee's arm. "We were just about to head out to the new coffee shop, Cups, to get better acquainted. I hope you can join us."

Merilee glanced at her watch, horrified to see how late it already was. "I would love to, but I have to work."

Heather smiled sweetly, but there was a note of disapproval in her voice. "We all work, honey. But it's important for our children that we moms take time out for ourselves."

"I know—and you're right. Maybe next time. It's just that it's going to be a busy day and I don't like to drop last-minute surprises on the nice people I work for."

"Where do you work?" asked the petite Liz.

"I work for Stevens & Sons in Roswell. I'm their marketing manager."

There was a short silence before another woman, indistinguishable from the others in her tennis whites, asked, "The jewelry store? The one where Usher is always in the TV ads?"

"Yes, he's shot a few ads for us, since he's local. Very nice man."

"He's so hot," one of the women said, and then slapped her hand over her mouth as if it had spoken without her permission.

Merilee jiggled the sign-up sheet. "I'll fill this out tonight and send it in with Lily tomorrow. And I'll bring dessert to the party on Saturday."

Everyone smiled and waved, and Merilee started for her car before she remembered something else. "Is there room for me to bring my son to the party? I'm not sure if I can find someone to watch him."

Heather smiled widely. "Of course—siblings are always welcome at my parties. We should have enough room for one more."

"Great—thanks again."

She said good-bye, then climbed into her minivan, pausing to hit her parents' phone number. She missed her Bluetooth from her old car, feeling like a dinosaur as she drove past the other mothers, smiling because she didn't have a free hand to wave.

It rang nine times before her mother picked up. Her parents had only a landline, believing for ten years now that smartphones were only a fad.

"Hello, Mama. It's Merilee."

"I know. You're the only person I know who would ever think to call this early."

Merilee took a deep breath, eyeing the pink gift bag on her passenger seat and wishing she'd stopped to look inside it before she headed out of the parking lot.

"Did I wake you?"

"Of course not. I'm up early every morning. I just don't enjoy having to have a conversation this early."

"I'm sorry. I'll make this quick. Do you remember when I was little and you used to make those amazing peanut butter fudge brownies to take down to the beach house at Tybee? I'd like to make those for a party for Lily's class—"

"No. And you know why. I'm surprised and not a little disappointed that you would even think to ask."

Merilee thought back to her Lamaze classes, focusing on her breathing so she'd stop feeling so light-headed. "Mama, they're only brownies, for goodness' sake. And they're so good. It's been such a long time—"

"Now I've got a headache. Thank you, Merilee, for starting my day off by bringing up Tybee and those horrible memories."

"They weren't all horrible, Mama. There were so many good ones, and I wish you'd reconsider—"

She heard a fumbling sound and then her father's voice. "Merilee? Why are you giving your mother a headache? I hope you're not talking about your divorce—you know how upsetting it is for your mother. I think it's best if we hang up now until you've calmed down and can talk about more civil subjects. Good-bye, Merilee. We'll talk to you soon."

Merilee hit "end" before she could hear the click from her father hanging up the phone. She pulled over onto the shoulder of the road, not trusting her shaking hands to hold the steering wheel straight. She practiced her deep breathing for a moment, until she was distracted by the bag on the seat beside her and picked it up. Being careful not to disturb the tissue paper too much—Lily would be able to tell—she parted it carefully and looked inside.

She'd expected a small bottle of blowing bubbles and maybe a bag of chips or a cookie. Instead, she pulled out a black-and-white gift card from Sephora worth twenty dollars. Merilee's first thought was to call a friend to discuss how odd this gift was for a ten-year-old, and if she should get a gift for Colin just in case his room mother hadn't seen the need for a little first-day-of-school lagniappe. And then she realized that she'd jettisoned all her old friends along with her marriage and house.

Not that she'd had any close friends—at least not since high school and college. She'd left her old friends behind along with her hometown and the memories it contained. Besides, she'd always worked full-time, which didn't allow time to build close friendships with the other mothers at school. She'd worked not because they needed her income, but because Merilee never wanted to be as dependent on her husband as her mother was on her father. But, as her mother had pointed out more than once, look where her independence had gotten her.

She took a deep, shuddering breath, feeling the trembling in her fingers begin to subside, then let her gaze fall to the floor on the passenger side, where a small box of her antique maps sat, apparently forgotten during the unloading. Reaching over, she picked it up and set it on her lap, resisting the urge to reach inside and follow a random map to an unknown destination. She couldn't, of course. There were Lily and Colin—the best things that had ever happened to her—and she had a strong suspicion that she needed them as much as they needed her right now.

As she put the car in drive and pulled out into traffic, she kept the box of maps on her lap, if only to remind herself that nothing ever stayed the same, despite all evidence to the contrary.

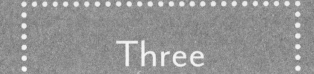

Three

SUGAR

Sugar squinted at her reflection in the mirror over the hall table as she carefully applied her lipstick. Until the day her mother decided to stop getting out of bed, Sugar had seen her mama do this at the exact same mirror every time Astrid left the house or someone came to the door. Always humming or singing, even when putting on lipstick. It was Sugar's earliest recollection of her mama, hearing her beautiful voice singing her to sleep. Her daddy called it singing sad, on account of the sorrowful tunes that she favored. He always said it like an accusation, looking at Mama as if he were expecting an apology.

The memory stung Sugar like a slap, causing her hand to shake and forcing her to lean against the table. She'd always thought that memories were supposed to fade as she got older. Only the good ones, apparently. The bad ones seemed to grow sharper, a knife blade pressed against her skin, threatening to cut her if she turned to look too closely.

She closed her eyes for a long moment, thinking she could hear the braying of the mules in the fields and smell the dust from the road churned up by the metal-rimmed wheels of a hay cart. Thought, too, she heard the shattering of breaking glass in a sleeping house and the sound of her mother's bare feet on the floor. The sharp shout of a name.

Echoes of a past that was like a shadow that stayed long after the sun disappeared.

Sugar's eyes snapped open, trying to focus on the reflection in front of her. The cotton fields had long since been plowed under, the mules gone long before that. And Astrid had been laid to rest more than sixty years before. Sugar leaned forward, blinking rapidly behind her glasses, peering into the old mirror. The woman who stared back wasn't her. She never would have allowed her hair to get so white, or her skin so wrinkled. Astrid used to say that Sugar was so strong willed a tornado wouldn't be able to shift her position on anything. Maybe time was more covert, slowly spooling the years until there was no thread left behind you and all that remained was a stranger's face in the mirror.

She glanced down at the plate of brownies she'd placed on the hall table, unsure why she'd made them or for whom. True to her nickname, she'd been born with a sweet tooth the size of Stone Mountain. But besides robbing her of night vision and her once-beautiful gold hair, old age had muted her taste buds, too. It put her out of sorts. It didn't seem fair how finally when she'd reached the age where she didn't have to worry about her figure anymore, she'd stopped craving sweets. If she somehow managed to make it to heaven, she'd demand an explanation.

The inability to sleep was another one of Father Time's little jokes on the elderly. For years now she'd wake up around three in the morning and would read either her Bible or the latest Harlan Coben novel or whatever thriller she'd found on the New in Print table at the new library in Milton. But the night before, she'd chosen to bake brownies instead. Despite her intentions of having nothing to do with her new tenants, her thoughts never seemed to stray far from the young divorcée and her two children. There was something so familiar about Merilee Dunlap, something sad and haunted about her that had nothing to do with her recent divorce. Most people would miss it when looking at her, but Sugar had lots of experience recognizing the perpetually haunted.

Now she had three dozen chocolate brownies that she couldn't taste arranged on a plate with plastic wrap, and, having survived the Great

Depression, she would not throw out anything, regardless of how un-wanted or useless it appeared to be. She'd seen Merilee's minivan rumbling down the drive an hour before and figured that they'd had enough time to have already had supper and she wouldn't have to deal with the awkwardness of being invited to join them. With a heavy sigh, Sugar picked up the plate and stepped outside.

Her hip hurt as she carefully made her way down the steps and onto the drive that connected the properties. Willa Faye called Sugar's ailments "visits from Arthur Itis," but giving it a funny name never seemed to ease the pain. Moving her joints and limbs regularly did seem to help, but the first step almost made Sugar think how much easier it would be to sit in a wheelchair all day, letting other people push her around. Maybe it was because Willa Faye had succumbed to such an existence or maybe it was because Sugar had been raised with four brothers, but she found that she had no desire to be pushed around all day.

Bright beams shone from the windows of the cottage as Sugar approached, the front lights forming warm puddles of illumination on the porch floorboards—a complete waste of electricity considering it wouldn't be dark for another hour and a half. The scent of the boxwoods distracted her from thoughts of Merilee's extravagances. They always reminded her of Tom and the short time they'd had together here, the pungent aroma of the small, shiny leaves like a switch on her memory that never turned off.

She tried not to think of Tom picking her up and carrying her over this very threshold as she climbed the front steps one at a time, taking a moment to catch her breath before knocking. The main door was open, the screen door allowing in the green scents of a warm summer evening. Not that she was surprised, but there were no smells of supper billowing out of the kitchen. As she lifted her hand to knock, she glanced down and spotted a small toy figurine partly wedged into a crack between floorboards, its sightless face turned up to hers.

There was something about it that made her pause. Maybe it was the wide unseeing eyes or the careful smile that made her feel sorry for it. It wasn't until after she'd placed the plate of brownies on a porch chair to free her hands that she realized it reminded her of Merilee. Ignoring the common sense that told her that her knees might get her down there but might not get her back up, she squatted down to reach it.

She was still crouched on the porch when the front door opened and the little boy, Colin, stood looking at her as if it were the most natural thing in the world to see her there. "I smelled cookies."

"They're brownies. And you can have one if you would please help me up. My knees seem to have forgotten how to stand."

Colin got himself on his hands and knees, forming a kind of bench. "Put your hands on my back, and I'll stand up slowly and you can stand up with me."

She did as she was told, not convinced it would work until her legs were straight enough for her to get her feet underneath her and they were both standing. "You're a very smart boy, Colin. I hope you're planning on being an engineer when you grow up."

He smiled brightly, illuminating a missing-tooth gap in his lower front teeth. "That's what Mom says, too. But I can't decide. I'd like to be an ice cream truck driver and eat all the ice cream I want. Or be a funeral guy like my dad's brother, Uncle Steven. He's really funny."

"Your uncle Steven?"

"Uh-huh. He's an unner-taker. He lets Lily and me ride in the long black car sometimes when we visit him and Aunt Shawna, except she's not supposed to know. He keeps mints and water in the backseat and he says we can have however much we want."

Sugar grimaced from the ache in her knees and from Colin's comment about his uncle. She'd had a lot of experience with undertakers in her ninety-three years and had yet to meet one who was particularly funny or generous. And she could only hope that the long black car Colin referred to was the limousine.

"Thanks, young man." She rubbed her knees and forced her back to straighten. She did yoga three times a week at the Prescott Bend Country Club—her lifelong membership part of the deal her brother had made when he sold the property it was built on. She probably wasn't the best advertisement, but she didn't care. It was free, so she was determined to use it even if it killed her.

Colin's gaze slipped to the toy in her hand. "Is that one of Uncle David's Lego people? Mom keeps them hidden in her drawer."

Sugar refrained from asking him how he knew about them if they were usually hidden. She wasn't sure how to speak with children, having had very little experience, but Colin didn't seem to mind. "I just found it here." She took an exploratory step to make sure her knees were functioning and picked up the plate of brownies, planning to give Colin the plate and then leave.

"My uncle died when he was a little boy. Can I have a brownie now?"

The door opened again and a frazzled Merilee stood there, framed in the doorway, an orange slant of late-afternoon sun lightening her hair like a halo. "Oh, I'm sorry. I didn't hear you knock." She opened the door wider. "Colin, aren't you supposed to be doing homework?"

"I was too hungry to concentrate and I smelled brownies. Look what Miss Sugar brought!" He pointed excitedly at the plate. "Could I have one while we wait for the pizza man so I don't die of starvation?"

"You're not going to die of starvation, Colin." She looked at Sugar, a small flush on her face. "I had a long day at work and I'm still unpacking. Not the most nutritious . . ." She gestured Sugar inside and Sugar allowed herself to be led into the small living room. She had no intention of staying, or really moving in past the front porch, but the boy and his mother were like a strong wind sucking her inside.

"Pizza's a vegetable now, 'member, Mom? So we can eat it every day."

"That's enough, Colin. Please go back into the kitchen to finish your homework."

"But . . ."

Merilee speared him with a look that made him turn around and head back toward the kitchen, his feet dragging against the floor.

Sugar remembered not to purse her lips, recalling her mother telling her it would give her wrinkles and make her look like a pawpaw that had been left on the ground too long.

She was still trying to make her excuses to leave when Merilee noticed the toy in her hand. "Where did you find that?"

"On the front porch."

Merilee took it gratefully, squeezing her fingers around it as her eyes blinked rapidly. "I thought I'd lost it."

Sugar waited for her to say more, maybe something about her brother. A long time ago, she would have pressed for more, carefully prodding like a doctor on a sore spot in the polite way she'd seen the women in her family do for almost a century. It was the Southern way, after all. But that had been before Sugar knew what it was like to be on the other end of the questions.

"The brownies smell delicious. I'm guessing Colin smelled them through the plastic wrap and the screen door. I swear that boy was a bloodhound in a previous life."

Sugar smiled politely, watching as the younger woman slid the toy into the pocket of her skirt, which seemed about a size too large. As if to avoid further questions, Merilee pressed on. "I have to bring dessert to a children's party this weekend. I know nothing more than the basics of cooking, but if the recipe's easy enough, could I borrow it? I was going to do a search on the Internet, but we seem to be having a problem getting a connection. Your friend Wade is supposed to come over later. I hope it's soon, because I'm afraid Lily might have a heart attack from the stress of not having Wi-Fi."

When Sugar didn't say anything, Merilee explained, "Wi-Fi is what we need to connect to the Internet."

"I've heard of it," Sugar said, allowing herself to be led back to the kitchen, where Colin sat at one end of the table with a textbook in front of him and Lily sat in front of a large laptop with her head in her hands. Sugar placed the plate of brownies on the table. "I'm sure Wade will have you fixed up in no time. He can do anything—except convince me to sell this property." She wasn't sure why she'd said that other than the fact that she loved Wade as much as she was capable of loving someone. She bragged on him as if he were her own flesh and blood.

Lily looked up at her with hopeful eyes, the crease between her brows not smoothing out completely. "Really? Because if I don't check in online, I'll get part of my grade taken off."

"Lily, it won't be the end of the world," said her mother. "I'm sure your teacher would understand. Or why don't you call that girl from your class—Bailey Blackford? Her mother is the class mom and I have her home number on the form I stuck to the fridge."

The crease deepened. "That's their landline. I don't have Bailey's cell number."

Sugar met Merilee's equally confused gaze for a moment before Merilee turned back to her daughter. "But I'll bet that whoever answers the phone will be able to give it to Bailey."

A look of hope crossed the girl's face as she slid back her chair before snatching a paper from the refrigerator door and racing from the room.

Merilee smiled tiredly. "Would you like to stay for pizza?"

Sugar started to purse her lips but stopped. "No, thank you. I've already eaten." Before she could close her mouth again, she said, "I've got more tomatoes and okra in my garden than I can eat. If you'd like some, I could bring some over."

"That's really nice of you—thanks. The tomatoes would be great for the kids' sandwiches and my salads, but I have no idea what to do with the okra."

This time Sugar's lips pursed before she realized it. *Pizza as a vegetable. Really!* "Why don't I come by Friday after you get home and we'll make cookies together—I've got a recipe that's so easy even you could make them—and I'll show you how to prepare okra. I'll bring some of my tomato sandwiches, too. I make them with white Wonder Bread, Duke's mayonnaise, and my tomatoes. Can't be anything life shortening with that since I've been eating at least one a day since I was a baby. If you tell me you're going to put my tomatoes on wheat bread, you can't have any."

"Did you have electricity way back then?" Colin asked, swinging his legs under the table, brownie crumbs clinging to his chin from a brownie she didn't remember Merilee giving him permission to eat.

Merilee still seemed to be struggling for words after Sugar's brown bread ultimatum. "Colin!" she finally managed.

"Yes," Sugar said, "we had electricity. And running water, even. Not too common in a rural farmhouse in Georgia, because none of my friends had an indoor bathroom. But my mama was from Savannah and had been raised in a nice house in town and had grown up with those things. So my daddy worked extra hard to give her every convenience."

She felt out of breath, as if the memories of her mother had wrapped their fingers around her neck and were squeezing slowly. She glanced out the rear window toward the woods, half expecting to see the ghosts that were never far from her.

The sound of a car outside bolted Colin out of his chair. "Finally!" he shouted through a spray of brownie crumbs. "I was getting ready to pass out from starvation."

"Colin! Don't open the door to a stranger . . ."

Merilee's words trailed off at the sound of the screen door being opened and then the timbre of a familiar voice. Sugar followed Colin to the front door, recognizing the tall, broad-shouldered form of Willa Faye's grandson, Wade Kimball. "I think this is for you," he said to Colin, holding out a large square box that smelled of garlic and red sauce.

Colin let out a whoop, then took the box before running back into the kitchen. The clomping on the bare wood drew attention to the fact that he was wearing his shoes. Inside the house. Sugar pressed her lips together, this time on purpose, so she wouldn't say something she might regret.

"Sugar," Wade said, giving her a tight bear hug only because he knew she didn't like them. And only because he was the one person in the world who could get away with it.

"Robbing old ladies of their homes and land isn't profitable enough, so you're reduced to delivering pizzas now?" she asked, her voice muffled against his shirt.

She heard his laugh rumbling in his chest and she had to hide her smile. Even as a baby he'd had the deep, throaty laughter that drew people to him like flies to a cow, in a seemingly universal desire to be enveloped in the warmth that surrounded him.

"Good to see you, too, Sugar. Butter still not melting in your mouth, huh?"

She pushed him away, pretending to be annoyed.

"I passed the delivery boy driving back and forth on the road looking for the driveway and decided to put him out of his misery." His gaze rested on Merilee. "I'm assuming it was for you? If not, I've got some apologizing to do to the family whose dinner I waylaid."

"No—it's for us. Thank you. But how much do I owe you?"

He let his arm slide from Sugar's shoulders to wave his hand in dismissal. "Just consider it a 'welcome to the neighborhood' gift—except this one doesn't come with a dish you need to clean and return." With an outstretched hand, he stepped forward. "Wade Kimball—I believe we spoke on the phone. I'm here to check on your router."

Merilee shook his hand without smiling or blushing or doing any of those things women usually did when meeting Wade for the first time. He must have noticed it, too, because he seemed to falter with his next words. But then he stopped trying and just looked at her, tilting his head. "Have we met before?"

"No," she said quickly. "Maybe you've seen me at the grocery store or something. I've lived in Sweet Apple for about six years."

He thought for a moment. "No, I don't think that's it. Where are you from originally?"

Merilee's response took so long, Sugar was pretty sure wild horses couldn't pull it out of her. Finally, she said, "Sandersville—in south Georgia."

He straightened as a smile stretched over his face. "Ah. That must be it. I lived in Augusta for about ten years right out of college, working for a developer. Good work buddy of mine had grandparents in Sandersville and we used to visit them occasionally to help with repairs and maintenance. Nice couple—you probably knew them since it's a really small town. I'm trying to think of their name . . ." His eyes squinted in concentration.

"Lily!" Merilee called out loudly—and unnecessarily, seeing as how the girl had walked into the room while Wade was speaking and stood next to her mother. "Mr. Kimball is here to fix the router."

Lily tugged on her mother's elbow. "I'm right here, Mom."

Merilee looked relieved. "Great. Why don't you show Mr. Kimball where the router is while I warm the pizza up in the oven? Assuming Colin has left us any." Ducking her head, she headed toward the kitchen.

She'd made it to the doorway when Wade called her name. She faced him, her expression reminding Sugar of an actress on one of her soaps, waiting for her doctor to give her the prognosis.

"West. William and Sharon West. Did you know them?"

After an almost imperceptible pause, she shook her head. "No. I don't think so." She quickly disappeared into the kitchen.

Wade stared after Merilee for a long moment. "I've definitely seen her before. I'll think of it. She has one of those faces—the kind you don't easily forget."

Sugar frowned. "Now, don't be stirring up trouble. I think she has plenty enough on her plate."

Wade turned to her with a smile. "Don't tell me you're getting soft in your old age, Sugar. Since when have you involved yourself personally in the lives of your tenants?"

She almost said that she wasn't, until she remembered not only her presence in their house but also the fact that she'd come bearing brownies, something he was likely to discover. It irked her that she'd succumbed to whatever it was that had dragged her down the road, and the fact that Wade had caught her annoyed her even more.

"I'm tired," she said. "I'm going home now. I'll leave a bag of my tomatoes on the front porch steps for you to pick up on your way out." She stood on her tiptoes and gave him a perfunctory kiss on his cheek.

"Can I drive you?"

She held up her arm to display a black wristband, a soul-stealing device he'd given her last Christmas despite her well-publicized disdain for most new technology. It was one of those newfangled ones that displayed everything right there on the screen. Wade was always telling her about all sorts of things it could do if she'd learn how to really use it, but she figured she already knew all she needed to. She'd pace the house each night just to get in her recommended number of steps, despite how much her hip hurt or how tired she was. It was evil, pure evil. "I need to get my steps in. But if you see me face-first in the road on your way back, I give you permission to lift me into your truck and take me home."

Lily, who was almost hopping up and down with her impatience to get working on the router, stilled for a moment as if trying to figure out if she was being serious.

"Hopefully I'll see you before I run over you." He winked. "And thanks for the tomatoes."

The furrow between the girl's brows deepened with concern as he moved in front of Sugar to open the door. Sugar put her hand on his arm and spoke quietly. "Don't go digging where you're not wanted. Most people have secrets. And most of them should be allowed to stay hidden. No good has ever come from poking a stick down a hole. Sometimes you get a garter snake, but sometimes you get a rattler."

He narrowed his eyes. "How would you know anything about secrets?"

She stepped carefully out onto the porch. "Good night, Wade. Don't forget to pick up your tomatoes."

She moved down the steps in the twilight, then headed down the drive, sensing him watching her until she heard the snap of the screen door closing out the approaching night.

Four

Installment #2: Where Is General Sherman Now That We Need Him?

I saw a chicken hawk yesterday (that's a red-tailed hawk for my neighbors who aren't from around here). I haven't seen one in years, not since all the building started up here in Sweet Apple. The thwacking of hammers and the constant roar of earthmoving equipment is deafening to me, and I can only imagine what it does to a hawk.

I heard its raspy scream from my car while I was stopped on the road behind a long line of SUVs in front of the elementary school (is there a shortage of buses? I don't understand why there were so many cars clogging the road at pickup time) and opened the window just in time to see the large bird swoop down and pick up a small brown bunny innocently chewing grass by the side of the road.

A young mother behind the wheel of her SUV actually dropped her cell phone from her ear so she could throw her hand protectively in front of the eyes of the little boy sitting next to her. I wanted to tell her that she should let him see it because this is the natural world and the circle of life and all that. And it's bound to be a lot more G-rated than what he probably sees every day on the Internet.

I was admiring the bird's proud profile and spread of red-stained tail feathers as it soared away with its prey, continuing to watch it until it ran smack-dab into the side of an oncoming moving truck approaching the intersection from the opposite direction. It dropped the rabbit, which had the good sense to scurry away, but the poor hawk lay in the middle of the road like a sacrifice, his talons lifted in silent supplication.

A woman in a Lexus convertible jumped out, jabbering loudly on her phone and probably calling some rescue group, while a young man wearing overalls and a John Deere hat climbed from a pickup truck and approached the bird with an eye out to eat it, I suspect. The moving van had long since left the scene. I wanted to stay longer to see who'd win that fight, but the woman in the SUV behind me had begun honking. She looked as if she needed that Starbucks grande latte with double whip more than I needed to see the argument, so I moved forward.

It was then that I noticed the cow pasture on the corner was devoid of cows, and a large backhoe sat in the middle of the empty field, along with a big sign announcing a new swim/tennis community. I think I preferred the cows. They don't drive on our roads or send their children to our already-overcrowded schools.

Speaking of moving trucks, there have been quite a few on the streets of Sweet Apple these last few months as families do their best to get settled into new homes before school starts. In one neighborhood, a family moved down from Pittsburgh, Pennsylvania, bringing with them an impressive assortment of snow shovels and other snow-removal equipment. A mutual friend said that they'd heard about the ice storm in Atlanta a few Januaries ago and wanted to be prepared. I hope somebody told them that the only thing they should be prepared for is to watch those shovels collect dust and go unused for at least a decade, since that's when the next storm will hit.

Another new resident has come all the way from Fullerton, California, and was overheard at the Pilates studio saying how excited she was to experience the real South. Honey, Atlanta isn't the real South. It's a hodgepodge of people from all over the place living in houses that have been built in the last twenty years. If you want to see the real South, watch *Driving Miss Daisy* or *Steel Magnolias*. Better yet, head to Rabun County. That's where that Burt Reynolds movie *Deliverance* was filmed. And if you hear banjos, keep driving.

I met another of our new neighbors recently—a young divorcée with two children. She's not new to the area, but she's moved from one side of town to the other for a change of scenery, I suspect.

Her children are enrolled in a local private academy (I'll let you guess which one), and from what I know of the other moms there, this could be interesting, as this young mother seems very unaffected so far, and not all that interested in the politics of parenting as so many of us practice it here. But it's only the first week of school, and a lot can happen in the span of a nine-month school year. A lot of time for surprises. A lot of time for things to happen.

This blog is coming to you late, as you are probably aware, because of the power outage we had last night due to one of our powerful summer lightning storms. I opened up all the windows and put towels on the windowsills just so I could smell the rain and catch the breeze, which smelled of summer nights. I sat on my front porch and watched the lightning zig and zag across the sky before leaving us all in complete darkness, smelling the burnt ions and the steam from the hot earth and cut grass, enjoying the earthy scent of the wet red clay.

The storm brought back so many memories of my childhood that I found myself wishing the electricity would stay off a little longer. I remained outside until the storm moved away with the clouds and the stars came out. And then the electricity came back on in all the houses nearby, flooding the sky and streets and yards with so much light that I couldn't see the stars anymore.

MERILEE

Merilee had just finished throwing on a T-shirt and a pair of shorts and was trying to hang up the dress she'd worn to work when Sugar knocked on the front door. It figured she'd be early. She heard Colin racing toward the door to throw it open, giving Merilee a few extra minutes to stash the dress in the closet carefully so it wouldn't get wrinkled. She'd accidentally put the iron in the box of things for Michael to take and she refused to ask for it back. She'd also drag her feet on buying a replacement, knowing that as soon as she did, Michael would show up at her door with the iron, since it was more than possible that Tammy Garvey didn't know what an iron was and entirely likely that she sent out all Michael's shirts and anything else that looked like it might wrinkle. Including the silk underwear Merilee imagined that Tammy wore.

She hurried into the hallway, realizing too late that she was barefoot. She usually did go barefoot inside in the summertime, but there was something about Sugar Prescott that made her think that adults would be expected to wear shoes. Merilee was about to turn around when Colin ran into the hallway.

"Mom! Miss Sugar's here!"

Merilee wondered how long it would be before one of the children would make a comment about how misnamed their landlady was. She spotted the older woman standing in the entranceway, holding two Kroger grocery bags. Rushing forward, she took the bags, noticing as she did the Fitbit on Sugar's arm. She looked twice, just to make sure that's what it really was. The woman didn't know what Wi-Fi was, for crying out loud. What on earth was she doing with a Fitbit?

Merilee smiled. "I didn't hear your car or I would have brought this in myself."

"I walked," she said with a frown. And then, most likely in response to Merilee's confused stare, she added, "I'm old, not dead. Exercise is good for me, according to my doctor, who I think might have been kicked in the head by a mule when he was younger." She headed toward the kitchen as if it were still her house, which, Merilee realized, it was.

Lily sat at the table with her laptop and greeted Miss Sugar with a smile. Feeling the need to explain, as if Sugar's opinion about her mothering skills mattered, Merilee said, "She's checking her Facebook page and other social media accounts. She's only allowed to do that when I'm with her."

Sugar regarded her with a blank face.

"Oh, sorry. Social media is what all the young people are into these days."

"Like talking but without the bother of being face-to-face." Without waiting for a reply, Sugar began unloading the bags onto the counter and storing a few items in the refrigerator, including what appeared to be sandwiches on white bread cut diagonally in half and wrapped in plastic, and several plump, dark red tomatoes that made Merilee's mouth water. A large clear bag of green okra was emptied into the sink. Sugar looked pointedly at Lily. "In my day we didn't have time for 'social media.' There were too many chores."

Feeling as if she'd just been scolded, Merilee turned to her daughter. "Lily, would you please wash the okra?"

Lily looked up, her expression like that of a sailor about to walk the plank. "But I still have half an hour of computer time. You said!"

Merilee kept her voice calm, aware of Sugar listening behind her. "You can finish your half hour when you're done. It won't take but a few minutes."

With a sigh, Lily slid back her chair and walked heavily to the sink, as if she wore leg shackles. Merilee refrained from saying anything, aware again of Sugar's scrutiny, and second-guessing her decision to ask the older woman for help. Her only alternative would have been to go to the local bakery, but, even if she'd decided to put the cookies on one of her own serving dishes, the other mothers would be sure to know they were store-bought, which was apparently *not done* at Windwood Academy.

It was a tidbit of wisdom passed on from Bailey Blackford to Lily from Bailey's mother, for which Merilee was absurdly grateful. It was bad enough that her children were from one of only two families in the entire school to come from a "broken home." Something else that had been passed on via Bailey. She would not bring store-bought cookies to a party so that her daughter from a broken home could be ridiculed or pitied. Even if it meant inviting Sugar Prescott and her disapproving presence into her kitchen to learn how to bake cookies from scratch.

Sugar was already rummaging under the cabinets, which annoyed Merilee. The house included clean and functional yet outdated kitchen appliances—so it made sense that Sugar would be more familiar than Merilee with what the kitchen contained. But still, it was technically Merilee's kitchen—even though so far she'd used only the utensils, cups, plates, refrigerator, oven, and microwave.

A movement out the window distracted her, and she looked up in time to spot Colin running in the direction of the woods. She quickly cranked the casement window latch to open it and called out, "Colin—stop! Where are you going?"

He stopped suddenly and faced her, and she tried not to cringe when she noticed he still wore his white socks—without shoes—and his uniform shirt, untucked from his pants, was streaked with something she couldn't identify. "I saw that dog again right by the woods and I was trying to catch him. I think he's lost."

"I told you to stay away—it could have rabies or something. And you know you're not supposed to go near the woods. Come back here. You are *not* to go past the tire swing."

He sent one last look toward the woods before turning back to the house. "Yes, ma'am. But if I catch that dog, can I keep him?"

Merilee snatched back the word "no" even though that's what she wanted to say. According to Lily and Colin, they were the only two children in the history of the world who didn't have a dog. Their father had allergies, which was why they'd never had one before, but now her only excuse was that she was too exhausted to add one more thing to her plate. An excuse she knew wouldn't be understood by anyone under the age of eleven. "We'll see," she said instead, closing the window.

Sugar continued to bang things around under the cabinets, pretending she hadn't heard the exchange. "Please preheat the oven for the cookies, and I'm pretty sure there's a cookie sheet in the drawer under the oven."

Merilee stood in front of the avocado green oven, trying to make sense of the knobs. "What temperature?"

Sugar stopped for a moment. "The universal temperature for baking cookies, of course. Didn't your mama teach you how to cook?"

Merilee kept her focus on the immaculate oven, clean not because it had never been used but probably because Sugar was an expert at cleaning. And baking. "No. She was a great cook, but she didn't like me to be in the kitchen because she said I got in the way. And then . . . well, she stopped cooking altogether. That's when I learned how to pour spaghetti sauce from a jar and turn on the grill."

When Sugar didn't say anything, Merilee looked down at where she was crouched in front of a cabinet. The elderly woman's eyes were focused on her, but her mouth was clenched in determination that had nothing to do with their conversation. "Do you need help?" Merilee asked.

Sugar nodded tersely and Merilee grasped her elbows to haul her to her feet. "Thank you," she said.

"You're welcome," said Merilee. "But it might have been easier if you'd just asked me to get whatever you need."

"I wasn't sure you'd know what mixing bowls are." Her lips pressed together, but not before Merilee was pretty sure she'd seen what might pass as a smile. "Three hundred and fifty degrees," Sugar said, indicating the oven. "At least by the end of the day you'll know how to bake cookies and fry okra. Because it might be against the law for a Southern-born girl not to know how. Along with changing a tire."

Lily, her hands still immersed in the sink with the okra, looked at her mother with a worried expression. "Really? You mean like we could go to jail?"

"No, sweetheart," Merilee explained. "It's just an expression. But Sugar's right—women should know how to do all sorts of things."

"So if their husbands leave them they can hang pictures and stuff?"

Sugar spared her from answering. "No, Lily. So women can make the choice to do it for themselves or ask for help." It looked like she was going to say more, but instead she turned her back and began opening up a sack of sugar. She slid it and a bunch of mixing spoons down the counter toward Merilee. "I need a cup of sugar. If you spill any on the counter, don't knock it on the floor. We can put any stragglers into a corner of plastic wrap and save them for your morning coffee. Waste not, want not."

Before Merilee could point out the handheld vacuum she'd brought from their house, which now sat on its charger on the counter, Lily asked, "I'm done with the okra, so can I do the measuring?"

"Absolutely," Merilee said, happy to have her daughter's attention diverted from her laptop. Turning to Sugar, she asked, "Where's the recipe? I could get to measuring out the next ingredients."

"There's no recipe. My grandmother on my daddy's side taught me how to make these and she didn't know how to write, so I learned by watching. Never saw the need to write it down."

"Is that what it was like during the olden days?" Lily asked, concentrating on getting the exact amount of sugar in the measuring cup.

This time Merilee was sure she saw a smile. "Living on a farm meant there wasn't a lot of time for schooling, especially for girls and mostly for everyone during the fall harvest and spring planting seasons." Sugar looked out the window above the sink, her smile fading as her gaze seemed to focus on the woods. "So much has changed. I sometimes wonder . . ."

Instead of finishing her sentence, Sugar began filling a small saucepan with water, then placed it on the stove and lit the burner.

"What do you sometimes wonder, Miss Sugar?" Lily's sweet, high voice seemed unusually loud in the quiet kitchen.

Sugar moved away from the stove and looked out the window again. "I sometimes wonder if people today understand what sacrifice means."

"I know what it means," Lily said with excitement. "It's one of our vocabulary words this week. It means to do without or give up something, usually to help someone else."

The old woman had gone very still, her gaze focused outside the window. "Yes, that's right." Addressing Merilee, she said, "When the water in the saucepan starts to boil, turn off the heat and put a half stick of butter in a bowl on top of it—just until it's soft; don't let it melt. And move fast, because I can't be here all night. My shows start at eight o'clock."

"Don't you have a DVR?" Lily piped up as her mother retrieved the butter from the fridge. "Then you can watch your shows when you want to and fast-forward through the commercials."

Sugar blinked slowly behind her glasses. "I like commercials. They give me time to get up and walk around the living room so I can get my steps in."

Lily shared a glance with her mother before Merilee quickly did as Sugar had instructed. "What else can I do?" she asked.

"Watch, and memorize, because I don't like repeating myself." She handed her a mixing bowl filled with flour. "Please cut the okra into half-inch pieces and then coat them in here. When you're done with that, shake off the excess flour in a strainer, and then we'll move on to the egg and cornmeal part."

"You know, they sell batter mix now, so you don't have to go through all the trouble of . . ."

She stopped when she saw Sugar's expression and took the bowl. They measured, mixed, and battered in silence punctuated only by Sugar's directions. Lily slowly migrated back to her laptop while Merilee played the dutiful soldier, grateful yet irritated all at the same time. She was irritated at Sugar for being the way she was, and at herself for letting her get away with it. And at her mother, who hadn't thought it necessary to share her kitchen secrets with her daughter, and then, after David died, had stopped pretending to care or make plans to do it later. As if his death weren't punishment enough.

Her back was aching by the time they took the last batch of cookies from the oven and emptied the fryer of the final pieces of okra. She was about to suggest that Sugar recite the recipe again so she could write it down when she was interrupted by Lily.

"Mom! Do you know what a blog is?"

Merilee used the back of her wrist to scratch her nose since her hands were covered with oven mitts. "I don't have time to follow any, but I know what they are. Why?"

"Because Bailey Blackford says there's a new blog that's all about Sweet Apple and that I might recognize some of the people mentioned in it."

"Really? What's it called?"

"The Playing Fields. Bailey's mom thinks it's because it's all about the families with kids here in Sweet Apple, and all the time we spend playing sports. But I think it's bigger than that, you know?"

Merilee frowned, unsure of what Lily was talking about, but amazed at her daughter's insight just the same. "Who writes it?"

"No one knows because it's just signed 'Your Neighbor,' but Mrs. Blackford thinks it's probably a mom at Windwood since the blogger seems to know a lot about it. That's called a-non-y-mous, when you don't know who the person is." She frowned. "Bailey says that I shouldn't tell you."

"About the blog? Why? Is it bad?" Lily understood that the word "bad" meant foul language, nudity, drugs, and pretty much everything she'd been exposed to in the brief snippet she'd seen of *The Godfather*.

"I don't know; I haven't read it yet. Bailey said she'd send me a link. Do you want to see it?" The frown lines that had disappeared during their cooking lesson reappeared.

"Yes, please. I'll read it first, okay? Just to make sure it's appropriate for a ten-year-old." She leaned down and kissed the top of her daughter's head. "And, Lily? Thanks for telling me."

Lily beamed, making Merilee's heart squeeze. Lily's need for approval, while always a part of her personality, had gone into overdrive since the divorce. Yet another reason to silently curse Michael in Merilee's nighttime rants when she'd wake up and couldn't go back to sleep.

Sugar stood at the sink, filling it with hot water, her back stiff and unyielding, without any sign of a dowager's hump. "Please," Merilee said. "You've done enough—I'll clean up. Can I send you home with some cookies and fried okra?"

The older woman appeared not to have heard her. She leaned toward the window, her gaze on Colin in the tree swing facing the woods. "What will you do if he finds that dog and it doesn't have a home?"

The question surprised her. "I have no idea. I try just to think about things as they come up. Otherwise I get too overwhelmed." Merilee tried to smile but quit when she realized it wasn't funny at all.

Sugar turned off the water and her hands gripped the edge of the sink. "Dogs don't live nearly long enough. It's too hard on a child."

"Did you never have a dog?" Lily asked.

A sad smile crossed her face before disappearing into a grimace. "I grew up with dogs. My brothers always had outside dogs, but my daddy let me keep a small one inside just for me—as long as I kept it away from Mama, since she didn't like them. Her name was Dixie. She—" Sugar stopped abruptly. Folding the dish towel into a crisp rectangle, she said, "My shows will be starting soon and I need to see to my supper."

Merilee felt somehow bereft, as if she'd just missed an opportunity for something she wasn't even aware of. As if this glimpse into Sugar's life had been the opening for not exactly a friendship but some sort of relationship that until today Merilee hadn't really considered. Maybe it had to do with Sugar's being on her own for so long, so that Merilee could imagine they had something in common. Could understand what it was like living alone. Could understand the loneliness, the emptiness and barrenness that haunted not just her bed but every waking moment of her day. The crushing weight of all life's decisions, joys, and burdens that she'd once imagined sharing. The sheer hatefulness of it all because the decision hadn't been hers. Sugar's husband had been killed in the war, but the desertion of the heart would have felt the same.

Merilee pulled out a chair. "You've been on your feet all afternoon. Why don't you sit down and let me pour you a glass of sweet tea. That's one thing I do know how to make—my grandfather taught me, and he was born and raised in south Georgia."

Sugar frowned. "It probably won't be sweet enough for my liking."

"Colin likes it, and he only likes really sweet things," Lily said over the laptop.

"Well, then," Sugar said grudgingly, "I suppose I could have a glass. Just one, though."

Merilee smiled to herself as she poured four glasses from the pitcher she always kept in the fridge. Placing two in front of Lily, she said, "Your computer time has expired. Why don't you take one of these outside to your brother and enjoy some fresh air?"

Sugar sent Lily a stern look. "Don't forget to stay away from the woods. I don't have time to drive anybody to the emergency room tonight, and I doubt your mama would be able to drive a car with you or Colin in the backseat with a water moccasin hanging off your leg."

"Yes, ma'am." Lily sent Merilee a worried look. She closed the laptop without argument before heading toward the back door, walking slowly so she wouldn't spill. She was always so careful about making mistakes that Merilee wanted to call after her and tell her to run with the glasses, that spilling tea was one mistake in life that was easily cleaned up. But she figured Lily would probably learn that all on her own. That was the one sure thing Merilee knew about life: You'd make your own mistakes no matter how many times you'd been taught better.

Merilee put the remaining two glasses on the table and sat down. "Sorry I don't have any lemons. I forgot to stop at the grocery store on the way home."

Sugar took a sip from her glass and let it sit in her mouth a moment before swallowing. "I've had worse."

"Thank you," Merilee said, hoping the older woman could hear the sarcasm that she didn't bother to hide in her voice. She watched as Sugar placed her left hand flat on the wide-plank pinewood surface of the table, a single gold band on her third finger her only jewelry.

"My daddy made this table—from the tall Georgia pines behind this house. It used to be in the big house, but my father gave it to me when I got married. Said that with my brothers going off to fight and me getting married, they didn't need such a big table anymore. I think it made him sad to see it so empty each night." A short, bare fingernail picked at a small nick on the edge. "This table could tell so many stories."

She glanced up as if waiting for encouragement, and Merilee noticed how blue Sugar's eyes were, and how her face was a perfect heart shape. She'd once been a very beautiful woman, Merilee decided. Whose husband had been dead for more than seventy long years. Merilee felt that bond again, the loneliness that stretched between them like sticky strands of a web, connecting them whether they wanted it or not.

"Tell me one," she said, leaning back in her chair.

For a moment, she thought Sugar would refuse. Would stand up and leave and resent Merilee for interrupting her solitude. Instead, Sugar took a long sip of her sweet tea, then placed both hands on the table. "When I was eleven years old, I watched a man bleed to death on this table. And I can't say either it or I has been the same since."

Five

SUGAR

Sweet Apple, Georgia
1934

I squatted by my brother Jimmy at the edge of the lake, my hands on my kneecaps slipping in sweat as I watched him drag his small net as deep as he could, hoping to find the tadpoles that were hiding from him. Grandpa's binoculars—the ones he'd used when he fought in France during the war—hung around Jimmy's scrawny neck, and I held my breath as they dipped close to the water.

Even though Jimmy was a year older than me, we were the same size, and one of his arms was shorter than mine altogether, and near useless. He walked funny, too, one foot turned the wrong way and nobody knowing how to straighten it. All this was on account of him getting stuck when he was getting around to being born. I didn't know exactly what that meant other than my brother Jimmy and I looked like we were the same age.

"Quick," he said. "Give me that jar."

I handed him the chipped Mason jar that Willa Faye's mama had given us to play with. We'd stuck lake muck and grass in the bottom of the jar along with some lake water so the tadpoles could be comfortable in their new home. Jimmy told me that once they grew legs we'd have to let them go because they couldn't stay underwater all the and skirted back a step or two as the pitchfork shimmied down the side of the barn like it didn't want to see any more and lay in the dirt on its back, staring up at the sky. I didn't scream this time because I was too scared, but Jimmy took a step forward. "Cut it out, Curtis. It ain't funny."

I didn't think to ask him how he knew the boy's name. Jimmy always seemed to know everything.

And then everything seemed to move fast and slow all at the same time. The first thing I remembered was hearing the sound of something ripping as Curtis pushed Will again. Except this time when he tried to pull him back, Will kept falling.

A wad of Will's red and blue plaid shirt was crumpled in Curtis's hand, his arm still stretched out like he still thought my brother should be attached to the shirt. And then Rufus was moving forward and we were all running and Harry was passed out on top of Grace and Will was falling for what seemed forever.

Rufus got there first and I was glad, because if anybody could catch Will and not get killed trying, it was Rufus. Except it didn't work out the way it was supposed to. Rufus caught my dumb brother, but his foot stepped on the bottom of the jug just as he put his arms out. There was a big whoof of air from Will or Rufus, or maybe it was from me because I was so relieved my brother hadn't broken his worthless neck. But then Rufus lost his balance because of that crockery and he fell backward with Will in his arms, landing right on top of that pitchfork.

"Pa!" Lamar was the only one of us who could move. The rest could only watch the slow stain of red as it poured out Rufus's side into the dark clay of the ground.

Lamar was punching Will on his arm, trying to push him off of Rufus, but Will's eyes were closed, a soft snore coming from his mouth. I ran over and kicked him much harder than I probably needed to, but I was scared and angry and I wanted to hurt him as bad as Rufus was hurt.

Throw-up bubbled into the back of my throat, the stink of blood making me think of the hog butchering we did every October. I'd stay up in my room with my head under the pillow so I couldn't hear the squealing of the pigs, but I could still taste the blood that seemed to paint the air red.

Will fell on his face in the dirt and stayed there. Lamar was crying and trying to wipe his daddy's face with his shirt, but Rufus didn't move, just lay there with blood bubbling between his lips, then dripping down his cheek. I glanced over at Harry, who'd fallen out of the saddle and was trying to stand. I wasn't getting any help there.

"Jimmy! Go run and get Mama and tell her Rufus is hurt bad and needs help."

He stared at me like I'd lost my mind, but that was because he probably wasn't thinking of before, when Mama was still herself and had once set Harry's broken arm and stitched a cut in Jimmy's cheek when he'd fallen from a tree trying to study a hawk's nest. She'd known doctoring stuff.

"I'm getting Daddy," he said, not waiting to see if I wanted to argue. He ran toward the fields, red clay dust puffing out under his feet like time was chasing him as he kept his hand over the tadpoles, the binoculars clinking against the Mason jar's side.

"Hey, you, up there. Curtis!" I shouted as I looked up.

Curtis stuck his head over the edge of the haymow, looking like he was hoping I'd forgotten he was there. Or what he'd done. "Go get your mama and tell her a man's hurt bad and she needs to come quick." The words got stuck in my throat for a second, and I hoped he didn't notice that I wanted to cry because I was scared. Scared that Rufus was hurt so bad he couldn't be fixed. And Lamar was making that awful choking sound as he kept wiping his daddy's face as if that would do any good at all.

Curtis slowly turned around and disappeared for a few moments as he climbed down the ladder. It took him so long that I wanted to rush into the barn and grab at the back of his overalls and yank him down so I could punch him in the face a hundred times like I'd once seen Harry do to Will.

"Run!" I shouted at him. "Run fast and get your mama or your daddy or anybody else who can come help!"

He smiled at me, and it was like a winter wind had just blown through me, front to back. "Do it yourself," he said, then turned his back on me and poor Rufus and Lamar and walked just as slow as he could toward the woods that sat at the far end of the cotton field.

My head hurt I was thinking so hard, and I was just about to leave Lamar so I could go find someone when I heard Jimmy shouting. He was coming from the direction of the house, Daddy close behind, and I near fainted with relief. Daddy must have been home for supper, which was how he got there so soon. Right behind him were two more field hands, and I had to bite my lip hard not to start bawling.

Daddy told Jimmy to run for the doctor as they brought Rufus to the kitchen table and laid him on top, while I ran to the pretty front bedroom to go get Mama. She sat in bed, leaning against the lacy white pillows that she was so proud of because they'd come with her trousseau from Savannah, and Bobby sat in the rocking chair next to her, reading.

I was running to and fro, telling her what had happened and that she needed to come quick to help, but she just sat there with a frown as if she didn't know who I was or what I was saying. Finally, she reached for my hand and gave it a soft squeeze, and I saw the opened medicine bottle on her night table, the little dribble of dried brown liquid in the corner of her mouth like she wasn't using a glass to drink it anymore.

"You'll be fine, Alice," she said with a voice full of sleep. She was the only one who ever called me by my real name. "You need to learn how to tend to people on the farm, and I'd say now is as good a time as any." Her finger pointed to her large armoire as if moving her whole hand was too hard. "My medicine box is on the bottom, with old linens you can use for bandages." She lay back against the pretty white pillows and closed her eyes.

Bobby helped me pull out the box and carry it down to the kitchen, which I hardly recognized. There was blood everywhere—on the table, on the men, on poor Lamar, who was still making those awful sounds. A red smear shaped like a hand was on the middle of the icebox door, a single bloody footprint right in front but facing the wrong way.

"Mama's not coming," I said as I began to unroll an old bedsheet. My voice warbled like a baby bird's, which I figured was better than crying. "I'm not sure what I'm supposed to do with this, but Mama said to bring—"

Daddy put a large hand on my shoulder. "Rufus doesn't need it now, Sugar."

"But he's hurt. It was the pitchfork. He—"

"I know. But it's too late. He's already gone."

I blinked up at him and then at the table. Lamar had stopped crying and was holding his daddy's hand like he wanted to go wherever Rufus had gone. Blood puddles slowly tiptoed to the edge of the table before falling over the edge in tiny drips. It was so quiet in the kitchen that each drop on the floor sounded like a shout.

"It was an accident." Harry stood in the doorway, his face whiter than a cotton boll. There was vomit on his shirt and I could smell the moonshine, but nothing was stronger than the smell of copper that covered my mouth and tongue.

"It was an accident," Harry said again, as if saying it again would make it true. His eyes met mine and I knew he was sending me a warning.

I looked over at Lamar, because he'd been there, too, and seen what I'd seen. His eyes were red and his face wet with tears, but all he did was give a little shake of his head, then turn away, studying hard at his daddy's hand like he was praying for it to move again.

Daddy looked at Harry, then back at me, his cheeks heavy, and he seemed a lot older than when I'd seen him that morning at the breakfast table. "It was a sad and tragic accident," he said to the back of Lamar's head.

I looked at the faces around me, trying to understand something I couldn't. I didn't know much, but there were two things I knew for sure right then and there: that truth was as sticky as molasses, and I was never going to be a little girl again. That part of my life had ended the minute Rufus had decided to go to the barn to see if he could help.

I ran from the kitchen, my elbow knocking the tadpole jar from the edge of the counter as I left, the sound of shattering glass following me out the door.

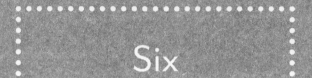

Six

MERILEE

The digital clock on the coffeemaker blinked as Merilee helped herself to another cup. A storm had blown in again the night before, shutting off the power for several hours. She frowned at the flashing numbers. It was one of those stupid things she didn't know how to fix because Michael had always had the job to go around resetting clocks after an outage. It wasn't that she was incapable of doing it, or too stupid or too lazy to learn how. It was that it was one more thing on the list of what made her miss the partnership of marriage. The unspoken *I'll make the coffee if you'll fix the clock*. Neither task was insurmountable on its own, but a day full of tasks that all fell on her now was simply exhausting.

The rumbling thunder had chased both children into her bed—thunder had never scared them into her bed before the divorce—and after a couple of hours of trying to sleep with various small elbows and knees poking her in the ribs and back, she'd come downstairs and sat on the front porch to watch the rain and think about the story Sugar had told her.

The old woman had left shortly afterward, looking up at the heavy clouds as a reason to leave right away. Merilee had offered to drive her, but Sugar had shaken her head and walked out the front door, her eyes the color of the ocean after a storm, as if the memories were stirred-up sediment.

Merilee's first thought had been to bleach the table, as if she could still see the dying man and the blood that had soaked into the ancient wood. But then she remembered that no matter how vivid the pictures in her mind, it had been eighty-two years ago. A long time, just not long enough to forget.

"Mom?"

Merilee turned to see Lily holding her laptop, wearing the *Frozen* nightgown she'd received from Merilee's parents the previous Christmas. It had been too small then and now hit her midcalf. It wasn't even a movie that Lily particularly liked. But she wore it because it made her feel as if the grandparents she rarely saw were part of her life.

Merilee kissed the top of her head, loving the way she smelled, wondering when that would change. "What are you doing up so early?"

Lily placed the laptop on the table. "Bailey sent me the link to that blog I was telling you about. I think you need to read it."

"When did this happen? Didn't I tell you I wanted to read it first?"

Lily nodded, keeping her eyes down. "I know, but when I called Bailey to ask her about our math test on Monday, she said I needed to look at the blog *right now*. So I did. And it's really bad and you need to read it. There's something in it about you. And the latest post is about Dad."

"Wait," Merilee said, wishing the caffeine would hurry up and reach her brain. "When was this?"

"Around midnight. I was worrying about the test and Bailey said she never turns off her phone, so I called her."

Merilee took a big swallow of coffee, not caring that she was scalding her tongue and the roof of her mouth. There were so many questions and things she knew she should be discussing with her daughter, but if some anonymous person was writing bad things about her and Michael, she needed to see it.

She sat down and opened the laptop. "Please pull it up, Lily. We'll talk about rules and consequences as soon as I'm done reading."

Lily did as she was told while Merilee downed the rest of her coffee. "Read the last two first, and then read this one. It was posted yesterday."

In ten minutes she'd read the first two blog posts, wincing at the mention of the divorcée, who was undoubtedly her, gratefully accepting the second mug of coffee from Lily without looking up from the screen.

"This is horrifying," Merilee said when she got to the end of the second one. "I feel as if I'm on a reality show with strangers watching me."

"It's not really talking badly about you, Mom. 'Unaffected' just means that you're not fake or insincere. I think it might actually be a compliment."

Merilee wanted to argue but knew Lily was right. She wanted to point out that it also said that the school year is long and a lot could happen, but she didn't want to add any more worry to Lily's full plate of things to needle over.

"You might need something stronger than coffee before you read the last one," Lily said quietly.

Merilee looked at her daughter over the rim of her mug. "It's only seven thirty in the morning. And how would you know about that anyway?"

"I watched part of *The Godfather*, remember?" She didn't smile.

Merilee's heart sank a little further. "Yeah. I remember." With a quick shake of her head, she returned to the computer and began to read.

• •

THE PLAYING FIELDS BLOG

Observations of Suburban Life from Sweet Apple, Georgia
Written by: Your Neighbor

Installment #3: Roundabouts: They're Not Rocket Science

I hope you all take the time to read our weekly local paper, the *Sweet Apple Herald*, which is conveniently delivered to our driveways (or sometimes they miss and it lands in the middle of the road or beneath a bush, where it's hidden until the next windy day, when all the pages are displayed on your front lawn, but I digress).

I read the paper from cover to cover, even the ads. And especially the obituaries. They're not meant to be amusing, but some of them are, unintentionally of course. Like the ones that try their hand at poetry and attempt to rhyme words like "Buick" and "quick," or "again" and "attain," and my favorite: "tricked" and "wicked." Neighbors, unless your last name is Wordsworth or Frost, you just shouldn't. And if your loved one was a party clown, don't put that picture next to his obit. It loses its sincerity, somehow. But if you do, rest assured I will clip it out and send it to my friend who collects amusing obituaries. Don't judge. Hobbies are good for you—like eating your vegetables and exercising. Only more fun.

In this week's edition of the paper, I was surprised to see that the entire front page—usually reserved for a groundbreaking story about the locations of new weather sirens or the increasing traffic woes on the Alpharetta Autobahn (Georgia State Route 400 for you newcomers, the nickname on account of the high proportion of German cars and the speed they manage to reach despite heavy traffic)—was completely given over to the three new roundabouts that are currently being constructed within our city limits.

I wasn't sure whether I should have been amused or horrified at the detailed drawing of one of the proposed roundabouts, complete with a diagram of cars entering and leaving the roundabout (with directional arrows just in case people were unclear about what side of the road to drive on), and an entire three columns of directions.

Neighbors, not to point out the obvious, but if you can't understand how a roundabout works from the overabundance of directional signs at said roundabouts, then perhaps you shouldn't be operating a motor vehicle at all. I would suggest a bike, but that's a whole different problem on our narrow and winding country roads and will undoubtedly be a subject for a future blog.

Speaking of news, I would be remiss if I neglected to mention more personal topics than what our fine local paper prints. This would include an observation of the high school's football team starters, who don't seem to fall under the socioeconomic spectrum of the rest of the school's—or Sweet Apple's—population. I'd be interested in learning where these young men actually live, and who's paying the rent.

Another touchy subject that won't be found in our local paper is that of a young third-grade math teacher who, rumor has it, is three months pregnant. This is wonderful news, of course, because there's nothing that we Sweet Appletonians love more than babies, but this teacher of our impressionable youngsters is a single lady. To make this news more than a little juicy, the presumed father of the baby was apparently not completely divorced when the pregnancy started. Yes, a divorce was in the works, but, for all intents and purposes, the man—father of two, I might mention—was still married to another woman.

I'm not trying to be mean-spirited toward any of the parties involved—especially to the recently divorced wife, who is the innocent victim in all of this. But hiding the truth is like putting perfume on a pig. That pig's still going to smell. And the sooner this is out in the open, the sooner everyone can move beyond this.

Before I sign off, I thought I'd bring up the topic of assimilation. No, this north Atlanta suburb is not technically "the South," but there are still quite a few natives among us, and although we appreciate the new transplants trying to assimilate into our culture, it's important to do it correctly. While having lunch at my club yesterday, I heard a woman from Michigan say, "Bless his heart," when the poor waiter spilled her tea (regular—not sweet—like I didn't need to hear that to know she wasn't from around here). It was incorrect usage of the term, and not the first time I've heard it used incorrectly. Correct usage would have been the waiter, after the woman asked for (shudder) unsweet tea, saying, "You're not from around here, are you? Bless your heart."

So I thought I'd be neighborly, and for each blog I'll end with a Southern saying and what it means. I hope y'all will enjoy this as much as I will.

"The new broom might sweep clean, but the old broom knows the corners." This can refer to a lot of things, including hiring someone older but with more experience, but as my example I'd like to use a newly divorced husband, with an ex-wife, two children, and a pregnant girlfriend. Seems to me he thought he was trading up for a younger model, the "new broom." Instead I think he's just getting more of the same—except it will take a few years before she gets tired of doing his laundry. And that's all I'm going to say about that.

Lily looked at her mother with wide eyes, the line between her brows a deep crevasse. "Do you think this means Miss Garvey is going to have a baby?"

It took Merilee a few moments before she realized to whom Lily was referring, having called Tammy Garvey all sorts of names in her head besides her actual one in the months since Michael moved out. "I don't know, Lily. There could be other pregnant single third-grade teachers . . ." She stopped at the look Lily gave her, a look that no ten-year-old should be familiar with.

Merilee put her arm around Lily's shoulders. "Still, let's not assume anything until I've had a chance to speak with your father, all right?"

Lily nodded and closed the laptop, the slump in her shoulders making Merilee hold off on talking about a punishment for disobeying. Finding out on a blog that her father's girlfriend was pregnant was punishment enough.

She took a breath, trying to ascertain how she felt herself. That nodule of pain that seemed lodged in her throat every time she thought of Michael was still there, but learning that Tammy was having his baby hadn't made it bigger. Maybe that was something. Maybe that was progress. And maybe the blogger was right about knowing sooner rather than later so she could move on. It was a good assumption that everybody at the lake party would know about it, so now she wouldn't be blindsided. She wondered if the blogger would be there and if she could guess who it was. And if the anonymous woman—she assumed it was a woman—had done her a favor.

"There're paw prints all over the grass outside! I think the white dog has been here! Can I go look for him?" Colin rushed into the kitchen, his eyes bright with excitement, his pajama shirt misbuttoned and his pants hitting him above the ankles.

Merilee stood and pulled out a chair at the table for him. "After your breakfast, and after you get dressed—and you can only go as far as the tire swing, remember?"

"But—"

"It could be a coyote. Or a raccoon." She didn't mention the word "bear," not wanting to scare either one of them. "There're all sorts of animals around here, and you don't need to be going too far from the house to find whatever it was."

"But I put an old dog bowl I found under the sink on the front porch and put cookies in it, so it must be a dog, right?"

"Colin!" Merilee stood suddenly, the chair scraping the floor.

"It's empty—I already checked. That's how I knew there were paw prints in the grass. And on the front porch, too."

Merilee tried to check her breathing as she knelt in front of her son, placing her hands on his shoulders. "Sweetheart, we cannot have a dog. And leaving food out on the porch to attract any wild animal is a bad idea. Do you understand me?"

He nodded solemnly, but the hope refused to leave his eyes. "Yes, ma'am. But what if it's a dog that needs a home? Then could we keep him?"

She sighed as she stood. "Why don't we cross that bridge if and when we get there? But no more food on the front porch; do you understand?"

He waited nearly a full moment, weighing his options, before he responded. "Yes, ma'am."

"Or the back porch," Merilee added. She went to the cabinet and pulled out two cereal bowls and placed them on the table.

"Why's Mr. Kimball here?" Lily called from the front room.

"What?" Merilee looked down at the oversized T-shirt she'd slept in; it barely concealed her braless breasts, which weren't as perky as they'd been before children. She put her fingers to her face, remembering that she hadn't washed it yet and that she'd put a blob of green toothpaste on a small pimple that had decided to appear on her chin the night before. She'd read this tip in a magazine somewhere and wasn't sure if it even worked but figured without anybody around to see her it couldn't hurt.

She was standing in the middle of the kitchen, trying to figure out if she'd be able to slip to her room without his seeing her from the front door, when she heard the knock on the screen door and then Wade Kimball's voice calling through it. "Good morning, Merilee. It's Wade. I'm here to build those shelves."

"Damn it," she said under her breath. He'd said he'd stop by on the weekend, but she'd assumed—incorrectly, it appeared—that he would call first to set up a convenient time.

She spotted Sugar's bib apron hanging from a peg on the wall and slid it over her head. "Hang on," she said as she tied it behind her, Colin already racing ahead to open the door.

"Hey there, sport," Wade said in greeting to her son. When he looked past Colin and saw Merilee, his eyes didn't register shock or revulsion. He was either very polite or needed glasses.

Crossing her arms over her chest, she said, "I wasn't expecting you so early."

He looked surprised. "I said I'd be coming this weekend. It's the weekend, right?"

"It's eight o'clock Saturday morning."

"Exactly," he said, moving through the doorway. "Carpentry is my hobby, which sadly gets postponed to the weekends so I can work my day job the rest of the week. If you'll just show me what you want done, I promise to stay out of your way."

Resigned, Merilee led him into the front room, which they used as their family room. It had wide-plank pine floors covered by soft cotton rugs and comfortable sofas. Everything was well-worn but loved, the bookshelves overflowing with older books, including an entire shelf dedicated to bird-watching. These were the oldest, the covers tattered and torn, the pages well read, with turned-down corners for easy reference.

"Here," she said, pointing to the space between the rear wall and the back of the couch. "We had built-ins in our last house, so I couldn't take them with me. But I need a place to keep my collection."

"Your collection?"

She nodded, always a little embarrassed when explaining it to other people. "Yes. I collect antique maps. Nothing really expensive or rare, but ones I find interesting for whatever reason. They're mostly smaller ones—I've never had room for the really big ones. I have a few I've framed, but the rest I keep rolled up and in archival-quality storage boxes. I need the shelves for those."

He studied her for a moment, and she found herself squirming under his scrutiny. "That's a lot cooler than my baseball cap collection; that's for sure." He smiled and she relaxed slightly. "What makes a map collectible?"

She shrugged. "Geography, mostly. Like if it's a place I'm familiar with. I like to see how things have changed. And I'm partial to the hand-drawn ones with pictures and sketches on them. It's almost like looking at old letters or diaries from another time."

"So you like old things? Or you like change?"

His last question was a little too close for comfort. Turning her back on him, she led him toward a stack of boxes she'd piled in a corner of the room. "Here are all the boxes, to give you an idea of dimension. I'm thinking something wide but short, so that it fits behind the couch. And I'd like to have a little extra space so I have room to grow."

He took a measuring tape from his tool belt. Pulling out the tape, he held one end toward her. "Hold that right by the leg of the couch."

He took several measurements, jotting them down on a small pad he kept in his belt. "You know, Sugar has some old maps. They belonged to her grandfather, I believe, and show all the land that used to belong to the Prescott family since the Civil War. Pretty impressive. Just about everything you see in a twenty-mile radius once belonged to them—including the land where the country club and golf course are now." Wade sat back on his heels. "My grandmother, Willa Faye, is Sugar's best friend, which is how I know all this, but every time one of Sugar's brothers would sell some parcel of land, Sugar would put a big black 'X' on one of her maps and go into mourning."

"That's pretty sad. But what about her nieces and nephews? Didn't they want to hold on to any of it?"

"You'd think with five children there might be grandchildren, but there weren't. Not sure what happened to the youngest brother, but I know one of them died in the war. The two oldest fought in Europe, and when they came back went a little wild. Took to all sorts of bad habits. Mostly horses. Never got married—too busy hanging around with the wrong sorts of women, according to my grandmother. The kind of women you spend money on but don't necessarily marry is how she put it. And nice women from good families were kept a good distance from them."

"So you don't know what happened to the youngest one—Jimmy?" It mattered to her, Merilee was surprised to find. She had such a clear picture of him, it seemed as if she knew him, and she wanted him to have a happy ending, even though from what Wade had just told her, it didn't seem likely.

Wade shook his head. "You can ask Sugar, but she might not answer. She's pretty closemouthed about her childhood—wasn't easy with her being the only girl and her mother pretty much out of the picture. Sugar had to grow up real fast during hard times. It's amazing she turned out as nice as she is."

Merilee made a face, making Wade laugh. "I know she seems crusty at first—that's just her nature, probably from having to deal with four brothers her whole life. But once you get to know her, you get to see how big and loyal a heart she really has. My grandmother once told me that Sugar would do absolutely anything for someone she loved. Anything. I've never had to test that theory, but I believe it."

"Yes, well, I guess I'll have to take your word on that. Why don't you finish up your measuring and figure out what you'll need in materials to write up a quote, and I'll go and throw on some clothes." She turned to leave.

"Oh, sorry. I thought you were already dressed. You should have told me."

She faced him, indicating the oversized T-shirt and apron. "Really?"

He shrugged. "I'm a guy. Besides, I was probably too focused on that green dot of dried toothpaste on your chin. You might want to wash that off if you decide to leave the house."

Trying to think of something to say and coming up empty, she turned again and headed back toward her bedroom.

When Merilee emerged from her room fifteen minutes later, she heard adult voices coming from the front room. She found Sugar running what looked like a dust rag over the coffee table, while Wade sat on the window seat with his pad of paper and a calculator. Sugar didn't even bother to look embarrassed at being caught dusting in her tenant's house and kept on with her work, interrupting herself only to say "Good morning" before resuming her task.

Merilee paused for a moment, listening for the children. "Have you seen Lily and Colin?" she asked.

"I told them to go get dressed and that they could watch television when they were finished," Sugar said without looking up. "You have that party at noon, and Lake Lanier is at least an hour away, depending on traffic." Preempting Merilee's next question, she said, "I forgot to bring over a tray for the cookies we made, and I know there aren't any in this kitchen, so I brought one over this morning. I took the liberty of putting the cookies on it, and I do believe they make a nice presentation."

Merilee wasn't sure if she should be annoyed or grateful. She had wondered how she'd bring the cookies to the party, thinking she'd probably stop off at a Walgreens on the way and get a disposable foil tray.

As if reading her mind, Sugar said, "It's sterling. From Mama's wedding silver. I trust you'll remember to bring it back."

"Thank you," Merilee said, feeling insulted and relieved in equal measure, a contradiction she was getting used to in her dealings with Sugar Prescott.

Wade stood and tore off the top page of the notepad. "This includes all materials, but I'll throw in the labor for free. Like I said, this is my hobby and I appreciate the opportunity to play a little bit. Beats cutting my lawn." He grinned.

Before she could argue, the children ran into the room and Merilee almost did a double take. Instead of the T-shirts and cotton shorts they'd normally wear on a Saturday, Colin wore a collared golf shirt and his nice pleated shorts, and Lily wore a sundress that had been at the back of the closet.

"Miss Sugar said it was a party so we should dress up a bit," Lily explained.

"Yes, but—"

"We're bringing our backpacks with our other clothes and bathing suits so we can change if everybody else is casual."

Merilee found herself speechless again. It wasn't that anything Lily said wasn't correct or that Merilee wished she'd thought of it herself. But she was angry. Not angry that Sugar had usurped her parental authority and Lily and Colin had actually listened and obeyed, but angry because she was just so darned grateful that somebody else had helped her out.

As if oblivious to any undercurrents in the room, Wade turned to Sugar. "When I come back tomorrow to get started on this project for Merilee, I'll bring more hay for the barn. I'll pad it extra high and show these kids how to jump from the hayloft. Maybe you can show them how it's done."

"Really, Wade," said Sugar, her expression stern. "Children aren't allowed to do those things anymore. At least not without some sort of padding and a helmet."

"What barn?" asked Colin. Lily just looked worried.

"Didn't Sugar show you her barn? It's on the other side of the woods from here, but it's just a quick hike. My sisters and I grew up jumping from the hayloft as soon as we could walk. Sort of a rite of passage around here." His face got serious as he eyed Lily. "Does this mean Sugar hasn't shown you her sheep? She puts red bows on their necks every Christmas."

"*You* put bows on the sheep. I just allow it because the police know who you are and won't arrest you for trespassing because you're practically my grandson." Sugar's lips pressed together in disapproval.

"There will be no jumping from haylofts," Merilee said firmly, remembering Rufus and the kitchen table and the boy Curtis. She met Sugar's gaze and knew she must be thinking the same thing. Eager to change the subject, she sent the children into the kitchen to eat their cereal. Feeling Sugar's disapproving stare, she told them to eat a piece of fruit, too.

Wade left to pick up the materials and get started in his workshop, promising he'd text her pictures to make sure it was what she wanted. Sugar declined his offer of a ride and headed toward the door.

Merilee called her name and the woman stopped, keeping the door open with one arm as if prepared to bolt.

"All those books in here on the shelves—the bird books. Were those Jimmy's?"

It took Sugar a moment to answer, as if she might be thinking of an answer that might not be the truth. "Yes," she said finally. "Those were his. He was a crack shot with his slingshot and would trade squirrels and rabbits for books because Daddy wouldn't have spent his money on anything as frivolous as a book. Jimmy was quite the entrepreneur."

"Has he been gone a long time?"

Sugar's lips pressed together and Merilee knew she'd gone too far. But she'd had to ask the question. Had to know what had happened to Jimmy.

"That's a story for another time." She let the door close softly behind her, then made her slow way down the porch steps toward the drive.

Merilee followed after her. "Would it be okay if we used the books? I think Colin would love to study the birds—there are so many around here, and he loves that kind of thing, and has the patience for bird-watching. I could buy our own set of binoculars—"

"I'll think about it," Sugar said, cutting her off. And without another word, she continued toward her house, her back rigid but her head bowed as if struggling under the weight of memories.

Seven

MERILEE

Lily sat in the backseat with the silver tray full of cookies on her lap while Merilee wished for about the tenth time that she'd asked Colin to hold them instead. Every time she took a turn or just went around a bend in the road, Lily looked like she would pass out from the burden of trying to keep the nicely arranged cookies in place.

"Sweetheart, it doesn't matter if they get messed up. We can fix them when we get there, okay?"

"But what if Bailey sees them before we have time to fix them?"

There were so many ways Merilee could choose to answer that question that it was hard to find one that would be appropriate for young ears. "You'll just have to tell her that they're delicious and she'll have to wait until she can have one."

Colin slumped in the backseat next to his sister. "What if the dog comes to the yard looking for me and I'm not there?"

"If a tree falls in the woods, and there's no one there to hear, does it make a sound?" She hadn't meant to be snarky, but she was feeling tense at the prospect of seeing all those people at the party and having them know more about her than she knew about them. Like how her ex-husband was living with his pregnant girlfriend.

"Huh?" Colin asked.

"Sorry," Merilee apologized. "I was just answering your hypothetical question with one of my own. And it's 'excuse me,' not 'huh.' I don't need people thinking you were raised in a barn."

"What's wrong with being raised in a barn? I think that would be cool. And I could have a dog and as many animals as I wanted, because it's a barn."

If the road up to Heather's house on Lake Lanier hadn't been so narrow and curvy, Merilee would have closed her eyes in frustration.

"Hypothetical means it's not based on fact, but on what someone *thinks* might be true," offered Lily. Merilee's hands gripped the steering wheel tighter.

Merilee had been up to this area, known as "Atlanta's water playground," a few times to take the children to the water park at Lake Lanier but had never been invited to one of the private homes. When Heather had told her that they should have enough room for Colin, Merilee was left thinking of a smallish cabin in the woods, with a distant lake view through the trees. Which was why when her GPS told her to take a left at a large gated entrance, she was surprised to be stopped by a man in uniform carrying a clipboard, and even more surprised when she gave him her name and it was on the list.

The road narrowed as it climbed past heavily wooded lots, quick slices of water views teasing them as they meandered their way until they couldn't go any farther because of all the parked cars. Merilee put the minivan in park as a young man wearing khaki shorts and a white button-down shirt ran toward her.

Merilee rolled down her window. "I'm looking for number eight thirty-six."

"The Blackfords?" He was already tearing off a ticket stub and handing it to her. "Just jump in one of those golf carts and one of us will be happy to drive you to the house."

"Oh, that's not necessary. We can walk," Merilee said, eyeing the heavy tray of cookies.

"Well, it's about three-quarters of a mile, mostly at a slope, so I'd

suggest you take advantage of the carts. That's what they're there for."
He smiled and opened her door.

"All right, then. Hang on, Lily, and I'll take the tray."

Lily looked more relieved than was warranted.

After settling themselves into a golf cart driven by another young
man wearing a uniform of khaki shorts and white shirt, they were
driven past two large stone pillars, each with an upright and angry-
looking lion perched on the top. She looked down at her shorts and
wondered if she should have worn a dress instead.

The driveway opened up, giving them an expansive view of the
lake and the large dock and boathouse and impressive array of motorized water toys parked around it. Several adults and children were
making their way down to the dock, but Merilee didn't have time to
try to identify anyone because she was too busy staring at the house.
Except it wasn't a house. Even calling it a mansion wouldn't have been
accurate. It was more like something from a Disney movie—sprawling
and turreted, with mullioned windows and lots of wrought iron. It
couldn't be described by any single architectural term. It was more like
someone had thrown a bunch of styles into a pot and stirred so that
instead of highlighting a single thing, the style muted all the elements,
creating something that was more surprising than beautiful.

The golf cart swooped around to the front of the house, blocking
their view of the lake, and stopped in front of wide stone steps leading
up to double wooden doors, the arched frame above them high enough
to belong to a castle with a moat. There was no moat here—only a
perfectly manicured lawn and garden that was so crisp and colorful
Merilee wondered if it could be fake.

"Merilee!"

She turned at the sound of her name, relieved more than she'd have
liked to admit to see Lindi Matthews. They hadn't had a chance to have
their coffee yet, but they'd had several phone conversations, during
which Lindi had essentially pulled Merilee back from the proverbial
ledge on the desperate matters of what to pack in the children's lunches
and whether she needed to reciprocate with gifts to the entire class
(whatever the kids wanted and no, respectively). Lindi's ability to listen

and consider all sides of a problem before offering solid advice probably made her a very good lawyer. Merilee needed to talk to another
adult about the blog and thought she'd ask Lindi out for lunch on a day
they could both manage it, because that conversation would last for
more than just a cup of coffee.

Lindi smiled, a small dab of pale pink lipstick on her front tooth.
"You've got a bit here," Merilee said, touching her own tooth with her
finger.

Lindi closed her mouth and swiped her tongue over her teeth. "That
will teach me not to try putting on lipstick while I'm driving. I don't
usually wear makeup, but one of the moms is a former Miss Georgia so
I always feel as if I have to be on my A game when I'm with this crowd."

"Which one?" Merilee asked, turning for the first time to study the
crowd of people. She hardly recognized any of them out of their tennis gear.

"The tall redhead with the legs up to here. It's one of the reasons
why you see a lot of dads at drop-off. For the sightseeing." She winked.
"Come on. Let me show you where to put the cookies. It's called the
dining room, but Jenna calls it the banquet hall."

They walked inside the house, and Merilee tried not to gape at the
wall of windows that faced them, framing the view of the lake, or at
the plush furniture and art that decorated the foyer and living spaces.
She looked down at the girl standing next to Lindi, a miniature version
of her mother. "Hello, Jenna. I'm Mrs. Dunlap, Lily's mother. She tells
me that you're very good in math; isn't that right, Lily?"

She turned to find that both of her children had left her side, seeing
that they'd deposited their bags with their bathing suits and change of
clothes on the floor next to her feet. Feeling a moment of panic that
all mothers seem to acquire at childbirth, she didn't relax until her gaze
settled on both children. Lily was already huddled in a group with
Bailey Blackford, and after a moment, she spotted Colin sitting cross-
legged in front of a large black Lab, reaching up to scratch it behind its
ears. Assuming it was the family dog, Merilee made a mental note to
ask Heather if they might ever need someone to dog-sit when they
went on vacation.

"I like Lily," Jenna said, her voice so quiet that Merilee had to lean very close to hear. "She's nice to me."

Merilee's eyes met Jenna's for a brief moment of understanding at the implication of Jenna's words.

"Sweetie, why don't you go say hi to Lily and she can introduce you to her friends?" Lindi offered.

A look of panic crossed the girl's face. "I'm hungry. Can I eat something first? And then I'll go say hi."

Lindi asked Jenna to scoop up the two discarded backpacks before the three of them walked into what indeed looked like the perfect spot for a medieval banquet. It was longer than most bowling alleys, as was the trestle table that ran down the middle of it. Wooden rafters bisected a cathedral ceiling, and four wrought-iron chandeliers with real lit candles dangled above the table. Cleverly disguised recessed lights and three walls of tall casement windows with leaded glass flooded the room with light that glinted off the plastic wrap on dozens of elaborate trays, bowls, and platters. Merilee gave a silent thanks to Sugar for the loan of the tray, trying not to imagine her embarrassment if she'd brought anything disposable or resembling plastic.

Leaning in discreetly toward Merilee, Lindi whispered, "Heather's husband is a doctor, but about six years ago he retired from practicing and opened up a bunch of those doc-in-a-boxes all around the state. It was so successful that they've branched out into twenty other states. In case you were wondering." She stepped toward the table and made room for her own large crystal salad bowl and Merilee's cookies.

A short, plump woman with olive skin and black hair was busily taking plastic wrap off the food and rearranging the silver boat of fruit that sat in the middle of the table, cascading grapes of three different varieties draping onto the lace tablecloth. She looked up and smiled at Lindi and Merilee without even pausing as she worked.

"That's Patricia—the house manager," Lindi said quietly. "You'll meet Claire, too—she's the assistant. You should probably get to know them both since you have children in both of Heather's kids' classes. She's very involved, so everybody gets to know Patricia and Claire."

It wasn't clear whether Lindi thought this was a good thing. The two mothers stood back from the table as Jenna put tiny pieces of food on a scalloped glass plate, studying each offering as if it were a specimen under a microscope.

"Did your husband come?" Merilee asked, noticing the large number of dads present.

"No, he stayed at home with the baby. Henry's only eighteen months and desperately needs his nap or we all suffer." She lifted her hand and waved to a dark-haired woman on the far side of the table. The woman smiled and approached them with two plates, both brimming over with food.

"Merilee, this is Jackie Tyson. She's the physical education teacher and girls' cheerleading coach. And no, she doesn't take bribes, so don't try." Lindi and Jackie both laughed, but it had an edge to it, as if somebody actually had tried.

Merilee introduced herself, trying not to smile as she realized she could have guessed the woman's occupation judging by the bike shorts and muscled thighs.

"Nice to meet you," Jackie said with a warm smile and another laugh. "Don't stand too close, though—my husband and I biked here. It didn't register that it would be so hot or so hilly." She lifted both plates. "But at least I won't have to feel guilty about all the calories."

Merilee nodded with appreciation. "That's impressive. I had a tough time driving here—thought my brakes might give out on a couple of those inclines."

"Will your Lily be trying out for the cheerleading squad?" Jackie asked.

"She hasn't mentioned it to me. She's never wanted to do one of those cheer camps or asked about trying out, and I never pushed it."

"I take it you weren't a cheerleader, then?" Jackie asked.

Merilee kept her smile in place. "I was. But it was a very long time ago." She took a deep breath, eager to change the conversation. "Lily would like to play tennis—maybe try the junior age-group of the Atlanta Lawn Tennis Association. Her dad plays on a men's singles ALTA team and I think that's given her the idea. She had lessons last summer and really enjoyed it and was actually pretty good, and because we're not in a neighborhood anymore, I thought ALTA would give her a chance to meet other girls her age outside of school."

"Bailey plays ALTA and is trying out for cheerleading, too," Jenna said quietly before biting a grape in half.

"Yes, well, the only way I can manage our schedules is to have the kids pick one sport per season to focus on, and that seems to work for us."

"Us, too," said Lindi. "It's the only way I can remain sane."

"Do you play tennis?" Jackie asked Merilee.

"Oh, gosh. No. When it comes to racquet sports I have the coordination of a toddler. I love the game, though. I was thinking of maybe joining the lowest level—I think that's C-9—where my lack of skills might not be noticed. More of a social outlet where we play a little tennis."

Jackie and Lindi exchanged a glance before Lindi explained, "There is no such thing as a social level in ALTA. They're all in it for blood. Or a bag tag—that's what you get to hang on your tennis bag when you win a championship. And they're in it for the food, too. The lower the skill level, the higher the quality of the food the players bring to each match. It's as competitive as the actual tennis. If not more so."

Merilee laughed, then stopped when she realized she was the only one.

"My husband must be wondering where his food is. He's on lifeguard duty down on the dock, so he can't leave," Jackie said. "And let me know if you hear of anybody who wants a cat. I just found a litter of kittens and my husband's being mean and saying I can't keep them. He says one Beagle and an orange tabby are enough." She nodded at Merilee. "It was a pleasure meeting you. Feel free to call me at the school if you have any questions about the athletic programs or need any advice—although if you're friends with Lindi, she's probably got you covered." She smiled again, then left to weave her way through the growing crowd, confirming Merilee's guess that the entire elementary school must have been invited.

A few women she knew by sight waved at her and she smiled and waved back, but she didn't approach them, afraid of any conversation that might mention the blog. And wondering if one of them might be the writer and not wanting to inadvertently give away any more blog fodder.

"Merilee! So glad you could make it!" Heather appeared in all her blond glory, her tanned and toned arms displayed to perfection in a white form-fitting sundress that showed off an impressive chest and lean body. Merilee found herself slouching as she crossed her arms, deciding that despite what Jackie had said, she'd join a tennis team and subject herself to humiliation if it meant looking like Heather Blackford.

Her bright blue eyes flickered over Merilee's sleeveless blouse and pleated shorts before settling briefly on her navy blue Keds. Turning her head, she said, "And good to see you, too, Lindi." She beamed at Jenna. "I understand you were the only one who got all the answers right on the first math quiz. I think we'll have to have you over to study with Bailey before the next test."

Jenna's eyes held a mixture of hope and terror. "That would be nice," she said quietly, her hand slipping into Lindi's as her gaze dipped to the floor.

Lindi smiled. "I'm going to take Jenna to change into her swimsuit. I'll leave Lily and Colin's backpacks in the pool house if they want to get changed later."

"Thanks, Lindi. And speaking of which, I need to go find my children—"

"Have you met my husband, Daniel?" Heather interrupted, pulling on her arm as Lindi sent her a quick wave before walking away.

"No, I don't think so." Merilee turned to see a tall blond man standing next to Heather. He was Ken to her Barbie, as fit and gorgeous and as comfortable in his skin as was his wife. Except he wasn't. Despite his warm greeting, and the way he really looked at her and said her name, there was something ill at ease in Heather's husband.

"She's a Georgia girl, too." Heather beamed. "That's how I can tell we're going to be the best of friends."

"A Georgia girl," Daniel repeated, studying her.

Merilee kept smiling, kept breathing. "You have a lovely home."

He turned his head as if seeing where he was for the first time. As if he weren't the one responsible for paying for all of it. "Oh, thank you. Yes, Heather's done a fine job with it, hasn't she?" It sounded like a real question, as if he was searching for reassurance.

"Yes, she has." Merilee was trying to think of something else to say when the piercing sound of a child's shrieking came from outside and seemed to go on and on and on. "That's Lily," Merilee said even before the thought fully registered in her brain. But recognizing your child's sounds of distress was another one of those things that appeared at childbirth, along with the eyes in the back of your head and the sixth sense that enabled mothers to know when something was wrong.

She began running toward the wide bank of French doors covering the entire back side of the house. Groups of people parted as she ran down the different levels of steps, following the shrieks, only half-aware of Daniel following close behind her.

She stopped at the trampoline, recognizing Lily's blond hair spilling over the side, the slight form of her daughter barely making an indentation on the black surface. A woman she didn't recognize was kneeling next to Lily, the little girl's bare foot being carefully manipulated in her hands.

"Lily?" Merilee called out before carefully pulling herself onto the trampoline.

"Mom!" Lily, whose screams had subsided into small whimpers by the time Merilee had arrived, burst into renewed crying. "My foot got stuck in the springs. I think it's broken, and now I can't try out for tennis or cheerleading."

The last part of what Lily said barely registered as Merilee crawled over to her daughter. She felt a heavier presence next to her and saw that Daniel had climbed up with her and was addressing the woman. "Thanks, Martha. What does it look like?"

"It's been a while since I did any nursing, but I don't think it's broken—it's either a sprain or a really bad twist."

He knelt by Lily's foot and took it. "I'll take over—thanks for your help."

The woman nodded and gave Merilee a brief smile before heading toward the edge of the trampoline as Merilee moved to Lily's side and took her hand. The sobs had reverted back to sniffles, although she still looked worried.

"Hi, Lily. I'm Dr. Blackford, Bailey's dad. I think what we have here is a badly twisted ankle. You're very lucky because it could have been worse, but it's not. I'm going to put a compression sleeve on it and an ice pack, but you'll need to rest it and keep it elevated for the rest of the day and all tomorrow, too. I know you don't want to hear this, but you should probably go home so you won't be tempted to use it. Otherwise, you could really make it much worse."

Colin appeared next to the trampoline with a large dripping ice cream cone in his hand and on most of his face and chin, the black Lab at his side as if they belonged together. "Do I have to go, too?" He lowered the cone and allowed the dog a few licks before licking it himself.

"I don't want to go home!" Lily began to wail.

Heather appeared, her elegant hands with pink-tipped nails resting on the edge of the trampoline. "You don't want to miss cheerleading tryouts, Lily, do you? You really should go home and rest your leg so that it gets better quickly and you're ready by Friday."

"Mom!" Colin protested. "I don't want to go!"

Ignoring the children's protests, Heather said, "Daniel can drive you. I wouldn't feel right making you take poor Lily home by yourself when I'm sure you're as shaken up as she is. There. It's settled. Daniel will drive you all home. I'll have someone bring your minivan back tomorrow morning."

A look that was either annoyance or surprise crossed Daniel's face so quickly that Merilee couldn't determine which one it was.

"Really, that's not necessary—," Merilee began.

Heather interrupted. "We insist. Don't we, Daniel?" She sent him a pointed look.

"Yes, of course," he said. "Let me go get the wrap and ice pack, and I'll carry her out to my car."

Both children were subdued as Daniel carried Lily to the four-car garage and carefully placed her in the backseat of a large black Mercedes sedan, asking Colin if it would be okay for Lily to rest her foot on his leg. To Merilee's surprise, he didn't argue, still despondent over having to leave behind his new best friend, who was standing on the driveway, looking at Colin and wagging its tail.

They pulled out of the garage and down the drive, all of them seemingly lost in their own personal miseries. "This really isn't necessary," Merilee said for what seemed like the hundredth time. "Lily's going to be fine, and I'm perfectly capable of driving."

"And all of that may be true, but I feel better knowing you all got home safely. We feel responsible because Lily got hurt on our property. This is the least I can do."

She held up her hands. "Fine. I won't say anything else about it, but I do hate making you leave the party."

He let out a soft sigh. "Those parties are more Heather's thing. Between you and me, I'd rather be at my fishing cabin on Lake Murray. Not a soul around, and the views are spectacular. It's what I call my piece of heaven here on earth."

"Sounds like heaven," Merilee agreed, enjoying the quiet inside the car, her ears still vibrating with the noise from the party. "I recently moved to a relatively secluded house, and I have to say I do enjoy the quiet. When my phone pings with a text message, it seems like an intrusion."

"At my fishing cabin, there's no cell reception or Wi-Fi. It's one of its perks."

He grinned broadly, as if he'd just shared a secret, and she found herself grinning back. Daniel Blackford was usually the kind of man she found intimidating—successful, self-assured, not to mention gorgeous.

"And please call me Dan. I've been Dan—or Danny to my family— my whole life until I met Heather. She likes Daniel better."

"I kind of like Danny," she said, laughing at the incongruity of it. "Does the rest of your family still call you that?"

"Just my older brother, but he's in Chicago now, so I don't see him too much. We were both born and raised outside of Macon, and he couldn't wait to leave. But I guess I'm a Georgia boy at heart and couldn't stand to live anywhere else. Wanted to raise my children here, to have the kind of childhood I had—swimming holes, fishing on a dock, catching lightning bugs in a jar on summer evenings." He was silent for a moment, and she watched his expression change so imperceptibly that she almost missed it. He'd gone from the Daniel Blackford she'd been introduced to, to a man defeated.

"It's hard to raise kids these days; that's for sure," Merilee said, trying to lighten the mood.

"Why's it so hard, Mom?" Lily called from the backseat.

Merilee turned to look at her daughter, the permanent frown line more pronounced than usual, her wrapped leg elevated on her sleeping brother's lap. "That's a discussion for another time. How's your foot?"

"It's fine—it hardly hurts. Do you think we could go back to the party? I was having a lot of fun." She sat up straighter, her eyes round. "Oh, no! We left the silver tray!"

Even Merilee sat up straighter, too, horrified at the thought. "Let's not panic. I'll text Jenna's mom and see if she can pick it up for me."

"I'll take care of it," Dan said. "I'll make sure it's delivered to your front door tomorrow, along with your minivan."

"I'm so sorry to be all this trouble. Really, I could call my ex to stay with the children, and I could drive back with you to get my car and the tray—"

"I'll take care of it," Dan said again, and Merilee knew he would.

"And our backpacks," Lily piped up from the backseat. "We left those, too."

"They're in the pool house," Merilee said almost apologetically, but she didn't offer again to retrieve everything herself. It was clear Dan was used to getting his way. Except in his own family.

They drove the rest of the way making easy conversation, which surprised her. She'd expected to be intimidated by him, but he put her at ease, asking her about her job and the children, skirting around her divorce and the reasons why her children had changed schools. He seemed so different from Heather. Not that Merilee knew either of them very well, but he was as quiet and introspective as she appeared to be social and outspoken. It was probably one of the reasons why they'd been attracted to each other.

As Merilee and Dan entered Sweet Apple, she gave him directions to her house. "Turn right here, and when you get to the white ranch rail fence, take a left onto the dirt road."

"This is Sugar Prescott's place," he said with surprise.

"Yes. I'm renting the cottage behind her farmhouse. She's my landlady."

"She's what my parents called 'good people.' Strong principles and convictions, that's for sure. Did you know she used to be the mayor of Sweet Apple? It was years ago—before I moved here—but I understand she ran against her own brother. That's something, isn't it?"

"I'd say. Have you met her?"

"Oh, yes," he said, a soft smile on his lips. "In my office, as a matter of fact. Didn't make an appointment, just showed up. Had to do with building a new clinic on Main Street. She wanted there to be a more aesthetic design to the building, and a lot more trees, more in keeping with the equestrian feel to the area. And I agreed. Because she was right. And because she didn't use the 'proper channels,' which is usually what people call the government bureaucracy, and I respected her for that."

"Yes, well, that silver tray belongs to Sugar."

His eyebrows lifted. "Then I will make sure it is returned to you posthaste. I might even polish it myself to make sure it gleams."

Merilee laughed at the image, believing that he actually might.

They drove past the large farmhouse, Merilee holding her breath until she was sure the front porch was empty, not wanting to confess she'd left the tray behind. Dan carried in Lily, who protested that she could walk herself, then settled her on the sofa in front of the television, her foot propped up on the armrest. He unwrapped it to check on it again, then rewrapped it, telling Merilee to put an ice pack on it for twenty minutes, then gave her his cell number to call if there were any problems.

She walked him out to the front porch. "Thanks so much, Dan. I can't tell you how much I appreciate it."

"Anytime. I mean it. And if that boy of yours wants to learn how to fish, call me. I've tried to teach my girls, but they're not too thrilled with sticking worms on hooks, and they're certainly not going to skin or gut a fish. I bet we can find plenty of fish in that lake at the front of the property. And since Sugar and I are such great friends, I'm sure she'd let us." He winked.

"Will do. And really, thanks again."

"Thank you, Merilee," he said. "I don't usually get a chance to know many of Heather's friends, but it's been real nice talking to you."

He said good-bye, then slipped behind the wheel of his Mercedes, making her wonder if he'd have preferred a pickup truck instead. Maybe he kept one for when he went up to his fishing cabin, hiding it from sight so Heather wouldn't have to look at it.

She watched until he disappeared around the bend, the puffs of red clay and a slightly unsettled feeling the only reminders that he'd been there at all.

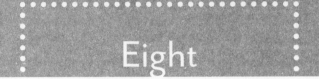

Eight

SUGAR

The shrill of the telephone startled Sugar from where she sat typing another letter to Willa Faye, her fingers paralyzed over the old round keys before she realized what the sound was. With her legs feeling rusty from sitting for so long, she wrested herself from her seat and made it to the rotary dial phone on the hall table on the eleventh ring.

"Hello, Sugar. This is Daniel Blackford. How are you?"

"Hello, Dan. Well, I'm still breathing. I hope you're calling about my tomatoes and not about me selling my land. I haven't changed my mind and don't plan to."

A low chuckle sounded in her ear. "I know that, Sugar. No worries. I'm actually calling about your new tenant, Merilee Dunlap. Her daughter, Lily, hurt her foot at a party at my house yesterday, and I was hoping you could go over and take a look and let me know how she's doing. I told Merilee to call me if she needed anything, but I haven't heard from her. You and I both know that doesn't mean everything is fine. I think Merilee would die of embarrassment if she knew I was asking after her. She seems very self-sufficient, and I don't think she'd take kindly if I called her myself."

She waited a moment before responding, biting back the first words that came to mind. Daniel Blackford was one of the few people she could still tolerate, and she knew he didn't take favors lightly. And she certainly couldn't explain her reluctance to talk with Merilee Dunlap, that every time she went over there it was like being confronted with a younger version of herself. It had been hard enough living through her youth the first time around, and she had no intention of reliving it. But standing on that front porch was like standing in a wind tunnel that sucked her into Merilee's life whether she wanted to go or not. "I'll go take a look and let you know. I suppose I could bring some of my tomatoes over, and some of my leftover corn bread from supper, so I have an excuse. If she thinks I'm just being friendly, she'll get suspicious. And she needs the food. I don't believe that woman knows how to cook."

"That's not considered a sin nowadays, Sugar."

"Well, maybe it should be. Back in the day I could feed my brothers and my daddy an entire meal with just a handful of collards, some flour, and a couple of eggs. I'm not saying it was tasty, but it put food in our bellies."

"I hear you. Please call me after you see Lily and let me know how they're getting along."

"I will. And, Dan? Please make sure my silver tray gets returned to me. It was my mama's, you know."

There was a small pause and Sugar smiled with satisfaction.

"How did you know about the tray?"

"I went to church today. You know the parking lot at First Methodist after services is better than a megaphone and a gossip column rolled into one."

He laughed out loud. "You don't miss a beat, do you, Sugar?"

"No. I surely don't."

There was a long pause on the other end of the line. "Good to know."

They said their good-byes; then Sugar placed the cover over her typewriter before heading to the kitchen to get the corn bread and tomatoes. The overcast sky gave her some respite from the hot sun, but still the driveway between her house and the cottage seemed to go on for miles. But she'd have to be crippled and forced to crawl before she'd spend the money for gas and take her car.

She looked toward the woods and for a moment she imagined she saw a mirage, a milky image of a small white dog by the edge of the trees. *Dixie.* She stopped, staring harder, pleased that she remembered the name even though she rarely thought of the sweet dog she'd had as a little girl. The last dog she'd ever had. She blinked and the dog was gone.

She wanted to believe that it had run back into the woods. Wanted to think it was safe. Poor little dog. They had both once believed the woods to be a refuge, shade on a hot summer day or quiet when too many voices in the house made your ears ring. A place to be alone. But it had stopped being that years ago.

It took her a full minute to catch her breath before climbing the steps and knocking on the front door. Colin opened the door before she'd rapped the second time. "Did you see the little dog? Did you? He was right there by the woods!"

Merilee came to stand behind her son, a look of panic widening her eyes.

"My eyes aren't as good as they used to be." Sugar pressed her lips together. "Can't be sure if I saw anything at all."

"Mom! I told you there was a dog! And if you won't let me feed him, he's going to starve!" He ran down the steps and headed around to the backyard.

"Don't go past the tire swing!" Merilee shouted after him. She looked at Sugar apologetically. "I'm sorry for shouting. It's not been a good weekend. Lily hurt herself at the party yesterday and is afraid she can't try out for cheerleading, which I had no idea she wanted to try out for until yesterday. She doesn't want to put any weight on it, so she's making me do her every bidding." Her gaze slid to the dish and the paper bag Sugar was holding. "Can I take those for you?"

"You may. The corn bread is left over, and I've got too many to-matoes for me to eat, so you might as well take them. Just make sure you bring back the plates."

Pink flooded Merilee's cheeks; no doubt she was remembering the silver tray. She opened the door wider. "Would you like to come in?"

Sugar was about to say no since she'd just learned what she needed to know for Dan, but her gaze strayed behind Merilee to the table in the hall and the small white book that sat on top of it. In a moment of weakness, she'd called Merilee and given Colin permission to use Jimmy's bird books if he promised to be responsible and take good care of them. They certainly weren't doing anyone any good sitting on the shelves. Sugar squinted at the book. She couldn't read the title, but she knew what it was. *Georgia Birds and Their Nests*. She knew on page forty-eight there was a picture of a summer tanager and on page sixty-two there was a black-and-white sketch of a chipping sparrow in its nest. They'd been Jimmy's favorite to spot, and below each picture were little pencil markings to keep track of how many times he'd seen one. And on page one hundred and six there was a small smear of blood on the bottom right corner, the ridges of Jimmy's fingerprint faintly visible.

She looked back at Merilee. "I suppose. If you've got some of your sweet tea, I'm thirsty enough to drink it. It's hot outside."

"Of course. Come on back to the kitchen." She opened the door wider to let Sugar pass through before taking the bag and plate and leading them both into the kitchen.

Sugar peered into the front room, where Lily lay on the sofa with her foot propped on the armrest, watching something on the television, a laptop open on her lap, her fingers furiously typing on the keys. Dirty plates and glasses and a bowl of popcorn littered the coffee table in front of the sofa. The girl was obviously not feeling too poorly.

Sugar sat down at the table while Merilee poured two glasses of her barely palatable sweet tea and placed the cookies on the table. She kept her back firmly against the chair, unwilling to get too comfortable. She was still trying to understand what had made her tell the story of Rufus and Lamar. And Jimmy. Maybe it was the boy, Colin, and how much he reminded her of her youngest brother, the soft lankiness of him. His enthusiasm for the world in which he lived and his unconcern for things like shoes and napkins and cleanliness. The *boyness* of him that made Sugar miss her brother as much now as she had when he was first gone. Just the whiff of boy sweat clinging to Colin's skin made her remember. Made her want to cry all over again. And that was something she was not prepared to do.

"Would you like a cookie?" Merilee asked, passing her the plate.

"No, thank you. I'm watching my figure." It wasn't true, but she said it anyway, trying to keep some distance from this woman and her children yet finding it more and more difficult. She took a sip of her tea, looking at the dark shadows under the other woman's eyes, the fingernails that were ragged and short. They had too much in common, and it unnerved Sugar. Made her feel as if she were standing on a red anthill and couldn't move out of the way.

Merilee cleared her throat and Sugar got an odd satisfaction at the thought of the younger woman needing to find the courage to speak to her. "Wade told me that you might have some old maps of your family's property, from before all the subdivisions and the golf course. I love old maps—I'm kind of a collector, actually. I'd love to see them if—"

"I don't have them anymore," Sugar said, cutting her off. "Or they're buried so deep in my attic that it would take weeks to dig them out. I'm sorry." Although she wasn't.

A movement outside caught her attention, and she turned her head to see Colin in the tree swing, holding what she was sure was another one of Jimmy's bird books, then looking up into the tangled leaves above him.

"Thanks for letting us borrow your brother's books," Merilee said, her voice not completely hiding the hurt she must have felt at Sugar cutting her off so abruptly. "I can't tell you how much Colin's been enjoying spotting the various birds. He saw a redheaded woodpecker yesterday. Can't stop talking about it. Which is a relief because I'm getting tired of hearing about how he needs a dog and if he finds a stray he's keeping it."

Something stirred in the place inside Sugar's chest where her heart was supposed to be. "I'll call animal control to come find that dog if you think it's real."

"I'm not sure if it is or not—only Colin's seen it. But I'm torn about letting him keep it—assuming it's real and he finds it."

"Don't." She hadn't meant to say anything. Hadn't meant to get involved. But there were some things that were hard to forget, despite the cushion of years.

"Why do you say that? Most of my friends say children—especially boys—should grow up with a dog. Teaches them about responsibility and how to care for someone besides yourself or your family."

Sugar allowed a soft smile to touch her lips, looking out at Colin but seeing another boy. Another time. "Jimmy had a dog, Dixie. She was just a small white mutt, and she was supposed to be mine, but every dog we had always chose Jimmy as its favorite. She slept at the foot of my bed as a sign of respect, I guess, and because I fed her, and loved her with all my heart, but she was always at Jimmy's side. Even at the end." Her voice slowed for a moment. "But that was my choice, not wanting to be there. My mama taught me that if you wanted to pretend that something never happened, then turn your head and don't look."

She didn't ask Merilee if she wanted to hear the story, because by then it was too late. She was already lost in the memories, a reminder that, in the end, that's all a person had left.

SUGAR
1935

I watched Jimmy and Lamar stomping on the maypops that had fallen from the pretty purple flowering vine that Daddy had once planted outside Mama's bedroom window in the years back before he'd given up on trying to make her happy. I sat on the back porch steps, just watching them and listening to the popping sounds as they splattered each round ball. I wanted to tell them that we could be eating them instead of squishing them, but I didn't. I was stuck somewhere between being a grown-up and being a little girl, and I was still trying to figure out which side I was on.

Since Rufus had died, more than a year before, I'd grown up. Not just taller, but inside my head, too. And in my heart. I used to love squishing the maypops, the soft liquid burst under my feet—just the sound making me happy. Jimmy and Lamar were practically the same age as me, but I was too grown up now to go over to the tree and start stomping.

I was so busy listening to the maypops that I didn't realize Dixie wasn't with us until I heard whimpering coming from under the porch, soft and breathy, like the sound of clean sheets sliding against each other when you're making a bed. I crouched down and that's when I saw her. Her white fur on her back paw was dark red, crusted with dry blood, but most of it fresh. She was trying to lick her bloody paw, but that must have hurt, too, because every time her little tongue would touch it, she'd whimper again.

"Jimmy! Lamar! Come here quick! Dixie's hurt."

Jimmy was the one who went under the porch to get her. I don't know anybody else she would have come to, hurt as she was. She was a small thing, and fit in his arms, but when he lifted her up I saw the animal trap still stuck on her, her small leg bent the wrong way.

Lamar put his hand under her muzzle and she rested her head on him, her eyes really dark, as if they were holding in all of her pain.

"Squirrel traps," Jimmy said, halfway between being angry and being about to cry.

"But Daddy told Harry not to set them out, that we have too many cats and Dixie and they could get hurt." I was crying now, too angry and sad to care. And too full of hate for my older brother to think about anything else.

Daddy opened the back door, his napkin still tucked into the top of his shirt from supper. "What's all this noise? Can't a man read his paper in peace?"

I ran up the steps, throwing my arms around his soft middle. "Dixie's hurt—she got her paw in one of Harry's traps, and her leg is broke. We need to take her to the doctor."

He seemed to get shorter then, his shoulders getting rounder, his chin closer to his chest. "I'm sorry, Sugar. We don't got the money."

"What about Dr. Mackenzie? He'd do it for free!" I didn't know that for sure, but he was Willa Faye's daddy and surely that would count for something.

He shook his head, looking over me toward Dixie, who'd stopped whimpering, like she was trying to be brave. "I won't be asking him for more favors. Besides, there's nothing that can be done." He patted my head like I was still a little girl, then looked behind me at Lamar and Jimmy, and it was like he said something that I couldn't hear.

"I can set it. I watched Mama set Harry's broken arm when I was little. I remember what she did. Most of it." I was already turning toward the porch steps, in search of a short piece of wood I could use as a splint.

Daddy put his hand on my shoulder, holding me back. "The dog's in pain, Sugar. It'd be cruel to let her suffer. Looks like more than just a broken leg, too. Seems she's been gnawing on it long and hard, which means a festering that'll just kill her slowly. You need to do the right thing by her."

He squeezed my shoulder, as much a sign of affection as he was capable of giving, then went back inside the house. Dixie was looking at me with her beautiful brown eyes, but I couldn't touch her. I couldn't. It would be like that Bible story about Judas. Even though that's what I felt like.

"I'll do it," Jimmy said, his words thick, like they'd been mixed with molasses. "I'll make sure she don't feel nothin'. I'll talk to her and pet her and let her know she's loved."

Lamar was frowning. I think he was, but it was too hard to see with all those stupid tears blocking my eyes. "I'll go, too. That way, you cain't blame one of us."

I nodded, then turned away, still unable to look at the sweet dog who slept at the foot of my bed every night and hated to play fetch but was good at telling when you were sad and would lick your face to make you feel better.

I listened as someone went inside the house to get Daddy's pistol he kept in his desk drawer in the study and then come back out. "You sure you don't want to say good-bye?"

It was Jimmy, and he was standing behind me, and I could smell Dixie, smell her blood and her breath, and hear her whimper. I closed my eyes and turned my head, then felt the soft, cool touch of her tongue as she licked my cheek one last time.

And then they were gone and I ran to my room to put my head under my pillow for the longest time just so I couldn't hear the single shot from a pistol from deep in the woods. When I came back downstairs to start fixing dinner, I wasn't the same person I'd been. If Rufus's death had made me grow up halfway, Dixie's had made me finish up right quick.

A person learns a lot about life living on a farm, and what I didn't pick up natural-like, Willa Faye's mother filled in for me as best she could. But I learned two things that day all on my own. The first was that my brother Harry would always be my enemy. The second was that I would never love anything again that I couldn't bear to lose.

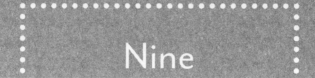

Nine

MERILEE

Sugar turned her head from the window and looked at Merilee as if suddenly realizing where she was and to whom she was speaking. And it was clear that both of them wished they could be anywhere else.

Sugar stood abruptly, holding on to the back of her chair. "I've got to go. You can bring back the plates when you're done. Just leave them on the front porch—no need to knock on my door and make me quit whatever I'm doing to answer it."

"Sure." Merilee stood and followed Sugar out of the kitchen.

Lily, who still had the laptop open—something Merilee really needed to say something about—turned to look at her mother. "Mom—Bailey just e-mailed me and told me that they're sending back all the cookies we made with the tray. I guess we were supposed to put a little sign on them or something saying they were gluten free, nut free, and dairy free."

"But they weren't," Merilee said.

"Exactly." Lily turned back and began typing furiously.

Merilee avoided looking at Sugar and was saved from commenting on the tray or anything else by the sound of a vehicle outside. She recognized Wade's pickup truck as it parked in front of the house and

Wade climbed out. For the first time, Merilee noticed how well his jeans fit and how nice a Braves T-shirt could look on a well-built man.

She closed her eyes briefly and gave herself a mental shake. She was barely divorced, and the mother of two. Not to mention the fact that she was definitely more a suit-and-tie type of girl. Always had been.

Merilee pulled open the door just as he reached the front porch, and just as Lily called out from the other room, "Mom—Bailey's dad says he thinks you're pretty."

Merilee cringed inside, wondering what else had been overheard in a conversation that probably wasn't meant for Bailey's hearing. And wondering why on earth he would say such a thing. It was . . . un-nerving.

"Why wouldn't he?" Wade said, stepping inside. "Speaking of pretty, good to see you again, Sugar." He leaned over and embraced the old woman while kissing her on the cheek. "It's a good thing you've sworn yourself to remain single or I might be asking you to step out with me."

Sugar made a good show of pretending to frown. "Your mama needs to give you a refresher course on manners, Wade."

"Nothing wrong with my manners. I just go a little crazy in the presence of so much beauty."

Sugar shook her head, but her cheeks flushed, which was better than the stark paleness of her face ever since she'd told her story in the kitchen. "That's enough, Wade. Why are you here?"

"I had an idea for another set of shelves that would fit in the hallway between the bedrooms and wanted to get Merilee's permission and do some measuring. She's got stacks of books along the wall that don't have a home, so I figured why not. I also noticed last time I was here that the cellar doors outside are rotting and need replacing. I wanted to get a better look and get you an estimate. We're in the middle of hurricane season, which always throws a tornado or two at us, and I want to make sure the cellar is functional."

"You do that. I'm going home to lie down a bit before *Southern Fried Homicide*. You can put your quote under my front mat. And please make sure you put more than zeros on it, because you know I'm going to send you a check anyway."

"Will do." He looked closely at her. "You feeling all right? You look a little pale. Why don't you sit down for a minute, catch your breath?"

She surprised all of them by actually sitting down in the stuffed armchair by the sofa. Merilee went over to Lily and, seeing she was on Facebook and not doing homework, closed the laptop. "We'll talk about this later," Merilee said quietly, watching as Lily's eyes refocused on the room around her and the fact that she was no longer alone. "Would you like some more sweet tea?" she asked Sugar.

"Not unless you're trying to kill me. But I would like a little tap water, please. Not too cold, not too warm."

Merilee made the mistake of catching Wade's gaze, his wide smile causing laughter to bubble in the back of her throat. She quickly left the room to get a fresh glass of tepid water for Sugar, then quickly returned.

Wade pulled out a measuring tape and stepped behind the sofa. "Just wanted to double-check a couple of measurements first," he said, the metal tape rattling as he placed it on the floor. "I've got a whole bag of sugar and ketchup packets for you to add to your collection, Sugar. I've been on the road a lot seeing to my new properties up in Forsyth County, so I've been eating at a bunch of those fast-food places. I'll leave the bag on your front porch when I drop off the invoice."

Sugar's chin went stiff. "I'm not embarrassed. Those things just get tossed out anyway. Might as well use them." She took a sip of her water, her eyes focused on Merilee as if expecting a challenge.

"So," Wade said as he moved the measuring tape to a new position on the wood floor, "I called my old work buddy I told you about, the one whose grandparents lived in Sandersville. William and Sharon West. They're in a retirement village in Hilton Head now, but still really active. He asked if they remembered you, but they didn't recall your name, either. It's funny, though, how you're from there and it's such a small town." He stood and hit the button on the tape so that it rattled as it was wound tightly into its casing, like a snake caught in a reverse hiss.

Wade tilted his head to the side. "What was your maiden name?"

"I really don't see how—"

"It was Talbot, right, Mom?" Lily interjected from the couch.

"Talbot," Wade said, slowly shaking his head. "Doesn't ring a bell, either. It just drives me crazy when I can't place a face or a name. Because I'm usually really good at both."

"Or I look like somebody you used to know. I promise you—we've never met." She wiped her hands on her shorts, feeling the sweat on her palms. "Why don't you come show me what you want to do with the hallway?" She led the way, glad for the dim lighting so he couldn't see her face.

While he was taking measurements, she heard another vehicle pull up in front of the house. Excusing herself, she walked quickly to the front door, knowing it could be only one of two people.

"Mom—Dad's here!" Colin called from outside, his voice seemingly amplified through the screen door.

She found herself tucking her hair behind her ears and smoothing her shirt, licking her lips so they wouldn't look so dry. She hated that she did this still, that she wanted to look nice for him. That she still believed she loved him. That she still wanted him back despite everything. She hated herself for this, but she couldn't seem to stop.

"Daddy!" Lily shouted from the sofa, forgetting that she was supposed to stay off her hurt foot and limping to the door.

And then Michael was there, all sandy blond hair and tanned skin, his hazel eyes looking green because of the emerald shade of his golf shirt. It was an expensive brand, a shirt she hadn't seen before. A brand he'd never worn. She tasted bile on her tongue, wondering if Tammy had bought it for him. Imagining the other woman helping him take it off.

"Hello, Merilee."

And that was all it took for her heart to squeeze, her knees to soften. Despite everything that was between them, he still had that effect on her. He was a bad habit she couldn't seem to break, reminding her of nicotine addicts who couldn't give up cigarettes even after they'd been reduced to breathing through an oxygen mask.

"Hello, Michael." Her voice sounded funny, but she wouldn't give him the satisfaction of swallowing first. "Did I mix up our schedule? I didn't think you had the kids this weekend."

"No, you didn't mix it up. Lily e-mailed me and told me she'd hurt her ankle. She told me she was fine, but I wanted to come see her my-self. I tried to call your cell to give you a heads-up, but it went straight to voice mail."

She frowned, trying to remember when she'd last seen her phone. It had been so crazy yesterday, with the party and then being driven home by Daniel Blackford. And today she'd been so worried about Lily and getting her situated that she hadn't thought to look for it.

"It must still be in my purse," she said, heading toward the hall table, where she'd left it when they'd come in the day before. Holding her breath, she searched the little pocket she always kept it in, and then the rest of the purse, before giving in to the inevitable. "I must have left it at the Blackfords'."

"I hope you locked it with a security code. It's situations like these when you wish you had."

She hadn't. It was so much easier not to have to enter a code every time she wanted to turn on her phone. When she was at work it was always turned off and locked in her office, so it wasn't something she ever worried about.

"Oh, Meri," he said, rubbing his hands over his face. "At least tell me that you deleted the contact name 'passwords' on your contact list with all of your passwords. Because if anybody can get into your phone, that won't be hard to find."

This time she did swallow, not caring that he saw it, because she was too focused on not crying. She wasn't sure why, but she thought it had something to do with feeling humiliated when all she wanted to do was appear strong and self-confident. To prove that he hadn't diminished her by his dismissal. And she had failed.

Wade appeared from the back hallway, walking slowly, as if he was familiar with his surroundings and supposed to be there. "I don't think her phone is in any danger at the Blackfords'. That neighborhood and those people are more likely to upgrade your phone before returning it than take it or mess with your passwords. Just saying." He offered his hand to Michael. "Wade Kimball. Nice to meet you."

He didn't bother to explain who he was or why he was there or why he was coming from the direction of the bedrooms. Merilee had a strong suspicion that he was doing it on purpose and she felt herself smile.

Michael shook his hand and introduced himself.

"And this is a good friend, Sugar Prescott," Wade said, indicating the old woman, who was still sitting but behind Michael and out of his line of vision.

"My landlady," Merilee explained. "Sugar, this is my hus—ex-husband, Michael."

Sugar stared at him with hard eyes, and Merilee had the strangest feeling that Sugar was doing it for her. The old woman didn't stand or say anything, just kept staring at Michael like she was waiting for him to disappear into a pillar of dust.

"It's good to meet you," said Michael, for once at a loss in a social situation.

"Hrum," said Sugar, not taking her eyes away from him, while he tried to keep smiling as if being given the evil eye were something that happened regularly.

Turning to Merilee, he said, "So, I was thinking if Lily was feeling up to it that I would take the kids to Cracker Barrel for lunch." He patted his pockets as if making sure he had his wallet, and Merilee noticed the bare finger on his left hand, a discernible indentation visible from where a wedding band had once been, worn every day for eleven years. This shouldn't have surprised her, shouldn't have made the lump form in her throat. Tammy wouldn't want any proof that the man sleeping next to her had belonged to another.

Colin started jumping up and down, shouting, "Cracker Barrel! Cracker Barrel!"

Lily hopped on one foot. "Yes, please, Daddy!"

Merilee stole a glance out the front window to Michael's car, relieved not to see a person in the passenger seat. "Won't Tammy mind not having you home for Sunday lunch?"

He looked a little sheepish. "She's . . . resting."

Merilee crossed her arms. "The first trimester is always the most exhausting." She didn't know she'd said it until it was too late, only Wade's widened eyes making her realize she'd spoken out loud.

Michael gave her an odd look. "You know?"

"Anyone who reads The Playing Fields Blog knows." She glanced at Colin, who seemed oblivious to the conversation and was still jumping around shouting, "Cracker Barrel!" Quietly, she added, "You and I will have to discuss this later, in private. We'll need to explain this to the children."

"Of course. But a blog? Who writes it?" His face darkened, and Merilee imagined him trying to organize his thoughts, to prioritize line items, to limit loss. It was what made him such a good corporate financial adviser.

"I don't know—it's anonymous. And I don't ask around because I don't want to publicize it. It mentions a lot of families in Sweet Apple, including ours—although not by name, thankfully—and it's not all that flattering."

"This isn't acceptable," he said, his face darkening further.

Neither is leaving your wife and getting another woman pregnant, Merilee wanted to add. But didn't. Michael had always been better at pointing out other people's shortcomings than at noticing his own.

"Well, freedom of speech and all that. The person isn't using names, so hopefully not everyone reading it will know it's us. And if nobody talks about it, then hopefully it will fade away."

Lily was now hanging on to her father's arm, breathing heavily from hopping, and a deep crease between her brows was now visible. "It now has over two thousand followers. Everybody at school knows about it, but Bailey doesn't think anybody knows some of it's about us. And she promised me she wouldn't tell." Her eyes widened as if a thought had just occurred to her. "But what if she does?"

After a deep breath, Merilee said, "That's for us to worry about and not you, all right? I'm thinking this is just a short-lived fad that will go away soon and we can forget all about it. Like Pokémon Go."

Her words did nothing to soften Lily's frown of worry.

"Look, why don't you all go out to lunch and forget about some stupid blog. It will give me a chance to do a little housework." She hadn't planned on it but felt the need to say it out loud in Sugar's hearing.

Michael glanced at Wade as if still waiting for an explanation for his presence, before turning back to Merilee. "I thought maybe you'd like to come to lunch with us. You know, like old times. Just the four of us."

She felt Wade and Sugar staring at her, making her feel that if she didn't have the right answer, they would provide it. "There's no 'four of us' anymore, remember? Besides, the kids have been with me all week. I'm sure they'd like some alone time with you."

"Mom—," Lily started to protest, but Merilee cut her off with a glance.

"We'll both be there for school and athletic events when we can, all right? But things are different now."

"Is Miss Garvey coming with us?" Lily asked, her voice so quiet that Michael had to lean closer.

His mouth tightened, understanding the meaning behind Lily's question. "You can call her Tammy now, Lily, remember? She's not your teacher anymore. And it'll be just you, me, and Colin. We can get sundaes for dessert, too, if you want."

"Sundaes!" Colin shouted, resuming his jumping, while Lily barely mustered a smile.

She sent Merilee a hopeful look. "But what about my foot? Dr. Blackford says I should stay off it."

"I'll carry you," Michael answered before Merilee could say anything.

As if conjured, the sound of tires on gravel came through the front screen door as Daniel's black Mercedes came to a stop next to Wade's pickup truck. She met him at the front door, relieved to see he had her phone in one hand, and horrified to see he had Sugar's tray full of cookies in the other.

She found herself flushing, remembering what Lily had said about Daniel thinking she was pretty, and hoping it had been a throwaway remark that he didn't recall. "Daniel—so nice to see you again. But really, I could have picked these up myself. You didn't need to go to all this trouble."

"No trouble at all," he said, grinning, looking very much like Brad

Pitt in his sunglasses and oxford-cloth shirt rolled up at the sleeves. "I was headed back to Sweet Apple before Heather and the girls were ready, and when she realized we had your phone, she said I had to bring it to you as soon as I got back to Sweet Apple. Claire and her husband will be here in about an hour to return your car." He looked sheepish for a moment. "You know, you really should have your phone password protected. It would have made it harder to find out who the phone belonged to, but anyone could have accessed all of your passwords and personal information."

"Yeah, I know." She looked at the tray, wondering how she was going to get it into the house without Sugar seeing, when she noticed that half of the cookies were missing. "I thought nobody ate them because I didn't include nutritional information."

He gave her a self-deprecating grin. "Well, nobody at the party ate them. But when Heather went for her run this morning, the girls and I enjoyed a few. For the record, we all agreed they were probably the best cookies we'd ever tasted—but don't tell Heather. She thinks her flourless carob chip cookies are to die for. And they would be if you like eating paper." He winked. "I thought I'd done a good enough job of hiding all the empty spaces on the tray."

She laughed, then pocketed her phone while taking the tray. "Would you mind doing me a favor? I need to get this tray to the kitchen without Sugar seeing, so if you could go in and say hello and introduce yourself to the men and distract Sugar for a minute, I'd appreciate it."

"I'm on it," he said with mock seriousness. "And I'd like to take a look at Lily's ankle, too, if that's all right."

"Perfect," she said, giving him a thumbs-up before running back toward the kitchen. When she returned a few minutes later, after having placed the cookies into storage bags and washing and drying the tray, Lily was back on the sofa while Daniel examined her foot. Sugar had thankfully stopped glowering at Michael and had stood as if preparing to leave.

"If you're ready to go, Sugar, I'll drive you back," Daniel said as he stood.

"Yes, thank you," she said, causing Wade and Merilee to exchange a worried glance. Sugar held up her bare arm. "I forgot my Fitbit, so why torture myself?"

"I think you're missing the point, Sugar," Daniel began, then stopped, realizing how pointless it probably was to argue. Facing Merilee, he said, "Lily is doing nicely—no problem with her putting weight on it, and Friday cheerleading tryouts are fine. Just let me know if you notice any swelling or bruising, but I think it's good. She can walk on it today, just no running or jumping, okay?"

Lily nodded, looking almost disappointed that her day of leisure on the couch was over.

Daniel offered his hand to Wade. "Good to see you again."

They shook and Wade nodded.

"You two know each other?" Merilee asked.

"Sure do," said Daniel. "We go way back to our single days right after we both moved to Atlanta. Lived in the same apartment building in Buckhead."

"And Wade dated Heather for a bit, too, didn't he?" Sugar said, projecting her voice so everybody would be sure to hear.

Wade gave them a tight smile. "Yes, a million years ago when we were just babies. And before she met Daniel, I might add."

"Small world," Merilee said, trying to picture the golden Heather with the pickup-truck-driving Wade and unable to.

Sugar's lips pressed together in disapproval. "That's when she still had brown hair and shopped at Penney's. Don't think she does that anymore, right, Daniel?"

Instead of answering, he tucked Sugar's hand into the crook of his arm. "Nice to meet you," he said to Michael as he led a straight-backed Sugar out the door.

"Wait a minute," Merilee said as she scooped up the tray she'd left on a side table and handed it to Daniel. "If you wouldn't mind."

"Not at all," he said with a wink.

There was an odd glint in Sugar's eyes. "When you return a serving piece, you're supposed to return food along with it."

Merilee thought of all the cookies in the storage bags sitting on the kitchen table, and the times she'd offered food to Sugar and each time been refused. "Thanks for letting me know," she said with a forced smile.

"I've got all that I need," Wade announced, following them outside. "I'll call you sometime this week to set up a time to come install everything." He said his good-byes, then climbed into his truck, leaving Merilee alone with Michael, the children having been told to go get their shoes.

They stared at each other for a long moment, strangers but not. She noticed for the first time the dark circles under his eyes, his slightly rumpled pants and shirt. "You have the iron," she said. "But if you take your clothes to the dry cleaner, ask for light starch. You like it that way."

"Thanks," he said. "So, how are you?"

"Just great. Fabulous." *Awful. Heartbroken. Lonely.* She said none of those things. He didn't deserve them. He didn't deserve to know how much she still hurt, or that all he had to do was say he wanted her back and she would be lost again, all her strength and resolve dissolved like smoke.

"Good," he said. "That's really good. You look great, by the way. Like you've lost a lot of weight."

She bristled. If she had it would be because she no longer had an appetite. A broken heart could do that to a person. "Thank you," was all she said.

"Oh, before I forget." He fished something out of his pocket. "I found this in your old nightstand. It had rolled to the back and got stuck behind a bunch of pens and pencils. I think it's one of David's."

He placed a yellow-hatted Lego construction worker in her outstretched hand. "Thanks," she said, unable to meet his eyes.

The children rushed out of their rooms, Lily limping to protect her ankle, kissing Merilee before jumping into their father's car.

"I'll bring them back in a couple of hours," Michael said as he opened his car door, then waited for a moment as if searching for the right words. "Call me if you need anything, all right? Anything at all."

She nodded, standing there and waving as they pulled down the drive, red dust blowing in her face. She clutched the Lego man in her hand, feeling all the losses in her life at once, and wondering how long it would take until the hurting and the missing would stop.

Ten

Observations of Suburban Life from Sweet Apple, Georgia
Written by: Your Neighbor

Installment #4: Memory Care and Botox Parties

As much as I avoid driving—what with having to dodge the families of deer and overly enthusiastic and road-hogging bicyclists on our narrow country roads—I do have to venture out from time to time to stock my pantry and do all the other errands needed in our suburban lives.

Something I noticed this week as I gritted my teeth and ran my errands—the excessive number of day care centers and retirement villages. Day cares and senior citizen neighborhoods are sprouting like mildew in our bucolic suburb. Does anybody else see the humor here? The same children raised by caregivers see a natural progression toward housing their aging parents in much the same fashion. Reminds me of something I read once, about being nice to your children because they will one day pick your nursing home. Don't get me wrong; these institutions are necessary given today's lifestyles. But it does make me think.

And what's with all these "memory care" buildings attached to the residential halls at the senior citizen villages? From what I've seen, memory doesn't need caring for after it's gone. Just call it "The Forgetting Place" or "Home for People Who Can't Remember" and be done with it. Because that's what they are. I think I've had enough of euphemisms.

Along the same lines as euphemisms is the overuse of the word "party." I've always associated the word with birthdays and retirements—things to be celebrated. No longer just for housewarmings and dinners, the word "party" is now being used alongside "karaoke," "Pampered Chef," and "Botox." This last one really confuses me. How could going to someone's house where a (hopefully) qualified person lays you down on a sofa and injects a botulism toxin into your face be considered—in any sane person's world—a party? And shouldn't a person be insulted just to be invited? Lastly, what does a person bring as a hostess gift for these gatherings—Band-Aids?

Yesterday in line at Kroger, the two women in front of me were talking about a Botox party they were going to that evening in one of our gated neighborhoods—that I won't name just in case you noticed your tennis partner looking less wrinkly today even after all those years in the sun. They kept looking back at me, and for a horrified moment I thought they were going to invite me, too. I was torn between slapping them if they did and pretending I didn't speak English. Luckily, I remembered that I'd been trying out shades of foundation in the drug aisle and had left two streaks of different-colored makeup slashing across my cheek, making me look like an Indian. Excuse me—Native American.

While at that same Kroger, I spotted the recently involuntarily downsized third-grade math teacher in line at the pharmacy counter. I assumed she wasn't there for birth control, seeing as how that ship has already sailed, but probably for prenatal vitamins.

I'd only seen her before at a distance, but up close it's easy to see why a married man—or any man with eyes—would find her attractive. And young. I think she's barely out of college. She's a dead ringer for a lingerie catalog model, with perfect skin, thick dark hair, and a warm smile. It's the smile that gives her away as a teacher, though. That slow and patient smile teachers of all small children use when explaining something in that way of theirs. I wonder if she was good at her job. I wonder if she misses it and regrets the choices she's made.

While I was there pretending to look at different shampoos, another woman, apparently the mother of one of her former students, recognized her, too. She'd bumped her cart into the teacher's, so she couldn't pretend that she hadn't seen her, and she spent the entire time not looking at the expectant mother's belly and not saying anything more than how hot it was outside.

And then I got distracted by free samples of Talenti gelato and lost sight of the teacher. If you haven't tried that gelato, don't. I think it must contain a controlled substance, because after one bite I found myself purchasing four small containers in different flavors. I guess the former teacher isn't the only one with self-control issues. Except if I gain a few pounds it won't wreck a family.

Speaking of life's upsets, we are smack-dab in the middle of hurricane season here in Georgia. We've had a hot and dry streak since June, which always gets me worried. And not just about the weather. If you read the arrest reports in the *Sweet Apple Herald* like I do, you'll notice there's hardly been a full column of late. And even though we're winding up for a hotly contested mayoral race, there hasn't been an ugly word or unsubstantiated claim made by either side as of today. I feel something brewing in the air, like a warm wind blowing westward over the Atlantic from Africa, the official birth of a hurricane. So check your hurricane shutters and stock up on bottled water. A storm is coming.

And now for today's Southern saying: "That's as handy as a back pocket on a shirt." I went to Walmart last week to purchase some necessary items and saw that they had hand soap on sale in those really big containers. Packaged with them was a hand pump to screw into the top when you were ready to use it so you don't have to go through the aggravation of pouring the soap into a smaller container. Except when I got home I discovered that the pump didn't fit on the container. I spilled about half the soap trying to get it to work. When I finish cleaning up all the soap off my bathroom vanity and the front of my shirt, I will be sure to take it back to Walmart (in a sealed bag). And when I dump that soap on the customer service desk, I will say, "This is about as handy as a back pocket on a shirt."

So when you're headed to Walmart to stock up on storm-preparedness items, don't forget the bread and milk, but for goodness' sake, leave the giant tub of hand soap on the shelf.

MERILEE

Merilee sat at a small table by the window of Cups, the local coffee shop, and closed her laptop. She hadn't been aware that Tammy had been fired. Not that she was surprised—Tammy was single and her students were young. Merilee just wasn't sure how in this day and age a woman could be dismissed for such a transgression. Maybe it was parental pressure and the promise of a full salary leave. Regardless, she found no pleasure in the news. She had once liked Tammy Garvey, when she was still the enthusiastic and fresh-faced math teacher who made Lily love math. Merilee hated what Tammy had done, but she couldn't bring herself to hate her. But that didn't stop her from thinking ill thoughts or calling her bad names in her head.

The aroma of fresh-brewed coffee and baking muffins against the visual backdrop of oak tables and brick and wood walls and floors made the coffee shop feel homey and charming; it was the place everybody congregated, since the marketing-genius owners had strategically placed it in close proximity to three public schools and Windwood Academy.

It was right after school drop-off, and Merilee used the opportunity to surreptitiously glance around at the clusters of moms at the various tables to see if any of them seemed to be reading the blog on their phones or other devices, or if any of them were trying not to stare or point. She could always tell when someone was talking about someone else, or trying to get them to look when they talked out of the sides of their mouths, as if moving their lips would give them away. And then the person being spoken to would pretend to admire the décor around the vicinity of where the object of the conversation happened to be.

Luckily, all the Windwood moms seemed to be buzzing about that morning's announcement at the parents' meeting about the fall gala. It was the school's biggest fund-raiser and also, according to Heather, the social event of the year. She was, of course, the head of the gala committee, and before the headmaster had even finished speaking Heather was already tapping people on the shoulder about being on the committee. Seeing the opportunity to bolt, Merilee had left before Heather could pull her into agreeing to do something she had absolutely no interest in or time to be involved with.

She spotted Lindi at the door and waved her over. "Sorry I'm late," Lindi said as she sat down. "I got a call during the morning meeting about an issue at work and I just now hung up." She dumped her large tote on the floor and smiled at the enormous ceramic coffee cup in front of her. "Wow, thanks. How did you know I like it black?"

"I passed Jenna and her class on the way to the media center as I left the meeting and asked her. I'd seen you leave and thought you might be a little late."

Lindi took a long and grateful sip from her cup. "I think you're my new BFF."

Merilee leaned forward. "You might have to fight Heather for that position."

Lindi's eyebrows raised. "Really?"

"That's what she said at her party, but she probably says that to everyone. She has a lot of BFFs, from what I can tell. Or maybe she didn't want me to sue her because of Lily. Although I'm pretty sure Lily hurt herself after Heather said that." She tapped her fingers on the lid of her laptop. "Have you read the most recent blog post?"

"Yep. Read it this morning over breakfast." She raised the cup to her lips, her eyes thoughtful. "Nothing really inflammatory, I don't think. Just observations—all pretty accurate, if you want my opinion.

I liked the part about euphemisms—I might have actually laughed. And the writer is vague enough that not everybody is aware of who's being discussed—or they don't recognize themselves, which is more likely. Most people don't see themselves the way other people do. Still no idea who might be writing it?"

Merilee shook her head, her gaze casually scanning the other occupants of the crowded room, smiling in response to a few waves from other moms from school—including her new carpool partner, Sharlene Cavanaugh. They weren't starting with their new driving schedule until the following week, but Merilee had her doubts. For starters, Sharlene had problems remembering Merilee's children's names and kept referring to Colin as Connor. Her optimism wasn't strengthened by the fact that this morning Sharlene was wearing flip-flops that appeared to be several sizes smaller than her own feet, as if she'd forgotten to put on shoes when she left the house and had found her daughter's in the backseat and made do.

"I don't have a clue," Merilee said. "I don't really know anybody well enough to guess. I know Heather the best, but she's so involved I can't imagine her having the time to write a blog and also squeezing in time to sleep."

Lindi took another sip of coffee, holding the giant cup with both hands. "Well, it's a very good thing you're on Heather's nice list. Your life—and your kids' lives—would be torture if you weren't."

"What do you mean?" Merilee leaned forward so they wouldn't be overheard.

Lindi shrugged. "Oh, you know. Invitations get 'lost' in the mail so you or your kids are never seen socially, or the committee you wanted to head either disappears or gets absorbed into a committee that's already being run by you know who. It's silly, and we're totally too old for this kind of behavior, but it happens. Heather likes to be in charge and call all the shots, and most of the time she does a really good job and tries to be as inclusive as she can—she even invited me to be in on the selection process for the new middle school science teacher, although I think it's because I'm on the board. But still. A little diversity would be nice."

Lindi turned to see who'd just come in the shop, then looked back at Merilee. "Dealing with some of these moms makes me feel like I'm back in high school, you know? Hoping to be invited to the popular table to sit with the mean girls. I have a law degree from Yale, for crying out loud, yet I always feel as if I don't quite measure up." She sat back in her chair, frowning. "Sorry—I don't mean to dump on you. It's just that Bailey has been giving Jenna a hard time—you know, excluding her from recess games and telling her where she can and cannot sit in every class they share together. It's just that in my experience, mean girls always learn it from their mothers, who were undoubtedly mean girls when they were younger."

The coffee on Merilee's tongue suddenly tasted bitter, but she held it in her mouth, unable to swallow. A memory of a much-younger version of herself on a school bus headed to summer camp, a plump brown-haired girl with thick eyebrows sitting next to her, the girl's sweaty thick thighs pressed against hers, had erased for a moment the coffee shop and the groups of women that surrounded her. But not the memory of the horrible things she'd said to that girl who'd made the mistake of sitting next to her. Things about the girl's appearance that, in retrospect, Merilee knew she'd had no control over. But she'd said the words. Had even made the girl cry, forever branding the episode onto Merilee's subconscious, from where it would emerge from time to time to keep her up at night. Merilee forced down her coffee and managed not to cough.

The sound of metal scraping against cement brought everyone's attention to the window facing the parking lot, where a giant and very ancient baby blue Lincoln had rolled its enormous front end over the sidewalk. The driver took a while to open the door, probably because the door was bigger than most cars nowadays and built of solid steel.

Lindi was already standing. "I should go help her."

Merilee looked back at the car and thought she recognized the white puff of hair over the steering wheel. "Is that . . . ?"

Merilee knew Sugar had a car, but it was usually kept in the carport on the other side of Sugar's house from hers, so she hadn't recognized it.

"Sugar Prescott," Lindi said, heading toward the door with Merilee close behind her. "I've offered a thousand times to take her car shopping for a more manageable car. Sadly, it's in perfect working order and she sees no need to replace it until it falls apart."

"How do you know Sugar?" Merilee asked.

"Everybody knows Sugar. We both volunteer at the senior center's jumble sale twice a year and are in charge of organizing all the donations. She finds a lot of good deals there, apparently. She has quite the selection of Christmas sweaters now."

Before Merilee could raise her eyebrows or question Lindi further, they'd reached the car and Lindi was holding open the car door. "Sugar—good morning!"

Sugar frowned up at her. "It was until I got here. Could barely find parking—why are all these people here?"

Merilee extended her hand to help her out, then quickly withdrew it when Sugar simply glowered at it. They waited a few moments as Sugar rocked herself a few times to get up enough momentum to propel her from her seat.

"There was a meeting at the school, so the moms are running about an hour later than usual," Lindi explained.

Sugar stepped up on the sidewalk and stopped to dig for something in her purse as Merilee shut the car door. "Let me see—maybe I can come back tomorrow." She pulled out a clipped coupon from an ancient purse that seemed to be of the same vintage as the car and thrust it at Merilee. "When does this expire?"

"Today."

Sugar sighed heavily as she looked through the window at the long line of patrons waiting to be served. "I don't even like coffee."

Lindi and Merilee's gazes met over Sugar's head.

"But every Monday there's a free cup of coffee coupon for senior citizens in the *Sweet Apple Herald*, so I come here once a week to use the coupon. Hate to see it go to waste."

Lindi pulled open the door to Cups. "Why don't I wait in line and get your coffee while you sit at our table with Merilee?"

Sugar pressed her lips together as she considered. "I suppose that would work." Merilee began to lead her to the table when Lindi asked, "How do you like your coffee?"

"Doesn't matter. It tastes terrible no matter how you try to disguise it."

Merilee held out a chair for Sugar before sitting down, aware of the glances sent in their direction. "I can't thank you enough for letting Colin use the bird books at the house. I think it's distracting him from looking for that dog. Yesterday, he saw an indigo bunting. He didn't know what it was until he looked it up. He really needs some binoculars—I just keep forgetting to go shop for them. The stores that sell things like that aren't on my usual round of errands."

Sugar remained straight-backed in her chair, and it seemed as if she might actually be offering a small smile. "Good to know that's one less child who's not rotting his brain on computer games."

Merilee just smiled, unsure how to respond.

Sugar smoothed the flats of her hands against the wooden surface of the table. "I sure was glad to see this place built."

"I thought you disliked all the new development," Merilee said, wincing as she took a sip from her now ice-cold coffee.

"I do." She was silent for a moment as her face softened in a contemplative look Merilee was becoming familiar with. "But this was where Curtis Brown's family lived. In a little house smack-dab on this spot. Burned years ago, which I can't say many people were sad to see. Mr. Brown had already been run out on a rail after he stole from the church offering box. Curtis had taken over running the farm, but he was so lazy he couldn't catch his breath if it didn't come naturally. I saw Mrs. Brown out in the field at harvest and planting times more than I ever saw Curtis, his little sisters running around half-starved because they were as poor as gully dirt and Mrs. Brown was too proud to ask for charity."

Sugar shook her head, her gaze focused at the window, the blue sky reflected in her glasses so they looked like a mirror on the world. "Mrs. Brown got sick one winter, and they had no wood for burning and wouldn't accept any from her neighbors. Then she died and those little girls got sent to the orphanage down in Atlanta. Or maybe it was to distant relations—I can't remember. I just know we never saw hide or hair of them again."

"That's so sad. There wasn't anyone closer who could take them in?"

Sugar shook her head slowly. "Times were hard. We barely had enough to feed and clothe our own families. Farms were failing every day, it seemed, and people were starving. We took care of Lamar after his daddy died, and my daddy tried to take care of Curtis and those little girls after his mama got sick, but Curtis didn't want us taking care of anything, and I was fine with that."

Merilee looked behind Sugar and spotted Lindi approaching the front of the line, wishing she'd hurry. She enjoyed Sugar's stories, although it had become clear to her that neither one of them was comfortable in the telling, and maybe even for the same reason. It was too easy to be dragged down into someone else's tragedies when you were barely treading water yourself.

"Whatever happened to Curtis?" Merilee asked, unable to stop herself.

Sugar's blue eyes darkened behind her glasses, her hands now clasped tightly on the table in front of her. "He joined the army, just like everyone else. Don't know what became of him, just that he never came back here after the war." Her eyes met Merilee's, and there was something in them, something unreadable and foreign. Something Merilee recognized but could not name.

She almost sighed with relief when Lindi reappeared with three cups of coffee, one in a to-go cup, and an assortment of sugar and creamers she pulled from her purse and dumped on the table. "I'm sorry to leave so soon—but I need to get back to the office to deal with an emergency. Good to see you, Sugar—and I'll talk to you later," she said to Merilee.

She held the door open for someone, and Merilee gave an internal groan as Heather Blackford entered, looking regal in purple workout gear. She wondered if she only imagined Sugar groaning, too. Heather spotted them immediately and headed to their table.

"Sugar!" she said, leaning down to kiss the older woman on her cheek despite Sugar's body language, which clearly stated she wished she were anywhere else but there. "It's so good to see you. This is so cute seeing the two of you together—landlady and tenant. It must be nice to finally find a tenant you get along with," she said to Sugar, who merely stared back at her with compressed lips.

Turning to Merilee, she said, "My first gala committee meeting is Thursday evening at seven thirty at my house in Prescott Estates. I'll put your name on the list at the gate so you'll have access. I'd like you to head the auction committee because I can tell you're smart and we really need a smart person to handle the solicitation of donations."

"But I—"

A look of concern crossed Heather's face. "You do want to help, don't you? This is for your children's school and for all the wonderful programs that will give them what they need to succeed in life. All of us moms need to do our part."

"Yes, I realize, but my work schedule—"

"I already asked Lily and she said you don't work Thursday evenings, so that's when I've scheduled all the gala committee meetings. See? It's all settled. See you at seven thirty on Thursday."

She smiled and started to leave before remembering something else.

"By the way, Sugar, your back tire is flat, so you might want to get that fixed. So glad we could talk. Bye-bye," she said, before turning around and heading toward another table, a short strip of toilet paper clinging to her sneaker.

Merilee half stood to go tell her, but Sugar held her back with a surprisingly strong arm. "Don't you dare. She broke Wade's heart in a bad way, and that's just karma."

Merilee had to bite her lower lip to keep from laughing. "Can I call someone to come fix your tire? I know how to change a tire; it's just that I'm wearing my last clean work blouse."

Sugar sighed heavily. "Just take me home. I'll call Wade when I get there. A buddy of his has an auto repair place—they can figure out what to do with it."

"I don't have to be at work until one o'clock, so that works with my schedule," Merilee said. "Thanks for asking," she added, knowing the sarcasm would be lost on the older woman. She indicated Sugar's untouched coffee. "We can wait until you're finished."

Sugar wrinkled her nose. "Ask for a paper cup that I can take home so I can drink it later."

Without questioning her logic, Merilee stood and broke into line at the front to ask for a travel cup before returning to the table to transfer the coffee. She held the door for Sugar, then followed her down the steps, keeping close to her elbow in case the older woman tripped, but being very careful not to let Sugar know.

As Merilee unlocked the minivan, Sugar pointed up to the sky. "I do think that's a brown-headed cowbird."

Merilee followed her gaze, spotting the glossy black bird with the chocolate head and gray beak.

"They're parasitic birds. Jimmy told me that—because they lay their eggs in other birds' nests and hope the other birds will raise them." Sugar leaned against the side of the minivan, as if the memories were weighing her down. "That was the best part about this particular patch of land—all the different birds Jimmy found here. There were thick woods back then, more than we had, even. When Jimmy wasn't working on our farm or doing his chores, he'd come over here. Couldn't ever pass up an opportunity to make a check mark in his book when he saw another bird."

Merilee pulled the door open and stood close to Sugar in case she wanted to lean on her to get in without asking for help. "Did Curtis not mind?"

"Oh, he minded. But that never stopped Jimmy." Her fingers, bony and sharp, dug into Merilee's shoulder as she hoisted herself into the passenger seat. "He minded a lot." Sugar turned to Merilee, an odd smile on her lips.

Merilee pulled herself into the driver's seat and started the minivan, then drove home slowly as Sugar began to speak.

Eleven

SUGAR

1939

I jiggled the reins attached to our old cart horse, Grace, trying to get her to go a little faster. I had a wagonful of chickens I was trying to sell, and if Grace didn't get a move on, they'd bake in their feathers under the August sun.

After the boll weevils ate all our cotton fields and most other people's, from what I could tell, Daddy had been busy figuring out what else he could do to make some money to at least pay the taxes on the farm and maybe buy up some of the abandoned farms dirt cheap. I thought he was crazy, and might have even said so, but he laughed and said the hard times wouldn't last forever and land would be worth something again. I hoped he was right, because if he kept on buying, we'd own most of the county pretty soon.

We still had our mama's vegetable garden—even though I did all the tending now—so we wouldn't starve to death, but he said we should get some more cows and hogs. We could keep what milk and meat we needed, sell what we didn't, and maybe even give a job to a few of the poor souls who knocked on our door just about every other day. Daddy believed in being a good Christian by practicing charity and letting Lamar stay in the house he'd shared with Rufus. Or maybe that was because he knew that the circumstances responsible for the way Rufus died weren't all accidental.

It had been my idea to sell chickens. We had so many, and I ended up giving away a lot of eggs. I told my daddy if we could sell chickens, people would at least have eggs to eat, and maybe something to fry up once in a while. When I was little it would have hurt to see my chickens go live with another family, but I was long past being sentimental. Watching farms get abandoned, and whole families walking barefoot down dirt roads, carrying satchels and looking for work and food, put everything in perspective. It helped that I'd stopped naming the chickens when I was a little girl after Harry told me I had just eaten my favorite hen, Martha, when I was still chewing.

Happiest day of my life was when Harry was sent to live with relatives in Cairo, Georgia, to work at the lumber-planing mill. Daddy could've used his help on the farm, but he'd begun to run a little wild with Curtis Brown, and this was Daddy's way of clipping his wings. At least for a little while, anyway. But we were stuck with Curtis, who was now running the little tenant farm my daddy owned. Running it into the ground, I'd heard Daddy say to Dr. Mackenzie more than once. But he felt sorry for poor Mrs. Brown on account of her husband running off, and couldn't see fit to turn her and her little girls out just because her son was a no-account. When Mrs. Brown got sick and died and the county people came and took the girls, Curtis promised Daddy he'd do his best to maintain the farm. It was a good thing Daddy didn't put much store in Curtis's words, because he would have been sorely disappointed.

The chickens were really just an excuse. Although it was Sunday and I wasn't technically supposed to be working on the Sabbath, I was on a mission to find Jimmy—and Lamar, since the two separated only when it was time to go to sleep—before Daddy found out that he'd run off still in his Sunday clothes right after church. To ruin a good pair of church pants was like a sin to Daddy, and I'd brought along a pair of dungarees for Jimmy to change into.

I knew he was off looking for birds, and that was why he didn't want to wait to go home and change before setting off. With Harry gone, everybody had to do more work, even Bobby, who did things so slowly and so poorly it was hardly worth having him take up space on the farm.

We were all working can to can't—from when you can see in the morning to when you can't see at night—which was why Jimmy never had the chance anymore to find his birds. I didn't blame him one bit, but if he got a hole in his good pants, there'd be trouble and more work for me to mend them. And if I passed a house and they wanted to buy a chicken or two, then my time wouldn't be wasted and I wouldn't be lying if Daddy asked me where I'd been.

Even if I hadn't known where I was, I would have known I'd reached the Brown farm by the fence that was supposed to mark the outside boundary. Or what was left of it. I knew they'd burned most of the rails last winter when it got so cold and Mrs. Brown was doing poorly. The woods were heavy and dark on the south side of the property, but Curtis was too lazy to lift an ax and get busy making firewood. I sure didn't want to be around when my daddy found out what had happened to the fence.

Grace stopped without me telling her—she was always looking for an excuse to stop—at the beginning of the drive. It was rocky and rutted because nobody had bothered to smooth it over, and it didn't look like a cart had passed over it in quite some time.

Pop. Pop. Grace barely raised her head at the sound of gunshots, but the air vibrated inside me like the string on a fiddle. What seemed like an entire flock of crows flew out of the trees on the edge of the woods just at the same time I saw something that looked like a person fall from one of the trees.

I'm not really sure what happened next. All I remember is how quiet everything was, like the birds couldn't sing because of their own sadness, and how I forced Grace into a trot before leaving her and the chickens under the shade of a half-dead oak. I remember that much. That tree, with the black slick of bark slashed across its trunk from a lightning strike. I remember falling against it as I jumped off the cart and began running as fast as I could toward the woods.

I ran past the run-down house, hardly noticing Curtis standing on the rotten back porch with the missing steps, his hunting rifle still resting on his shoulder like he wasn't done. I kept running, daring him to shoot me in the back. Because if he did, I'd have a reason to tear him apart with my bare hands like I wanted to.

His angry voice shouted at me as I ran. "Tell your idiot brother and his nigger friend to stay out of my trees if he don't want me to think he's a squirrel. And if you all don't get off my property I'm gonna shoot you for trespassing."

"Go to hell, Curtis," I shouted without slowing down, knowing he was too much of a coward to shoot me in the middle of a field, because then he couldn't say he thought I was a squirrel in a tree.

I was a fast runner, most probably because I had older brothers who were always chasing me down, trying to put dead snakes (sometimes live ones) and other irritations like that down my dress. I thought this was normal until Willa Faye told me her boy cousins (she only had a sister) would have gotten a whipping if they'd ever tried such a thing.

I ran so fast that I didn't notice Lamar until I almost stepped on him, squatting down near the ground. It was a good thing his face was so dark, because it was easier for him to hide in the woods. I don't have a single doubt in my mind that Curtis would have shot him, too, if given half the chance. That's when I noticed he was squatting next to Jimmy, my brother's face looking up at the tree toward his beloved birds, his legs turned at places they shouldn't have been.

"Are Granddaddy's field glasses all right?"

I almost cried to hear him talk, because I thought he surely must be dead from a fall like that. There was no blood or anything, so I was thinking he must have fallen on a big pile of leaves and as soon as he caught his breath again, we'd walk out of those woods and tell our daddy what Curtis had done.

And then I got angry because Jimmy could've died and all he cared about was those glasses not being broken. Because Granddaddy had given them to him and told Jimmy to take care of them.

The glasses still hung around his neck, resting on his chest all in one piece as if he'd put them there on purpose. "They're fine. Are you hurt?"

Lamar gave me a funny look but didn't say anything.

"I don't think so," he said, his eyes moving from me to Lamar. "I don't feel no pain," he said with a little laugh, like he couldn't believe his good luck at falling from a tree without getting hurt. "He missed me," he said. "He's got such a bad aim he'd miss the water falling out of a boat." He laughed again. "Startled me some, so I let go of the danged tree."

He put his hands flat down on the ground, then bent his elbows like he was trying to sit up, but then he stopped. "Are my legs still there?" His voice sounded like that time we'd seen a comet streak across the night sky like a ball of fire. Sort of a mixture of excitement and fear and the knowing that the universe was a much bigger place than we could ever even think about.

"Of course they're . . ." My eyes moved over to where his legs were still attached to his body, but looking like my favorite rag doll after Harry and Will had gotten hold of her.

Lamar reached over and pinched Jimmy's leg. "Can you feel this?"

"Feel what?" Jimmy asked, his voice sounding very far away.

My eyes met Lamar's. "We got to get him home," I said, my own voice sounding like somebody else's. Somebody who knew what to do. "Lamar will run get Dr. Mackenzie and he can fix your legs." I swallowed. "He will. I know he will." I said it twice, like that could make it true. I kept thinking about Daddy's favorite horse, Horatio, who'd broke his leg jumping over a fence. I remembered what the leg had looked like, and how my daddy had been pretty close to crying. And how Rufus had been the one to put poor Horatio out of his misery. It was the first time I'd learned that not all broken things could be fixed. But that didn't mean I couldn't try.

Lamar looked over to the porch, which was now empty of Curtis and his rifle. "I can carry him on my back."

I nodded. "Jimmy, you got to use your arms to hang on real tight, you hear? I'll help Lamar get you up there, and then we'll put you in the cart with my chickens. They're real sweet and won't bother you, so pay them no mind." I was talking fast as I moved, like I always did when I was scared or nervous, but it seemed to calm Jimmy—and

Lamar—as we pulled him up and onto Lamar's back, his legs hanging funny. I could now see the dark patches of blood on his Sunday pants but didn't say anything because I didn't want him to notice his legs. I don't think I could have stood it if Jimmy had cried.

We got him home, and Dr. Mackenzie came to look at him, but there was nothing he could do but set the broken bones. Whatever it was that made the legs work had been broken in the fall from the tree.

Curtis didn't go to prison because he told everybody it was an accident and he'd been squirrel hunting, and Willa Faye's mama gave Jimmy an old wheelchair that had belonged to her aunt, and everybody sort of thought things had worked out in the end. Except for me.

That's when Bobby, with all his book learning, told me about karma and how all good and bad things come back to you sooner or later. It put some of the joy back in my life, knowing that sooner or later, Curtis Brown would get what was coming to him.

Twelve

MERILEE

Merilee watched the lamps in the house flicker on and off as the storm dumped rain while performing a rather impressive percussion and light show in the sky. The children were with Michael tonight so she could go to the gala committee meeting. She hoped that Lily wasn't scared and that Michael knew enough to keep Colin from running outside with a kite and a metal key.

Glancing at her watch, she realized she had fifteen minutes before she needed to leave and still be early. It was amazing how fast she could get dressed and ready to go without two children in the house. She glanced into the hallway, where the stacks of books still waited for Wade's shelves in piles against the wall, her four high school yearbooks now sitting on top of one of them.

Wade was due back that weekend, and she wanted to be prepared for any curveballs he might unintentionally lob at her about where he thought he'd seen her before. Without thinking too much about it—mostly so she couldn't talk herself out of it—she picked up her cell phone and dialed her parents.

Her mother answered, and for a brief moment Merilee considered hanging up and trying again to see if she could get her father. Usually, but not always, he was easier to speak to and could smooth the transition to her mother.

"Hello, Mama. It's Merilee."

After a short pause, Deanne said, "Well, it couldn't be anyone else calling me 'Mama,' could it?"

The sting began in the back of Merilee's nose, traveling up to her eyes. She wondered how old she'd have to be before her mother could no longer make her cry. "How are you and Dad?"

There was a long sigh, as if her mother barely had the energy to force out words. "Nothing's changed. Your daddy's gout has been aggravating him a bit, and I have a doctor's appointment on Monday to examine a spot on my neck that I don't like the looks of. We both try to stay busy to keep our minds off of . . . unpleasant thoughts. Daddy's golf game is improving, my garden is looking beautiful, and my bridge partner and I won a trip to Branson, Missouri, for winning the most hands in last month's bridge tournament."

She sounded almost manic as she listed everything, as if she was trying to prove that despite Merilee and "unpleasant thoughts," they were still managing to have productive lives. The clink of ice cubes in a glass carried through the phone, and Merilee knew the drink they were cooling wasn't sweet tea.

"You'd know all this if you called or visited more often. It's not like anybody knows you here."

At least the rush of anger made the stinging stop. "It's hard for me with my job and the children's schedules. You know you're welcome to visit anytime. Colin's going to be playing flag football this fall, and Lily's going to be playing tennis. She's also trying out for cheerleading." Merilee had almost left that part out but changed her mind. She was so tired of doling out and holding back in her conversations with her parents. It was exhausting. "I'm sure they'd both love for you to come and watch them—"

"Cheerleading? Now, that surprises me. You always told me you hated it and resented me for pushing you to try out. Remember that? Even though it was the best thing that could have ever happened to your social life, not that I ever got any thanks for that. Whatever changed your mind?"

A crack of thunder shifted the air around Merilee, and she was fourteen again and her mother was piercing her ears with needles and ice cubes because all the popular girls had pierced ears. It had hurt, and then both ears had become infected, but she'd always worn earrings after that, irrationally believing that her mother might like her more if she did.

"Because Lily's new friend is trying out, so she wanted to try out, too. She didn't ask my opinion. I'm more excited about her playing tennis. When she played it at summer camp, she was really good and enjoyed it."

"Yes, well, there's nothing quite like being a cheerleader, especially captain, as you know."

"Oh, right," Merilee said, hoping her mother could hear the sarcastic note in her voice. "Look what it did for me."

"It did everything for you." She paused, and Merilee held her breath, waiting for it. "And watch your tone with me, Merilee. Dave's not here anymore to tell me I'm not the terrible mother you always told me I was." The clink of ice cubes was louder now, and Merilee pictured her turning the glass upside down to make sure she'd drained all the vodka.

"I didn't call to argue with you, Mama."

"Then why did you call?"

"I wanted to ask you a question. About Sandersville."

"Why on earth would you need to know something about Sandersville? We haven't lived there in twelve years. Sadly."

Merilee took this last dig without comment. "I just wanted to know if you remembered a William and Sharon West. They're older than you and Dad, but they lived there for a long time, so I was just wondering if you knew who they were."

"Of course we knew them. Not well, because they were older, but they belonged to the country club, too, so we knew them in passing. Why are you asking?"

Merilee waited for a moment, searching for the right words. "Do you know if they were still living there when you left?"

"I don't know. Really, Merilee. What is this all about? I feel another one of my migraines coming on."

"It's just that somebody here knows them. And wanted to know if I knew them. And when he asks the Wests about me, I wanted to know what they might tell him."

She could picture her mother holding on to her crystal tumbler, her long, painted nails wrapped elegantly around it, the tips bloodless from pressing too hard. "Yes, well, I guess it would depend on how good their memory is. And how much they read. It's been fourteen years, so it's quite possible they don't remember. We can at least hope so." *Clink-clink.* "So, when are you and Michael getting back together?"

Merilee bit her tongue before she told Deanne about Tammy's pregnancy. She didn't have the strength to deal with her mother and that bit of news just yet. "Not anytime soon. We're . . . still working things out."

"Good. A woman shouldn't be on her own. Thank goodness for your father. I don't know what I would have done without him. At least you have a son." She waited for a moment to let the arrow find its target. "Before I forget, I thought you should know that we've decided to sell the Tybee house."

The room seemed to dim, and Merilee wasn't sure if it was because of the storm. "No, Mama. You can't. It's been in your family for so long. And we have so many happy memories there."

"Nobody goes there, and it's senseless to keep paying taxes and maintenance on it."

"But I've told you, I want to bring the children there. So it's as much a part of their childhoods as it was of mine and David's."

"I told you not to mention his name to me. You have no right. No *right*." She'd slurred the last word, allowing Merilee to pretend that it was the alcohol that was making her say these things. Except she knew it wasn't. Because she'd been saying them for years.

A burst of rain hit the side of the house as the lights flickered again. "I have to go now, Mama. We're having really bad weather and I have a meeting tonight." She hung up the phone before her mother could say anything else.

It was only seven o'clock in the evening, but pewter clouds dimmed the remaining light, throwing the dirt road and sodden grass into premature dusk. Merilee concentrated on the drum of her wipers, hoping to erase the conversation with her mother. She wondered how much longer it would be before she could have a conversation with Deanne and not feel depleted afterward. Probably around the same time her mother would forgive her.

There wasn't a lot of traffic, and Merilee took her time driving to Prescott Estates, hoping to be in the right frame of mind to deal with a committee meeting by the time she arrived. She knew the neighborhood, of course, having dropped off both children at various times for playdates over the years. The topography was mostly flat, owing to its previous incarnation as farm fields, but those humble beginnings had long since been erased by the sprawling mansions playing coy behind gated drives, heavy foliage, and the occasional giant gas hurricane lamps giving the impression of vintage. It was like, Merilee mused, a discount store hiring a Neiman's window designer without changing the contents of the shop.

She stopped at the stone-and-iron front gate and waited for the uniformed guard to slide open his door before opening her own window. Despite the money apparently spent on the front entrance, they'd skimped on providing an overhang to protect visitors from the elements. Leaning back as far as she could so she could still be heard but not get drenched, she said, "I'm Merilee Dunlap, here to see Heather Blackford."

Moving as slowly as she thought a person could without actually being asleep, the guard picked up a clipboard and studied a sheet of paper on top, running his finger down the line with such a lack of speed that Merilee wanted to grab it from him. Eventually he found her name, then took so long to make a check mark next to it that she assumed he must be drawing a sketch of her.

"You know where to go?" the man drawled.

Heather had only mentioned that the meeting would be at her house but hadn't given her the address, so Merilee had looked it up in the school directory. "I got it," she said, already raising her window.

"Stay dry!" he called out helpfully right before it shut.

"Thanks," she mouthed, feeling the drenched inside of her door and seat, the damp strands of hair sticking to her face.

The professionally landscaped streets were lit by replica gaslights, the bulbs inside valiantly flickering to give the impression of authenticity. They were pretty, she conceded. Much nicer than the generic electric lights in her previous neighborhoods.

Her wipers thwacked back and forth as the rain increased in intensity. She allowed a groan as she realized she'd left her umbrella at work and that she would show up at the meeting looking like a drowned rat.

The GPS on her phone told her to take a right and then an immediate left, leading her directly in front of open iron gates with stacked-stone pillars on either side, a ginormous flickering gaslight on top of each. Moving forward, she studied the steep incline of the drive, hoping her tires and brakes were up to the challenge.

She followed the driveway to a wide, circular drive in front of what appeared to be an exact replica of Tara—except much larger. With the rain and now full darkness, Merilee couldn't tell what color the shutters were, or if there were cotton fields behind the house, but she did notice that while the house wasn't completely dark, there were only sporadic lights on inside, but at least the large light hanging over the front door was illuminated.

The lack of parked cars didn't alarm her, as she was a good fifteen minutes early, and there might have been cars parked on the street that she hadn't noticed because she'd been concentrating on not running into anything in the deluge.

Grabbing her purse and hugging it close to her chest, she dashed out of her car to the covered front entranceway. She hadn't locked her car door but figured she probably didn't have to in this neighborhood. At least the doorbell was lit up so she didn't have a problem finding it to press. She heard deep, gonglike tones inside the house, using the time while she waited to wring out her hair and wipe what she knew had to be smeared mascara from under her eyes.

When she was done, she waited for another full minute, straining her ears to see if she could detect the sound of faraway footsteps. She stood there for a little longer, deciding whether it was rude to ring the bell twice, then waited for another minute before she pressed the bell again.

The distant sound of tires on wet asphalt made her turn around to see if someone else had decided to tackle the steep driveway, but she was disappointed at the sound of the car driving away. She rang the bell one more time, then checked her phone to see if there were any text messages from Heather to let her know they'd changed the date of the meeting, then double-checked her calendar to make sure that it was actually tonight. She even considered texting Heather to let her know she was at the front door, but she didn't want to appear to be completely inept.

Merilee took a deep breath. The woman she'd been before Michael had left her would have simply opened the door. But that was when she'd still had a modicum of confidence. She heard her mother's voice again from their phone conversation, the memory alone draining her of what little self-confidence she still possessed. She'd half turned to leave when she recalled what her mother had said about selling the Tybee house because no one used it; remembered the dozens of times she'd begged her mother to allow Merilee and her children to go there. The anger flooded her like a rush, the blood hot in her veins. *You have no right.*

If only to block out the voice and the anger, Merilee whipped around and pushed down the door latch. She had meant only to test it to see whether it was unlocked, but instead she found herself standing inside a cavernous foyer, the black-and-white marble tile reflecting the dim light from an opening at the far end.

"Hello?" she called, stepping inside, hesitating a moment before closing the door behind her. She heard herself dripping onto an area rug, no doubt antique and expensive, but she stayed where she was, unsure if it would be better or worse than dripping on the marble floor.

The distant sound of voices was coming from a lit doorway, and Merilee let out a huge sigh of relief. Carefully walking across the marble to avoid slipping, as well as to limit the amount of water she deposited on the floor, she made her way to the opening, realizing it must be the basement when she saw the wrought-iron railings and the carpeted stairs leading down.

"Hello?" she called again as she headed downward toward the sound of voices, pausing on the bottom step to admire the space. Calling it a basement would be like calling Buckingham Palace a house. Because of its position on a hill, the home's basement was actually the garden level, with tall ceilings and walls of windows and French doors. Nothing was illuminated out back, but Merilee imagined it would be a gardener's haven, complete with infinity pool, outdoor kitchen, and comfortable outdoor furniture that was probably nicer than what Michael had taken from their living room when he'd moved in with Tammy.

The inside was furnished in the kind of style Merilee had always loved but had never been sure how to put together. It was some kind of a cross between Restoration Hardware and Arhaus, with gray distressed wood, nubby-textured upholstery, curved legs, lots of metal and glass—way out of Merilee's price range. It made her like Heather a little more, feeling as if they at least had this one thing in common.

She followed the voices, walking through an area that appeared to be a replica of an Irish pub—or maybe simply a transported one—complete with benches, tables, and upholstered seats, and toward an ajar door that was almost hidden behind the bar.

Relieved at having finally found the meeting, she pulled open the door and stopped abruptly. It wasn't that the décor was so fundamentally different here from that in the rest of the house or that the room seemed completely empty except for the giant screen airing an episode of *Hogan's Heroes* that made her hold her breath. It was the fact that she felt as if she'd stepped back into her own childhood and into a room that had so obviously not been professionally decorated but perhaps filled with objects that had been consciously acquired over the years.

It contained a collection of beloved items—an electric guitar, a scattering of beanbag chairs in various Atlanta sports team colors, a John Smoltz shirt framed on the wall; even a Magic 8 Ball sat in a place of honor on a shelf. A life-sized cardboard cutout of a Christmas-light-bedecked Chevy Chase from *Christmas Vacation* dominated a corner of the room near the screen, and a neon Guinness sign blinked cheerily on the opposite wall. Merilee turned toward an alcove at the back of the room and spotted an air hockey game, a vintage Pac-Man arcade machine, and a floor-to-ceiling shelving unit containing nothing but vinyl LPs, a Nirvana album propped in front. Stacks of *National Geographic* magazines sat on an adjacent set of shelves, the top two shelves covered in what appeared to be an *Ally McBeal* dancing baby and several Lego structures. An authentic pay phone was attached to the wall, a thick white-pages book dangling from a metal chain next to it. A popcorn machine with a spotlight highlighting it like a celestial being sat next to a Coke machine, each space filled with a different Coca-Cola product.

This was apparently a man cave, but to Merilee it was clearly much more than that. It was like the last holdout of an old life, one that the new life was encroaching upon little by little, with plans for complete obliteration. Merilee recognized this within the first few seconds of standing inside the door; recognized it because the room was so startlingly similar to her bedroom at her parents' house after David had died.

Something wet touched her knuckles and she let out an involuntary shout as she looked down and saw the Blackfords' dog nudging her hand for a scratch.

A movement from the line of theater seats in front of the screen distracted her as Daniel Blackford stood and looked at her, his surprise matching her own. "I'm . . . sorry," she stammered. "I didn't mean to disturb you. I think I took a wrong turn . . ." She stopped as the dog nuzzled her hand again.

"Great guard dog, right?" Dan asked, his smile breaking the tension.

The dog turned its head, clearly expecting to be scratched behind an ear. "Truly ferocious," she said, obliging the request. "What's your name, handsome fellow?"

"Puddles," Dan said with a straight face.

"Puddles? Well, no wonder he's so docile. No dog named Puddles would ever dare to question an intruder's authority to be here."

"True." Dan shoved his hands into the front pockets of his jeans, and Merilee noticed that he was barefoot. It made him seem oddly vulnerable, and she warmed to him. "I've always had black Labs, but that's where my input ended. The girls named him."

"Well, that's a relief. I was afraid you'd say that it was your idea."

He laughed, and she relaxed. She wondered if he had that effect on everyone, putting them at ease no matter how awkward the situation.

"I'm so sorry to have bothered you. I'm looking for Heather. We're supposed to be having a gala committee meeting at seven thirty."

His eyebrows lifted. "Well, there is a meeting—but it's at the club-house. Did you check there first?"

Heat rose from her chest, slowly engulfing her throat and face. "I . . ." She opened her calendar on her phone, double-checking it. "I put down that it was at the house. I must have misunderstood." She shook her head. "I'm so embarrassed. I should have called Heather when nobody answered the doorbell."

"Please. Don't be embarrassed. I don't mind the company. The girls are out to dinner with their grandparents, so it's just me and my favorite non-PC old sitcoms that nobody else will watch with me."

She felt a smile tugging at her lips. "If it's any consolation, I love *Hogan's Heroes*. And if non-PC is your cup of tea, then I suspect *F Troop* and *I Dream of Jeannie* are also favorites. I grew up watching reruns on TV."

"You can stay and watch, if you'd like," Dan offered. "I'll make popcorn and call Heather to let her know you've taken ill and can't make the meeting."

He looked hopeful enough that for a moment she believed he might be serious. Or at least a little bit. "Trust me, you have no idea how appealing that sounds. But, as Heather pointed out, I have an obligation to my children to be a part of the gala. She wants me to head the auction committee."

"Ah," he said, nodding. "She must think you're very smart, then."

"That's pretty much what she said, but she might have just been sweetening me up."

"Don't sell yourself short, Merilee. Heather's very shrewd and a lot smarter than most people give her credit for. She knows what she's doing."

A large framed photograph hanging on a wall behind Dan drew her attention. "Is that the Cockspur Lighthouse on Tybee?" As she drew closer, she recognized Heather with Bailey and Brooke in the foreground of the photo with the whitewashed brick structure behind them, the wind pushing their blond hair across their faces, nearly obliterating their matching smiles. A perfect, beautiful family.

"It is," Dan said. "We have a place there, so I have lots of photos of the island. I like to think of myself as an amateur photographer, when I'm really just giving the girls fodder for when they're older and they say I never did anything with them. I'm the perpetual photographer, so it looks like my widow and orphans in most of our photo albums." His tone didn't match the lightness of his words, and Merilee recognized something about it. Something in connection to this room. "Are you familiar with Tybee?"

She nodded. "My grandparents lived there full-time, so I spent most of my school vacations there as a child. Happiest moments of my life, I think. Until . . ." She stopped, unable to finish.

"Until what?" he asked, his voice kind. It had been so long since anyone had spoken to her with such care and concern that she felt the sting in the back of her throat again. And the need to talk to someone. The last person she'd confided in had been Michael, before they were married. He'd never asked her about it again, so she'd put her grief aside, wrapped it up in the Lego men and tucked it away.

"Until my brother, David, died. He . . . drowned. There on Tybee. He was younger than me, and I was supposed to be watching out for him." Her voice caught, and she was aware of how close to tears she was.

"I'm so sorry." He touched her arm, and she knew if she rested her head on his shoulder he would let her, and he would say the right words and make her feel not so alone anymore. But she couldn't, of course. Not here, and not with Dan, no matter how innocent or well-meaning it might be.

"I've really got to go," she said, backing up so that he dropped his hand. "Heather is probably already wondering where I am." She smiled brightly. "Thanks for the offer of popcorn and a screening of my favorite TV shows, though."

"Anytime," he said, walking her out of the basement and up the stairs, turning on lights as they went. He opened the front door and held it open for her. "Good night, Merilee."

"Good night. And thanks again," she said as she stumbled out into the rain, realizing only after she'd driven down the driveway and onto the street that she had no idea where she was going.

Thirteen

Observations of Suburban Life from Sweet Apple, Georgia
Written by: Your Neighbor

Installment #5: Clubbing at Costco

Until they opened up that new Costco near us here in Sweet Apple, I never for the life of me would have thought I needed a six-gallon jug of Tide or seventy-two rolls of toilet paper "just in case." I resisted getting my own membership card for the longest time, but like all the other lemmings here in Sweet Apple, I caved and got one. It's got a big gold star on it (I thought I was special until I saw everybody else had one, too, so I stopped bragging that I was a "gold star Costco member"), and I proudly flash it whenever I enter the store in need of a jar of nuts the size of my head or breakfast cereal in a container large enough to feed a third world country for a week.

During my trip earlier this week (where I was nearly taken out by a white Lexus SUV because the driver had her cell phone glued to her ear), the artificial Christmas trees had just been delivered.

I'm not going to use this blog to comment on people who choose artificial trees, because I'm sure they already know that they're sellouts, lazy and unimaginative people with no desire to foster happy memories for their children. Because, really, with all the hustle and bustle of the holidays, what could be easier and more time-saving than hauling up a fully lit tree from your basement and plugging it in?

I heard of one mother who even keeps the ornaments on and just sticks the tree in a corner of her guest room with a sheet thrown over it. I don't want to be the guest waking up in *that* room in the middle of the night with a hulking triangular-shaped blob looming over me. Granted, that mother has three boys all playing on travel baseball teams year-round (which we all know you can do in Georgia), so she's busy playing chauffeur, so who can blame her for cutting corners on the biggest family holiday of the year? Bless her heart.

At the Costco there was quite the scuffle between two women fighting over the last twelve-foot tree (in a box—how convenient!). A Costco employee was making a valiant effort to referee, but I think it was obvious to all spectators that those two women were willing to fight to the death and that blood would be spilled if he got too close.

I missed the outcome of the battle because I was distracted by a group of women nearby hovering over an enormous pallet of boxes filled with cotton athletic socks at the unbelievable price of ten for five dollars. I didn't need athletic socks, but even I gave them a closer inspection, because the price was just too good to ignore.

That's when I heard the words "gala committee" and my ears perked up. There is no better source of scandal, drama, hysterics, and hurt feelings than a gala committee. And occasionally they even manage to throw a pretty darn good party, too. Apparently, one of the members arrived late to a recent meeting, having mistakenly gone to the house of one of the other women first, saying she believed the meeting was there.

There was quite a bit of back-and-forth about whether this was a mistake or intentional, as the very good-looking husband was home alone at the time and it took a good thirty minutes for the latecomer to discover her mistake and make it to the actual meeting. I believe in giving someone the benefit of the doubt. The woman is new in town, after all, so I'm inclined to cut her a little slack. Even if she is single and beautiful, which is what I'm thinking is the real reason behind all the tongue wagging. Nothing like single and pretty to get a room full of married women as nervous as a long-tailed cat on a porch full of rocking chairs.

When I left the store later with my cart full of things I'd had no idea I needed when I entered the store (the prices really are that good!), I stopped again at the thinning display of artificial Christmas trees. There was no blood on the floor, so I imagined the altercation had ended amicably. I stared closely at their nine-foot model and I will admit it looked most lifelike.

But if I bought it and brought it home, I'd know it wasn't real. Just like those committee members gossiping about that poor woman. They know, deep in their hearts, the truth of the matter. But sometimes it's just easier to go with the cheap imitation and ignore reality.

And that, dear readers, brings me to this week's Southern saying. When listening to people wag their tongues on a subject they're not informed about, or judge a person they barely know, just say, "You'd better clean up your own backyard before you start talkin' trash."

Because I would bet money—and I'm not a betting person—that each one of those women has something in their closets they'd rather not air. Everybody does. Especially those who are always eager to cast the first stone.

SUGAR

Not for the first time, Sugar cursed her own vanity and wished for a cane. Or at least the courage to wear flat shoes with a dress. Not that her heels were that high, but even her inch-high heels made the walk along the drive between her house and Merilee's more like an exercise in torture. And the nylons simply added insult to injury. But she would rather be turned into a pillar of salt than show up at an Atlanta Woman's Club meeting without either.

Apparently, there was more wrong with her car than just a flat tire, and it would take at least a week until she had it back. Merilee had been with her when she'd received the diagnosis from Wade and had offered to take Sugar to today's meeting. Her offer seemed to have surprised them both. Because that was something that people with a connection did. Something a friend would do.

Sugar spotted Wade's truck out front with the tailgate down, meaning he was probably in the middle of a delivery. It distracted her so that she didn't at first notice Colin sitting on the front steps, staring at something on one of the wooden railings.

She stopped in front of him. "Good morning, Colin," she said.

He didn't look up. "Good morning, Miss Sugar. Have you ever watched what happens when you put a thumbprint of syrup somewhere and wait for the ants, to see what they'll do?"

"I can't say that I have," she said, staring dubiously at the steps and wondering if she could manage them without humiliating herself by taking off her shoes.

"Do you need help up the steps?" he asked.

He was looking up at her, his wide blue eyes so much like Jimmy's that for a brief moment he *was* Jimmy. And he was telling her about a nest he'd found, and how careful he'd been not to touch anything.

"Yes," she said, her voice weak. "That would be very nice. Thank you."

He held out an elbow and she took it, admiring the way he waited for her on each step until she'd reached the top.

"You're a real expert on this," she said. "Have you had a lot of practice?"

"Not a lot. But when we visit my grandma, I have to help her get out of her chair and stuff like that all the time. She's not as old as you, but she likes to pretend she is."

Sugar made an effort not to smile. "Is this your mother's mother?"

Colin nodded. "Uh-huh. She says she's had a tiring life so it's hard for her to walk."

"Do you visit a lot?"

Colin shook his head. "No. I think visits make Mom pretty tired, too, so we don't go too much."

"Have you seen the dog lately?"

"No, ma'am. But I did see a hawk yesterday. I couldn't tell what kind it was because it was too far away, but it was definitely a hawk."

Wade spotted them through the glass on the front door and hurried to open it for them. After kissing Sugar on her cheek, he crossed his arms and gave her a stern look. "You walked in this heat?"

"I've lived in Georgia since long before you were born, young man, and I'm not going to give in to it now. And I have my hat." She patted the feathered and netted concoction on top of her head. She kept it in a special box wrapped in tissue, bringing it out only for special occasions.

"Oh, yes," he said. "It's beautiful enough to keep you from having heatstroke."

Merilee appeared from the bedroom hallway. "I thought I was going to pick you up."

"I did, too, but you're late. I don't want to be late for my meeting. It's frowned upon at the Atlanta Woman's Club."

Merilee checked her watch. "But I'm not supposed to pick you up for another fifteen minutes."

"Exactly. In my day, on time didn't mean showing up at the last minute. I waited on my front porch for five minutes and you never appeared, so I figured I might as well come here so you don't have to waste more time by making a stop."

Merilee blinked slowly, like a person trying to control her anger, which confused Sugar, because all she was doing was stating a fact. "Well, we have to wait a few more minutes because Heather Blackford is coming to pick up the kids and take them all to the movies. And I have to find my shoes."

Sugar's eyes met Wade's. "Heather Blackford is coming here?" he asked.

Merilee lifted her head from where she'd been looking under the couch. "I can meet her outside if it'll be awkward, Wade. I forgot you two dated."

"They more than dated," Sugar interjected. "They were engaged. Invitations had already been sent out, as I recall. And then she found what she thought was a bigger fish, even though it was obvious to everyone that she was still madly in love with Wade."

"Sugar . . . ," Wade warned.

"I'm just stating facts. Someone has to. No need for everyone to get upset."

"I'm not upset," Wade said.

"Neither am I." Merilee's cheeks flushed.

"I'm upset," Colin piped up helpfully. "We were supposed to go skating, but Lily and Bailey said they didn't want to break any legs because then they couldn't be on the cheerleading team."

"It's true," Lily shouted from the hall. She was sitting on the floor with what looked to be a thick album opened on her lap.

Colin rolled his eyes. "She doesn't even know if she made the team yet."

"Please sit down, Sugar," Merilee called from the kitchen, apparently still looking for her shoes. "This might take a few minutes."

Sugar sat down on the edge of the sofa and waited for Merilee to hobble back into the room with one shoe on before pointedly staring at her watch.

"Is this what you're looking for?" Wade asked, holding up a strappy low-heeled sandal. "I found it behind a stack of what looks like high school yearbooks."

Merilee's expression changed slightly from harried to wary, her gaze moving from the shoe to the book Lily was looking at.

"Lily, I thought I told you that we would look at them together. You really need to ask permission before touching someone else's things." Merilee took the shoe and the book in one quick movement, shutting it without looking at it. "Sorry."

"It's just a book," Lily said, her voice wavering. "I didn't know I had to ask permission."

Merilee squatted down next to her daughter. "I'm sorry, sweetheart. I didn't mean to snap at you. But they are private, and I'm not sure I'm ready to share them with you yet."

"I've got some scary photos of me in high school, too, so I can't say I blame you, Merilee." Wade's tone was light, but Sugar knew he was lying. The boy had never taken a bad picture in his life. But if he thought his confession would make Merilee open up about why she didn't want her daughter to look through the yearbooks, they were both disappointed.

Merilee stood, then gathered the yearbooks into her arms and stepped back to examine Wade's shelves. "You've done a beautiful job, Wade. Thank you."

"My pleasure. And if it's all right with you, I've brought stuff over to fix the cellar door, too."

"Yes, of course. Thank you."

He looked at her closely. "You've got . . ." He lifted his hand and moved back a strand of hair. "Your hair was stuck in your lipstick."

Her cheeks reddened. "Oh. Thanks."

The hallway was narrow, leaving little room for her to back up or look away. Sugar watched as Merilee's eyes widened, as if she was really noticing Wade for the first time. Noticing him as a woman would notice a man. *It's about time,* Sugar thought, suddenly remembering Tom and the first time she'd seen him.

Wade backed away first, allowing Merilee to carry the yearbooks back to her bedroom, which was followed by the sound of a drawer opening, then closing with a solid thud. Letting everyone know exactly where to find them.

Colin was already running to the door before the rest of them heard the car outside. "I'll go see who it is!" he shouted as he yanked open the door, followed closely by Merilee and Wade.

Merilee smelled Heather's perfume before she appeared in the doorway, her halo of golden hair seeming to illuminate the room. She smiled brightly at the small group of people. "Well, if I'd known it was a party, I'd have come sooner and brought a dish."

Without waiting to be invited, she stepped forward and enveloped Merilee in an embrace. "Don't you look charming today, Merilee? I absolutely *love* your haircut—so flattering." Straightening, she winked in Wade's direction. "And your skin is practically glowing. It must be the company."

As Merilee stammered incoherently, Wade's arm made its way to Merilee's shoulder. "Hello, Heather. It's been a while."

"Yes, it has. You're looking good, Wade. And so are you, Sugar. You must tell me what vitamins you take, because you never seem to age." She wisely didn't approach Sugar for a cheek kiss or hug, most likely owing to the fact that Sugar was doing her best to stare her down with a glare that might have turned some women into ice.

Heather continued to smile as if nothing bothered her, but Sugar knew she'd seen Wade's arm. Knew it from the brief flash of those perfect blue eyes.

"Before I forget," Heather said to Merilee, "I need you to go ahead and block off next Saturday on your calendar so we can both go shopping for our gala evening gowns."

"Oh, I don't think—," Merilee began.

"It's all settled and I won't take no for an answer. It will be *so* much fun. And it will give us the chance to get to know each other better." She looked down at her watch and then behind Merilee. "Are the kids ready? I don't want to be late—I want to make sure we get the best seats."

"Yes, but—"

"Great! I can't tell you how much I'm looking forward to our shopping trip. I'll text you when the movie's over. Y'all have fun!" she said, wiggling her fingers.

A flurry of activity curtailed any argument, and after just a few short minutes, the door closed and the house descended into silence.

Sugar stood, leaning heavily on the arm of the sofa to push herself upright. "May we go now? There won't be any of the chicken salad sandwiches left if we don't hurry. I can't taste them anymore, but I can still feel the crunch of the pecans on my good teeth."

Merilee picked up her purse from the back of a chair and spoke to Wade, carefully avoiding his eyes. "Please lock up when you leave."

"Yes, ma'am," he said. "But I'll probably still be here when you get back."

Merilee looked startled, which had clearly been his intention. "I'll . . . okay," she said, turning so fast that she nearly bumped into the chair on her way to open the door for Sugar.

Merilee held open the door of the minivan for Sugar, and then drove down the driveway without speaking, although her jaw was twitching, as if she was thinking about all the things she could have said to Wade but hadn't. It was her generation, Sugar suspected, raised with computers with backspaces and "delete" buttons that made them believe they always had a second chance to say the right thing.

"So, what's this Atlanta Woman's Club?" Merilee asked suddenly, as if realizing Sugar could ask her about Wade any minute.

"Well, let's see," she said, thoughtful. "It's an old and venerable Atlanta institution. We've been around since 1895 serving our communities in all sorts of philanthropic ways. Wasn't too popular with the men when it started, but they soon accepted it, knowing these strong and independent women wouldn't be told no anyway, so they might as well at least pretend to go along with it."

"Doesn't sound like your kind of group at all," Merilee said, the corner of her mouth twitching.

"Humph," Sugar muttered. "It was the AWC who convinced the mayor back in the twenties to buy the land for an airfield—which just happens to now be the busiest airport in the world."

"Impressive," Merilee said, signaling a turn onto Georgia 400, then heading south toward midtown Atlanta.

"Oh, that's just one small thing. We also established the Atlanta public kindergarten system and mobile libraries in the area, just to name a few. Not a lot of people know about us because we prefer not to toot our own horns like some other organizations that I will not name." She pressed her lips together to show Merilee that she meant it, even though she couldn't quite remember the names of the other organizations anyway.

"Your husband, Tom—was he supportive of your membership?"

Sugar looked down at her hands, neatly folded in her lap, and the single gold band on the third finger of her left hand. "He would have been. He died before I became a member."

Merilee was silent for a moment, chewing her bottom lip. "You were so young when you were widowed. Did you ever consider re-marrying?"

"Have you?" Sugar shot back.

Merilee sent her a sharp glance. "It's been less than a year. To be honest, I still feel as if I'm married."

"Humph. Your husband apparently doesn't." She pressed her lips together again. "Wade is single, you know, and about your age. And not too hard on the eyes, either, just in case you haven't noticed, al-though I suspect you probably have. He's a wonderful craftsman, but you should know that he's also a very successful developer. Very."

Merilee had reddened to the tips of her ears. "I don't care about that. Being kind and considerate and having a sense of humor is important. And being good with kids. And faithful."

Sugar studied Merilee, a soft smile teasing her lips. "Is that what you'd look for in your next husband?"

"Yes," Merilee said without pause. "Hypothetically, anyway, since I'm not looking for another husband. But especially the faithful part." She was silent for a moment. "What about you? What would you look for in a husband if you were to marry again?"

Sugar pretended to think. "You know what I'd want?" She regarded Merilee over the tops of her glasses. "I'd want a man who could drive at night."

The minivan veered out of the lane for a brief moment as Merilee barked with laughter. "I suppose our needs change as we get older."

"That they do," agreed Sugar, feeling the aching place inside her chest again, the place where her heart had once been.

Merilee plucked a pair of sunglasses from the dashboard and adjusted them on her nose. "So, what was Tom like? And how did you meet?"

Sugar's hands tightened in her lap. She never talked about Tom to anyone. Never. Especially not to someone she barely knew. She wanted to ignore the question, to dismiss it as simply an effort to divert a dis-cussion about Merilee's own life. Except Sugar knew that wasn't true. Despite all her attempts to keep her new tenant at arm's length, a ten-uous connection had been formed, its foundation loosely based on proximity and loneliness, and a stubbornness to survive a life that wasn't of their own choosing.

Sugar turned her head, wishing she had her own sunglasses to block the glare from the window. "I was nineteen. And the first time I saw him, I thought that if I could ever fall in love, it would be with him."

"What about Tom? Did he feel the same way?"

A small smile lifted her mouth. "Oh, no. The first time he saw me, I was trying to kill someone. I suppose you can say he saved two lives that day." She looked up at the bright blue sky, and remembered.

Fourteen

SUGAR

1942

I looked down at the top of Jimmy's head as he sat in his wheelchair, taking a moment to catch my breath. His beautiful reddish blond hair was a total waste on a boy, but beautiful to look at from where I was usually standing behind him. It was just like our mama's, which was why she probably pretended he didn't exist. Nobody wanted a mirror image of themselves that was less than perfect.

I was panting from pushing the wheelchair toward the granite Goliath known as Stone Mountain. Some people actually drove their automobiles up the gentle slope all the way to the summit, but all the pleading from Jimmy and bullying from Harry couldn't get me to do something so foolish. Instead, I parked at the bottom of the trailhead and began walking, planning to continue until the path got too rocky or I ran out of steam.

It was cold for April, and my breath made smoky puffs as I exhaled; the sky had started out with timid clouds, but they now seemed to be gaining confidence as they grew in size and color, nearly obliterating the sun as we climbed. I'd never been to Stone Mountain before. Only the carving of General Robert E. Lee had been finished since the entire idea had begun back in the twenties, and I had enough to keep me busy rather than spending my day looking at what happened when people didn't have the wherewithal to finish what they started.

Today was supposed to be just Jimmy and me on account of Lamar being sick. It was just a little cough, but he said he felt poorly enough to stay home. He was now living with another family of tenant farmers, the Scotts, who didn't have children and treated him like a son. They'd moved into the house he'd once shared with Rufus, and it all worked out since now he had a family again.

I suspected that Jimmy might have caught whatever Lamar had, but he was too stubborn to admit it. That was how people could always tell we came from the same family. I saw him shivering and made him put on a sweater, and he didn't fight it, which should have told me to make him stay home. But that would have been like making a cow stop producing milk just by talking to it.

We heard the whoops and hollers from Harry and Curtis behind us, and I started pushing again, not wanting them to catch up. They'd not been invited, but Harry had said it wasn't fitting that a girl should be driving all by herself (even though we both knew I was a better driver than he was) and I would more than likely wreck Daddy's Plymouth because I was a girl. I knew they were both looking for a place to smoke where Daddy wouldn't find out—Daddy could not abide tobacco, most likely on account that his tobacco crop had failed ten years ago and set him back in a bad way. But even Harry knew that Daddy wouldn't have let him take the car if I hadn't been with them.

It was our big family embarrassment that Harry and Will were of age yet not in uniform. They'd managed to avoid the draft so far, but after Pearl Harbor, when just about every able-bodied man had voluntarily enlisted, they remained civilians. Even Bobby, my quiet, smart brother, whose favorite thing to do was read, had signed up. Bobby promised he'd come back, but I didn't see how he could promise such a thing. Three boys from the county had been lost in France already, and they thought they'd be coming home, too. Mama took it hard when Bobby enlisted and hadn't spoken a word to anyone since.

"Go faster," Jimmy said, leaning forward. "I want to stop up there and look through my binoculars."

Granddaddy's field glasses hung around his neck, the strap fraying now. I didn't know for sure, but I thought he still slept with them. Harry and Will teased him, saying he was a baby because he still slept with a toy. Jimmy never defended himself because we both knew he did it so Harry or Will wouldn't steal them while he slept.

With a quick glance behind me, I started moving as fast as I could. The path at the base was wide and mostly smooth, so I didn't have to struggle too much, although the muscles in my calves had already begun to burn. I passed a young man—not too much older than Harry—in uniform who turned to look at us, which wasn't an unusual occurrence owing to Jimmy's bright hair and my running like I was being chased.

He didn't look away as we passed, and I felt like I had to turn my head to look, too. The first thing I noticed was his eyes. They were dark brown, almost black, but they were turned up a little bit at the corners like he'd smiled so much that they got stuck there. He wore a khaki navy uniform, which wasn't a rare sight because of the nearby Naval Air Station in Chamblee. Willa Faye was always swooning over a man in uniform, which I told her was silly because they were still just boys under the uniform, and there was nothing special there from what I could tell. Maybe I saw things differently because I was raised with so many brothers and she just had one sister.

But it wasn't his eyes or his uniform that made me take a second look. It was the way he looked at me. Not like he wanted to whistle at my backside, but like he wanted to know my story.

I suddenly felt self-conscious that I wore saddle shoes and bobby socks that made me look younger than my nineteen years. Willa Faye sometimes painted a line on the backs of her legs when she went out dancing so people would think she wore nylons, but only after she left her house so her mama wouldn't see. There wasn't enough privacy at my house to do such a thing, plus I didn't have the patience. But at that one moment, when his eyes met mine, I wished I'd given a thought to what I looked like.

I kept going, pushing Jimmy to the point where he wanted to stop, then waited while he put his binoculars to his eyes. "Do you see anything?"

He shook his head. "Not many birds—no trees up on the mountain, so I wasn't expecting to. But you can see pretty far—I think that's the road we drove up on."

He handed me the glasses and I took them, aware of the man in the uniform still watching me, his hands in his pockets, his hat at an angle that made him look mysterious as well as handsome.

It took me a while to get anything to come into focus, my fingers clumsy as I attempted to adjust the binoculars. I just saw lots of blue sky and then, lowering the glasses, a road and a single car moving slowly across a background of green grass.

"See it?"

I nodded, following the progress of the car, seeing how I could make out the occupants of the front seat even from this distance.

"I like the way things look through my binoculars," Jimmy said. "No matter how different something looks from up close or far away, objects don't change. They're still the same. Just like people." He tugged on my arm and I relinquished the binoculars.

"Jimmy!"

Curtis suddenly appeared beside me, taking hold of the wheelchair while Harry grabbed me around the waist and pulled me backward. They smelled of cigarettes and alcohol and I turned my head in disgust while quickly grabbing for the handgrips of the wheelchair.

Harry pulled me back. "It's not fair that Jimmy gets a free ride up the mountain, so we're going to take turns rolling him back down."

"Stop it, Harry. Don't be like that. He might get hurt."

Curtis pretended to be upset. "What about us? Don't you care about what happens to us?"

Ever since Jimmy's accident, I had avoided being in Curtis's company. It was a sin to hate, but I thought God would make an exception for Curtis. The boy was pure evil, and if I was Catholic like Willa Faye, I would have found some holy water to sprinkle on him.

"No, I really don't. Now, give me back the wheelchair."

Jimmy looked at me with wide, terrified eyes behind smudged glasses. "Come on, Harry. Quit it."

Curtis grinned, then sat down on Jimmy's lap. "Come on, Harry. Give me a push and climb on."

"No!" I shouted, trying again to reach the handles, but Harry held me back, laughing like it was the funniest thing in the world, which just made me madder.

I stomped on his foot with the heel of my shoe—grateful now that I had on my saddle shoes—and he let go just as the wheelchair started to roll slowly back down the path, heading too close to the edge. I grabbed hold of one of the wheelchair handles and brought it to a stop. I launched myself at Curtis, grabbing at his face, his hair, anything to give me the grip I needed to cause damage. I wanted him to roll to the ground and slide off the mountain, not that we were high enough to do much damage, but maybe I'd get lucky and he'd hit his head. I wouldn't care if I went to jail for murder if it meant that he was dead.

I felt strong hands on my shoulders, and then the man in uniform yanked Curtis to his feet. Without even a how-de-do, he punched Curtis in the face, knocking him to the ground. Kneeling down, the man looked up at Jimmy, who was shaking from fever and fear, his face an awful chalk color.

"Are you all right?" he asked.

Jimmy and I both nodded.

The man stood, rubbing his knuckle, and I saw that he still had a boy's face, the uniform making him appear older. "I'm sorry about that, but I was afraid things were getting out of hand and you needed assistance." He surveyed the scene, eyeing Harry, who looked like a bull refused by a cow, and Curtis, stumbling with his hand to his face. Turning back to me, he said, "May I escort you back down? I brought my Jeep, and I'd be honored if you'd let me bring you home."

"Yes, please," I said, not caring that I didn't know this man and I'd just agreed to let a stranger take Jimmy and me home. But I trusted him. There was something in his face that made me think I'd known him my whole life.

The man slipped off his cap, showing shortly cropped, thick brown hair, and tucked it under his arm. "Lieutenant Tom Bates, ma'am. I'm currently training pilots at the Naval Air Station, but my home is Dothan, Alabama." He smiled, and all of a sudden I felt much calmer.

I introduced Jimmy and me, then began walking back down the

path. I turned at the sound of footsteps, no longer afraid with Tom there. Harry called to me with the belligerent tone he used when he knew he'd already lost a fight. "You can't leave with a stranger, Sugar. You ain't too old for Daddy to tan your hide."

Tom stood between Harry and me, and I saw how he was taller than Harry, making my big brother seem puny. "I've introduced myself to her, so we're not strangers. And I'd say she's in better hands with me than she'd be with you and your friend." We all looked over at Curtis, who was squatting down now while blood poured from his nose and painted the dusty trail with red.

"I forbid you to go, Sugar." Harry tried to look tough, but I could see the worry in his eyes, probably remembering how Daddy had sent him to Cairo and how he'd hated every minute, only returning after he'd promised Daddy he'd do better and not be so mean and hateful to everyone.

We turned our backs on him and I allowed Tom to guide Jimmy's wheelchair as we made our slow way down the mountain. We told Tom about the farm and our family, and he told us about his own family back in Dothan. He was an only child, and his parents were much older than ours. His daddy owned the general store downtown, and his mama loved his daddy so much that she went to the store every day to help him. It said a lot about Tom, I thought, that his parents loved each other enough to want to spend all their time together, and then poured all that love into their son.

It wasn't until much later, after I'd put Jimmy to bed and given him something to bring his fever down, that I lay in bed thinking about Tom Bates, and the way he'd smiled at me, remembering something I'd promised myself a long time ago, a promise that I would never love anything again that I couldn't bear to lose.

A mockingbird cried out into the cold spring night, and I wondered if Jimmy had heard it and was sitting up in his bed by the window with the binoculars. I rolled over, my back to the full yellow moon, and closed my eyes, wondering if it was already too late.

Fifteen

MERILEE

Merilee parked her minivan in front of the cottage, embarrassed at the little jolt of excitement she felt at the sight of Wade's truck. Another club member had already planned to drive Sugar home after the AWC meeting, so after dropping Sugar off at the Wimbish House on Peachtree Street—Sugar having declined her offer of assistance to walk her to the front door—Merilee drove straight home, relishing the idea of the rare peace and quiet of an empty house for at least another hour.

She found Wade in the kitchen, kneeling in front of one of the cabinets and unscrewing the hinge. He smiled at her when she walked in, and she hoped the blood rush in her chest didn't mean she was having a heart attack.

He stood, brushing his hands on his jeans. "The cellar door has been replaced—I'll have to show you how the new lock works. I thought you might need help moving all those books onto the shelves, so I figured I'd make myself useful until you got back. These kitchen cabinets are pretty warped, so I've been making some adjustments to make them easier to open and close."

"Wow, thanks. I'm really not used to having things in good repair. My husband wasn't very good with his tools."

"Really?" Wade said, his mouth widening to a grin.

"Oh," Merilee said, feeling the blood rush to her face. "I meant, he wasn't, you know, handy . . ."

Wade held up his hand. "I know. I'm just teasing. You're so serious that I couldn't resist."

She frowned. "No, I'm not. I just have a lot on my plate and have to be in charge all the time . . ." She stopped when she saw he was still grinning. "What?"

"I see where Lily gets her frown."

"Oh." She raised her hand without thinking, using her forefinger to massage the crease so it wouldn't stay. Just as her mother had shown her when she was a teenager.

He moved to the back door. "Come on—let me show you the cellar." He held the door for her and as she passed him she wondered if she'd only imagined the crackle of electricity that seemed to spark between them. She smoothed her hair with her hands, imagining it shooting up in all directions.

They walked to the side of the house, where two large wooden doors covered what looked like a giant slice of pie glued to the house's foundation. "These doors are pretty heavy, so make sure you give them a good yank—you should probably practice, so if there ever is a tornado and you need to get in here in a hurry, you won't panic."

She nodded, hoping she'd never have to use it for real. She was petrified of dark spaces and spiders, having somehow inherited those fears from David after he died. She'd always been the one to comfort and pretend bravery when he was alive. After he died, she found she couldn't bear to be inside small, dark places, David's death ramming home the fact that monsters really did exist in the dark spots right outside the edge of the light.

He squatted down. "I've attached a few new sliding bolts on the outside, but I also gave you an easy four-digit combo lock as a deterrent to keep people out of it—you don't really need anything more secure unless you're putting valuables in there."

He raised his eyebrows in question and she shook her head.

"This way, nobody has to hunt for a key in an emergency. I would make it easy to remember—and suggest making it the same code as your cell phone access. I'll even program it for you if you'd like—or show you how to do it yourself."

She smiled hesitantly. "I don't even have a pass code on my phone."

Wade frowned. "Still? That's not a good idea, but you probably already know that. But it's your decision." He indicated the cellar door again. "I've installed several secure bolt locks on the other side of the doors to keep them shut in strong winds, but they can only be locked and unlocked by hand from the inside." He stood back. "You want to give it a try?"

She shook her head. "Not particularly. I'm not a fan of . . . cellars."

He nodded sympathetically, which made her like him a little more. "Is it the critters or the dark?"

"Both."

"Hm. Well, maybe this particular cellar won't be so scary to you if it's familiar. And if you go down with someone you trust. But it would be a good idea to do it before you have to go here in an emergency and your kids need you to be calm."

She knew he was right, and even appreciated his offer of help, but she couldn't bring herself to say yes.

"Here, I'll open it the first time—you have the rest of the summer to practice. And then we'll just go down there to poke around for a few minutes, see if there're any supplies you might want to store down there, like bottled water and blankets, and then we'll come right back up in the sunshine. I've got a flashlight in my tool belt that I'll leave down there for you. I could even hold your hand if that would make you feel better."

Zing. She swallowed. "I'm sure that won't be necessary. I've survived childbirth twice, after all."

He chuckled, the sound low and rumbly in his chest, the chest that was currently covered by a close-fitting T-shirt that showed off a rather impressive outline of muscles. She looked away.

"Let's get this over with. I still have to move the books and start dinner before the kids get home."

Wade leaned down and yanked on the metal handle of each door, swinging them open so that she could look down a short set of rocky steps that led to absolute darkness. As promised, he pulled a flashlight from his tool belt and flipped it on, the triangular slice of light illuminating a low ceiling covered with dark wooden beams and thick cobwebs. "You ready?" Wade asked, holding out his hand.

She hadn't meant to, but she eagerly accepted it, allowing herself to enjoy the little sparks of heat as his skin touched hers, and let him lead her down the steps. It was cooler down there and smelled of dirt and dust and old air. Merilee took an involuntary step backward, bumping into a solid chest that had the opposite effect from calming her down.

He aimed the flashlight's beam upward. "Pull on the chain—let's see if the lightbulb works."

She gave it a tug and nothing happened.

"Remind me to bring a supply of lightbulbs, too—in case the electricity doesn't go off in a storm."

Wade put his hand on her arm and aimed the flashlight around the space, illuminating several pieces of broken furniture, a small table with a metal box of candles sitting on it next to a rusted bread box. He'd examined the perimeter of the room, and was turning back to her to speak, when she noticed something on the far wall, a dark rectangular shape crouched against the floor.

"Shine it over there," Merilee said, guiding his hand to the shape. She was eager to leave this dark place, but his nearby presence gave her enough courage to look around and even be a little curious.

"I sure hope that's not a coffin," Wade said as he moved forward.

Merilee frowned, temporarily aware of the darkness around them. "If you're trying to reassure me, it's not working."

Up close, with the flashlight trained on the object, she could tell whatever was underneath was covered by several heavy blankets, and she was relieved when Wade started removing them without asking her to help. He pulled off four of them, piling them on the ground, eventually revealing what appeared to be an army footlocker.

Wade moved closer to the trunk and stared at it for a moment, contemplating. "It might not be a coffin, but a body could definitely fit in there."

Merilee was ashamed to admit that the thought had crossed her mind. "We should go. Maybe Sugar knows what's in there."

"Hang on," he said, handing her the flashlight. "I doubt she knows or would remember, and we can answer that question right now." He popped open the two latches on the front, then paused, a locked padlock barring access.

"Well, this dog won't hunt." He gave a strong tug on the lock, then leaned over the lid. "Shine the flashlight on top. This looks like an army trunk, which might give us an idea who it belonged to. Maybe jar Sugar's memory."

She moved the flashlight, the yellow circle of light catching on what remained of the tips of white stenciled letters that had at some point been scratched out with a sharp object. "They're unreadable," she said, her need to state the obvious something she'd acquired since becoming the mother of two young children.

"Sugar might know where the key is. If not, I can break the lock. Aside from curiosity, I'd like to make sure there's nothing dangerous in there—like ammo or rifles or anything curious kids shouldn't be messing with."

Merilee nodded, looking around her and suddenly recalling where she was. "Can we just go now? I think I've seen all I need to." The flashlight flickered, then dimmed. She grabbed his arm.

He put his hand over hers. "I'll make sure there's a good stock of batteries and some camping lights down here in case of emergencies." He looked down at her for a long moment, giving her the chance to explain.

"Thank you," she managed, quickly turning and heading for the steps.

Once they'd emerged into the warm sunshine, Merilee felt her equilibrium return and led the way back into the house. She poured them both glasses of sweet tea and handed him one, which he accepted gratefully.

"So, were you really engaged to Heather?" She hadn't meant to say that out loud, but she was trying to clear her head of the damp, still air from the cellar and it was the first thing that crossed her mind. It had been plaguing her more and more since she'd found out and was one of those things that her mind rested on when she woke up in the middle of the night and couldn't go back to sleep.

The light in his eyes seemed to dim. "Yeah. We were. But a long time ago. Back when she wasn't even a blonde."

"Hard to imagine Heather without blond hair."

"True. Not that she will ever admit that it's not natural. She used to look a lot different. Personality kind of changed, too. It's like she was happy just being herself until she found out she could be someone else, someone she considered better, and she jumped at it. Kind of left me in the dust. Or at the altar, as Sugar likes to say, although it wasn't that bad. Only the invitations had been sent out."

"I'm sorry," Merilee said, meaning it. "At least she saved you the trauma of a divorce. And being stuck with a whole bunch of mono-grammed towels you can't use."

"I guess you'd know." He spoke softly, and he was so close that without having to lean very far she could stand on her tippy-toes and press her lips against his. And when she looked in his eyes, she could see that his thoughts were probably running in tandem with hers.

But she held back. He wasn't Michael. He didn't look like Michael or smell like Michael. He wasn't the father of her children. He also hadn't broken her heart. Maybe because he'd admitted to suffering from the same affliction, she imagined there was something between them. Some unspoken agreement that their scar patterns might fit to-gether like pieces to a puzzle. But he still wasn't Michael. She stepped back and imagined she heard them both exhale a sigh of regret.

He cleared his throat. "I'll just finish that last cabinet in the kitchen, then help you with the books, and I'll be out of your hair."

"Sounds like a plan," she said, like she really did want him to leave. One thing she did know for sure was that she didn't want him there when Heather returned with the children. She remembered the ques-tioning looks she'd received from Heather and the other committee members the night of the gala meeting, and she wasn't interested in repeating the ordeal of unasked questions and innuendos.

"I'll get started with the books," she said before leaving the room, hanging on to her empty glass so she wouldn't have to brush by him to put it in the sink.

Merilee sat in the back of Dan's Mercedes next to Heather, a mimosa in her hand, while Claire sat in the driver's seat, acting as their chauffeur for the day.

"I told you this would be fun," Heather almost squealed as they headed toward Buckhead, with its high-end boutiques and the luxury shopping meccas of Phipps Plaza and Lenox Square.

Merilee smiled and took a sip from her glass, self-consciously tucking her feet out of sight. When Heather had mentioned going shopping, Merilee hadn't thought it was something one would need to dress up for. She hadn't realized her error until she'd seen Heather in head-to-toe couture, right down to the red soles of her Louboutins. She had pointedly ignored Merilee's khaki shorts, Jack Rogers sandals, and oversized Ann Taylor blouse, which was a lot roomier on her now than it had been when she'd bought it four years before.

"There's a designer consignment shop I found online," Merilee said. "I really don't have a lot of money in the budget for a ball gown, so I was thinking that would be a great place to start . . ."

"Oh, don't be silly," Heather said, opening up a thermos and topping off Merilee's glass. "You can't wear something somebody else has already worn! It could be from someone else at the gala, and as your friend I couldn't bear to see you embarrassed like that if someone recognized the dress." She looked very serious, and for a moment, Merilee tried to picture her as the "before," the brunette with hidden ambitions Sugar had spoken of. But with Heather's expertly highlighted and colored hair, bronzed and glowing skin, and perfect makeup, Merilee couldn't imagine her being anything other than the beautiful and wealthy pampered suburban wife and mother she was. Still, she wondered if the before or the after was the "real" Heather, and if Heather ever missed the girl she'd been when she was engaged to Wade.

The champagne was beginning to muddle her brain a bit, but she knew she needed to have this conversation before she did something she'd regret, like squander her children's college educations for the perfect ball gown she'd only ever wear once.

"That's just a chance I'll have to take," Merilee continued. "I really don't have any room for anything extravagant in the budget—remember, I'm a single mom, and even though my ex is very generous with child support, I still have to provide food and shelter for myself from what I can earn. I don't want to be in debt."

Heather waved her hand in dismissal. "I know, and I so respect you for all that. Which is why I want to reward your hard work and sacrifice by, shall we say, subsidizing a dress. The mothers on my committee have to look the part. If we want people at the auction to bid big money, we need to be front and center looking like big money." She pressed her hand to her heart and shook her head. "I know it sounds contradictory, but it's true. Money begets money. If we look like we don't need the money, the bids will come in higher than if we were wearing khakis and old blouses."

She looked Merilee directly in the eye, and it was all Merilee could do to not hold her hands across her chest as if she'd just been discovered buck naked in public.

Heather continued. "I like you a lot. I think we have so much in common, and I just know we will be great friends. Which is why I have chosen you as my 'project.' Not that you need more than a spit and shine, but I think it's been a while since you've really taken care of yourself—and you deserve to be pampered. I mean, look how hard you work, and without help! It would be my absolute joy to do whatever it takes to get you up to speed. That includes a trip to my hair salon, the Saks cosmetics counter, and my favorite boutique to find you a suitable gown. My treat. If you'd like to pay what you think you can afford, then that's fine. But what is having money if I can't use it for good and to spoil my friends?"

Merilee fervently wished they'd had this conversation when she was still stone-cold sober. Or even way before that, before the divorce, when she still had a modicum of self-confidence and wasn't so desperate to be valued again. The old Merilee might even have been annoyed to be considered anybody's "project." Because she now found herself on the verge of saying yes. She grasped frantically for her last thread of self-respect. "No, I couldn't possibly—"

Heather tucked in her chin. "I know. I understand. You're a strong woman and it's hard for you to accept help."

Merilee sat back, relieved that Heather *did* understand. It had been too long since anybody had even tried.

Heather continued. "But maybe . . ." She tapped her finger on her chin, thinking, and eventually a slow smile spread over her face. "But maybe you'd feel better about it if I let you do something for me, too."

Merilee found herself nodding eagerly while trying to figure out what she could do for Heather. "Of course. Anything."

"Well, as luck would have it, my wedding anniversary is on the night of the gala. And since you work at the most fabulous jeweler in Atlanta, maybe you could help Daniel choose something wonderful for me. He and I don't have the same . . . taste in jewelry. He thinks a small knickknack is sufficient to show his love, but I disagree." She threw her head back and laughed, revealing a diamond pendant necklace that had to be at least four carats. "I know you will be able to better direct him to something more my taste. Something big and shiny."

"I'm not really a salesperson—"

"Oh, honey, I know that. You're the marketing genius behind their advertising. But you're there every day and know what they've got. And Daniel will trust your judgment. I promise you it will be a big-ticket item and earn you a lot of respect from your employers." She smiled broadly, her teeth white and perfect. "See? It would be a win-win. I scratch your back, and you scratch mine. And everybody's happy!"

Heather tilted her slim neck back and downed the rest of her mimosa, the diamond winking against her tanned skin, and Merilee followed suit, making a promise in her fuzzy brain that she would choose the cheapest dress she could find even if it looked like a burlap sack.

Twenty minutes later, Merilee was ushered into the private dressing room of Fruition, a store she wouldn't have known existed if she hadn't been with Heather. There were no signs outside the nondescript mid-century brick one-story building, just a single doorbell that Heather had pushed with an elegantly manicured finger. It was opened immediately by a very tall, very thin, very blond woman who ushered them in with a secret smile.

Merilee found herself in what could have been a chic apartment's living room, with low, white leather couches, glass-and-steel tables, and a dais in the middle of the room, three sides of it bordered by gilt-edged mirrors. "Merilee, this is Yvette—a woman of exquisite taste and knowledge of fashion who also happens to be brutally honest. She will be in charge of finding you the perfect gown."

"Nice to meet you, Yvette." Merilee glanced around, wondering where the dresses were so she could shop by looking at price tags first. "If you'll just lead me to the racks so I can browse, I'm happy to let Heather go first."

"Oh, I've already got my gown," Heather said with a dismissive wave before opening her purse to pull out a tube of lipstick. "This visit is all about you. When we've decided, then we'll head to La Perla and Louboutin to accessorize. I promise to buy things for me, too, because I also have to look the part."

"Really, Heather, just the gown is fine . . ."

"Oh, no!" Heather cried out, reaching into her purse and pulling out a man's wallet. "I forgot to give this back to Daniel. We were at the club last night at a pool party and he had his wallet in his bathing suit pocket. The girls begged him to go swimming with them, so I stuck it in my purse." She grimaced. "I should call him, but my phone battery is completely dead." Heather gave Merilee a wink. "I might even use his Amex so he doesn't see the charges on mine. Not that he minds, but he's always making comments when the bill comes in. I don't even think he checks his own!"

"Here—use my phone," Merilee said, pulling hers from her purse. "I just programmed the code so I'd remember it—it's one-one-one-one."

"Thanks." Heather closed her eyes in relief as she held Merilee's phone. "You really should have a more secure code, you know."

"I know, but I can't remember any of them, so I just decided to use the same code for everything. Maybe when my brain cells recover from this year, I'll go back and reset everything. But this works for now."

Heather nodded sympathetically as she reached over and patted Merilee's hand. "I understand."

"Are you ready?" Yvette asked. "Heather already prepped me prior to your arrival this morning, and I have several selections waiting for you in our dressing area. Let's go see if any are to your liking, and we'll try on whichever ones strike your fancy."

Merilee tried to think clearly enough to come up with a protest that didn't sound ungrateful. "Okay, so if I don't like anything, is there a room with other dresses where I can browse?"

Heather laughed. "No, Merilee. This is one-of-a-kind couture. Let Yvette do her job, and I promise you won't be disappointed." She reached over and gave Merilee a reassuring squeeze on the arm as a man in a tuxedo appeared with a bucket of champagne and two glasses. He immediately filled the two glasses, then handed one to Heather and one to Merilee.

"Here's to the perfect evening," Heather said, raising her glass to clink with Merilee's.

Merilee took a sip, needing more sustenance and fortitude for what was becoming a surreal adventure, then turned to follow Yvette. "Hang on," she said, turning back and handing Heather her purse. "Can you hold this for me? Just stick my phone in it when you're done."

"Of course." Heather smiled. "You go have fun now—and let me see your favorites."

By the time the car was headed back toward Sweet Apple, the trunk was stuffed with packages and Merilee's head was swimming with champagne. She was now the proud owner of a midnight blue silk-and-chiffon concoction that felt like a cloud and showed off more skin than anything she owned—except her bathing suit.

It was being altered to fit her as if it had been made for her (Yvette's words), and Merilee had no idea how much it cost and was afraid to even guess. None of the dresses Yvette had selected had either price tags or sizes written anywhere on the gowns or on their padded hangers, which alone probably cost more than everything together in Merilee's closet. Merilee had used her own money for the matching shoes, spending more than she'd originally planned to spend on the dress. But, as Heather had pointed out, she couldn't wear Jack Rogers sandals with a couture gown.

Merilee turned to Heather. "Thank you—for all of this. It was really fun, and I truly can't express how much I appreciate this."

"I just wish you'd let me take you to Spa Sydell. Nothing like a facial and massage after a hard day of shopping."

Despite the effects of the champagne, that had been Merilee's only successful compromise with Heather. "And I do appreciate the offer, but I need to get back. Michael's bringing home the children at six."

Heather tapped an elegant finger against her champagne glass. "Will you be bringing Michael as your escort to the gala?"

Merilee almost choked on her mouthful of champagne. "Oh, gosh. No. Do I need a date? I was planning on going solo."

Heather moved her head from side to side, as if weighing options. "Well, I suppose you *could*, but you would most likely be the only single woman there. Plus it will make my table lopsided. I've decided to put you at the head table with Daniel and me and some other VIPs— but it will look out of place if we have an odd number of chairs."

"Can't you just put an extra chair at the table? Then we can pretend that my date had to cancel last minute because of some emergency."

"Surely you have a male friend you could bring," Heather said, her eyes narrowed in concentration, as if going through a Rolodex of possibilities in her mind. She looked up suddenly, her eyes now wide with excitement. "Or, as a last resort, do you have a brother?"

The champagne in Merilee's mouth turned suddenly sour. "I did," she said slowly. "But he died when he was a boy."

Heather grabbed her hand and squeezed, and Merilee found herself squeezing back. Maybe it was the alcohol, or maybe it was the look of compassion in Heather's eyes, but Merilee found herself drawn to her,

and maybe even hopeful that this could be her first real female friendship in her new life.

Heather drew back, her head tilted to the side the way some people
study artwork. "Just to throw it out there, but what about Wade Kimball? And let me tell you, that man knows how to fill out a tuxedo."

Merilee drained her champagne glass, more to give herself a chance
to come up with a response and less because of her need for more alcohol. She placed her hand over the rim when Heather picked up the
bottle to pour more. "Wade?" She shook her head, thinking of a thousand reasons why not and then grabbing at the most obvious. "Wouldn't
that be awkward for you? And Dan? You once had a . . . relationship
with Wade, from what I understand. We'd be at the same table."

Heather flicked her wrist in the same way she'd done at La Perla
when dismissing a particular bra as being too lacy. "We're all mature
adults, and Daniel and I have a very secure marriage—neither one of
us will have a problem, and I know Wade won't. Our relationship was
forever ago—when we were practically children. I once thought Wade
was the man for me—way back when. Before I realized that who you
think you want and need in your twenties isn't always the same man
you want and need in your thirties and forties."

Merilee wanted to tell her that, yes, it could be. That she'd once
imagined being with Michael in the nursing home, where they'd park
their wheelchairs next to each other and talk about their grandchildren.

"That may be," Merilee said instead. "But I don't really know Wade.
And I certainly don't want to give him the wrong impression by inviting him. It would be like going on a date when I have absolutely no
intention of dating. Not for a long while, anyway."

"Ah," Heather said, tapping her nails against her glass. "You're
imagining you're still in love with your husband."

The way she eagerly nodded in agreement reminded Merilee of why
she didn't drink very often. It was humiliating the way she became
such an emotionally open book whenever alcohol was involved. "If he
asked me to come back tomorrow, I have this terrible feeling that I'd
say yes."

"The same man who left you for your daughter's teacher and then knocked her up?" In response to Merilee's surprise, Heather added, "I read that blog, too, so I know. And I think what they did to you is despicable. He didn't deserve you and you should be glad to be rid of him."

Merilee reached for a tissue from a box in the center console and wiped her eyes. "I know. But I still can't imagine going out with another man. Not for a while. Besides, what would my children think?"

Heather raised an eyebrow. "Well then, it's settled. You have to invite Wade. I think he's the *distraction* you need right now. Trust me, I know what I'm talking about. I'm sure the children like him and won't have any objection, and Michael will get the comeuppance he deserves when he hears about it or—better yet—sees photos from the gala on Facebook. You really need a page, by the way. It's the best way for Michael to see what you've been up to without him. I could even set it up for you if you'd like. Just let me know what password you'd like to use, and then all you'll have to do is post beautiful photos of you having fun at the gala with Wade. And anything else you'd like to post." Heather sent her a wicked smile that would have made Merilee blush if she'd been sober.

As sick as the entire idea was, it did have a certain appeal. Merilee removed her hand from the top of the glass and allowed Heather to refill it. After taking a healthy sip, she said, "All right. I'll invite Wade. It's just one evening, right? And if you and Dan are okay with it, then I say let's do it."

They raised their glasses again and clinked them together before Merilee sank back into the seat of the car and let the glow of the champagne and the day wash over her, allowing herself to ignore the niggling thoughts of how Heather knew she didn't have a Facebook page and how she was going to ask a guy for a date after being out of practice for more than a decade.

Sixteen

Observations of Suburban Life from Sweet Apple, Georgia
Written by: Your Neighbor

Installment #6: Biker Chicks and Football

Long before there's a snap in the air, we here in the South are regaled with SEC football in all its glory. You will be considered unpatriotic if you don't have your school flags flapping from your car windows or at least an affiliation bumper sticker or license plate to show your allegiance.

To our newcomers from outside the Southeast, learn to live with it. SEC football is as much a part of us as sweet tea and grits. In September, start planning your tailgate party menus, because that's the only way you can expect any kind of social life on a Saturday for the entire season. Or at least have the biggest TV screen in the neighborhood. The good thing about football is that you don't have to understand the game to enjoy a good tailgate party.

And don't dismiss family loyalties. I know of a couple where the husband went to Alabama and the wife went to Auburn, and they had to seek marriage counseling after every season. Their daughter started at Alabama and then finished up at Auburn because she couldn't take the stress of choosing one over the other. Now, that's loyalty.

Another thing I've been noticing, now that the weather has gone from one hundred percent humidity to only ninety, and the temperature is now safely down from the heatstroke-inducing nineties, is that the bikers are out in force. Not motorcyclists—we don't have many of those in our little Sweet Apple suburb. I'm talking about the foot-pedaling, Lycra-wearing (whether they can pull it off or not), sweat-covered bike people who love to travel in packs and exercise their right to use the roadways for their recreational use.

Now, I'm all about being healthy and making good lifestyle choices. Obviously, a lot of my neighbors are, too, judging by the number of Pilates, yoga, and fitness studios that have spread like kudzu within our city limits in the past few years. But I can't help but wonder if these bike people might also have death wishes. In a town where many of our roads are narrow, winding, hilly, and with no shoulders, it does give you something to ponder when you're coming around a bend going forty-five and nearly run into a herd of them, their little fanny packs shifting from side to side as the riders pump their muscled calves to make it to the top of the hill and, presumably, make their hearts stronger. I wonder if they have any idea how close they just came to making their heartbeats permanently stop.

Luckily, we have a lot of roads with bike paths, and even the Greenway, which goes on for miles, through several counties, with no motor vehicle access. It's made for those of you who like to exercise outdoors either on foot or on a bike that probably costs more than your monthly mortgage. I'm not judging. Perhaps we motorists should hand out flyers with a map of these locations every time we pass a biker. We could be saving a life.

Speaking of all this exercise brings me to another, slightly related note. Have you ever noticed how gaining weight or losing weight directly impacts a person's personality? Like how when a person gets down to the point where they don't take up two seats at the movie theater they become more outgoing, more free with their opinions, more likely to ask for a raise or ask someone out for a date. It's like their real personality has been hiding under all those fat cells, waiting to have its day. And all it takes is one day for a person to simply look in the mirror and decide they've had enough. Sometimes, earth's little earthquakes—like a divorce— do that, too, but it's only fair that something so awful can have a good side effect, right?

And that's a good thing—most of the time. We should all be given the opportunity to be our real selves, regardless of how much we weigh. And sometimes having a stronger, leaner body is just the push we need to break out of our shells. Unless your real self is the spawn of Satan and you've been waiting years to wreak havoc on those who overlooked you in your chubbier days. That just means you're a hateful person, thin or fat.

And that brings us to our Southern expression of the day: "You can't tell the size of the turnips by lookin' at their tops." I know a married soccer mom and mother of two who is involved in every corner of her community and school. She is All That. But what she allows the rest of us to see is just the top of her, sticking out of the ground. The rest of her she keeps hidden, so nobody really sees the all of her. And from what I know, the all of her is not a pretty sight. It's like judging a book by the cover—you've got to open it up and see what's written on the inside before you form your opinion.

SUGAR

Sugar looked up from the television with annoyance at the knock on the door. Pushing herself to a stand, she waited for her body to register that she was upright before heading to the front door to open it.

"Good morning, Miss Sugar. We brought you groceries." Colin smiled as he thrust out two Kroger bags.

Sugar looked behind him to see a similarly burdened Merilee.

"It's a teacher workday, so no school for the kids. Lily had cheerleading practice and I took the day off to run some errands, and since your car still isn't back, I figured you'd need a few necessities."

Sugar raised an eyebrow, pretty confident that her idea of necessities was nothing like Merilee's. "Thank you," she said. "But I'm watching the weatherman on HLN. I never miss a weekday morning." She was hoping they'd understand and just drop off the bags and leave so she wouldn't miss any more than she had to.

"Oh, I didn't know you had cable," Merilee said, stepping forward so that Sugar had no choice but to open the door further and let them in. She paused to stare at the screen. "Are you watching the weatherman or the weather? Bob Van Dillen is pretty cute."

Sugar closed her mouth in what she hoped was a look of disapproval. "I meant the weather, of course." Which was a complete lie. The weatherman was the main reason she got up every morning. He was easy on the eyes. He also looked like Tom.

"Why don't you come in?" she said as Merilee and Colin passed her on the way to the kitchen.

Merilee was already unpacking the grocery bags on the counter when Sugar entered the kitchen. There was her half gallon of whole milk—the Kroger brand because it was cheapest—the jar of Duke's mayonnaise, a jar of Maxwell House instant coffee, and a bag of sugar.

"I forgot to ask you what you needed before I left for the store, and for some reason I don't have your number programmed on my phone yet, so I had to guess. I remembered seeing these things in your kitchen before, and I know you've used a lot of sugar in the cookies and brownies you've brought over to us, so consider this me returning a favor." Merilee spoke quickly, avoiding Sugar's eyes, her hands busying themselves as she stowed the emptied bags inside another bag. As if she was afraid she'd be rebuked.

Sugar felt ashamed, embarrassed that she'd become so unapproachable. She attempted to redeem herself. "Why don't you sit down and let me finish that? I've got some freshly made sweet tea in the icebox if you'd like to see what sweet tea should really taste like." She couldn't help it. There were just some things that old age granted that she was bound and determined to take full advantage of. Like removing any filters before she spoke the truth.

"Too late," Merilee said with a smile as she stowed the last of the bags. "But I'd love some tea. Although it will be tough to beat my grandfather's." She said it like a challenge.

Sugar poured two glasses and placed them on the table, then turned around to ask Colin if he'd like some, but the boy had disappeared and Merilee seemed unconcerned.

Merilee picked up her glass. "Wade fixed the cellar doors at the cottage, then took me down to examine the cellar, and we found what looks like a locked army trunk. The markings have all been scratched out, and it was covered in blankets. Chances are it was just being used as a table in case the cellar had to be used in an emergency." Merilee took a sip of her tea, smiling in appreciation and oblivious to the rush of blood in Sugar's ears or the very real threat that Sugar was about to have a heart attack. "Not bad," she said, swirling the ice in her glass. "Almost as good as my grandfather's."

Sugar could barely hear because the buzzing in her ears was so loud.

Merilee continued, like a bee prepared to sting, unaware of the damage about to be done to both parties. "Do you have any idea who it belonged to or what might be inside?"

Sugar took her time sitting down, then sipped her tea. "Wade already called me, and I told him I have no idea what it is or why it's there." She stood again so suddenly she thought she might faint. "Where's Colin?"

"He's probably looking for more bird books on your bookshelves. I didn't think you'd mind . . ."

But Sugar was already walking as fast as she could out of the kitchen, turning right at the front door toward her father's old study. Her heart fluttered in her chest when she noticed the door partly ajar. Had she left it open? She usually closed it, but sometimes, especially lately, she found herself forgetting small things like that. "Colin?" she called, facing the door.

"He's in here," Merilee called from behind her.

With one hand pressing against her chest, Sugar closed the door, making certain it was latched, before she turned around and walked into the front parlor. She ignored Merilee's expression of concern, her gaze settling on Colin, who was sitting on the floor in front of her mother's cedar chest, which had once held Astrid's wedding trousseau. The top was still shut, owing most likely to the crystal lamp and ceramic dog figurine on the top. But one of the two drawers had been pulled open, and Colin was occupied with examining an old jam jar, the lid still intact and showing a smattering of punched holes.

"Colin!" Merilee called out, her son either too engrossed to hear or purposefully ignoring her. "I'm so sorry," Merilee said to Sugar, attempting to remove the jar from Colin's hands. "He's generally pretty curious, but I thought I'd taught him better than to invade someone's privacy—"

"Jimmy used to catch tadpoles in that jar," Sugar said, cutting her off. "I'd forgotten that was in there." She stepped forward to look inside the opened drawer, half-afraid of what else she might see. What memories might nudge sleeping ghosts.

Colin relinquished his hold on the jar. "Apologize to Miss Sugar for invading her privacy," Merilee prompted.

"I'm sorry for invading your privacy," Colin parroted, his tone making it clear that he had no idea why what he'd done was wrong. He was like Jimmy that way. There were no sins against curiosity, and the world was full of things to explore.

Sugar took the jar from Merilee and handed it back to Colin. "You can have it. I bet there are still tadpoles in the lake—just make sure you have an adult with you if you decide to catch any." Not that she and Jimmy had ever required adult supervision. But that had been in the days before bike helmets and seat belts. According to popular belief, it was a surprise anybody had survived childhood back then.

"Did this come from the drawer, too?" Merilee asked her son, bending forward to retrieve something from the floor next to Colin.

It took a moment for Sugar to recognize the printed map in the painted wood frame. "Yes," she said. "It was a wedding gift," she added, remembering. "From my daddy. He made the frame himself. It shows the land and the cottage you live in now."

"You should hang it in the cottage," Merilee suggested. "I think there's a perfect space for it in the bedroom hallway, on the short wall between the two bedrooms."

Sugar wanted to be angry. Her privacy had been invaded, after all. And she was missing the weather report on the television given by that handsome weatherman. But Colin was looking up at her with Jimmy's eyes, and Merilee was saying the exact same words that Sugar had said to Tom long ago. It seemed there really was no way of escaping the past, no matter how far down you tried to bury it. It was there, invading the present when you least wanted it to. "It used to hang there. I took it down."

Sugar pursed her lips to show Merilee that she didn't want to discuss it any more, but as Sugar was discovering, Merilee wasn't necessarily the quiet and unassuming young divorcée she'd first appeared to be. There was something deeper there. Like another person entirely, hiding inside. Sugar just wasn't sure if she'd been pushed there or had been deliberately hidden.

Completely unaware of Sugar's interest in closing the subject, Merilee tapped on the glass, then turned it to face Sugar. "What's this spot here without trees?" she asked, pointing to the edge of the map, which had been cut off to fit into the frame. "It almost looks like a clearing, but there's not enough to tell."

Sugar took the frame and pretended to study it as if she'd never seen it before. As if she had no idea there was a clearing in the woods. She was trying to come up with an answer when Colin gave a yelp of surprise and turned around, holding Jimmy's field glasses up like a prize. "Look what I found!"

Merilee sighed. "Colin, really. You need to stop now. That doesn't belong to you."

Tucking the frame under her arm, Sugar took the glasses from Colin. "She's right. They don't belong to you. Where are your manners?"

She was sorry she'd spoken so harshly even before the little boy's face crumpled and Merilee bent down to place her arm around him.

Merilee looked up, her eyes flashing. "You're right, he shouldn't be touching things that don't belong to him. And I'm sorry for allowing him. But you could have said it more nicely." Merilee pulled Colin up and he buried his face in her side.

Sugar found herself in the rare position of feeling the need to explain herself. "Those were my grandfather's from the First World War, and then they were Jimmy's. They were his most favorite thing. It's a small thing, I know. But seeing someone else with them was almost like losing my brother all over again." She swallowed. "I'm sorry."

Merilee's eyes were bright as she hugged her son. "David, my brother—he collected Legos. He always had a fistful of pieces and the little Lego people. Even his pockets bulged with them. He had so many toys, but he loved them the most. I saved a few of them after he died and I always think that if my house ever catches on fire, and I know the children are out safely, those are the first things I'd save."

Their eyes met in mutual understanding of loss and regret and the debris of their interrupted childhoods. Sugar looked away first, unwilling to form an attachment that would break sooner or later. They always did.

"I'm missing my show," Sugar said stiffly. "Thank you for the groceries."

Merilee's face matched the look of hurt on Colin's, shaming Sugar to her core. But not enough to ask them to stay.

"You're welcome," Merilee said. She began leading Colin to the front door, but she paused as the boy ran back to replace the jar in the drawer, even though Sugar had said he could keep it.

Sugar sat down on her sofa long after the front door had been shut quietly behind them, holding the field glasses in her hands, trying to keep them from trembling.

Seventeen

MERILEE

Merilee took a turn off the main road where an old farmhouse crouched on pilings, its foundation having been removed along with the horses in the pasture and the white ranch railing fence that had once surrounded the farm. It was almost like looking at a once-distinguished old man who'd been stripped of his dignity and was forced to stand naked and exposed, like he'd done something wrong.

The brand-new brick signpost announced what was happening behind the old house and felled trees: THE MANSIONS OF SWEET APPLE. She'd never paid much attention to all the development going on around her, always too busy with her job and the kids and Michael. But since meeting Sugar Prescott, she had a whole new perspective on what all the new development might mean to the older residents who remembered what it had once been like.

Merilee paused for a moment as a long truck laden with tall Georgia pine trunks lumbered past her. She remembered a time from when she was small and her grandfather had taken her to his favorite fishing hole, only to discover that the surrounding landscape was so altered, he couldn't find it. *Once it's gone, it's gone. There's no bringing it back.* She looked at the gaping holes of Georgia clay that would soon become the foundations for new homes, thinking they resembled deep wounds more than progress.

She'd been unsuccessful reaching Wade on his cell phone and had called the office number on his business card. His secretary had explained he was on a jobsite that morning and then happily told Merilee which one. Since she passed it every day on the way to and from work, she figured it would be better asking him in a place where he'd be easily distracted and perhaps not notice her embarrassment or abject humiliation. She'd been under the delusional assumption it would be easier than asking him over the phone.

She picked up her phone and dialed his cell number one last time, waiting until it had rung enough times to go to voice mail before hanging up. With a resigned sigh, she pressed her foot on the gas and moved forward to two construction trailers parked at the edge of the site. Two men wearing jeans, collared shirts, and white hard hats stood next to the trailers with a partially unfurled paper, one man pointing at it and then gesticulating toward where a backhoe was slowly digging another large hole.

He looked up as she got out of her car, feeling self-conscious in her skirt and blazer, then found herself smiling in response to Wade's own smile as he began walking toward her.

"Merilee! Now, this is a surprise. Did Sugar send you to sabotage my site?"

She frowned. "No. Would she want me to?"

He shrugged. "This was Willa Faye's old homestead. My mother was born here."

Merilee's gaze turned toward the house, its white clapboard siding now fully exposed to the sun, without the shade of the old-growth trees. It reminded her of an old high school classmate of hers who'd walked to the front of the class to give a book report with the hem of her skirt inadvertently tucked into the waistband of her underwear, her wide backside visible to everyone. Merilee couldn't even remember the girl's name—only her nickname, "Daisy." But she remembered the skirt incident and how she and her friends had laughed. It haunted Merilee with shame every time she remembered it. And now the exposed siding on the house made her wonder if the house might be feeling the same kind of embarrassment.

"Wow. What a way to thank a family home for its years of service."

Wade frowned. "Maybe you shouldn't be spending so much time with Sugar. For the record, I'm moving it to another piece of property I own a couple of miles down the road. I'm going to restore it and then live in it. It's in really bad shape now—needs a completely new roof and there's a bit of termite damage. If it stays here, it will disintegrate and be lost forever. Even Sugar thinks I'm doing the right thing."

"My apologies." She smiled up at him, loving the way his eyes turned up at the corners like he was always secretly laughing at something. She was still trying to think of a way to bring up the subject of the gala when the man Wade had been speaking with called out.

"Hey, Wade—while you're talking, I'm going to check out that new backhoe you have over there. She's a beauty."

"Come here for a second, Bill. There's someone I want you to meet."

As the man approached, Wade said, "I want you to meet an old friend of mine—the one whose grandparents are from Sandersville. He happened to be in town on business and wanted to drop by one of my construction sites to find out the secret to my success."

Merilee considered for a brief moment pretending she hadn't heard him and making an excuse to leave before she realized that she'd never be able to walk far enough away from her past. It was always there, lurking in the shadows. So she turned slowly, squinting more than the sunlight required.

"Merilee Dunlap, please meet Bill West. Another developer who wishes he'd thought to buy up land in north Fulton County when I did."

They shook hands and Merilee did her best to smile. "Nice to meet you."

"It's always good to meet friends of Wade's. He always knows how to pick 'em. Well, with a few notable exceptions."

Wade elbowed him. "Now, now. Be nice."

Bill grinned. "So, you know Heather."

Merilee glanced over at Wade, wondering why she and Heather

might have been a topic of their conversation. "Yes, she's a friend of mine. Through the kids' school." She wasn't positive that was true, but she hoped that by saying it, it would make Bill stop talking.

He chewed on his lower lip. "Then I'm not saying a word. I just knew her when she was dating Wade. When she was still a nice person."

"Watch it," Wade warned.

Bill held up his hands in surrender. "All right, all right. I'll stop."

Merilee wondered at the use of the past tense, but before she could say anything, Wade said, "So, doesn't Merilee look familiar to you? I swear I know her from somewhere but can't place her. Maybe you can. Of course, you sowed a lot more wild oats than I ever did in my misspent youth, so maybe you've got fewer brain cells than I have."

"Ha," Bill said before turning to study Merilee. She continued to squint and smile, trying not to make it obvious that she was holding her breath. "Yep. Definitely looks like someone I should recognize. Or maybe that's just wishful thinking that I should know so many beautiful women that they all start to run together."

Merilee exhaled, feeling the sweat roll down her spine beneath her jacket.

"Right," said Wade, slapping his friend on the back. "You let me know if it comes to you. Go check out my backhoe and make sure you tell me how jealous you are."

"Nice to meet you, Merilee," Bill said, tipping the rim of his hard hat as he left.

Wade turned back to her. "I saw you called me a bunch of times on my cell. Sorry I couldn't talk—it's been a crazy morning already." He crossed his arms. "So, what can I help you with? Is there a problem with the cellar doors? Or the shelves?"

"Oh, no. They're both fine. Really. You did an amazing job on the shelves—you finished them off just beautifully. You're a real craftsman."

"Is this about the army trunk in the cellar? I called Sugar and she had no recollection of it."

"I've been thinking about what you said—about there maybe being ammunition or rifles or something dangerous in there. I just don't like the idea of my kids—or anybody's kids—snooping around and breaking a lock. If you could ask Sugar if it's okay to open it, then we probably should," she said, her smile now plastered on her face as she realized that the time had come. She mentally kicked herself for not waiting until he'd called her back on the phone.

"So . . . ," he prompted.

"So . . . yes. Well, there's this gala fund-raiser at Windwood. Heather is the committee chair and she asked that I head up the auction committee."

"No, I'm not giving anybody free land, if that's what you're here to ask for."

"No, not that—unless you really want to. I, um, she's putting me at the head table with her and Dan, and when I told her I was planning on going solo she said that wouldn't work because then she'd have an uneven number of chairs as well as the girls-to-boys ratio at the head table. Personally, I don't see a problem, but clearly it's an issue for her."

He was scrutinizing her closely now, apparently now anticipating her question and enjoying her discomfort. "Clearly," he said.

"So, having absolutely no interest in bringing my ex-husband, mostly because it would be awkward explaining it to his pregnant girlfriend, I brainstormed with Heather for somebody else who might want to come as my escort."

"Go on," he said, enjoying himself immensely.

She swallowed, feeling the heat rise in her cheeks. "And, she, um, we, thought that maybe if you were free that night—the twenty-ninth of October—and had any interest in going, that maybe you could sit at my table."

"And be your date."

Merilee shook her head vigorously. "No. Not a date. My escort. A table filler."

"You make it sound so appealing, and it's obvious that you want me badly."

She sighed and closed her eyes briefly. "No—that's not how I meant it. It's just that I don't want you getting any ideas of, well, you know. You-and-me-as-a-couple kind of thing. I'm sure you don't consider me in that way, and to be honest, I'm still getting over my husband

and our nasty divorce and have absolutely no interest in dating anyone right now. Maybe never.

"And I thought I should mention that Heather wants us to sit at her table, with her and Dan. I know it might be extremely awkward, so I wanted you to know up front, and I will completely understand if you say no."

He smirked. "What was between Heather and me was practically a lifetime ago. I'm completely over it, and sitting at a table with her and Dan won't bother me at all."

She felt enormously relieved for some reason. "That's very good to know."

"So you want to date me. For this one night."

"I guess, if you want to put it that way . . ."

"Then, yes. I'd love to go. Text me the date again so I don't forget and I'll get it on my calendar. I even own a tux, so that's already taken care of."

She raised an eyebrow in surprise, and then found herself blushing again as she imagined him in a tux.

"Great, then. Thank you. I'm sure I'll see you between now and then to discuss details." She glanced at her watch. "And I need to get going. Traffic's a nightmare this morning and I really don't want to be late for work."

"All right. I'll see you later. Thanks for the invite."

She smiled and said good-bye, then started to walk away.

"Merilee?"

She turned.

"Don't assume that I haven't considered you-and-me-as-a-couple kind of thing."

Without another word, he turned to join his friend, leaving Merilee too flustered to move for an entire minute.

Merilee looked up from her computer, where she was working on the ad layout for Stevens & Sons' holiday extravaganza and promotions. Seeing as how they usually did about thirty percent of their business in the month of December, it was imperative that their party was successful in show-casing all the blingiest bling that might be considered an appropriate Christmas gift for a spouse, loved one, or mistress. She tried to unthink that last one, but every once in a while, the whole Michael-Tammy thing reared its ugly head in her subconscious, with interesting results.

"Come in," she called when she heard a knock.

The door opened and she was surprised to see Gayla Adamson, their top sales associate. She was short and slim, with overprocessed blond hair and enthusiastically plucked eyebrows. She had a reputation among the other salespeople as being a bit of a vulture, but Merilee had never had enough experience with the sales force to know if that was just jealousy talking or if it had some root in the truth. Regardless, it was odd to see her in her office.

"Can I help you with something?"

Gayla didn't smile. "Daniel Blackford is here asking for you. I must admit I was a little surprised, seeing as how the Blackfords have been clients of mine for years."

Merilee slid her chair back. "Oh, please don't worry. I'll make sure you get this commission. I'm doing this as a personal favor for Heather just this one time. When it's time to complete the sale, I'll come and get you."

Gayla still looked miffed. "I just don't know why Heather didn't ask me. I always help her with her selections. She even called me yesterday to let me know he'd be coming—just like she always does. Except Daniel says he only wants to deal with you. I'm just confused, I guess."

"That's odd—I don't know why Heather would have called you. But I'm sorry—I really am. Actually, I didn't even know the Blackfords were clients here or I would have asked who their salesperson was. It's just a—I don't know—favor-for-a-friend kind of thing. Just a onetime deal. And if she suggests doing this again, I'll tell her that you are more than capable of helping her, as she well knows." Merilee smiled, trying to be ingratiating and friendly. From what she'd heard about Gayla, she figured there was a chance she'd walk out to the parking lot and find four flat tires on her car. Or a pipe bomb in her desk.

"Fine. Should I show him in? He said he'd like to speak with you in private first." She raised a skinny eyebrow, showing Merilee what she thought of the whole idea.

"Oh." Without thinking, she put her hands to her hair and her gaze to her top desk drawer, where she kept her lipstick, neither action missed by Gayla.

"He's *married*," Gayla hissed as she left the office, leaving the door slightly ajar.

Merilee took a deep breath to compose herself before Daniel appeared in the same spot Gayla had just vacated. "Dan. So nice to see you again." And it was. Not just because he was nice to look at, but also because she genuinely liked him and enjoyed his company. Still, she stepped behind her chair just in case he wanted to kiss her cheek in greeting. As Gayla had so helpfully pointed out, he was married, and Merilee was overly sensitive about stepping over that line. After what she'd been through in her own marriage, she wasn't interested in having any misunderstanding, whether it was warranted or not.

Dan closed the door behind him, sending Merilee an apologetic smile. "Sorry—I don't want Gayla overhearing. She and Heather always work together, so I'm sure her nose is all out of joint about this. I just want to let you know that I know this isn't your usual thing, and I appreciate you taking the time with me to select the right gift." He grinned, a real grin that reminded her of why he was called "Danny" by those who knew him well. "And I'm so relieved that I don't have to work with Gayla. I think all she cares about is her commission and not about finding the right piece. It gets my goat every time."

"I understand—and it will go no further than this room." She headed around the desk on the opposite side from him to get to the door. "I asked Heather about her preferences and had some time this morning to pull a few things I thought might work. I'll let you be the judge, of course."

She turned the knob, falling backward as the door refused to open, as she pulled and it slipped out of her grasp. He caught her by the shoulders. "You should try weight lifting," he said.

Despite her embarrassment, she grinned. "Yeah. I think it's the door—I can't tell you the last time I shut it. It must have warped or something."

"Allow me," Dan said as he reached for the knob at the same time she did, his hand covering hers. They both jumped back, and it was unclear to Merilee who was more surprised at the warmth generated by the brief touch of skin.

She held up her hands. "It's all yours."

He pulled on the knob several times before the door swung open with a loud *whoosh*. When they exited the office, Merilee noticed that most of the people on the showroom floor were looking in their direction.

"So," she said, walking toward one of the locked display cases, "let me show you what I've got." She bent down, and using the key she'd obtained from the store manager, she unlocked a drawer and pulled out a large velvet tray where several sparkling baubles winked up at them from the overhead lights.

"Wow," Daniel said, picking up a diamond-and-sapphire emerald-cut ring, then putting it down quickly. "Lots of big and shiny. Just like Heather likes to wear." His tone matched Merilee's own thoughts, but she kept them to herself. It wasn't her job to comment on Heather's taste, or lack thereof. She was here to do a favor for a friend.

His gaze wandered briefly over the pieces she'd selected, then strayed to an adjacent case, where a lesser-known jewelry designer's latest line was being displayed. Merilee adored this designer, loved his use of semiprecious stones set in metal shaped to mimic the natural world. He pointed to a ring with the base of a platinum oyster sheltering a saltwater pearl resting gracefully on top. "May I see that?"

"Of course," she said, quickly unlocking the case and pulling out the ring. She handed it to him. "This might be my favorite piece in the entire store. It's exquisite—understated yet undeniably elegant." She shrugged, suddenly at a loss for descriptive words. "It's simple— and yet manages to be just gorgeous." She looked up at Dan with a frown. "But I didn't think it would be to Heather's taste."

He shook his head with a grimace, examining the ring. "It's not really—although she might like it. But I love it. It actually reminds me of her—she's the pearl, so beautiful and valuable. And the shell is the life she has made for us and our family." His eyes met hers. "Can you try it on so that I can see what it looks like on a woman's hand?"

"Of course." And because she no longer wore a ring on her left hand, she slid it onto her third finger. The wide band was hard to get over her knuckle, so Dan had to help her slide it the rest of the way onto her finger. It was such an intimate gesture that she found she couldn't look into his face.

Holding up her left hand and staring at her palm, she said, "How does it look?"

"Perfect," he said. "Absolutely perfect." And when she did finally look up, she saw that he was looking at her. "I'll take it."

She had to clear her throat to speak. "Are you sure you don't want to see anything else? I have a whole tray of jewelry that I—"

"No. I don't always know what I'm looking for, but when I see it, I know that's what I want."

As she fumbled to get the ring off her finger and look at the price tag, since neither of them had any idea how much it cost, Gayla approached. "Have you made your decision?" she asked, her tone of mock interest more than mildly grating.

"Yes," Dan said, taking the ring from Merilee, then handing it to Gayla. "Can you put this on my account and wrap it up? I think Heather will be surprised."

"I'd say," Gayla said, not bothering to hide her dismay at the relatively low price point or the less-than-sparkly choice. "Are you sure this is what you want? Perhaps I can show you—"

"I'm sure," Dan said. "I've got a meeting I need to get to. I'll pick it up later."

"Oh," said Merilee. "If it helps, I can bring it home and meet you at the school or something, if that makes it easier."

He smiled warmly. "That would be nice. Thank you."

With barely concealed disappointment, Gayla excused herself and hurried to the back office to ring up the purchase and have it gift wrapped in the store's signature silver and gold paper.

"Thanks again for your help," Dan said, reaching into his pocket to retrieve his phone.

"You're more than welcome. And if you need to return it . . ."

"That's odd," he said, staring at his phone, a frown puckering his eyebrows.

"What's wrong?"

"My phone's off. I was wondering why it wasn't buzzing." He pressed the "on" button, and while he waited for it to power up, he said, "I won't be returning the ring. It's something Heather and I agreed on when we got married—we never return a gift. We decided that if you love a person enough, you'll love anything they get for you if you know it comes from the heart. That's how I know she'll love this ring— if not initially, then she'll grow to love it."

Merilee almost asked if they were speaking about the same Heather. "That's a beautiful sentiment—something I'll have to remember."

Dan was staring at the screen of his phone, a deep crease between his brows. "Looks like I accidentally picked up Heather's phone again. She just bought a new one that's exactly like mine, so now we have the same phone with the same case. Never happened before, but now it's happening a lot, it seems." He smiled up at her, but his expression was lacking in warmth. "Guess I need to run and find Heather and swap phones before my meeting. Thanks again."

Before she could step away, he'd leaned down and kissed her on the cheek right there in the middle of the showroom floor. She turned back to the case and began replacing all the jewelry she'd gathered, still feeling his lips on her cheek and wondering how many people had seen.

Eighteen

SUGAR

Sugar sat in front of the open window, her fingers stilled on the keyboard in midthought, startled the way a breeze could carry with it so many memories. It was the first whiff of cooler air, heralding the lingering death of a Georgia summer. It was only early September, but the unpredictable weather always liked to tease people into thinking it was time to air out last year's wool coats. She was sure it confused a lot of the transplants, but after more than ninety summers and falls, she knew what to expect.

Fall had always been her favorite time of year, the crunch of leaves reminding her of pulling out favorite sweaters and sitting in front of a roaring fire. Of her first kiss, right out there on the front porch, but only after Tom had made sure her daddy wasn't looking.

It was Jimmy's favorite time of year, too, when he would mark the flocks of birds flying from up north, some to stay, others just resting before taking off to parts farther south. Exotic places like South America and the Caribbean. Places Tom had promised he'd take her after the war, a plan to which she'd agreed but only if he promised he'd bring her back to their home in Sweet Apple. Back to where she knew each fall the weather would turn, the fields would lie fallow, and the crimson and russet leaves of the maples and black gum trees would fall and crunch under her feet. But the leaves of the live oaks that lined the drive would stay green. It was the one constancy she could always count on.

She began to type again, but stopped at the sound of banging on the front door. Maybe it was more like knocking, but it was so rare to have someone come to her house unannounced that it always sounded like banging to her.

She stood and went to the door, peering through the door's windows to make sure it wasn't one of those people asking her to buy something or here to save her soul. She didn't need to buy anything—unless they were Girl Scouts selling cookies—and the state of her soul was between her and Jesus and was nobody else's business.

It was Merilee, waiting patiently as Sugar made her way to the door, something cradled in her arms, her minivan parked behind her. "I'm sorry to bother you, but I need to ask you something."

Sugar raised her eyebrows—or what was left of them. They had once been golden blond, with arches Bette Davis would have envied. Now they were practically invisible, the pale white color having leached the gold away years before. "I thought you had my phone number now."

Merilee extended her arms so Sugar could see the Mason jar in one hand and Jimmy's binoculars in the other. "I found these on the porch. Colin's denied it, but I'm assuming he took them, so I'm here to return them."

Sugar opened the door wider but didn't step forward to take either item. "He's not lying. I left them on the porch for him. They're not doing anybody any good sitting in that cedar chest, so they might as well go to good use. He can keep them."

"You're giving them to him?"

Sugar crossed her arms. "I am. Tell him to take care of them."

"Well, thank you. After I apologize to him for believing him to be lying to me, I'll have him thank you in person."

"That's fine," Sugar said, waiting to close the door so she could go back to her typing, but Merilee didn't appear to be done.

"I, uh, also have a favor to ask, if that's all right."

Sugar raised her nonexistent brows again. "Well, I guess I can't stop you from asking, but that's no guarantee I'll say yes."

A spark of humor flitted across Merilee's gaze, causing Sugar to frown harder. It wouldn't do to have people not fearing her.

"Yes, well, Heather has called an emergency meeting of all the gala committee heads tonight—as in thirty minutes from now, and I'm just hearing about it because I was at work all day. None of my babysitters or people I would normally call to watch the kids are available on such short notice—although one of them told me she could be here in an hour—and Michael is out of town on business. I would rather skin myself and swim in rubbing alcohol than ask Tammy."

Sugar's mouth twitched at the image. "And you'd like me to babysit."

Merilee looked genuinely relieved. "It would just be for an hour or so—their old babysitter can make it here by then."

"I see," Sugar said. "And if I said no?"

"I could bring them with me, but Lily really needs to get to bed early and I have no idea how long I'll be. But it'll be easy—I promise. I've got Colin sitting in front of the TV watching a show about dogs, so he's good to go for at least an hour. They've got my cell number, and I told them they could call for pizza. I left them a couple of twenties. Or I could bring them here so you don't even have to leave your house . . ."

Sugar was already walking out onto the front porch. "Give me those," she said, reaching for the jar and binoculars. "I'll stay with them until your babysitter arrives, and make them a proper meal. Regardless of what the government is saying these days, pizza is *not* a vegetable."

"Get in the minivan and I'll drive you."

"No need." She held up her arm with the Fitbit. "I need my steps." She began walking toward the cottage, hearing Merilee return to her minivan and start the engine only after she'd made it to Merilee's front steps.

"Hello?" Sugar said after knocking, then opening the front door. She looked into the empty front room, where the TV screen was showing a litter of puppies nursing while a narrator in a sickly sweet voice was explaining what was going on. "It's Miss Sugar. Your mama asked that I look in on you." She waited for a response, and when none came she closed the door behind her and moved into the front room, placing the Mason jar and binoculars on the coffee table. "Your mama said I could use thumbscrews and red ants if needed, and the first young person who shows themselves will get to help me make cookies."

A high-pitched giggle came from behind the sofa as Colin peered over the back. "I win!" he shouted.

"Nuh-uh," Lily shouted from the kitchen doorway. "I was here first."

"It's a tie," Sugar said. "So you both get to help me. But first we're going to make a real dinner and you will be expected to eat your vegetables. Trust me, you will want to, because the way I prepare them is guaranteed to be unlike anything you've tried before."

She ignored their groans as they trailed her back into the kitchen. "As long as we have fresh vegetables, we're in business." She had to restrain her own groan when she saw that the produce trays in the icebox were empty except for a soggy partial head of iceberg lettuce. And then she felt almost physically ill when she opened the pantry and noticed the name-brand cans of vegetables. She wasn't sure what offended her the most—the fact that Merilee wasted her money buying the name brand, or that there wasn't a fresh produce bag to be found either in the pantry or in the icebox. It was a travesty. With a deep breath, she pulled out a can of green beans and set to work, not even bothering to waste her time hunting for any fatback for the vegetables.

After they'd eaten and the cookies were in the oven, the phone rang. It was the babysitter, explaining she'd been in a fender bender and wouldn't be able to make it. Glancing at her Bulova, Sugar figured she had enough time before *Law & Order: SVU* came on and that Merilee would, hopefully, be back by then. Because now that the necessities were done, she had no idea what else she was supposed to do with the children.

She looked down to find two pairs of blue eyes staring up at her expectantly. "Don't you have homework?" she asked.

"I finished mine and Colin doesn't have any," Lily said. Colin just nodded, like he was used to having his older sister speak for him.

Sugar thought for a moment. "Maybe I can read you a story?"

Lily shook her head. "We don't like the same kinds of books." She frowned, then shared a conspiratorial glance with her brother. "But there's one book . . ." Without waiting for comment, Lily ran down the short hallway toward the bedrooms, returning shortly with a large hardbound book that looked vaguely familiar.

"It's Mom's senior year high school yearbook from 1998."

Sugar looked at her dubiously. "I thought your mother didn't want you to look at these without her permission."

"Oh, she changed her mind," Lily said.

"Did she really?"

Lily nodded emphatically. "She said it was just a silly yearbook and there was no good reason to not let us see it."

Colin nodded, his attention distracted by the sight of the jar and binoculars. "I didn't steal those."

"I know," Sugar said gently. "They're yours now—as a gift from me. I already explained to your mother that you didn't take them."

He grinned up at her. "So they're mine? To keep?"

She nodded. "To keep. But I need you to promise me that you'll take good care of them. They used to belong to somebody very precious to me." She picked up the binoculars and placed the strap over his head so the glasses hung over his chest.

Colin nodded solemnly. "I will. Can I go look at birds now?" he said, the yearbook forgotten. "I promise to stay on the tire swing and not go anywhere else."

"Sure. And let me know what you see."

He ran toward the kitchen and the back door, not pausing long enough to put on shoes. Sugar figured that was something Merilee would need to address. Sort of like Sugar was the grandmother, whose only duty was to have fun with the children, leaving all the heavy responsibility of rearing the children to their mother. As it should be.

Lily tugged on her hand, leading her to the sofa, where they sat down together, the yearbook across their laps. Lily used a fingernail coated with chipped pink polish to open the front cover. "Look at all this writing from her friends. She must have been really popular when she was in high school."

She said it with an air of reverence, and almost with disbelief, as if she couldn't imagine her mother having so many friends. "Mom always says that being popular isn't important. It's being nice to everybody that's important." She frowned a little at the book opened on her lap. The inside of the book was indeed so full of signatures and little drawn hearts and stick drawings in all different colors of pens and markers that it was hard to find any white space. There were lots of *Go Bulldogs* and *See you in Athens* scribbled everywhere, like graffiti, in red and black, the colors of the University of Georgia.

It surprised Sugar. Most UGA grads had an overabundance of red and black among their household items—pot holders, bumper stickers, throw pillows. Maybe all that was in storage. Or maybe she hadn't gone to UGA—although Sugar remembered the Realtor, Robin, mentioning that she'd graduated with Merilee from UGA but hadn't known her well in their college years. Not that that was so surprising—UGA had around thirty thousand students, so it was more than possible to never cross paths with a fellow student, or to overlook a fellow student completely. Although, judging by the enthusiastic comments on these two pages, Merilee didn't seem to have been the kind of person one might overlook.

"They all say 'To Tallie,'" Lily pointed out. "Maybe this isn't my mom's."

"No—look, there's a few addressed to Merilee, although it appears those are from teachers or administrators. Her friends all used 'Tallie.' That must have been your mother's nickname."

"Maybe from her last name, Talbot. That was her last name before she got married to Daddy."

Sugar nodded. "I think you're right. You're very smart, Lily."

Lily blushed before turning the page and pausing. Only one person had signed this page, right in the middle, with a bold, black marker, and it appeared that this page had been reserved, a VIP seat at a crowded stadium. *I love you, Tallie. Can't wait to marry you. John.*

"Who's John?" Lily asked, her whole body recoiling. "My dad's name is Michael."

"Well, most likely John was an old high school boyfriend of your mother's. Remember, a person usually graduates from high school when they're only about seventeen or eighteen—still pretty young. It's very rare these days that a girl marries her high school sweetheart—especially if she heads off to college and a career and meets other people."

"Like my dad."

"Yes, exactly." Sugar turned the page quickly, realizing why Merilee might have originally not wanted her children to have access to her high school yearbooks.

They turned the pages slowly, commenting on the funny hairdos and clothing styles and the complete lack of selfies or any reference at all to Facebook. At least Sugar noticed it with an almost nostalgic glow.

"Look—there's Mom!" Lily pointed enthusiastically at a group photo of the varsity cheerleading squad in an impressive pyramid, Merilee on the ground in front doing a perfect split. "She was the captain—see?" Lily's chipped nail tapped on the photo's caption: *Merilee "Tallie" Talbot in her fourth year as team captain for the Eagles varsity squad.* "She didn't tell me she was captain," Lily said, her voice filled with awe. "I can't wait to tell Bailey."

Sugar raised an eyebrow but didn't say anything.

"Look how pretty she was," Lily said.

And she was, Sugar had to agree. Shiny dark hair; long, lean limbs; and skin that glowed—the kind that didn't need makeup or a dermatologist's care. "She still is," she said, because it was true. Merilee Dunlap was still a very attractive woman. But she was different, too, from this girl in the photo. Not just older, but changed in a way that was hard to quantify. Sugar thought it was in the eyes, the way the cheerleader had once looked out at the world as if she knew who she was and what her place in it was.

Sugar leaned forward, looking through the bottom of her bifocals to magnify the photo. She could now see the shadow of a furrow between Merilee's eyebrows, lending her face an almost haunted look that prevented her from appearing completely carefree. Yet her smile defied anyone to think that she was anything but.

Sugar sat back. "Do you know when your uncle died? How old your mother might have been?"

Lily shrugged. "She doesn't like to talk about it. But I think she said she was in high school."

Sugar nodded slowly as they continued to turn the pages, pausing at the page devoted to the football team. A large heart had been drawn around a single player's face, an arrow going through it, complete with feathers at the tail. Sugar leaned closer to read the name: *John D. Cottswold, Varsity Football Captain.* She quickly turned the page before Lily could focus on the picture of the square-jawed teenager or the name.

They continued to turn pages, looking at these strangers' photos, noticing how many times Merilee appeared in them in various groups, clubs, and committees. And Sugar saw how many times John D. Cottswold appeared next to her.

"Look!" Lily exclaimed before Sugar's eyes could focus on a new page. "It's senior prom. And Mom is prom queen."

It wasn't surprising, really, to see Merilee standing next to John wearing coordinating evening wear in shades of blue and black. They were both wearing cardboard crowns and grinning at the camera in a series of photos, one picture showing Merilee's lips pressed against John's cheek. *Marry me, Tallie!* was written underneath the first photo in the same bold black handwriting they'd seen before.

Sugar was bracing herself for Lily's comment when Lily slammed the book shut. "I think Mom's home."

"I thought you said your mother had given her permission."

Instead of answering, Lily slid off the sofa and ran back to the bedroom, leaving Sugar in the dreaded position of either tattling on the girl and admitting her own complicity, or pretending that she believed they hadn't done anything wrong. Lily *had* said that she'd received her mother's approval, after all. And Sugar had chosen to believe her.

"Hello, I'm home," Merilee called. "I'm so sorry the babysitter didn't show—she called me and said she'd already spoken to you and that you were okay with staying a little longer. Still—I'm so sorry."

"No harm done," Sugar said as she managed to stand. "There're cookies in the oven."

As if on cue, the oven timer began to beep and Merilee rushed to the kitchen to take them out, Sugar eventually catching up. "You didn't have to do this, Sugar, but I know the kids loved it."

"Well, someone has to teach them kitchen skills, and I happened to be here."

The sides of Merilee's mouth twitched. "It's a good thing you were." She slid off the oven mitt she'd grabbed from the counter. "It's a lovely evening outside—hardly any humidity. Why don't you go sit out on the front porch and I'll join you with some iced tea and cookies? Just give me a minute."

Sugar pretended to give it some thought. Something about seeing the girl Merilee had once been had added a whole new dimension to this woman. Made Sugar realize that she wasn't the only one with shadows in her past. "I suppose so. *Law & Order: SVU* is a repeat tonight anyway."

Sugar began making her way to the front porch as Merilee called out to her daughter. "Lily, please go get your brother and tell him it's bath time and then bedtime, but before he brushes his teeth he can have a cookie."

Merilee soon joined her with the promised iced tea and cookies on one of Sugar's serving plates. "Sorry," Merilee said, following Sugar's gaze. "I haven't had a chance to bring it back to you yet. You can take it and the cookies when you leave."

Sugar almost said something about how people nowadays had no idea about manners, but she remembered the cheerleader in the photo, the haunted look behind her eyes, and remained silent. Instead she took a sip of her tea. "Almost there but not quite. Needs more sugar." She felt the younger woman watching her but didn't turn to meet her gaze. "Your brother, David, the one who collected Lego people. How did he die?"

It was another one of the few things that made getting older worthwhile, the ability to speak without preamble. Being old was a good excuse for getting away with almost anything. And she wanted to know. Not because she was nosy—she wasn't. But because she had a deep-seated belief that the shadows she saw behind Merilee's eyes were similar to her own. She simply didn't have enough years left to wait until she knew Merilee well enough to ask.

When Merilee turned to her in the dimming light, she didn't feel guilty. Because instead of being upset or affronted, Merilee wore the expression of somebody who'd been holding her breath for a very long time and been finally told it was time to breathe.

"He drowned. My grandparents had a house on Tybee, and we went there for most of our vacations. I loved my grandparents—especially my grandfather. He's the one who bought me my first old map." She smiled at the memory, looking down at her glass as she sloshed the ice back and forth. "David was seven years younger than I was, so I was always the designated babysitter. Not that I minded—I adored him. We all did. I knew he was my mother's favorite, but I didn't mind because I understood. He was funny and smart and sweet—since the moment he was born. Everybody loved him."

Merilee looked out toward the white fence, the rails gleaming in the yellow light of the moon. Sugar didn't say anything, not wanting Merilee to stop. "We were kayaking in the ocean—but keeping really close to the shore because I'm afraid of sharks and things I can't see." Her smile faded as quickly as it had appeared. "He had on a life jacket—he'd put it on himself, saying that he knew how to do it and didn't need my help." Her voice caught. "He was seven years old, and I figured he did probably know how to do it. He was such a smart kid."

Sugar sat back in her rocker, the wood creaking against the floorboards of the porch.

"I didn't see the wave in time to turn us around to face it head-on, and it hit us broadside, knocking us out into the water. It couldn't have been more than six feet where we were, and if his life jacket hadn't slid off of him in the water, I could have pulled him up. I wasn't even worried at first because he was such a great swimmer. But the boat hit him on the head when he was tossed out, and he must have lost consciousness.

"I searched and searched for him. Even after the rescue people came, I refused to stop, though I was so tired I could barely hold my head above the water anymore. They pulled me out of the water, saying that I would drown, too, if I didn't get out. I used to think that I would have been better off if they'd let me drown. My mother blamed me, you see. And my father always takes her side, so he blamed me, too. My grandparents died shortly after that, so all I was left with was the blame and the disappointment of my parents that I was the child who'd survived. I don't have a good relationship with my parents still, because they will never forgive me."

Sugar was surprised at the anger she felt toward people she'd never met. Maybe because she couldn't help but picture her own daughter. And how she would have given anything to be able to watch her grow into adulthood. To be given the chance to cherish her.

"I suppose your mother had no business having a daughter." Sugar stopped talking, except the words pressed against her throat, demanding to be let out. If there was anything she still believed in, it was fairness. "I had a little girl. I named her Mary, after Tom's mother. She lived less than a day." She paused, waiting for the familiar sting in her chest, which never faded no matter how many years had passed. "Sometimes I think I should be glad that she didn't survive, because I might have treated her the same way your mother treated you because I didn't know any better. I think some women are just born without that mothering instinct."

Merilee reached over and squeezed Sugar's hand. "No. That's not true. I see how you are with my children, and with me, and I know that the person you show to the world isn't the real Alice Prescott. You have a huge heart, and you would have been a wonderful mother."

"A huge heart?"

Merilee nodded. "But I promise not to tell anybody."

Sugar pressed her lips together, but only so Merilee couldn't see her smile.

The sounds of a late-summer evening lent the night a melody, the song of the tree frogs and crickets filling the trees in the woods behind them, cocooning the two women in the illusion of friendship and a shared past.

"What about Jimmy, Sugar? What happened to Jimmy?"

Sugar stared out toward the woods, imagining the dark shadows that lingered among the tall Georgia pines, smelling again an autumn evening and the coppery tang of blood.

"In the end, I guess you could say it was his heart that finally gave out. At least that's what the doctor said. But that's not the real story. That's not the real story at all."

the arrowheads belonged to him. Not that I wanted to stand there and argue. Stupid people rarely want to hear the truth.

"Good-bye, Curtis," I said again, this time closing the front door in his face.

His visit had unsettled me, but I didn't have time to dwell on it. I made supper and fed Mama, then returned to the kitchen table, where I ate with Jimmy. His field glasses hung around his neck as always, and he ate in a real hurry, barely taking time to chew his food.

"Is there a fire somewhere that I don't know about?" I asked.

He replied around a mouthful of mashed potatoes. "Nope. Just spotted a whippoorwill nest in the woods I want to study tonight. I found the perfect tree and Lamar's gonna help me get into position. I expect to spend the night out there, so I'll bring a pillow." He swallowed, then coughed. He'd never completely gotten over the chest cold he'd had when we'd met Tom that past spring. Dr. Mackenzie said it had weakened his heart and lungs in a bad way and that he needed to take it easy. Not like anything like that would ever slow Jimmy down. For a boy in a wheelchair, he was probably more active than the average person. His arms were so strong I'd once watched him climb a tree with his legs dangling beneath him.

"I wish you wouldn't do stuff like that, Jimmy. You could really get hurt. And it's going to get cold tonight—and you know what that does to your chest."

"Lamar'll be with me and I'll wear a sweater and bring a thick blanket, all right? So you can quit your worrying."

I slid my napkin across the table toward him. "Clean your glasses. I swear I don't know how you see anything."

He smiled as he took the napkin, his face so sweet and precious to me. I figured that even if I never had any children, just having Jimmy in my life would always be enough.

Despite his assurances, I did worry. I lay in bed, sure I wouldn't be able to sleep, but the exhaustion of the day must have overtaken me, because when the scream awoke me it was full dark.

I sat up, shivering in the cold, wondering if I had imagined it. But then I heard it again, muffled this time, and then something crashed and shattered as it hit the floor.

"Mama?" I shouted as I slid from the bed and ran downstairs to her bedroom. Her door was shut but not latched, and when I pushed it open I could see my mother's white nightgown on the floor. It took my eyes a moment to register in the dark and see the shadows on top of the bed.

"Bitch," a voice said, and I recognized it. *Curtis*. "You ain't supposed to be able to talk." And then the unmistakable sound of a slap against skin, and my mother whimpering.

My fingers fumbled on the wall for the light switch, but he was faster, the sound of broken glass crunching under his feet before he grabbed my wrist, squeezing until my fingertips tingled. "Let go of me," I shouted, desperate to pull away, and even more desperate to get him away from my mama.

His other hand threaded through my hair, and he pressed wet lips against mine. "I'd prefer something younger and sweeter, anyway."

Without even having to think about it, I raised my knee and slammed it into his crotch. He let go immediately, but I didn't run. I needed to make sure that he chased me, that he left Mama alone.

I listened to his breathing, reminding me of a bear my daddy had once caught in a trap. And that scared me, finally. Because I remembered how it had taken three shots to finally kill that bear.

"Bitch!" he screamed at me, and I was glad, because that meant he'd recovered his breath. I turned and ran toward the back door in the kitchen, glancing over my shoulder to make sure he was chasing me. With my bare feet slipping on cold, damp grass, I ran as fast as I could toward the dark woods.

The full moon guided me until I was deep inside, the thick canopy of trees hiding the light, surprising me with random bursts of yellow on the forest floor as my feet pounded, the skin tearing on rocks and sticks and me not feeling any of it. I could hear Curtis, his feet crunching dead leaves, his breath panting behind me. I didn't turn around, stretching my arms out to protect me. I was half-aware of my nightgown glowing like a beacon, making it easy for him to follow me. But there was nothing I could do about it. I had lost all sense of where I was, simply searching for a place to hide where he couldn't see my nightgown. My hand struck the bark of a tree, the snap of bone so loud I cried out. I fought to catch my breath, seeing red spots against the inside of my eyelids, before turning in what I hoped was a new direction.

And ran right into Curtis Brown.

He was like that wounded bear in his anger, ripping at my nightgown and howling with rage and pain and victory. He squeezed my broken hand and I dropped to my knees, and that made it easy for the rest of what happened. I don't remember much. Just his hands on my breasts and then my thighs, the smell of the pine straw beneath my head, the pain that made me feel like I was being ripped in two. He wanted me to cry: I could feel it each time he struck me with his fist and each time he invaded me. So I bit my lip until I tasted blood, telling myself I would rather die than give him the satisfaction.

And somewhere through the river of pain, something big and heavy rustled through the woods toward us, the pounding on the ground vibrating in my ear. I kept my eyes shut tight and clung to that pulsing sound, focusing on it so that I could ignore everything else, and prayed it was a bear seeking vengeance.

A scream like I'd never heard erupted from the shadows, and I forced open my eyes as something huge charged toward us, making a sound that was part wounded animal and part devil. I'd never believed in the devil until that moment, and I didn't care whose soul he was there to steal as long as it meant all this would be over.

"Get off of her!"

It was Jimmy, riding on the back of Lamar, who'd grown as big as Rufus and could carry Jimmy like he weighed no more than a leaf. Jimmy threw something at Curtis and it struck the side of his head with a sickening *thunk*, knocking him off me. My broken hand forgotten, I crawled backward, pulling what was left of my nightgown over my legs and across my chest.

Curtis lay still, his eyes closed, but his breath wheezed in and out so I knew he wasn't dead. Lamar had stopped running, and with another scream, Jimmy launched himself on top of Curtis and picked up a large rock—the one that he'd thrown the first time—and held it over Curtis's head. Lamar grabbed Jimmy's hand and pulled him back.

"Don't do it, Jimmy. Don't do it. That be murder on your head, and he ain't worth it."

Jimmy waited a long moment before letting the rock fall. He rolled off Curtis, his breath thick with liquid. He began to cough, the kind that wore him out and bent him over. When he'd finished, he began crawling toward me, his binoculars dragging through the dead leaves and pine straw. "We came as fast as we could, but it was so dark . . ." He started to cough again.

"I know. It's all right. He didn't hurt me. Just my hand—I think it's broke." I grimaced with the pain, hoping neither one of them noticed. "I need to get back for Mama—I need to make sure she's all right."

Lamar crouched next to me, and I could smell his sweat mixed with the stink of my own fear. "Can you walk? 'Cause if you can, I'll carry Jimmy back to the house."

We all looked at Curtis, who was moaning quietly. "Leave him," I said.

There was something in my voice, something stronger and older that hadn't been there before. They must have noticed it, too, because they didn't argue. We left him there, and when Lamar went back the next day to check, he was gone.

We told my daddy that I'd gotten hurt falling from a tree where I'd been watching birds with Jimmy. He was too preoccupied with the farm and Mama's constant crying to pay any heed to how that didn't make sense. But we'd figured that Daddy would have killed Curtis if he'd known the truth, and like Lamar had said, it would have been murder on Daddy's head. And we all knew that Curtis Brown wasn't worth it.

I put Jimmy to bed and laid camphor compresses on his chest, but nothing worked. Even Dr. Mackenzie said there was nothing to do for him, that his heart was too tired to keep going. I sat by his bed and read to him from all his bird books, and I knew that made him happy because he smiled a lot. But it didn't make him better. I knew it was near the end when he asked me to take those binoculars off him and put them around my own neck.

"Keep them safe," he said. He began to cough, and I waited until he could speak again. "You don't really need them, Sugar. You see pretty good already. Except sometimes, when it's real dark"—he stopped to clear his throat, his voice thick—"remember that everything's the same. You just can't see it. You can figure out which way to go, or wait until somebody turns the light back on."

He started coughing again, and there was so much blood on his pajama shirt that I sent Lamar for Dr. Mackenzie. But by the time they got back, Jimmy was gone. I was still holding his hand, and all I could do was look at him and his dirty glasses and want to yell at him for never cleaning them.

Tom helped me with my grieving, but he couldn't put back what had been stolen from me that night. But he tried, and he was so gentle and caring, and I knew that if I still had a heart, it would love him. So when Tom asked me again to marry him, I said yes.

Twenty

Observations of Suburban Life from Sweet Apple, Georgia
Written by: Your Neighbor

Installment #7: Preparing for the End of the World: Snow

Did you all know that this month is National Preparedness Month? There seems to be a month for everything now: National Physical Fitness and Sports Month, Colorectal Cancer Awareness Month, Teen Dating Violence Awareness Month, National Childhood Obesity Awareness Month, National Safety Month. I could go on and on until my calendar was so filled with reminders that there would be no room to put doctors' appointments or friends' birthdays—the two things that are pretty much the cure-all for most of what ails us.

Shouldn't we always be aware of society's issues so that we can look for solutions? Or maybe we do need to be reminded because most of us are getting our news from Facebook these days instead of a legitimate newspaper written by real journalists.

I'm not saying the attempt to bring people's attention to these worthwhile issues isn't important. I'm just thinking that perhaps the overabundance of them might make people pay less attention—and our attention spans are pretty short already. Or that perhaps the sheer quantity of issues might lessen their importance. Like that high school in a neighboring county that I shall not name that appointed twelve valedictorians because they didn't want to hurt anyone's feelings by selecting just one. What's one standout when there are eleven "good enoughs"?

Which brings me to my next (loosely related) topic. A group of women—presumably mothers since it was right after school drop-off—sitting next to me in the local coffee shop last week were talking about millennials and how the world will certainly end when they're old enough to take over and run things. One woman joked that the easiest way to confuse a millennial was to show them a first-place trophy.

I wanted to turn around and ask them if they'd ever rushed back to their child's school to bring PE shoes or a forgotten homework assignment. Or if they'd ever stepped in to finish a science project because their child had left it until the last minute and was worried about getting a lower grade because it was late. Because a sense of entitlement and a lack of responsibility dont't just happen by accident. They are taught. Just something to think about.

Back to National Preparedness Month. Did you know that FEMA has an app for this? There really is an app for everything. They pretty much have it covered, so I don't need to elaborate. But I do have a request to my fellow Sweet Appletonians: Be prepared for snow. No, we probably won't have another storm like we had a couple of winters ago during Snowmageddon, when people were stranded on I-285 overnight and we became the laughingstock of the country.

Do yourselves a favor and head to Costco now and buy lots of kitty litter and extra blankets to throw in your car. Maybe even a snow shovel or two if you can find them. It makes no sense for the city of Atlanta and its environs to buy more snow-removal equipment for an event that rarely happens more than once a decade, so don't look to the government to help you out here. Go ahead and have a good supply of bread in your freezer and bottled water in your garage so you can beat the rush to Kroger when the first flurry signals the end is near.

My hat is off to our northern transplants, who actually know how to drive in snow. It's the locals who seem to muck it up by doing things like stopping on the upside of a hill or braking too hard. I would suggest heading to Colorado in January and taking a driving class, or make a promise not to get behind the wheel of your SUV if there is so much as a snowflake in the sky. Hopefully the mayors of Atlanta and Sweet Apple have learned their lesson from the last snowstorm and know not to close all businesses and schools at the same time, thus orchestrating the biggest hot mess any of us have ever seen on the roadways. So do your duty and be prepared. And for heaven's sake, if you see what we Southerners refer to as "the devil's dandruff" falling from the sky, stay home.

October is also Breast Cancer Awareness Month (don't forget to schedule your mammogram and do your self-exam), in addition to being the month of the fall gala at several of our local schools. Time for moms to remember their prom days and wear pretty dresses and high heels, and for their husbands to be forced into tuxedos.

Overheard in the same coffee shop were several planning meetings for various school galas. One event is being held in the school gym, one in a tent on the school's football field, and one on the lawn of a grand Lake Lanier estate, fully catered (no home-brought chafing dishes for this school fund-raiser!) and under a rental tent that was actually used at a wedding for one of the "stars" (quotation marks intentional) of *Real Housewives of Atlanta*. I choked on my coffee when I heard the rental fee.

I couldn't help but wonder if it might be more efficient for the attendees to simply donate the money to the school instead of spending the money up front in the hope that people would donate it back. Am I missing something? Of course, that's no fun, and I do appreciate dressing up and having a good time as much as the rest of you. But I also don't mind making a batch of shrimp and grits to bring to an event to keep down costs.

All this planning, and meetings, and discussions—it all brings me to today's Southern saying: "It's fixin' to come up a bad cloud." Sometimes it's easy to see when a storm is brewing. The clouds lie low and angry, the heavens rumble, and flashes of lightning streak across the sky. You don't need to be a weatherman—or weatherperson—to know a storm is brewing.

It's the subtle signs that most of us miss. A drop in air pressure. A breeze that springs out of nowhere. A friend who starts acting differently. Unreturned phone calls. An invitation that never arrives. There are all kinds of storms in life you need to watch out for. The next time you suspect something is unsettled in the atmosphere, either high above or right around you, just say, "It's fixin' to come up a bad cloud." And then take cover.

MERILEE

"Go, Cavaliers!"

Bailey Blackford did an effortless split in front of the line of cheerleaders, holding her pom-poms up in a V. Merilee adjusted herself again on the hard metal bleachers at the football field, watching the end of the girls' practice with other mothers. Several clutched pumpkin spice lattes, which had recently appeared on the menu at Starbucks, while others had giant-sized tumblers of iced water. Of course, it could have been vodka and Merilee wouldn't have judged. She could use a stiff drink herself.

She restrained herself from checking her watch. Lily's tennis team practice was directly after this, and Merilee had to somehow manage to drive Lily across town in rush-hour traffic, pick up dinner at whatever drive-through they passed, and then be back at the rec center to pick up Colin from flag football practice. All in half an hour.

She slid an envious glance over at Claire, Heather's assistant, sitting nearby and looking calm and relaxed because all she had to do was take Bailey to tennis. The thought had occurred to Merilee to ask Heather if it might be possible for Lily to ride with them, but then she'd have to worry about Lily not eating (she knew Bailey would have a nutritious meal packed by Patricia waiting for her in a cooler), thereby letting Heather know that she actually *didn't* have it all together despite what Heather kept telling her. If she did, she would have a nicely prepared dinner for her daughter, probably tied with neat blue and orange ribbons to show her team support. And a note of encouragement tucked inside. Because that's what Heather would have done. Or had one of her minions do for her.

But Heather hadn't had a horrendous day at the office and been stuck in a traffic jam that ate up forty-five valuable minutes on her way to watch Lily's practice. Lily had sent her a disappointed glance as Merilee attempted to find a spot on the bleachers that wasn't already taken by the other mothers watching their daughters. She'd found a place separated from the other mothers by a turn of the bleachers and sat down next to Lindi Matthews. Lindi wore a suit and heels, leading Merilee to believe that she'd also come straight from work and arrived long after the other mothers had already hunkered down in the prized front-and-center seats.

"Go, Jenna!" shouted Lindi as her daughter did back handsprings down the field.

"Wow," Merilee said. "You didn't tell me she was such a gymnast."

Lindi smiled proudly. "She's been working on those handsprings all summer. She didn't tell me, but I think she really wanted to be on the squad and this was her way in." She leaned over conspiratorially and whispered, "She's not the most coordinated in the clapping routines and such, but she can do flips and handsprings with the best of them." Sitting up, she added, "And because she's so small, she's perfect for the tops of the pyramids."

"Good for her," Merilee said, meaning it. She remembered how Bailey and the other girls had ignored Jenna at the lake house party before school had started.

"Heather asked me where she goes for gymnastics, and I'm pretty sure she thought I was lying when I told her the Y. They have great classes there for kids—and they're cheap. I have a feeling Heather was prepared to hire a personal coach for Bailey."

Merilee said, "She hired a tennis coach for Bailey and asked if Lily would also like to be coached. When I told her I couldn't afford it, she said she was paying the coach for the hour anyway, and it would help Bailey to have a strong partner during the lesson. So I agreed."

Lindi nodded. "She can be generous. And she's always so put together. If she weren't always so nice, it would be easy to hate her."

"Well, if it's any consolation, it must be hard to stay gorgeous and perfect at all times. But she probably does wake up like that." Merilee grimaced. "Actually, I know she does. She's forced me to be on Facebook and she's my only friend on there, so I get to see all her selfies—of which there are a lot. There are several of her waking up in her various houses, and she looks better in all of them than I probably will the night of the gala after having actually spent lots of time and effort on my face and hair."

Lindi held up her hand for a high five. "Amen, sister. And here I was thinking it was just me. And you didn't tell me you were on Facebook. I'll look for you."

"Don't expect to see much. I honestly don't see the point of Facebook."

"Well, one good thing is that friends from way back can find you and reconnect. At least that's been the case with me."

Merilee pretended to study the field.

"Don't you think?" Lindi persisted. "I mean, my best friend from third grade found me and we now do a girls' retreat at her beach house every spring. We actually have even more in common now than we did back then."

"That's nice." Merilee forced a noncommittal shrug. "Although I can't really think of anybody I'd like to be in touch with that I'm not already. Sometimes you just need to move on and meet new people. Besides, I don't use my maiden name on Facebook, so they wouldn't be able to track me down anyway."

Merilee felt Lindi looking at her but didn't turn her head. Changing

the subject, she said, "How's it going on the food and alcohol procure-
ment for the gala? I'm not even going to pretend not to be curious how
you snagged that gig. I have the enviable job of begging people to
donate stuff for the auction. I even bullied my boss into donating a
really nice diamond tennis bracelet."

"Good for you. I'll ask around to see if anybody I know might have
a Rembrandt or something hanging on the wall they might want to
donate for a good cause." Lindi grinned. "As for how I landed my gig,
one of the owners of a local distillery—Old Fourth Distillery—is a
family friend and I happened to mention that in passing to Heather
when I first met her. Remember that—the woman's mind is a steel
trap. She never forgets a thing. That's why she thought I might be able
to wrangle a good discount for their Southern Dry Gin. She especially
liked it because it goes with the *Gone with the Wind* theme she's
planning—the juniper berries in the gin are cultivated at Oakland
Cemetery in Atlanta."

"What's that got to do with the gala's theme?"

"Oakland is where Margaret Mitchell is buried. You really need to
get out more, Merilee."

Jackie Tyson, the cheerleading coach and biking enthusiast Merilee
remembered meeting at Heather's lake house, cupped her hands around
her mouth and shouted, "Okay, team—take a quick water and bathroom break and come right back so we can go over the halftime routine
one last time before I let you go."

She spotted Lindi and Merilee and waved before approaching and
sitting down on the seat in front of them. "Hello, ladies. Your girls are
doing great—they're both real assets to the team."

Merilee smiled, wondering if she said that to all the moms.

"That Jenna," Jackie continued. "She's a little powerhouse. She's
quiet, but she pays attention. Even the other girls know that when Jenna
speaks, they should listen. It's like she's already weighed all the pros
and cons in her head, studied the facts, and has prepared her case before
she opens her mouth."

Lindi nodded. "She's been like that since birth, so I can't take any
credit."

"And your Lily," Jackie said. "She's the peacemaker. I know she's the oldest child, but she really acts more like a middle child, always wanting everyone to be happy. I actually wanted Lily and Jenna to be cocaptains, but they both told me they'd rather have Bailey as captain. Probably because Bailey's been asking for it since the first day of practice and they didn't want to deal with any flak if she didn't make it. I think that says a lot about your girls and the way you've raised them. Good job."

"Thanks," Merilee said. "Although I think a lot of that is by accident."

"Ditto," agreed Lindi.

"True, environment is important," continued Jackie. "But a mother's influence is huge. For instance, I know Heather tries so hard to get Bailey interested in the shyer and quieter girls—and to invite them to sit with Bailey and her friends in the lunchroom. And I commend her for trying. But on that class trip to spend the night at the aquarium last week, I actually heard Heather tell Bailey to be nice to the ugly girls. I appreciate the sentiment, but . . ." She shrugged. "I'm sorry. We're all Heather's friends and I shouldn't have said that. It's just after a day of dealing with schoolgirls and all their drama, I needed to let off some steam."

Lindi leaned forward and patted her shoulder. "No apologies needed. I only spend a fraction of the amount of time you do with my girl, and you have all my sympathies."

Jackie turned to Merilee. "How's the carpooling situation going?"

Merilee gritted her teeth. "It's been . . . interesting. I can only carpool in the mornings because afternoon sports have sort of blown carpooling out of the water. And when it works, it's fabulous. But when it doesn't—like when Sharlene takes her kids to the dentist first thing and forgets to tell me so that I'm sitting in her driveway for fifteen minutes wondering what's going on . . . My kids think she's funny— probably because she brushes her teeth in the car and uses a cup to spit in—but they're not crazy about rainy mornings when she's driving, because she makes them walk all the way to the end of the driveway instead of picking them up at my front door."

"Seriously?" Lindi asked. "Why?"

"Because I think she might be afraid of Sugar. She said Sugar just sits on her porch and gives her the stink eye every time she drives past."

"That's ridiculous," Jackie said. "For your kids, anyway. But I know what she means about Sugar. She once tried to run me off the road when I was on my bike. She's got that enormous car and she pretended not to see me on Birmingham Highway. I had to run off the shoulder of the road and ditch my bike. I swear she meant to run me over. Didn't even look back to make sure I was okay."

Lindi and Merilee shared a glance, knowing without a doubt that Sugar had been fully aware of what had happened.

Merilee's phone rang. She'd left it faceup on the bench next to her, so all three of them looked at it when the generic tone sounded. Daniel Blackford's name popped up on the screen, confusing her for a moment because she couldn't remember programming his name and number into her phone. Nor could she imagine what he was calling her for, but then she remembered Heather's ring and wondered if he'd changed his mind.

"Excuse me a second," she said, ignoring Jackie's raised eyebrows. Lindi, thankfully, had been diverted by the ringing of her own phone. When Merilee was out of hearing distance, she answered it and said, "Hello?"

"Hi, Merilee. It's Heather. I'm so sorry to have confused you— Daniel and I accidentally switched phones again. I really need to get one of us a different case, don't I? Although mine's brand-new and Daniel loves his, so I guess we'll have to draw straws and the loser gets a new case." She laughed, something oddly familiar to Merilee. She'd had the thought before, but this was the first time she really paid attention to it. "But I wanted to call you to see if Lily wanted a ride to tennis practice. It's silly for you and Claire both to be driving, especially when I know you have your son to collect, too."

"That's so kind of you, Heather, but I'm already here—"

"And don't worry about feeding Lily. I took the liberty of packing a nice dinner for her, too—grilled chicken with roasted tomatoes and whole wheat pasta. Lots of protein and good carbs for practice! I hope you don't mind."

"Mind? Not only are you offering to save me from the torture of driving through rush-hour traffic, but you're also planning on feeding my child a much more nutritious dinner than I could have put together. You're really too kind, and I have no way to repay you."

Heather laughed her little tinkling laugh again. "Merilee, we're friends. And there's no keeping score in friendship. I know how hard you work, and how unsettled you must be with the divorce and trying to figure everything out. I'm excited that I have the means to help you; that's the biggest thanks I could ever get—knowing I've helped a friend. So don't say anything more about it—just say yes. I've already texted Claire, so she knows, and she'll bring Lily home after tennis. Sound good?"

"Sounds wonderful."

"Great. So I'll see you at the next committee meeting—tomorrow at Cups, right after drop-off."

"I'll be there. Thanks again."

She was about to hang up when Heather spoke. "Oh, one more thing. Your boss called me to let me know about the diamond tennis bracelet he's donating for the auction. Good job, Merilee! And I was thinking—to thank you for all your hard work and to give you the break I know you need, I thought I'd let you use our house on Tybee for the Columbus Day weekend. You can have four days of R & R all to yourself. How does that sound?"

Merilee could hardly breathe for a moment.

Heather continued. "If you don't feel like you can accept, I could say that I'm going down for a needed break, and I don't want to be lonely so you should come with me. Would that make it easier for you to say yes?"

"I . . . wow. Can you let me think about it? I need to check with Michael and the kids first, and I'll let you know. Does that sound all right?"

"Of course. See you tomorrow."

When Merilee returned to her seat, practice had just ended, and Jackie and Lindi were gone, leaving her without the chance to explain to Jackie that it hadn't been Daniel Blackford calling her. As she stood waiting for Lily to gather her things, her mind was drawn back to her conversation with Heather, and a niggling thought about something Heather had said.

She frowned, trying to think of what it was. It wasn't until much later when she was lying in bed tossing and turning and trying to find sleep in a bed made for two people that she remembered what it was. It had been Heather's laugh. And how it had reminded her of something from a long time ago. Something that she thought she'd forgotten. And wished that she had.

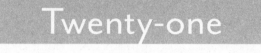

Twenty-one

SUGAR

Sugar stood on Merilee's front porch with her arms akimbo, frowning at Wade. He was pointing at two ancient metal hooks on the porch's ceiling, and he was trying to tell her that a swing had once hung there, and how the porch really needed one and he would be happy to make one.

She stared up at the hooks, vaguely remembering a swing but not remembering when it had gone away. Ever since she'd told Merilee about the night of the full moon and Jimmy's death, her memories had become fuzzier, a kindly survival mechanism, she supposed.

She only wished it had kicked in before she'd opened her mouth. It had felt good to finally tell someone. Only Willa Faye knew the whole story, but she'd known Curtis and knew where the blame lay. But in telling Merilee, it had been like a forgiveness of sorts. Because Merilee had listened and not blamed or accused or sympathized. Instead she'd squeezed Sugar's hand and told her she was the bravest and strongest woman she'd ever known.

Sugar had always wanted to be brave and strong but had convinced herself that she was a survivor not because she was either, but because she didn't have a choice. To have Merilee say it made Sugar believe maybe it was true. And it made her feel beholden to another human being, something she was pretty sure she'd never been in her entire life and didn't particularly like.

Wade was still speaking. "The direction the house faces would make this a perfect spot to sit in the afternoons and catch a cooling breeze. I'm just sorry I never noticed those hooks before."

She blinked a few times, seeing Tom sitting in the swing in his uniform, his duffel bag by the steps, his hand reaching for her. She forced her gaze to Wade's face. "I don't care what you do. If it makes you happy, then go whole hog. Just don't expect me to sit in it. I get vertigo. A rocking chair is about all I can handle at my age."

Wade tried to hide a smile. "I understand. But I thought Merilee and the kids might enjoy it."

Merilee, who kept avoiding looking at Wade and whose face flushed every time her eyes accidentally settled on him, nodded in agreement. "It would be nice. It would give me the excuse to get the kids away from the TV, and since the Wi-Fi doesn't reach out here, it would be a win-win."

"Can I go now?" Sugar asked, not sure why she was feeling so cranky. "I told Willa Faye that as soon as I got my car back, I'd give her a prison break and take her out to lunch."

Wade's eyebrows lifted. "Now, now, Sugar. You know Grandma is in a gorgeous place where they take really good care of her, and the food is so good I go there every chance I get, and if they took people my age I'd be moving in any day now. Think how much fun you two would have if you lived in the same place. Just something to think about for the future—for when you're old."

"If this is another way for you to get me to sell you this land, you've got another thought coming. I'm not selling—ever. You know that."

"I do know that, as I discovered the first and last time I ever asked you, and I promise you I rarely make the same mistake twice. Although I do hope one day you'll tell me why you're so desperate to hang on to all this land. I'd say it was for sentimental reasons, but you and I both know that despite all your many virtues, sentimentality isn't one of them."

He leaned down and gave her a quick peck on the cheek before she could avoid it. And she wanted to tell him then. Tell him the full story. She let her gaze travel over to Merilee, remembered how free she'd felt to tell part of the story. *You're the bravest and strongest woman I've ever known.* She had a brief memory of looking at Merilee's yearbooks, and the picture of the young man, John, who'd wanted to marry her. There was definitely a story there. A story Sugar was sure she didn't want to know. Maybe the only reason Merilee thought Sugar was so brave and strong was because she recognized a little bit of herself.

"Good-bye. I need to get Willa Faye." She grasped the railing and stepped down from the porch onto the first step.

"Hang on," Wade called after her. "The other reason besides the porch swing I asked to see you and Merilee this morning was about that trunk in the cellar. Did you ever find the key?"

Something fluttered in her chest. "Sorry, I forgot."

She began walking again, hoping to make it clear that she wasn't interested in pursuing the conversation.

"Well, I brought something to jimmy the lock, if that's all right. Merilee and I were worried that since it's an army footlocker there might be guns or ammunition or something that might be dangerous if kids got into it. Not just Merilee's kids, but any future tenants. So if you have no objections . . ."

Turning to face him, she cupped her hand over her eyes to shade them from the sun. "Remember what curiosity did to the cat."

He laughed, that little-boy laugh that had always made her smile. "Unless you think it's really an Egyptian sarcophagus, I think we're safe. So is it all right if we go ahead and open it?"

She knew what happened when a person said no enough times to Wade. He eventually turned it into a yes. She wasn't even sure why she didn't want them to open it. She wasn't the one who'd put the trunk in there or locked it, so it had nothing to do with her. But it did. In the same way a single drop of water was in the end responsible for the flood. *You are the bravest and strongest woman I've ever known.*

"You might as well," she said quickly, before she could change her mind. "But I'm coming with you. Just in case there's anything valuable inside."

Wade frowned. "Don't you trust me?"

"Almost as far as I can throw you."

He winked at her, then offered her his elbow. "I hope it's not a body. I don't think I could carry two unconscious females back to the house by myself."

Sugar stared straight ahead as Merilee followed behind them. "Really, Wade?" Merilee said. "I don't think so."

Wade hugged Sugar's hand against his side. "I'm just speculating. Nobody could live as long as Sugar without a skeleton or two in the closet."

Sugar pressed her lips together and allowed Wade to lead her around the corner of the house to the cellar. He let go of her arm and leaned over the padlock. "You pick a good code?" he asked Merilee.

"Um . . ."

Without asking her to elaborate, Wade starting dialing numbers. "One-one-one-one. I sure hope that doesn't unlock this—" The lock snapped open.

"You said you wanted it to be something easy that both the kids and I could remember," Merilee protested. "It's the same password I use on my phone so we don't have to think during an emergency."

"This isn't so critical," Wade said as he slid the lock from the metal loops of the door. "But your phone?" He shook his head. "Pardon me for saying this, but that's just not very smart. Did you know there are people trained to hijack phones and make your life a living hell? Of course, a toddler could hijack your phone, because there's no challenge to getting past your password."

"I know, I know. Give me another month or two, when I should be able to free up a few more brain cells to devote to things like changing passwords and balancing my checkbook."

"You don't balance your checkbook?"

Merilee gave him a pointed stare, and Sugar wanted to say something about the importance of always knowing what the bank was doing with your money, but she couldn't. The sight of the opened cellar doors seemed to be restricting her ability not only to speak but also to breathe.

"Do you want to stay here?" Wade asked her. "The steps are kind of steep and narrow."

She shook her head, avoiding his gaze. He took her arm again and led her into the cellar, one step at a time. Merilee paused for a long moment, then ran down the steps as if someone might be chasing her.

He turned on several camping lamps, giving a bright glow to the small, cramped space. "It's over here," he said, leading them to a spot against the wall. He moved aside several blankets that had been piled on the floor in front of the trunk. Picking up a lamp, he held it closer. "Looks like a standard-issue army footlocker—but any identifying marks have been removed."

She'd already seen enough. Backing up, she struck the side of a chair with her leg, and she gratefully sat.

"Who else had access to the cellar?" Wade asked as he removed a long, pointed tool from his tool belt and crouched in front of the trunk. "If it's full of cocaine or something, I'll need to explain it to the authorities."

Sugar pressed her lips together again to show her disapproval. "Until my tenants, just my daddy. After Tom died, I moved back to the main house to take care of my mother, and he pretty much took care of the place after that. I didn't cross the threshold until I hired you to clean it up before my first tenant moved in about ten years ago."

Merilee stood within the circle of light from the lamp, glancing behind her every once in a while, watching as Wade moved the tool back and forth several times before a loud click sounded in the damp cellar.

The fluttering began in her chest again, and she had to close her eyes and take a deep breath before opening them. Placing the lock on the ground, Wade grabbed hold of the sides of the trunk lid and lifted it. "Oh."

Both Sugar and Merilee leaned forward to see what Wade was looking at. The trunk was completely empty except for wadded clothing shoved in a corner and a pair of russet brown lace-up boots sitting in the facing corner, as if they'd just been placed there, awaiting their owner.

"Here," Wade said as he handed Merilee the lamp. "Hold this up so I can see better." He reached inside and lifted up what appeared to be a uniform of khaki shirt and trousers.

The first thing she noticed was that there weren't shoulder loops on the shirt, meaning it had belonged to an enlisted man and not an officer. And then Wade turned the shirt around to the front, and they all stared at it without saying a word.

A dark hole stared back at them like a sightless eye, a crusty russet stain covering most of the front of the shirt, a thick river of it coating one side as flakes drifted toward the ground in the beam of the light.

"Looks like a bullet hole and blood to me," Wade said.

Merilee held the lamp higher. "Is there any insignia or identifying marks on the shirt or inside the trunk?"

"Not that I can see." He stood, sending Sugar a worried glance. "I'm going to need to take the trunk out of here to get a better look. Merilee, could you please take Sugar back to the house and get her some water?"

"Of course."

Sugar allowed Merilee to help her to a stand without protest. She led her carefully up the stairs and into the front room, where she insisted that Sugar sit down, then put her feet up.

Sugar felt queasy and light-headed, but not enough to not be embarrassed by the hole in the toe of her stockings. She'd put nail polish on the hole to stop it from running, but nobody was supposed to see it.

Merilee went to the kitchen and brought back a glass of tepid water and handed it to her, keeping her hands near the glass while Sugar drank.

"You don't need to hover," Sugar snapped.

"Glad to see you're feeling better," Merilee said with an uncertain smile as she sat back on her heels. "Just didn't want you choking to death on my sofa. Hard to explain to the children."

Their eyes met in mutual understanding, both clinging to a normalcy that might neutralize what they'd just seen and what it might mean.

Sugar took another sip of water, then handed the glass back to Merilee.

"Still no idea who that trunk belongs to?" Merilee asked gently.

Sugar met Merilee's eyes. "I know it's not Tom's. He wasn't army. Harry and Will didn't return to Sweet Apple until 1950, when our daddy died and they took over the farms. Kept their houses in Atlanta, so they never saw the need to store anything here."

"And Bobby?"

Something fluttered in her chest again. "He died in France. The only thing of his I remember Mama keeping was his dog tags. We buried her with them."

Sugar turned her face toward the back of the couch, anticipating Merilee's next question.

"What about Curtis?" Merilee waited, as if thinking Sugar might say something so she wouldn't have to. Merilee continued. "That night, you said you left him there in the woods and when Lamar went back to check on him, he was gone."

"And that was the truth. As much as I wish he had died that night, he survived to be shipped off to fight in the Pacific. Lamar, too." She closed her eyes again, seeing Lamar's face that night in the woods, remembering all his kindnesses and his friendship with Jimmy, and found herself very close to tears she'd promised herself long ago she would not shed. "I don't know what happened to him, although I suppose he'd be dead now even if he wasn't killed in the war. I hope not, though. He deserved a long and good life."

Merilee stood and looked down at Sugar with concern. "Is there anything else I can get for you? Maybe call a doctor? You're looking pale."

Sugar considered for a moment. "You can bring me some of that iced tea. Just don't forget to add some sugar. Yours is never sweet enough."

She could see relief in Merilee's face. "I'll be right back."

She was halfway to the kitchen when Sugar called her back. "Do you think we should call the police?"

Merilee stopped and turned around. "I hadn't thought of that, but probably. It's an old shirt and an old stain, but that's still a bullet hole. It could be a hunting accident for all we know, or even a combat injury, given that it's a uniform—it's impossible to tell. I imagine the Sweet Apple PD has never seen an old case like this, but they'll know what to do. I wouldn't worry, though." She smiled. "I'll be right back with your tea—extra sugar."

Sugar nodded and closed her eyes, the fluttering in her chest softer now, like little secrets whispered in the dark, searching for an escape.

Twenty-two

MERILEE

Wade met Merilee at Sugar's house right before Officer George Mullins of the Sweet Apple Police Department arrived. Sugar hadn't asked for them to be there, had actually made it pretty clear that she didn't want them there. But both had agreed they should be there after Wade pointed out that the sight of the bloodstained shirt was the one thing he could recall having ever subdued Sugar Prescott.

When Wade had called Merilee the previous night to plan the meeting, Merilee had been relieved to know that the topic of Sugar was the purpose of his phone call. The awkwardness of their conversation at the construction site was one of those scenes that played over and over in her head at night, pushing out all thoughts of sleep and filling her with mortification. She had no idea how she'd agreed to ask him to the gala. It had been either the champagne or her sheer loneliness, or simply Heather's powers of persuasion. Most probably all three.

"You look nice today," Wade said as Merilee approached the steps.

She glanced down at the blue silk blouse Lily had said looked pretty on her, trying to pretend she hadn't deliberately pulled it out of her closet to wear because she knew she'd be seeing Wade. "Thank you," she said, trying very hard not to notice how nicely his golf shirt fit, or how something zinged in her brain when he smiled at her. She must *really* be lonely. Time to binge watch Nicholas Sparks movies on Net-flix to cure her of her romantic fantasies, assuming it would work in the same way that her children couldn't bear the sight of candy for at least two weeks following their Halloween gorging.

Sugar answered the door wearing lipstick and a frown. "I can't visit now. I have an appointment." Her lips pressed together as the police cruiser pulled up in the drive. "You'll just have to come back later."

"Or we could stay," Wade said as he leaned forward to kiss her cheek, then gently moved past her so that he was standing next to her when Officer George Mullins reached the porch.

Merilee and Wade introduced themselves, and despite Sugar's pro-tests that they were just leaving, they all settled themselves in the front room, a plate of cookies and glasses of sweet tea in front of them. Even in her annoyed state, Sugar remembered her manners.

Sugar smiled at the officer. "I believe I knew your grandmama—Betsy Rucker. I was in her wedding when she married your grand-daddy, Vern—probably have a photo somewhere I can show you. Nice people. I went to your parents' wedding, too—just as a guest, though. Beautiful dress and flowers, I do remember that. It was over at the First United Methodist—that first wedding after the big fire." Leaning for-ward, she slid the plate of cookies across the table. "I remember you as a baby, too. Fat little thing. I don't think I'd ever seen so many rolls in a baby's legs before. You might just have been the cutest baby I've ever seen."

The officer grinned as he took a bite from his cookie, and if Merilee had to take a guess, she'd say that Sugar Prescott had never once re-ceived more than a warning for any traffic offense.

The officer began asking Sugar the same questions Merilee had asked her the day they'd discovered the trunk, and Sugar responded without appearing to have to think about her answers—no, she didn't know who the trunk belonged to, and no, she didn't know how it had ended up in the cellar. Yes, tenants had access to the cellar, but to her knowl-edge none of them had ever had a reason to use it.

Officer Mullins was thorough and respectful of Sugar's time, asking all his questions and jotting her answers down in a notebook in less than twenty minutes. "I think that's all the questions I have for you, Miss Sugar," he said as he stood and pocketed his notebook. "We're going to do a cursory search of the property and the cellar. One of our detectives is going to come out and ask you a few more questions and do a mouth swab just to see if there's a match with any trace evidence they can pull off the trunk or the shirt. My guess would be no, owing to how old everything is—any trace evidence would probably have degraded by now, but we have to be thorough."

"That's fine, young man. You do what you have to do, and I'm not even going to ask that the trunk and its contents be returned. You may dispose of it as you see fit whenever you're done with all the testing and scientific whatnot you'll have to do to it."

Merilee met Wade's gaze behind Sugar's head. They both knew she watched *Forensic Files* and the Investigation Discovery channel religiously and could probably lead a forensic investigation by herself.

"Yes, ma'am. It won't be me doing all the lab work, but I promise you it will be in good hands." He picked up his hat from the hall tree, then tipped the brim as he left the house.

Sugar was right behind him, picking up her netted hat—the same one she'd worn to the Atlanta Woman's Club—and then pinning it to her hair.

Looking in the mirror behind her, she said, "If you wouldn't mind moving your truck, Wade, I need to get to Bible study. If the police need to get inside, tell them the door's unlocked."

"Bible study? Since when?"

"Since I turned ninety-three. Figured it was time to start studying for my final exam."

Wade grinned, then held the door open. Merilee began to follow but paused in front of a low chest she hadn't noticed before, two silver-framed photographs standing neatly on top.

"Is this you?" Merilee asked, holding up one of the photos. "I recognize the hat." It was a black-and-white picture of a stunning young blond woman—not really more than a girl—tall and elegant, wearing clothes in the style of the nineteen forties, surrounded by three men.

One was considerably older, the other two in their mid-twenties. All three wore suits and ties, looking uncomfortable, as if they were used to wearing more casual clothes.

Sugar stepped closer to see, then nodded. "That was taken at my mother's funeral. My daddy wanted a keepsake. And he was right—this is the last photograph taken of him before he died just a few months later. That's Harry and Will. That scar on Harry's cheek—he received that at Normandy. That scar and his medal's all he came back with. He left any sense of decency and honor back on those beaches, pretty much."

Merilee studied the photograph, especially Sugar. She had always suspected that Sugar had been a beautiful woman, and this confirmed it. She was Hollywood-glamour beautiful, the kind of face and body you'd see on pinups at the time. Not that Sugar Prescott would ever have posed for a pinup. But there was something else about the photo of the woman with the three men. About the way she stood a little in front of them, the father's hand on her arm instead of the other way around, as if she were the one offering support. And guidance.

"And this one?" Merilee asked, holding up a photo of an impossibly young Sugar with a handsome man in uniform. She was wearing a white suit with a matching hat and carrying a bouquet of flowers. "You and Tom on your wedding day?"

Sugar nodded. "I'm going to be late."

"Sorry—coming," she said, giving the photograph one last look. There was something about it that made Merilee pause. Both Tom and Sugar were smiling, but it was more than that simple expression. It was something that reminded Merilee of herself.

"Coming," Merilee said again, carefully replacing the frame before following Sugar and Wade out the door.

Wade settled Sugar into her car and watched as she began to drive away before climbing into his truck. Leaning out his window, he called to Merilee, "Do I need to get you a corsage or something for the gala? Or coordinate the color of my cummerbund?"

"Nah. Let's pretend we're adults for one evening and dispense with all that."

"If you say so." His smile brightened. "Would it be nerdy to admit that I'm looking forward to the evening?"

She felt that zing again and made a mental note to check out Netflix as soon as she got home. "Yes," she said.

"Yes?"

Before she could respond, she noticed a black Mercedes coming down the drive toward them, and Wade turned to look, too.

The car stopped and the window rolled down. "Good to see you again, Wade." Turning toward Merilee, Dan said, "You said you were free Monday morning, so I thought I'd stop by and pick up that package you've been holding for me. But if you're busy . . . ," he said, indicating Wade and the patrol car pulled up in front of Sugar's house.

"Not at all—this is perfect timing," she said as she walked toward the car. "If you give me a lift to my place, I'll get it for you."

She waved good-bye to Wade, ignoring the question in his eyes, then slid into the passenger side of Dan's car. It smelled faintly of leather and a light scent of cologne that she thought was quite pleasant. Michael hadn't worn cologne, maybe because he didn't think he could carry it off. But Dan could. He was the kind of man who could get away with wearing a pink shirt or carrying his wife's handbag without dinging his masculinity.

"You look pretty," he said, and Merilee smiled, noticing the lack of a zing, for which she was grateful.

"Thank you. And don't mind the police. We found an old trunk in the cellar complete with an army shirt and bullet hole. Sugar doesn't know anything about it, so we're not worried. It's been there awhile."

"So's Sugar," Dan said with a half smile, making Merilee laugh.

Dan continued. "Sorry to hear that Heather's making all her committee heads work over the weekend. I hope you didn't have any plans."

Merilee was startled for a moment before she remembered that Heather had told Dan that she was staying home to work on the gala over the long holiday weekend. It was a white lie, Heather had confessed to Merilee, told only because Heather knew that Dan had been itching to spend time at his fishing cabin drinking beer and not shaving for four whole days, and if Heather hadn't said she'd made plans to stay home and work, he wouldn't have gone for a much-needed break.

Merilee found it sweet, the way Heather worked so hard to make sure her husband had a break. So completely different from Merilee's now-defunct marriage, in which Michael called all the shots and everybody did what Michael wanted to do. Maybe if they'd seen Dan and Heather's exemplary marriage, they might have been able to save their own.

Merilee smiled. "Yes, well, I love her dedication. It's going to be an amazing event and I'm glad to be a part of it. And I'm thankful she's not making us wear hoop skirts and corsets to go along with the theme."

"Oh, I'm not so sure. I think you'd look lovely in a hoop skirt and corset."

Merilee grinned. "Well, thank you, suh. But what about the curtain rods?" she asked, recalling the famous Carol Burnett skit. "Should I leave them behind?"

He laughed, and Merilee felt relieved that he'd recognized the reference. But she figured anybody who loved *Hogan's Heroes* as much as he did probably would have. She was glad to have found another friend, especially one she respected. She remembered what he'd said about Heather, and why he'd selected the ring for her. It had touched Merilee, to see that kind of devotion from a husband toward his wife.

He stopped the car in front of her house. "Stay here, and I'll run in and get it." Without waiting for a response, she went into the house and pulled out the beautifully wrapped box, glowing in its iridescent gold and silver paper with coordinating ribbon. As she closed the drawer, she looked up through the side window by the fireplace in the front room and saw a small white dog in the yard.

It was just standing there, looking toward the drive, where Dan's car sat idling, its tail wagging slowly, its little pink tongue hanging crookedly out of its mouth, as if it had just run a long distance and was catching its breath.

Merilee slammed the drawer shut and raced out the front door and down the steps, looking out toward the side yard. But it was empty, with no sign of the little dog.

Dan opened his door. "Anything wrong?"

"Did you see the dog?"

He raised his eyebrows. "A dog? What did it look like?"

"It was small and white, and he was right there in the middle of the side lawn, but now he's gone." She shook her head. "Colin's been seeing a little white dog and I'd begun to think he was imagining it. And now I think I am. Maybe it's a mirage."

"Maybe," he said, his face thoughtful. "It's not always easy to recognize what's real and what's not."

His expression had changed, almost as if he were closing something off from her. She focused on the package as she handed it to him. "I wish somebody had told me that years ago. Might have saved me some heartache."

"Nah. You still would have made the same mistakes. But how are we going to learn if we don't make a few mistakes along the way?"

She studied the package for a moment before lifting her gaze to meet his. "True. Thanks for stopping by—and I hope Heather loves the ring as much as we do."

"Me, too." They said good-bye before he closed the car door and drove away.

Merilee walked back to the side yard and around the house, looking for the little dog, thinking about what Dan had said, and wondering if she'd ever learned anything from the mistakes she'd been making her whole life.

The gate guard at Prescott Estates waved her in, the barrier going up as soon as her car rounded the corner into the entrance. She was there so often these days that she was now on a first-name basis with all the guards.

She parked in front of the multicolumned clubhouse, then headed inside, her purse and water bottle tucked securely under her arm. It was Thursday evening and they were supposed to be having their weekly committee-head meeting, which was why she'd been confused when Heather told her to wear her workout gear and bring water and then had refused to answer any more questions.

The guard on duty in the reception area stopped her and rerouted her from the dining room, where they usually met, to the workout room on the lower level. Merilee opened the door and stopped, her eyes blinking under the bright fluorescents, ten or so vibrantly colored rubber mats covering part of the floor like a patchwork. Two eager-looking women stood in front of the mats, smiling toothy grins.

"Merilee!" Heather shouted, nearly hopping over to the door. She was wearing what only a model might consider workout gear—a marbled tank with a small bow in the back and matching capri pants with a flattering wide white stripe going down the sides, delicate ruching at the calves. It was in stark contrast to Merilee's old UGA gym shorts and the ratty T-shirt she'd pulled from the ragbag when she realized she didn't actually own workout gear.

"You look like a college coed," Heather gushed. "You'll need to share your secret on how you stay so youthful." She pulled on Merilee's arm. "Come on over and meet Laura and Lauren—they're my Pilates trainers, so I've hired them tonight as a nice break from all the hard work we've been doing. They're going to teach us some core-strengthening exercises we can use to look great in our evening gowns. And other reasons, too, but sometimes it's easier to get started on something if you set short-term goals."

Heather continued to speak as she led Merilee across the room. "They have their own teaching styles, but tonight I told them they need to have only one style—mine." She grinned. "I love these ladies, and they've brought their business cards so that if anyone wants to continue, all they need to do is call. And first class is on me!"

"That's very generous of you, Heather."

Heather gave her a serious look. "This is what friendship is, Merilee. And I choose to be generous with my friends. Besides, everybody should take fitness very seriously. It's not only important to our own minds and bodies, but it's also important for our children—especially our daughters—to see us taking care of ourselves. Being fit isn't an accident. And we certainly don't want inactive, overweight children any more than we want to be inactive or overweight ourselves."

Heather introduced Merilee to Laura and Lauren—she couldn't remember which one was which. Laura—or was it Lauren?—was the tall, slender one with extraordinarily long arms and legs, and the other instructor, presumably Lauren, was shorter, with dark hair and a small yet efficient and well-toned body. They both made her nervous, like they could tell at a glance that she'd once been slim and fit and had let everything go. Not that she was overweight, but there were definitely lumps where there hadn't been before, and if she had any muscles, they were hiding.

"No need to be nervous," the taller one said. "We won't push anybody to do anything they're not ready for. It can actually be very relaxing—especially a mat class, which we're doing here. If you come to the studio, you can see the other kinds of equipment we have for all levels." She smiled warmly, making Merilee believe that she might actually enjoy exercising again.

"I love your lipstick," the shorter one said. "It really brightens up your face. I always tell my clients that on days when they don't feel like exercising to put on a pretty shade of lipstick, and it's an instant pick-me-up."

"Absolutely," Heather agreed. She faced Merilee, her expression earnest. "What lipstick is that? I want to try it."

Merilee dug in her purse and pulled out the tube of lipstick that she'd bought on a whim at Kroger. "It's Revlon—nothing too exciting, I'm afraid. But the color does stay on for hours and I love the texture. Doesn't dry out my lips."

"Don't you hate that?" Heather exclaimed. "There's nothing worse than dry, cakey, so-called long-wearing lipstick that doesn't last. And believe me, I've tried every single brand—from super expensive to drugstore—and I'm still searching. If this works, I will owe you bigtime." She took the tube from Merilee and glanced at the bottom. "Do you mind if I borrow this for a minute? I want to run to the ladies' room and give it a swipe. I promise I'll wipe off my germs when I'm done." She winked, then speed walked herself in the direction of the restrooms.

Laura and Lauren were occupied speaking with two other women, leaving Merilee to glance around. She noticed several of the other committee members in the room, some of whom had already claimed a mat and most of whom were all dressed in coordinated workout outfits not dissimilar to Heather's. Merilee self-consciously tugged on the hem of her shorts, feeling like Daisy Duke in a room full of Patty Dukes.

She spotted her carpool partner, Sharlene, behind a table near the far wall; little triangles of fabric covered the plastic folding table in front of her. Curious, she headed over to say hello.

"Hey, Sharlene. What's all this?"

"Oh, didn't I tell you? It's my new business venture—Canine Couture. I'm making kerchiefs for dogs. I've always bought cute fabrics and made little kerchiefs for my own dogs, and then friends started asking me to make some for them, and then I just had this idea that maybe I could charge money and start a business."

Merilee fingered through the fabrics, admiring the wide-ranging themes—school logos, autumn, Halloween, Christmas, florals, cartoon characters, and even—surprisingly—cats. "How's it going?"

"Pretty well. I mean, not as much as if I were an interior designer or real estate agent, but not too shabby if I say so myself. I bought my ball gown using my own money. I'm thinking of expanding into a line of dog car seat covers, too."

"Dog car seats?"

Sharlene nodded enthusiastically. "Yes. If you love your dog like family, you need to treat him like family and be concerned with his safety, just like a child's. Coordinating your dog's kerchief with his car seat cover will just make it more fun."

"Good for you," Merilee said, and because she felt bad walking away without making a purchase, she bought a UGA-themed kerchief for the dog she did not own.

Lindi Matthews arrived shortly afterward, and they each claimed a mat in the last row. Lindi wore running shorts and a tank top, which showed off her muscled legs and arms, but made Merilee feel better by complimenting her on how nicely shaped her legs were. Merilee had forgotten that, and even hated wearing clothes that showed off her legs. It had taken her years to figure out that it was probably because her legs were what her mother always told her were the only pretty thing about her.

They survived the class, and Merilee was feeling optimistic enough at the end to take a business card from each of the instructors and promise she'd call. As she headed toward the exit, Sharlene ran after her. "You forgot your kerchief," she said, waving it in front of her.

"Oh, right. Thanks." She said good-bye to the other mothers as they filed out into the parking lot. It was only when she got to her car and was fumbling in the dark for her car keys that she realized Heather hadn't returned her lipstick. She looked up and saw Heather deep in conversation with one of the other tennis moms, whose first name Merilee thought might be Liz.

Not wanting to interrupt, she slid behind the wheel and shut her door, realizing that in the grand scheme of things, a tube of lipstick was a small way to begin to repay Heather for all of her kindnesses.

She waved as she drove out of the parking lot, and Heather waved back, a big grin on her face.

Twenty-three

SUGAR

"Joyful, joyful, we adore thee . . ." It was the closing hymn of the Sunday service and Sugar sang as loudly as she could. She'd been told often that she couldn't carry a tune in a bucket and for many years had kept silent during the hymn-singing portion of the service. At least until the day she'd stood next to a tone-deaf child who belted out the words with such joy and abandon.

She'd learned two things that day: that singing in church had nothing to do with how good a singer you were, and that she was too old to care what she sounded like, anyway. So she belted out her favorite hymns and paid no attention at all to the heads turned in her direction.

Merilee sat next to her, also singing, and occasionally going off pitch, but most likely due to Sugar leading her astray. Merilee had a good voice, strong and clear and probably in tune if standing next to like-talented individuals. She was there because Sugar had needed a ride to church and Merilee had obliged.

Not that either of them had been looking to ask a favor or to fulfill one, but Merilee had been on her way to the grocery store—the children at their father's for the weekend—and had passed Sugar just as she'd delivered a swift kick to the back tire of her car. It wasn't that she was angry at the car. It was old, after all. She was irritated because she would probably have to buy a new car at this stage in her life, when her chances of getting her money's worth were next to nil.

When the hymn ended and Merilee made to move out of the pew, Sugar put her hand on her arm. "Just wait until they've all left. I can't stand the jostling and the crowds." She sat back and waited for the people to step around them, patient smiles on their lips.

After everyone had left and the organ had stopped, Sugar took a deep breath. Her family had been coming to this church for more than a hundred years. The church had built a new, larger sanctuary a while back, but one service a month was still held in the old one, and that's the one Sugar went to.

"Is this where you and Tom were married?" Merilee asked in her church voice.

"Yes. And my grandparents. Not my parents, though; they were married in Savannah, where Mama was from. All the funerals were here, too. Just memorial services for Bobby and Tom, though, since they're buried overseas. Mine will be here, too. I've already worked out all the details with the pastor. Wade has a copy."

"Of course you have," Merilee said. She stood and moved into the aisle and waited for Sugar to haul herself up, even waited patiently while the blood began to flow again into Sugar's extremities so she could move. Sugar assumed she was used to waiting on small children, so it probably wasn't something Merilee had to think about.

"Nothing wrong with being prepared. That's the problem with the young people today. Everybody thinks nothing bad will ever happen, so they don't plan for it."

Merilee held up her elbow and Sugar surprised them both by taking it. "I don't know if you're including me in 'young people,' but I'm prepared. You should see your cellar. I could live there for a month without having to come up for air once."

"How old are you?" Sugar asked. "Just in case I need to change my classifications."

A corner of Merilee's mouth twitched. "Thirty-six. But remember that thirty is the new twenty."

"Humph. And ninety is still the old ninety."

Merilee laughed out loud, then slapped her hand over her mouth when she remembered where she was. They were silent as Merilee led Sugar down the front steps one at a time, Sugar's other hand clasped tightly to the banister. The older she became without falling, the more nervous she became that she might.

A slip and fall on her front steps was the whole reason Willa Faye's daughter had decided it was time to move her mother out of her house and into that retirement community with the ridiculous overblown name—the one Wade was always telling Sugar she should consider. As if she had any inclination to move into what was basically a dormitory for the elderly, complete with rubber chicken at dinner and motorized scooters.

Willa Faye was happy there, had even started sharing meals with a younger gentleman of eighty-seven. But Sugar couldn't leave her home, not while she still had breath in her. And not just because she was stubborn and liked things her own way, and had no interest in doing anything on anybody else's schedule. If only her reasons were that uncomplicated.

"I don't mind taking you straight home, but if you need anything at Kroger, I was headed that way . . ."

Sugar shook her head. "Seniors' day is Wednesday and the store has coupons and discounts for the old people. I'll wait to go then."

"Oh, of course. I didn't know." Merilee began walking in the direction of the parking lot, but Sugar held her back. "I'd like to walk a bit, if you don't mind. I get stiff sitting for an hour. I should tell the pastor he should write shorter sermons."

"Sure." Merilee moved in beside her and tucked her hand in the crook of Sugar's elbow. "Lead the way."

She'd thought they'd walk down the sidewalk adjacent to Main Street for a block or two—just enough to get her hip joints moving again. But her feet seemed to have another idea entirely, and they ended up on the path leading them to the graveyard. She was a frequent visitor here, her friends now seeming to die with alarming regularity.

They walked slowly, admiring the old-growth trees that shaded the paths and the leaves that had just started wearing their new autumn colors. "Is this where your family is buried?"

Sugar stopped, suddenly tired. "No. We have a family cemetery. Pretty much everyone, except for Bobby and Tom, is buried there."

"Is it nearby?"

"Near enough." She spotted a bench and began leading Merilee toward it, eager to get the pressure of standing off of her knees and hips.

Merilee waited for her to sit before joining her. "I can take you sometime, if you'd like. I mean, if you don't want to drive or go alone, I'd be happy to take you."

"I can go by myself." Realizing she'd been rude, even for her, she said, "Thank you. But I go there to talk with Jimmy and Mary. They don't answer—I suppose I'd need to seek a doctor's advice if they did— but I try to make up for all the conversations we didn't get to have." She paused. "And I speak to my mama sometimes, too, for the same reason."

She felt Merilee looking at her. "I wasn't aware that you had a good relationship with your mother."

Sugar started to press her lips together, wondering what it was about this woman that made her share so much. Maybe it was the simple truth that there was so much unsaid, and too few people remaining whom she could tell. "I'm no doctor, but I'd say my mama had depression or one of those mental diseases they all talk about today, and there's now probably some pill she could have taken to make it go away. But all we had then was something to make her tired so she didn't notice how unhappy she was. I wish I could go back with all I know now and apply it. Then maybe I could have the kind of conversations I always imagined a girl would have with her mother."

"If you figure out how to do that, let me know."

A limb of crimson maple leaves shuddered with excitement above them as a bird stretched its wings and flew away, the temptation of a blue sky more interesting than their conversation. "That's a red-winged blackbird," Sugar said with confidence. "They've usually gone down to the coast by now—don't like the colder weather." She pressed her back against the bench, thinking of Jimmy and of her deal with God that he'd be the last loss in her life. As if, in the stupidity of the young, she believed she had any bargaining power at all in the grand scheme of things.

But as part of her reasoning there'd been what Jimmy had taught her about the migrating birds, about how they came back year after year, and how that always filled him with hope that despite storms and losses, the opportunity to start again was always there. It was why she'd said yes to Tom. If only to show Jimmy that maybe he'd been right. She stopped and turned to Merilee. "Did your life change after David died?"

Merilee seemed surprised by the question, as if she'd never thought about it before. "Yes. Of course." She waited a moment, but Sugar didn't interrupt. "Everything changed. And not just in the obvious ways. We were all so sad; we all grieved in our own ways. We were the family who'd lost a child, and you could see it in the eyes of our neighbors and my teachers. I was the girl who'd lost a brother. But my mother had lost her son, and she stopped noticing that she had another child. That's what changed, really. Because after that I became the girl desperate for her mother's attention and approval. That pretty much defined me for a long time."

Merilee had been wearing red knit gloves with little bows at the wrists—very impractical for keeping hands warm, but nobody had asked Sugar, who'd prefer warm fingers to silly embellishments—and she pulled them off a finger at a time, wadding them angrily in her hand. "According to a shrink I saw when I was in my twenties, I was so desperate for my mother's approval and affection that I did things I'm not proud of. Things that still haunt me."

She leaned against the back of the bench, the gloves held tightly in her fists. "There was a girl I remember from summer camp. She had the misfortune of being overweight with bad skin, and her only offense was sitting next to me on the bus and then being assigned to be my bunkmate. I made her life hell. And it got worse when she moved to our school and I recognized her. I don't even remember her real name— my friends and I all called her Daisy, because of those dairy commercials about Daisy the cow. The name stuck because we were relentless, and pretty soon the entire school called her Daisy."

"Was she really so awful that you couldn't see anything good about her?" Sugar asked, trying to understand this part of Merilee and finding it difficult.

"That's the really awful part. Because Daisy was funny. And really smart. I actually invited her to my house a few times to study for exams—I just made sure that none of my friends knew. In return I'd give her advice on how to dress, and the best hairstyle for her face— stupid stuff like that, but she was so grateful. She always seemed . . . eager to be my friend. Not that I'd treat her any differently when we were back at school, but she seemed to accept it.

"I still feel physically ill when I remember her, and the way I treated her. I've tried to analyze my dislike of her, and in some part of my psyche I think it's because I saw me when I thought of her. I saw the girl my mother saw every time she looked at me. And I wanted to punish myself for being so unlovable."

"So you became a 'mean girl'?"

Merilee frowned. "How did you ever hear that term?"

"They were playing that movie with that young actress who's since lost her mind—Lindsay somebody—at the little movie theater at the place where Willa Faye lives, so we watched it. Showed me how much things have changed since I was a girl. And how little."

Merilee slowly unfurled her fists and watched as the gloves regained their shape. "Our junior year Daisy and I were in the same English lit class and I intercepted a note she passed to a friend. It was all about how in love she was with the football quarterback, and how she dreamed he'd ask her to our junior prom. I might not have even paid attention to the stupid note except I'd been dating the quarterback since freshman year, and I'd already bought my dress for the prom— a dress I didn't particularly like but one my mother had picked out for me. It made me . . . unreasonably angry."

"Was this the boy John from your yearbook?" Sugar asked.

Merilee looked startled. "How do you know about that?"

"Lily told me she had your permission—I'm assuming that she didn't?"

"No. There are . . . things I'm not ready for her to ask me about."
She closed her eyes. "Like why I allowed my friends to write the word
'moo' on Daisy's senior page. But yes, it was the same John. He'd stood
up for her in the lunch room once when a bunch of the jocks were
tormenting her, and he became her hero. And, in my stupid teenaged
brain, it made me mad and so I was even more despicable in my behavior toward Daisy."

Sugar felt her lips pressing together. "You were horrid. I'm disappointed in you, Merilee. Somebody should have taken a switch to
you—of course, they would have been thrown in jail, but it would
have been the right thing to do."

"I wish someone had. But, according to that same shrink, teasing
Daisy fed my popularity. And my popularity in turn increased my
mother's interest in me. When I remember Daisy now in the middle of
the night, I can't go back to sleep because of the shame I still feel. In some
ways I'm glad. At least that way she can wreak a little deserved revenge."

Sugar squeezed the handle of her pocketbook, which was sitting in
her lap, wishing Merilee hadn't told her all this. It was a secret shared,
and Sugar felt beholden to Merilee again, as if it meant she'd be expected to share her own.

Sugar sniffed, the first warning of her fall allergies. "That's the
problem with people today. They think professionals know all the
answers. They make everyone believe that every bad deed is forgiven
if you have a good enough reason."

"You don't think that's true?"

Sugar closed her eyes, remembering a moon-filled night saturated
with the sound of running feet. "No. Because then we wouldn't have
anything to keep us up when we awaken in the middle of the night."

Merilee's fists tightened over the crumpled gloves, and Sugar could
tell she wanted to argue with her, but someone at some point had told
her it was rude to argue with the elderly. "I sometimes wonder if I
should try to find Daisy, apologize to her. I doubt it would make her
feel better about the years she suffered through, but maybe then I'd
stop having nightmares."

Sugar wanted to snort but wasn't sure how. "Maybe an apology might help *Daisy* not have so many nightmares." She sniffed again. "Lily didn't see the photo of Daisy. But we did see the picture of someone named John with the heart around his face and him asking you to marry him. What happened to him?"

Merilee's cheeks, which had been pink from the chilly wind, suddenly turned the shade of wet flour. "He died."

Sugar nodded, afraid to say something that might make a connection to Merilee's loss. She'd learned that shared losses didn't divide them, but added to one's own pile.

"Wade tells me that the two of you have a date and that Heather's behind it."

"It's not a date," Merilee protested. "It's for the gala, and Heather needed an even number for her table."

Sugar blew air from her nose, hoping it sounded like a snort. "Heather has never done anything without a reason, and needing an even number doesn't sound like a good one. I wouldn't go, if I were you."

Merilee turned on the bench to face her, trying very hard to keep her anger in check. "Your experiences with Heather aren't mine. She's my friend. She reached out when I was at my loneliest, has introduced me to lots of new people, and has been nothing but warm and kind to me and to my children. There's nothing that she could possibly want from me in exchange for being so nice except my friendship, so I wouldn't worry."

"It's not you I'm worried about. Heather carved her initials on Wade and it took a long time for him to heal. I'm just afraid somebody's going to get hurt."

Traffic whizzed by on nearby Main Street, reminding Sugar that she had things to do—bills to pay. Letters to write. But her memories seemed to weigh her down, press her into the bench. She thought of Tom and the porch swing, and how she'd made the mistake of believing she could ever be done with losses.

"Does Wade really put red bows on your sheep at Christmas?" Merilee's voice brought her back to the present, and she felt an odd gratitude. It also made Sugar think that Merilee must be procrastinating going home, too.

"Yes. He's incorrigible."

"You love him like your own grandson."

Sugar's lips thinned as she molded them against her teeth. "I allow myself to care for him because he's not mine to lose. I can live with that."

"He said his grandmother once told him that you would do anything for those you loved. I think that means you don't do a good enough job of hiding your indifference," she said with sarcasm, as if unsure someone so old would understand it.

Sugar grunted, unable to find a suitable sound. "Or maybe I'm immune to the need to perform heroics. No need to rush into a burning building to save someone."

Merilee gave her a sideways glance. "Well, that's a good thing. Someone your age shouldn't be doing that kind of thing anyway." Merilee stood slowly. "I need to get going. Are you ready?"

Sugar nodded and Merilee helped her to stand. They were walking back toward the parking lot when Merilee asked the question Sugar had been expecting. "What about when Jimmy died—did your life change?"

Sugar took a long time to respond, not sure how much she wanted to tell. Or how much Merilee was ready to hear. "It was because of Jimmy I married Tom. I know Jimmy wanted me to approach the rest of my life with hope. So I promised myself I would never shed another tear. And I haven't. I just wish he'd been around to warn me what it would cost."

SUGAR

1943

Willa Faye grabbed my left hand, looking at the fingers, which were healed but still didn't look the same as they had before my "accident."

"Where is it?"

I allowed myself to share a little of her excitement. "It's Tom's grandmother's ring and his mother has it in Alabama. I don't think it would fit over my knuckle now, anyway. His mama's too ill to travel, and with Tom being called up, we're not going to have time to have a proper engagement party. I'll let you break the news to your mother."

"She will be so disappointed. Especially since it doesn't look like either one of her daughters will ever get married. She *lives* to entertain and this could have been her one chance to throw a real party."

I slapped her on the arm. "Don't be ridiculous. This war will be over soon, and all the men in the county will come running back looking for wives."

"Have you told President Roosevelt about the war being over soon? He should probably know."

"All I know is what Tom says, and I'm choosing to believe him."

Willa Faye gave me a sympathetic smile, but I looked away, not wanting anyone's sympathy. Despite all I thought I'd learned about life and all its disappointments since Rufus's death, I had decided to hope. To allow myself to believe that I was truly done with tears. Maybe if Jimmy were alive, he might have told me that I should stop promising myself things I had no control over. Like who to love and when to cry. Because only stupid people did that. Or the kind of people who didn't believe themselves strong enough to bear one more loss.

"Daddy's already started building the house—wants it to be ready in time for the wedding. He's got the house framed and the roof on. Don't know how he managed that so quick, but I guess Daddy's got lots of friends who owe him favors from back when times were hard and he put food on their tables."

"But why so close to the main house? You love those woods so much, I thought for sure that's where you'd want your house with Tom."

I rubbed the swollen knuckle, feeling a residual ache, imagined I could hear again the snap of bone. "Daddy said the same thing." I met her eyes. "But I said no. I wanted the house to be close to theirs so I could take care of Mama. She doesn't sleep very well at night anymore, and with Daddy having to travel so much now, I'd feel better."

"I understand," she said, reaching over to squeeze my hand, and I wondered if she really did. If anybody really ever could. "I'm just wondering what's the rush to get married. If you wait until Tom comes back, we'll be able to throw you a proper wedding, with parties and presents and a trip into Atlanta to buy you some new and pretty things."

I found I couldn't look at her as I shook my head vigorously. "No. We need to get married now. Before he leaves."

"Are you afraid he won't come back? But surely . . ." She stopped, and I still couldn't look at her. Couldn't look at the understanding dawning in her eyes. "Oh, Sugar. Does Tom know?"

I nodded. "Yes. I couldn't marry him without telling him the truth. But I didn't tell him it was Curtis."

Her hand squeezed mine. "Why not?"

"Because Tom would hunt him down and kill him, and I don't want Tom to pay the price for Curtis's sins. He'd never tell the police the reason why for the same reason I can't. I've got to live here and hold my head up. So I told Tom I didn't recognize the man, that it must be one of the temporary farmworkers who'd helped with the harvest and that he must have moved on because I hadn't seen him again."

"But what if Curtis comes back?" She pulled away, lowering her voice. "What will you do?"

"I'll kill him myself." The words were spoken before I knew I'd given them permission to leave my mouth.

Willa Faye released her hold on my hand. "What did Tom say about the baby?"

"He says he'll love it as if it were his own, even though I'm not sure that I can. But Tom's so sure that his love will be enough. And that I'll grow to love the baby in time."

"And you will, Sugar. You will. You'll see."

I chose to believe her, and once I'd made that choice the rest seemed easy.

I watched the house being built and the birds in their migration patterns decorating the sky, seeing them both as symbols of hope. Before he left to join the colored troops to fight in the war, Lamar built me bird feeders to place in the trees around the new house, and I kept them filled with corn and seeds, remembering what Bobby had told me about karma. I figured if I fed the traveling birds I was doing my part of being good to the universe, and that in repayment it would be good to me.

As it turned out, Tom had less time than we thought. He got two days' leave, which meant that Mrs. Mackenzie had to make do with magnolia leaves from her backyard instead of the flowers she'd planned to get in Atlanta to decorate the church. At least I'd had time to shop for a suit to wear. Mrs. Mackenzie had said every bride should have a gown, but I was hardheaded and practical like my father. And I remembered the hard times and could not bear to waste money on something I'd wear just once. I suppose I could have worn my mama's dress, but nobody mentioned it. Maybe because they wanted to think I should start my own marriage with better karma. Not that anybody would have called it that—I'm sure there's some Christian word for it—but we were all thinking the same thing.

Tom and I got married at the church where I'd been baptized and where we'd had Jimmy's funeral less than two months before. My daddy was there to give me away, and Mama came, too, her hair washed and combed by Mrs. Mackenzie, her dress hanging on her because she'd gotten so small. My brothers couldn't get leave, and that was just as well. Mama had Dr. Mackenzie's arm to lean on and that was all she needed.

Tom was so handsome standing at the front of the church in his uniform, but I think it was his smile I noticed the most, reminding me of the first time we'd met on Stone Mountain and I knew then there was something special about him.

There was a small reception afterward in the church hall, and I knew it would take a long time for me to come up with the right words and the right way to thank Mrs. Mackenzie for everything. But right then I was in too much of a hurry to get Tom alone. It might not have been more than an hour after the ceremony, but it seemed like a century had passed before Tom helped me into his Jeep, then slid in next to me.

"Congratulations, Mrs. Bates," he said, kissing me gently on the lips.

It was the first time I realized I wasn't going to be a Prescott any longer, and I pulled back as if he'd made a mistake. But then I smiled and put my arms around him and pressed my lips against his, and that made the wedding guests on the church steps—mostly Willa Faye and her sister and also, I suspected, Mrs. Mackenzie—start shouting and hollering.

We waved good-bye as Tom put the Jeep in gear and we headed toward our new home, ecstatically uncaring of the ruts and dust of the unpaved road. But the road Tom chose took us by the old Brown homestead. Daddy was working the farmland now, the cotton fields replaced by rows of corn to grow what the government needed him to, to supply the war effort, but the house had fallen into disrepair, the front porch all but gone to wind and rot, and most of the windows broken or missing altogether. I suppose if I'd been paying attention, I would have told Tom to go another way like I always did. It was longer, but then I didn't have to pass the house and remember who'd once lived there. But Tom would have wondered why.

"That doesn't look right," Tom said, slowing down the Jeep.

I'd been looking in the other direction like I usually did when I accidentally went this way and had to pass the house, but Tom's words made me turn around.

"See?" he said, pointing toward the lone chimney and the unmistakable column of smoke rising into the early-evening air. "Isn't this your daddy's property?"

I nodded, struggling to find my normal voice. "Nobody's lived there in a long time. But sometimes Daddy will turn the other way if one of the migrant families needs temporary shelter. That's why he keeps it stocked with wood. If they decide to stay and work his land, he'll find a better place for them to live."

This was the truth, although nobody had been inside the house for more than a year. And I wondered if Tom noticed that there were no lights on in any of the rooms that might indicate more than one person living there.

"Let's go," I said, as eager to get home as I was to leave this place behind me.

Tom smiled and took my hand to kiss it, then put his foot down on the gas pedal.

There'd been no time to finish our house. Only the walls in the bedroom and kitchen had been Sheetrocked—something new Daddy said would be quicker than plastering and just as good—and the outside hadn't yet been painted. But when we pulled up to the front, Tom laughed.

"I told Lamar that I wanted a front porch swing. I didn't think they'd have time to build one and hang it, but I guess I was wrong."

He opened my door and swung me up in his arms like a baby. He kissed me properly this time, the kind of kiss that made me forget things like the woods after nightfall. "I'm going to carry you over the threshold for good luck, and then we're going to rock a bit in the swing. Because that's how I want to think of you when I'm over there, fighting. I want to picture my beautiful wife sitting here on this swing, saving a seat for me beside her."

We sat in the porch swing and huddled under a blanket and talked until the stars disappeared from the sky and the light turned pink. Then we went to bed and Tom made me forget, for a little while, about the war being waged on the other side of the ocean, and the smoke rising from a house that should have been empty.

Twenty-four

MERILEE

As the rear door to the Odyssey lifted, Merilee stifled a groan. Colin's game tablet—given to him by Michael as a consolation prize for the divorce and disguised as last year's Christmas present—sat in the middle of the trunk. She slid in her suitcase and picked it up, thinking she could just put it into Michael's mailbox on the way out of town as she headed to Tybee.

Or not. She couldn't remember the last time she'd seen Colin playing with it. Since Sugar had given him the field glasses, they were rarely parted. A few times he'd gone to sleep with them around his neck, and it reminded her of Jimmy. As Merilee had carefully removed them to his nightstand, she'd understood what a gift they had been from Sugar.

She tossed the tablet back into the car, then closed the door. It would be there if Colin wanted it when she got back. Returning to the house, she made sure the coffeemaker was turned off and unplugged, the thermostat set to sixty-six degrees—five degrees warmer than Sugar had suggested she set it to if she ever had to leave the house for a long period of time—then checked all the windows to make sure they were shut and locked.

As she locked the front door behind her, she saw again the porch swing hooks and recalled what Sugar had told her about Tom. When she'd reached the part in the story where Tom left to go overseas, Merilee had been pulling up to Sugar's house and she'd stopped talking. Merilee had turned off the ignition and moved to the other side of the car to help Sugar out—but only because it was too high up; otherwise, Sugar insisted, she could do it herself. Merilee had expected Sugar to invite her inside for some sweet tea so she could finish the story.

Instead, Sugar had thanked Merilee for the ride and had gone inside by herself, closing the door firmly behind her. For a brief moment, while sitting on that bench in the cemetery, Merilee had imagined they'd made a connection. Maybe even had the foundation for a friendship. Or at least found a substitute for an absent mother and a lost daughter. Instead, it appeared that Sugar might not be the only one attempting to fool herself.

Merilee spotted Wade's truck coming up the drive as she walked down the steps and found herself trying to remember if she'd put on lipstick. She even considered opening up the passenger door, where she'd already put her purse on the seat, to sneak a swipe of color. Luckily for her self-respect, he drove quickly and was pulling up beside her before she could even open the door.

"Hey, Merilee."

She almost did a double take to make sure it was Wade and not some businessman in a suit who'd stolen his truck.

Seeing her glance, he tugged self-consciously on his tie. "I know—weird, huh? I'm headed to a zoning meeting. They probably expect me to appear wearing a hard hat and towing a bulldozer, but I hate to be stereotyped."

"Well, if you want them to take you seriously, I think you've got it covered."

"Thanks," he said, flashing that smile that wouldn't look out of place on a magazine cover.

"I'm heading out for the long weekend—is there anything you need?"

"Actually, I brought you something." He reached through his truck's window and pulled out a brown-paper-wrapped package. "I was stuck at the light at the Crabapple intersection in front of that antiques store on the corner. I don't know if you've noticed, but there's a sign in the front window that advertises old maps. I had a little time to kill between appointments, so I parked and went in."

"What did you find?" she asked, feeling pleased he'd thought of her, and also excited to see what was under the wrapping.

"Check it out," he said, pulling off the paper and wadding it in one of his hands.

Her eyes widened. "Wow. I think I've seen this before. Well, part of it, anyway." The old map was framed in simple pine, the glass covering it sporting a small crack in the top right corner. She used her finger to trace the edge of the small lake at the front of the property and the road that skirted around it.

"You have?"

Merilee nodded. "Sugar has the other half. It was a wedding present from her father. That half shows the farmhouse and the land where this house was built and the surrounding acres. Pretty much leaves off where this one starts."

"They might have been connected at some point—I think they might have been surveyors' maps back in the day, showing property lines and such."

"Yeah, I was thinking the same thing." She frowned, noticing the other half of the clearing in the middle of the woods she'd noticed on Sugar's map. "What do you think this is?"

He studied it for a moment, then pulled back. "I have no idea. Considering how old the map is, it's probably been covered over by now. I bet Sugar knows. There's nothing about those woods she's not aware of."

"I bet." She smiled. "Thank you for this. The other one used to hang in the bedroom hallway of this house but Sugar took it down, so she's still got it. I'll ask her if I can hang them together."

"Or maybe I should. It's hard for her to tell me no." He took the frame from her. "And I'd be happy to have them put in matching frames, if you'd like."

"Only if you let me pay for it."

"If you insist." He returned the map and the wrapping paper to his truck. "I was going to ask you if I could work on the swing this weekend. I guess if you're not going to be here, it won't bother you if I set up shop in your yard."

"No, you won't bother me. But Sugar . . ."

"I know. She told me about Tom and the swing. But she thinks you and the children would enjoy it." He started to say something else, then stopped, a slight flush coloring his cheeks.

"What?" she asked, curious. "What else did she say?"

He met her gaze. "She also said that you and I might enjoy some 'canoodling'—yes, she used that exact word—on the swing, especially as the nights get colder."

It was her turn to blush. "Well, I've always wanted to hear how that word could be used in a sentence, and I guess now I know."

"Yeah, now we both do." He grinned again. "So, where are you headed?"

"Tybee." Even just the name filled her with a mix of joy and sadness and trepidation. She'd been there to visit her grandparents many times after David's death, never to kayak or swim in the ocean, and always without her parents. Once her grandparents had died, both while she was in college, she hadn't been back. Her parents still owned the house, but she had no idea if they ever visited. She never asked.

"You staying at your parents' place?"

She realized that Sugar must have told him about her connection there, and probably about David. She was glad she didn't have to explain the whole story to Wade and thought that maybe that had been the reason Sugar had told him. She'd never pictured Sugar as a gossip; Sugar had even asked Merilee to find a way to block the Entertainment Television channel because it was all unsubstantiated gossip.

"Actually, no. They've recently put it up for sale." She swallowed the lump that seemed to creep into her throat whenever she thought about the house being sold. "I'm staying with Heather at their home there. Just the two of us for a girls' weekend."

"Really?" he asked.

"Why are you so surprised?"

"I don't know. It's just, well, I wouldn't think that you and Heather had a lot in common. At least the Heather she is now. I'd say you'd be more compatible with how she used to be—when she was more relaxed and natural and not always trying to be perfect."

"Gee, thanks. I'm so glad you see that I've given up trying to be anything close to perfect."

"That's not what I'm saying . . ."

"I know," Merilee said as she opened her car door and climbed behind the steering wheel. "But did you stop to think that the reason why she relates to me could be because she's still the same person? And that too many of you are judging her because of her glamorous lifestyle and ignoring the person she is? Remember, it wasn't me she left at the altar, so my opinions aren't clouded by what she did years ago."

His eyes narrowed for a moment. "I'll keep that in mind," he said as he closed her door.

She rolled down her window. "If you need anything in the house while you're working, the spare key is under the planter with the orange mums."

"Well, aren't you just the model of security. A security code that anybody with half a brain can crack, and a spare key in the most obvious place on the planet, where anybody who's ever watched an episode of *Murder, She Wrote* would know to look."

"Are you done? It's a five-hour drive and I'd like to get there before it gets dark."

"You're driving? I'm surprised Heather would consider driving in a Honda, even as a passenger."

"I don't know if you realize it, but you just insulted not only Heather but also me, since I purchased this car and drive it every day. And, to answer your question, we're driving separately. She has a lot of stuff for the house and didn't think there'd be room for me and my suitcase in her car. And I don't mind. I find long drives relaxing, and I've downloaded an audiobook to listen to on my phone."

He held up both hands, palms out. "Sorry—really. I didn't mean to be offensive, and I apologize. I hope you have a good and relaxing time. You deserve it."

Mollified, Merilee thanked him, then started the car.

"Just in case I don't see you beforehand, what time should I pick you up for the gala?"

"I don't know—I'll have to ask Heather since she might need me there early. I'll text you once I speak with her."

"Sounds good—have fun. Feel free to call me if you need anything."

"I'll be with Heather at her well-stocked house. I think I'll manage."

"Yeah, well, just in case. Heather seems to attract drama." He held up his hands defensively. "I know—sorry. Heather's your friend and it's none of my business."

"Exactly." She said good-bye again, then drove away from the house, trying to decipher what he meant by Heather attracting drama.

Merilee headed south through and past Atlanta and had just taken the exit to I-16 east toward Savannah when her phone rang, Heather's name displayed on the screen. She hit answer, then raised the volume so she could listen to it on speaker.

"Hi, Heather. Are you there yet? I'm making good time and should be there in about two and a half hours."

There was a brief pause, and then: "Actually, there's a problem. And I apologize for waiting so late to call you, but I was hoping I'd be able to still come. But it's just impossible."

A horn blared from behind her and Merilee realized that she'd braked suddenly. She waved an apology and returned her foot to the accelerator. "You can't come?"

"I am so, so sorry. Brooke woke up this morning with a fever, and I kept expecting it to go away, but it hasn't. It's not so high that it's worrying, and I don't think she needs to go to the pediatrician—yet— but she's just miserable and all she wants is her mommy. You know how that is. I'd still consider going if Dan were here—he's so good with the girls—but he left yesterday for his fishing cabin on Lake Murray and I'd hate to make him come home. I'm sure you understand."

Merilee was already looking ahead for the next exit, to turn around. "Of course I do. I know how helpless it feels when one of your kids is sick. Michael has the kids all weekend, so I'll just hang around my house enjoying the peace and quiet . . ."

"Oh, don't be ridiculous. You can still go—I *want* you to go. Trust me, enjoying the peace and quiet at the beach is a lot more fun than staying at home. I've had my property manager stock the fridge and wine cellar—and there's even champagne chilling in the fridge. And orange juice. I remember how much you enjoyed our mimosas."

Merilee murmured an assent, remembering how easily the champagne had affected her judgment.

"I've already remotely reset the alarm code to one-one-one-one—see, I remembered!—so you won't have to use a single brain cell when you're there. And I had the property manager leave the front door key under the mat. I know that's stupid, but it's just for today, and besides, I have an alarm."

"Oh, I do the same thing—except I put our key under the flower-pot. I think that it's so overused and obvious that burglars today don't bother to look there anymore."

Heather laughed, something about it triggering that same unreachable memory again. "See? I knew we had a lot in common! Anyway, I know you're driving, so I'll text the steps on how to work the alarm so you'll have it with you later and don't have to remember anything or write it down."

"I feel so bad staying in your house without you. If Brooke is better tomorrow, will you come down? You need a break, too. Seriously, I don't know how you do all you do."

Heather laughed again, and Merilee bit down on the inside of her cheek, trying to remember why the sound made her wince. "I will—but don't worry. If I end up staying home with Brooke, I promise to not get out of my pj's, all right?"

"Deal. And thanks, Heather. I really can't tell you how much I appreciate this."

"Don't give it another thought—just enjoy yourself."

Merilee hung up, feeling disappointed but excited, too. It had been a very long time since she'd spent any time away by herself, without housework or errands or kids or work to occupy her time—much less in a gorgeous oceanfront home. When Heather had given her the address to plug into her GPS, Merilee had out of curiosity searched for it on one of the real estate apps. The house was huge, and brand-new, with every amenity and upgrade—so different from her grandparents' cottage on Chatham Avenue, which had been built around the turn of the last century and was one of the few remaining beach resort cottages built along the back river and beach.

She was glad Heather's home was on the east side of the island and she wouldn't be passing the old house that held so many memories for her. Seeing a FOR SALE sign would have probably made her cry.

By the time Merilee reached the Islands Expressway, she'd opened all the minivan's windows and was listening to a classic rock station she'd found on the radio, the volume turned up embarrassingly high. She remembered from her fall breaks from school that October was the best time to be at Tybee—with most of the tourists gone, along with the pressing heat and humidity of summer. She sang along with Mick Jagger about getting no satisfaction, belting it out in a way that reminded her of Sugar singing in church.

When she passed Fourth Street the GPS told her to prepare to turn left. Merilee found her shoes on the floor of the car with her feet and slipped them back on as she lowered the volume on the stereo and looked for her turn. Right past Sixth Street she turned left toward the ocean and onto a cement-and-brick driveway.

She knew what to expect from the photos online. But when she stepped out of the car and heard the ocean and smelled the salt and sea island air, she knew she'd found her way back home. Even without her grandparents, the wild scent of this place would always calm her soul and bring her back to the once-happy little girl she'd been a long, long time ago.

Quickly sliding out her suitcase and locking the minivan, she headed up the wide stone steps to the wood-and-leaded-glass front doors. She knew there was an elevator in the garage she could have used for her luggage, but she was so used to doing everything herself that it didn't occur to her to use the elevator until she'd already reached the top step.

Lifting the mat, she found the key, then studied the directions Heather had texted her before disarming the security alarm. She stepped through the door into a huge great room and stood there for a few moments, taking in the tall ceilings and the sweeping staircase, the marble floors and the beautiful art on the walls. Leaving her suitcase, Merilee closed the doors and moved forward through the house to the wall of windows that overlooked a stone patio and, beyond that, the Atlantic Ocean. She opened a set of French doors and left them open, wanting the house to be filled with the salt-drenched air, which seemed to wrap her in its arms and tell her everything was going to be okay.

She explored the house, relieved that she didn't have to decide on a bedroom, because there were two master suites on the main floor, one just as luxurious and huge as the other, and both with French doors leading onto the balcony. She picked the one without the toiletries in the bathroom, assuming that was Heather and Dan's room.

Kicking off her shoes, she found the remote for the all-house stereo and plugged in her phone to stream Pandora before heading to the kitchen. She'd stopped being wowed and impressed by the time she'd entered the kitchen, because it was all too overwhelming. No detail or convenience had been spared, and the kitchen was so beautiful and welcoming that Merilee thought that if there was any kitchen that might convince her to enjoy cooking, this one might be it.

She opened the refrigerator and found it stocked with all sorts of goodies, including a fruit and cheese plate and the promised bottle of champagne and carton of orange juice. Feeling like a kid playing hooky from school, she hunted around the cabinets before she found a glass pitcher and made mimosas, going heavy on the champagne. She wasn't driving anywhere, nor did she have to be a good example for her children, so she was going to enjoy herself.

After closing all the doors and resetting the alarm, knowing she probably wouldn't remember to do it after the mimosas, she found the media room with the large screen upstairs. She settled herself into one of the relaxing plush leather chairs, the pitcher on one side and the cheese and fruit on the other, and proceeded to binge watch a sappy romance DVD Heather had conveniently included in her collection— lasting almost to the end before she couldn't take it anymore.

Unsteady on her feet, Merilee returned the remnants of the food back to the fridge and, because there was only a tiny bit left in the pitcher, finished the rest of the mimosas without bothering to use her glass. She left both in the sink, planning to wash them in the morning and not trusting herself to hold on to anything right now without dropping it.

Feeling inordinately pleased with herself and happy with the world in general, she retired to her suite, forgetting her suitcase in the hall and, being too tired to retrieve it or her pajamas, stripped down to her bra and underwear before crawling into the ridiculously high-thread-count sheets. Leaving the curtains open despite the convenient button located by the side of the bed, she fell into an alcohol-induced sleep, looking forward to being awakened by a Tybee sunrise.

Something loud and blaring was interrupting her sleep. She didn't remember setting a wake-up alarm—she didn't remember much of anything except drinking an entire pitcher of mimosas—and thought if she could just ignore it, it would eventually stop. But it didn't. After opening her eyes briefly before tightly shutting them again, she burrowed her head under the pillow, ignoring the chalky feel of her mouth and the fact that there was no light coming in from the windows. Either it was still the middle of the night, or she'd somehow pushed the button for the curtains and closed them.

But somewhere through the pulsing alarm, there was a thud, and then a door slamming. Merilee sat up, the room swimming around her, and it occurred to her that she was still very, very drunk.

Maybe Heather had come after all, and Merilee had a coherent thought about dirty dishes being left in the sink. And then she had the stray thought that Heather must have forgotten the alarm code because she'd changed it to something Merilee could remember. Except at that exact moment, she couldn't.

She slid from the tall bed and padded barefoot across the wood floor of the bedroom, running into a dresser and a wall before she found the bedroom door. Opening it, she stood in the doorway for a moment, trying to remember the floor plan of the house. And where a light switch might be.

The screaming siren sound was louder in here, the marble floors scooping up the sound and throwing it back in her face and into her ears and pounding head. She slapped her hands over her ears, trying to make it stop, then lowered them again. *The alarm.* Had she set it incorrectly? She did remember closing the doors and heading to the alarm panel to reset it, but had she actually done it? Or did she not close a door completely and an ocean breeze blew it open? She recalled up-ending the mimosa pitcher for the last drop and wished that she hadn't. Maybe then she'd have more of her brain to work with.

"Heather?" she started to say, but it came out as a burp. Why wasn't Heather turning off the alarm? *And where is the damn door?* She stumbled forward, going where there was a red pulsing light across the room. It had to be the alarm panel. And if it wasn't, she'd find a phone and call someone. If only she remembered where her phone was. A phone began to ring somewhere, but she was pretty sure it wasn't hers, just as sure that she wouldn't be able to find it if she couldn't find a light switch.

She was slowly making her way across the great room toward the flashing red light, her arm stretched out in front of her, when some-thing hit her hard against the entire side of her body, throwing her sideways against what felt like the large sofa she'd seen earlier, its back facing the front door.

The air flew from her lungs as her body landed; then, just as quickly, whatever it was that had hit her lifted off her and backed away. She slid from the edge of the sofa and onto a plush rug, the room still spin-ning as every single bone in her body screamed, somehow obliterating her need to feel fear.

"Heather?" she managed, tasting blood on her cracked lips.

"What the . . . ?" It was a man's voice, but it was a familiar one. "Where's the damned light switch?" The man moved away from her, followed by the sound of a lamp crashing to the ground, and then a moment later the overhead spotlights and chandelier sprang to life, illuminating with brilliant clarity her lying on the ground next to the sofa, the remains of a crystal lamp lying scattered nearby. And some-where, a phone continued to ring.

"Merilee?"

It was Dan.

"Oh, my God. Are you all right? Don't move—let me make sure you don't have any serious injuries . . ."

But she was already struggling to sit up, moving each limb to make sure she could. "I'm fine. Just bruised a bit from the fall." Or maybe both arms and legs were broken but the alcohol was blocking her pain. She blinked up at him. "What are you doing here? Is Heather with you?" She was embarrassed to hear her words slurring together.

"No. I'm assuming she's at home, where she said she'd be."

Merilee pressed her hands against her ears again. "Can you shut that off? I think my head might explode."

"I tried—but the code's been changed."

She leaned her head against the sofa, trying to stop the pounding. "It's one-one-one-one. Heather changed it for me." She wanted to smile at her ability to remember but was afraid she might look like a lunatic.

He left her to go to the alarm panel as she closed her eyes, then immediately popped them open, not liking the way the room rocked. After a few seconds the house was blessedly silent—even the distant phone had stopped ringing. "Thank you," she murmured.

Dan squatted down next to her. "Are you sure you're all right? Did you hit your head? I don't see any blood."

"No. Thankfully, the sofa broke my fall. I think I'm just stunned. And a little drunk."

He nodded, keeping his eyes focused above her neck. "I've been trying to reach Heather but haven't had any luck. Neither has the security company." He blinked at her, as if he thought she was a mirage. "What are you doing here?"

"Heather invited me for the weekend, and then Brooke got sick and she had to cancel."

"Brooke's sick? Heather didn't tell me."

Merilee pulled herself closer to the sofa, afraid to stand just in case she couldn't, and searched for whatever sobriety she had left. The fall had at least shaken her awake. Dan was examining her head and looking into her eyes—to check for a concussion, she assumed—but his examination ended there.

"Brooke's fine—just a little fever, but she was asking for her mom. And Heather didn't want to bother you." It was her turn to blink at him. "So why are you here?"

"The security company received a remote emergency call and they couldn't identify the phone number or caller, so they called Heather to verify. When she didn't answer, they called me. Heather insisted on getting me a satellite phone at the fishing cabin for emergencies, and I guess she gave them the number. Anyway, I had no idea what they were talking about, so then I asked them if they could see if there'd been any activity in the house and they said it appeared that both the front and back doors had been opened but the alarm wasn't going off."

Merilee groaned, rubbing her hands over her face as if that might help her think more clearly. "That was me. I opened up all the French doors as soon as I walked in. But I know I disarmed the alarm correctly because it gave me the green light and no alarms sounded."

"You did it correctly—no alarm was going off until I got here and punched in what I thought was the right code. But when I first got the call, I just assumed we'd forgotten to set the alarm last time we left and the wind had blown open some of the doors, which would account for the activity and for the lack of an alarm sounding. Being on the ocean and having two little girls who don't always remember to latch the doors means it happens a lot."

He smiled and Merilee wondered why he'd only look at her face or around the room, and why he hadn't offered to help her up. Which was fine, because her head had finally steadied itself and she wasn't sure how it would do at another elevation.

"Anyway," he continued, "I'm only an hour away, so I told the security company I would check it out and not to call the police yet. The alarm wasn't going off, so I didn't have to worry about annoying the neighbors, so I figured I had time to get here, close everything up securely, reset the alarm, and get back to my cabin."

In the distance, the distinct sound of a police siren began to wail. Their eyes met in mutual understanding. "Damn it!" Dan quickly stood. "The alarm! The security company always calls here first when the alarm sounds. Did you hear a phone? That was probably them calling to see if everything's okay before they call the police."

"Oh, no," Merilee said, rolling onto her front so she could use both hands to hoist herself up. She took a few tentative steps toward the front door, relieved to see that she still could. "I heard it but didn't . . ."

She stopped, aware of two things at once: The first thing was that the sound of sirens was directly outside and she could see through the front-door windows two men climbing the front steps, silhouetted against the bright lights of their cruiser. The second thing was that she was standing there wearing only her bra and panties when Dan opened the door to greet the two officers. Behind them was a middle-aged woman wearing a bathrobe and slippers, her look of annoyance at being awakened at whatever hour of the night it might be changing to one of surprise once it alighted on Merilee. She looked vaguely familiar, and Merilee prayed she wasn't from the school. But they'd definitely met before.

"Daniel?" the woman asked.

Merilee immediately grabbed two throw pillows from the sofa and held them in front of her, belatedly realizing that she most likely appeared nude from the visitors' point of view.

"I'm sorry, Officers," Dan began as he fished his wallet from his back pocket. "There's been a mistake. The alarm code got changed and I wasn't aware, so I set it off accidentally—and I was distracted and didn't hear the phone ringing, nor did I think to call the security company to tell them you weren't needed."

He held out his ID and one of the officers inspected it. "Thank you, Dr. Blackford." He turned to Merilee. "Mrs. Blackford?"

"Oh, no. I'm not his wife . . ." And then she stopped, realizing her mistake before the last word was uttered.

"Are you . . . all right?"

Dan must have seen Merilee's look of acute embarrassment as she registered what the police—and the familiar-looking woman—thought they were seeing.

"Yes, of course. I'm fine." She spoke slowly so her words wouldn't bump into one another. "I'm his wife's friend." And then she stopped talking altogether, realizing she couldn't make it right now, no matter how hard she might try.

One of the officers turned toward Dan. "This is the eighth false alarm we've had from this residence so far this year, sir."

"I know. And I'm sorry. I'll have the door latches fixed and I'll straighten everything out with the security company so they have my emergency number to call from now on."

"You do that. Good night, sir." He faced Merilee and she wondered if it was a trick of the light that appeared to make him smirk. "Ma'am."

The woman in the bathrobe attempted to move forward but was effectively blocked by the two officers. "Daniel, is there anything I can do? I'm just next door if you need me."

He said nothing, just closed the doors and leaned his forehead against them. "I am so sorry . . ."

Dropping the pillows, Merilee ran to her room and shut the door, wondering if she could live in that room for the rest of her life.

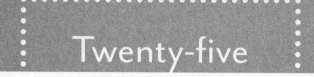

Twenty-five

Installment #8: Friendship: The Ties That Bind. And Strangle.

I have noticed how few grown children live near their parents anymore. Especially in the great suburban cities like Atlanta, where there are so many jobs and things to do for young people that it draws them like a spider to its web.

I'm not saying this is a bad thing—it's wonderful that our cities can offer so much. But I think it's the extended families that pay the price. There are a lot of grandchildren being raised who never get to know their grandparents and vice versa. And there's so much to be learned from both generations.

Skype and FaceTime are wonderful inventions because they're better than a phone call and it's the next best thing to seeing your loved one in person. It strengthens the connection between separated family members. But there's still a void to be filled in our lives, and most of us are able to do that with friendships.

Friends are the ones we turn to in a pinch when we need a babysitter, or advice, or an exercise partner. Even someone who will accompany us to the doctor and hold our hand. Friendships can be golden. They can also be toxic. And it's not always clear who's who until a bomb explodes and the dust clears.

But let's not confuse real friends with Facebook friends. With few exceptions that I've noticed, Facebook friendships seem to be about one-upmanship, more than most of us have seen since elementary school. And about the illusion of having lots of friends. Sure, posting photos of you having a wonderful time is a great way to get back at an ex, but be careful. Everything always comes back around. It's one of life's guarantees, for which those of us who've been maligned in this life are eternally grateful.

Speaking of friends, the local coffee shop is abuzz with gossip about an incident that occurred over the long weekend between friends. It appears to be a huge misunderstanding, but it's not clear as to who the wronged party is. According to popular gossip, the winner of the "wronged" designation had an incredible arrangement of flowers delivered to the friend who'd allegedly wronged her.

I won't say that I'm siding with one or the other, or even claim to have insider knowledge of what actually transpired at a beach house along the Georgia coast. All I know is that there's more here than meets the eye, and one should look further into a person's character and get to know her before making assumptions.

I read something on the Internet the other day about how women who have close friendships live longer than those who don't. I think it should be added that the quality of the friendships makes the difference. See above my comment about toxic friendships. In this same article, it gave the definition of what the difference was between a good friend and a best friend. Apparently, a good friend helps you bury a body. A best friend brings their own shovel and doesn't ask questions.

And now on to our Southern saying: "You can put your boots in the oven, but that don't make 'em biscuits." As I mentioned in a previous blog, it's gala season here in our neck of the woods. Don't try getting an appointment at your local hair or nail salon near the end of the month, because they are plumb full. You might have to go to another county if you're desperate and can't manage on your own.

I was at my local dry cleaner's the other day and a mother whom I shall not name but could was pitching a hissy fit with a tail on it because the poor man had not steamed the pleats in her evening gown the exact way she'd wanted and had apparently explained to him previously in excruciating detail. A rack of dry cleaning was between us, so she didn't see me, but I'm quite sure if she had, she wouldn't have wanted a witness to her bad behavior and would have ended her tirade.

Because that's how you can tell the true character of a person. See how they speak and behave toward those who work on the other side of the counter and vacuum their rugs. A woman who can scream at a dry cleaner, then turn around and act like a person of good character and smile at all of her acquaintances and even nod to strangers in church is not a good person. And those boots she just stuck in her oven will never be biscuits, either.

SUGAR

Sugar sat at the table in Merilee's kitchen, wondering once again how she'd found herself there. Knowing it was Merilee's day off and that this was when Merilee usually ran her errands, Sugar had walked down the drive to ask Merilee to take her to the grocery store. However, instead of being a quick visit ending with them both piling into the minivan, Sugar's trip had ended with Merilee answering the door with puffy eyes and reddened nose and explaining the problem without Sugar professing any interest in knowing. Which wasn't necessarily true, but it irked her that Merilee would assume she cared.

Merilee had read the blog post aloud—twice—then closed the lid of her small computer before looking across the kitchen table. "Everyone knows—or thinks they know—what happened. But they don't. I promise you, Sugar, there was nothing going on. It was exactly as I told you and anyone else who asked. It just sounds like a complete lie. And just my luck that the middle school secretary has a family beach house next door to the Blackfords'. I don't think I can leave my house again. Ever."

"Well, you're going to have to because I need to get to Kroger and I'm not driving that death trap of a car Wade found for me."

Merilee blinked at her through puffy eyes. "It's a Camry, Sugar. One of the safest cars around."

"Humph. I don't drive foreign cars; he should know that. And it's so small I feel like I'm going to get crushed like a bug by all those huge trucks you mothers are driving these days."

Merilee closed her eyes, and Sugar noticed how pale she was, and the dark circles under her eyes, which were more pronounced than usual. "This is not about you, Sugar. My whole life was turned around and inside out and I ended up here. I was lonelier than I'd been in a very long time, yet I was finally starting to make real friends and get involved again. And now . . ."

Sugar waited for Merilee to open her eyes before delivering the look she'd once reserved for her older brothers, or for the town council when she'd been mayor. The look that gave her the power to believe that she was stronger and braver than she probably was. "It's not all about you, either, Merilee. Do you think you're the only woman who's ever had to live a life she hadn't planned on? Or even wanted? Life is a hard business; we both know that. Sometimes you're the bug, and sometimes you're the windshield, and that will never change, no matter how old you get."

Merilee's face had paled and then flushed pink with anger. And then, to Sugar's surprise, fat teardrops sprang from the corners of Merilee's eyes. "I suppose I deserved that."

"Yes, you did. And I'll be danged if I'm just going to sit here and watch you feel sorry for yourself instead of getting back up on that horse. Don't ask me what horse—it's the horse you've been riding on ever since your divorce, afraid to fall off. Well, now you have. It's not a sin to fall, you know. It's only a sin if you never get back up."

"I can't pretend this didn't happen. Somebody put it in a blog, for crying out loud."

"There are worse things in life." Sugar regarded her steadily and Merilee had the good sense to look contrite. Sugar continued. "Regardless, I believe the whole point of the blog was to urge people to learn the facts first before gossiping with half-truths. Whoever wrote that blog is on your side. And Heather did apologize, admitting—at least to you—that you were the wronged party." Sugar frowned, looking at the enormous bouquet on the kitchen counter that had been delivered to Merilee with a handwritten note of apology from Heather.

"But I'm not you," Merilee said. "I still claim to have a heart. I can't just brush myself off and carry on like nothing's happened."

Whether or not Merilee had intended it, those words struck Sugar hard. She took a deep breath and straightened her back, listening as it popped in protest. "You and I and your real friends know that you did nothing wrong. Just like everybody knows that I have no business driving a little car. So pull up your big-girl panties and let's go to the store. I'm out of sugar and if you force me to drink this dishwater one more time, I'll complain to someone about elder abuse." She slid her iced tea glass across the table toward Merilee.

Merilee was in the middle of sipping her tea and choked on a laugh, a few drops running down her chin. "Did you really just say that?"

Having succeeded in lightening Merilee's mood, Sugar leaned heavily on the table and stood. Picking up her pocketbook, she hung it over her forearm and walked to the front door, peering through the screen. "Speak of the devil," she said under her breath as Merilee joined her at the door.

A shiny halo of blond hair appeared over the steering wheel of a familiar black SUV—foreign, of course—the various country club and neighborhood gate stickers plastered in a row on the side of the windshield. It would be convenient to have those as an easy reference just in case a person ever forgot where they lived.

"I wonder why she's here," Merilee said.

Knowing how Heather liked to hear herself talk, Sugar found her way to one of the front room chairs to wait. "Whatever it is, make sure you let her know that you're madder than a wet hen about what happened."

Merilee looked at her with surprise. "I'm not . . ." She stopped, the crease that had formed between her brows not disappearing as she turned to face Heather. She stepped back to open the door as Heather reached her, crossing the threshold with a long garment bag.

"Hello, Sugar," Heather said sweetly. "Always nice to see you." She smiled brightly, making something curl in the pit of Sugar's stomach.

Sugar grimaced in response.

Heather then turned to Merilee and opened her mouth to speak, but Merilee cut her off. "I want you to know that I'm still madder than . . . uh, very upset about what happened. Mostly because it could so easily have been avoided if you'd just communicated with Daniel. Or anyone, really. Even your beach house neighbor, Rachel Evans. Something so easy as a phone call would have made a world of difference."

Heather's shoulders sagged, although she was careful not to let the garment bag sag, too. Instead, she moved forward and placed it carefully across the sofa before turning to Merilee. "I know, I know, I know. I have been beating myself up about it ever since it happened. There's just been so much going on with the gala and all, and with Brooke being sick I let some of the details fall through the cracks. And I have made a vow to myself to never let my cell phone out of my sight so that I am reachable twenty-four/seven. Especially on days when I've given both Claire and Patricia time off. I can't tell you how awful I feel."

Heather began to tear up and Merilee hastily grabbed a box of Kleenex off the counter and thrust it at her. If Sugar could move a little quicker, she'd whip the used tissue from Heather's hand and analyze it for actual moisture. She wondered for a moment if, with all the scientific advances these days, they'd developed a test for crocodile tears.

"I really am sorry," Heather said, embracing Merilee in a bear hug. Completely unmoved, Sugar just stared at her.

Heather pulled away but kept her hands on Merilee's shoulders so she could look directly in her face. "All forgiven? We're still friends?"

Merilee nodded. "Of course. I am upset, but I do understand how these things happen."

Heather beamed. "Wonderful. We'll have to plan another girls' trip when Daniel is at home so we can go and have a truly relaxing trip. Deal?"

With a look of relief, Merilee said, "Deal."

Sugar just rolled her eyes.

Heather turned around and lifted the garment bag. "Want to see your surprise?"

"Is it my dress?"

Heather nodded enthusiastically as she began to unzip the bag from the top. "Yes. My dress was ready and when I got there they said yours was ready, too. If there are still alterations to be made, I'll be happy to run you up there for some adjustments."

She pulled the gown free from the bag and lifted up the hanger. "What do you think?"

The gown hardly looked real. It was something Ginger Rogers or Carole Lombard would have worn in one of the old black-and-white movies or to the Oscars. It was refined and elegant, with a kind of material Sugar had no words for.

"It's more beautiful than I remember," Merilee said, her hands over her mouth.

Heather looked more than pleased with herself, as if she alone held the strings to Merilee's happiness.

Sugar smiled. "It is lovely. Wade will have a hard time keeping his jaw off the floor, much less doing anything else but look at you. You might want to hire a driver."

Sugar was gratified to see Heather's smug look drop from her face. Finding her composure, Heather said, "I think everyone will find it hard to look anywhere else. She really does look stunning in it." She thrust the gown at Merilee. "Here—try it on."

Merilee took the gown but shook her head. "Not right now. I've been cleaning the house all morning, so I'm sweaty and need a shower, and I was about to take Sugar to Kroger."

Heather looked disappointed. "All right. But call me immediately if you need anything altered and we'll run it back to the shop." She pulled her phone out of her purse and held it up like a prize. "See? I have it with me, and it's not only fully charged, but it's turned on."

"Very impressive," said Sugar. "Which one of your assistants charged it, turned it on, and put it in your pocketbook?"

Ignoring her, Heather leaned over to hug Merilee again. "Thanks for being so understanding. And again, I'm so, so sorry."

"Apology accepted. In fact, it's already forgotten," Merilee said, and Sugar almost had to bite her tongue so she wouldn't shout out that she hadn't forgotten and she hadn't even been there. But only because she was afraid it would make Heather linger even longer, and Sugar had already waited so long that she needed to visit the ladies' room before they headed out to the store.

Merilee walked Heather to the door to say good-bye as Sugar slowly stood, then headed toward the back hallway to the bathroom. She'd almost reached it before she stopped, noticing the two framed maps hanging on the wall. She hadn't heard Merilee approach and jumped when she spoke.

"Wade hung them this morning. Thanks so much for letting me hang them both. It's amazing that he found the second one, isn't it?"

"Yes," Sugar said slowly. "Amazing."

"Did you know that your map had another half? I was thinking your daddy might have mentioned it to you when he gave it to you."

She shook her head. "No."

Merilee pointed to the clearing in the middle of the woods. "Wade and I can't figure out what this is. Any idea?"

She didn't speak right away. "Wade asked me the same thing, and I told him I didn't know."

"Because you don't know, or because you don't want to tell us?"

Without turning to look at her, Sugar said, "Because when he asked, I didn't want anyone to know. But now, I think I've changed my mind."

She did turn this time, and noticed her glasses were dirty, because there was a smudge in the middle of Merilee's cheek.

"What made you change your mind?"

"I'm old. I'm allowed." She paused, taking a deep breath. "It's the family cemetery. It's where I visit Jimmy and Mary. I just had the horrible thought that if something happened to me, nobody would know to go visit them. That nobody would care. So I want you and Wade to know."

Merilee touched her arm, then quickly withdrew, unsure of whether Sugar wanted the interaction. "Is that why you don't want to sell the land? Because of the cemetery? I'm pretty sure there would be ways to preserve it so that it remains the way it is, surrounded by the woods. I know several neighborhoods with an old cemetery tucked away off the beaten path . . ."

"No. That's not the reason." She excused herself and headed into the bathroom, letting the door snap shut behind her.

Twenty-six

MERILEE

"Daddy's here!" Colin's shout was followed by the thump of his overnight bag hitting the floor and then being dragged toward the front door. Although both children kept clothes and toothbrushes at their dad's house, Colin's stash of books went with him everywhere, along with the field glasses around his neck. He'd wear them in the shower and to school, too, if he were allowed.

Merilee finished clasping the faux drop-diamond necklace Lindi had lent her, looking in the mirror behind her to where Lily sat watching, apparently impervious to the news that her father had arrived to pick up her and Colin for the weekend.

"You look beautiful, Mommy," she said, her voice filled with awe, her use of the word "Mommy"—something she hadn't called her since around first grade—making Merilee smile.

"Thank you, sweetheart." She turned around to kiss Lily on the forehead, but Lily held her arm out, stopping her.

"You don't want to mess up your lipstick." She slid from the bed, picked up the lipstick tube from the dresser, and dropped it in the tiny black velvet evening bag—also on loan from Lindi. "Don't forget to reapply after you eat or drink something."

Merilee gave her daughter a questioning look. "How do you know so much about lipstick?"

"Bailey. She's not allowed to wear anything more than lip gloss now, but her mother wants her to know the proper way to wear makeup so she doesn't look like a clown when she's allowed to wear it the first time."

"Ah. I guess that makes sense. In an odd, never-would-have-thought-about-that kind of way, but it works." She winked at Lily, making her giggle.

"And Miss Sugar's here, too," Colin called out.

Merilee glanced nervously at the door. "Better go intervene before a fistfight breaks out. I have no idea why she has taken such a dislike to your father."

"She doesn't like most people," Lily said as she pulled open the bedroom door. "She says she finds most of them a vexation to her spirit—that wasn't a vocabulary word, but I looked it up and it means annoying."

"Does she, now?"

"Uh-huh. But she says there are a few exceptions. Like Colin and me. Dr. Blackford and you and her friend Willa Faye and Mr. Kimball."

As Merilee walked down the short hallway, her long silky skirt swishing around her ankles and her incredibly high and sexy shoes tapping on the wood floor, she found herself feeling secretly pleased that Sugar Prescott found her to be one of the few people she didn't find to be a vexation to her spirit.

She found Sugar and Michael facing off in the front room, Colin wearing a fight-or-flight expression. "Colin, why don't you go put some of those cookies we made last night into baggies for you and Lily to take to your dad's? And don't forget to share with Dad and Tammy."

She wondered why she'd added this last. Good manners had something to do with it, but she also didn't think a few extra pounds on Tammy's young—and pregnant—body would be amiss.

"Wow." Michael was looking at her, his mouth slightly ajar.

"You like it?" she asked, giving a twirl because she loved the way her skirt billowed when she did, the light changing the color of the fabric as it moved. "It's just something I found in my closet."

"I bet," he said. "I don't remember anything like *that* in your closet."

"Yes, well, maybe you didn't look close enough."

She hadn't meant it to sound so confrontational but wasn't upset that it had. She was feeling more confident—most likely due to the time she'd spent at the hair and nail salon with Lindi and Sharlene. They'd even taken her to the Lancôme counter at Belk's, where a lovely lady named Lupina had done her makeup and shown her how to do it herself. It had been years since she'd spent that much on makeup, but when she'd looked in the mirror, she knew it was worth it.

"You look beautiful, Merilee," Michael said, and she knew he meant it. She stared at him for a long moment, wanting to see regret, to see him recognize what he'd had all along and hadn't appreciated. To have him ask her to come back and admit he'd made a horrible mistake. But he didn't, and she was glad. The thought surprised her. But in that brief moment of clarity she'd realized that she didn't want him back. It was as if she'd suddenly understood that during her marriage she'd never exceeded his expectations of her. She took full blame, knowing she'd been the one to set the bar so low. But a marriage had to be more than a simple safety net below a tightrope life. All it had taken was distance and time to realize it.

Something had changed in the last few months. A shifting of perspective. She wouldn't go so far as to say that she was stronger and braver, but she was different. Maybe that was the good that could come from divorce.

"I hope those are sitting-down shoes you're wearing with that standing-up dress," Sugar said, eyeing Merilee's gown over the tops of her glasses. "You'll need a walking stick by the end of the night if they're not."

"Thanks, Sugar. No need to worry. Heather's providing a bin of flip-flops for those of us who might need to change for dancing."

"How nice of her. I suppose she would know about feet. She's spent so many years in those high heels that her feet look like they've been caught in a wheat thresher. Bless her heart."

"Can we wait until Mr. Kimball gets here to pick you up?" Lily asked.

"No," Sugar and Michael replied in unison, the only thing Merilee could ever imagine them agreeing on.

"Let's not keep Daddy waiting," Merilee said. "I know there will be lots of pictures taken so you can see us all dressed up and earning money for your school."

"Y'all ready?" Michael asked, shouldering Colin's hefty bag. "Say good-bye to your mother."

"Don't touch her dress," Lily shouted, pulling on Colin's arm mid-run. "And she can only blow you a kiss."

Colin looked at his sister as if she'd lost her mind. "She's my mom, too."

Merilee squatted in front of her children and blew them both kisses, then gave them gentle squeezes on their shoulders. "There—that should preserve my dress and makeup and last until I see you Sunday, and I'll give you extra hugs and kisses to make up for these. All right?"

Colin grinned and nodded and Lily let go of his arm. Merilee stood, not an easy feat considering her four-inch heels. "Y'all behave, all right?"

"Yes, ma'am," Colin said.

Lily frowned. "It's not like we can misbehave in front of Miss Garv—I mean Tammy. I still think she's my teacher."

Michael raised his eyebrows, then ushered them both toward the door. "Good-bye, Merilee. Have fun tonight."

She smiled. "I will. Thanks."

He turned to Sugar. "Good night, Miss Sugar. Always a pleasure."

"Humph," she said before turning toward the children with a wide smile. "Let me know if you see any new birds, Colin. Most of the migrating birds should be here by now. And when you get back, I think it will be time to make us some pumpkin bread."

"Yay," they shouted as they rushed to Sugar and gave her hugs while she pretended to be annoyed and pushed slightly off-balance by their exuberance.

When they were gone, Sugar turned to Merilee with an appraising eye. "I suppose that beats those yoga pants you usually wear on weekends." She studied Merilee's ears, where she'd put in the tiny diamond stud earrings that Michael had given her when they were still dating. They were the only sparkly earrings she owned.

"I brought these on the hunch that you didn't have anything appropriate to wear." She opened her palm. "It seems I was right."

Merilee looked down at Sugar's outstretched hand. A pair of large clip-on earrings in the shape of starbursts and encrusted with tiny sparkling clear stones winked up at her. "They're beautiful," she said, her hand reaching for them, then drawing back, afraid she'd misunderstood Sugar's intentions.

"They're costume, but good costume. They were made back when people still cared about quality and workmanship. Willa Faye and her mother bought these at Rich's department store in downtown Atlanta for me to wear on my wedding day. I figured they weren't much use sitting in my jewelry box, so you might as well wear them."

"I'd hug you if I weren't wearing this dress."

Sugar simply looked at her. "Well, are you going to try them on?"

Merilee was already pulling out the studs from her ears and placing them on an end table by the sofa. Then she carefully took the earrings from Sugar's palm and stood in front of the small hall table by the door and snapped them in place. Moving her head from side to side to admire the effect, she smiled. "I think these might be the most beautiful earrings I've ever seen. And I work in a jewelry store, so that says a lot." She faced Sugar. "I don't know how I can ever thank you enough."

"You can start by not losing them."

Merilee studied Sugar, seeing the young bride with the sparkling earrings on her wedding day, how happy she'd looked in the photo. And tried not to think of all that had happened since to change her. "That night—after you got married and Tom drove you home and you saw smoke in the chimney of the old farmhouse. Did you ever find out who it was?"

They both turned toward the door at the sound of another car pulling up. "That must be Wade," Sugar said, and Merilee wondered if that was relief she saw in the old woman's face.

Merilee felt that zing that was becoming much too familiar start in her toes and shoot its way to her brain before turning around and zipping back through her body. If she didn't know any better, she would have thought she might be having a hot flash.

Because she was standing near the door, she opened it before Wade could knock.

"Well," he said, eyeing her appreciatively. "Who'd have thought you could clean up so nice?"

"Thank you, Wade," she said, moving back so he could enter. "I think."

He smiled down at her. "Maybe I should try that again. Hello, Merilee. I do say that you look good enough to eat."

The zinging was now bouncing between them like a rubber ball, and she wondered if they turned off the lights if it would leave an electric trail.

"You don't look so bad yourself," Merilee said, her voice unexpectedly husky as she admired his broad shoulders and long limbs inside his black tuxedo.

"Do I need to chaperone you two or can I go home now and watch my shows?" Sugar interjected.

Merilee stepped back, wondering why she was so out of breath. "I think I'm safe with Wade, but thank you, Sugar. May we drive you back since we're heading that way?"

Sugar frowned. "Only because you need something for your shoulders besides that old wool coat that's two sizes too big for you and I happen to have an evening wrap. Otherwise I'm afraid you're going to get new-monia and old-monia before the night is through."

She headed outside, followed by Merilee and Wade, who took Merilee's key and locked the door behind them. "I have no idea why I'm doing this, since all anybody needs to do to get inside is look under the flowerpot."

"Wrong," Merilee said. "I've moved it to beneath the front mat."

"That makes me feel so much better," he said, placing his tuxedo jacket around her shoulders. "Don't want you to catch old-monia," he said, and they both shared a giggle that earned them a glare from Sugar.

Merilee stopped short in the drive, staring at a sporty Audi sedan. "Where's your truck?"

"That's for business. This is for pleasure." He sent her an evil grin.

"I just hope none of my friends see me driving around in this foreign show-off car," Sugar said as she waited for Wade to open the passenger door.

"Since we're just going to your house, I don't think that will be a problem, Sugar," Wade said. "But I must say you look mighty sexy sitting in the front seat."

"Harrumph," was all Sugar said in reply.

Wade caught Merilee's gaze in the rearview mirror. "Remember my friend Bill West? You met him when you came to my construction site."

Merilee kept her face passive. "Of course. Your friend with the grandparents from Sandersville."

"That's right. He says he thinks he knows why we both find you look familiar."

"Really?" She was glad she was sitting in the backseat, where she could hide in the shadows.

"Yeah. He thinks you were in the news or something some time ago. Like your picture was in the papers a lot. Bill thought maybe you won a beauty pageant or something."

"No. I've never won a beauty pageant."

She felt him watching her, so she smiled and let her gaze slide away.

They'd reached Sugar's porch and Wade opened both her door and Sugar's, then led Sugar inside to retrieve the wrap. Merilee closed the back door, then waited for him to return, welcoming the frigid air as she breathed it into her lungs, then exhaled in white puffs. By the time Wade got back to the car, Merilee's equilibrium had returned and she'd made a promise to herself that she'd forget about everything and just enjoy herself tonight.

Although Sugar's mink wrap smelled vaguely of mothballs, Merilee was glad for its warmth and for the fact that the head and paws were no longer attached. Sitting back in the plush leather seat, she allowed herself to truly relax for the first time since that awful night at the Tybee beach house.

On the way up to the Blackfords' Lake Lanier house, Wade drove them through downtown Sweet Apple, where scarecrows sporting different themes—provided by local schools and businesses—were attached to all the lampposts lining the road, giving Main Street a festive fall air and filling Merilee with a sense of contentment and possibility. She turned her head toward Wade. "I hope you don't mind getting there a little early. Heather said I didn't need to, that she had plenty of people to help, but I just want to make sure that all the auction bidding forms are filled out accurately and everything's in place."

"Not a problem. Although with Heather in charge, I don't think you need to worry about everything not being perfect."

"True." She continued to look at him, admiring the way the streetlights traveled across the strong planes of his face, accentuating a shadow on his nose where he'd broken it playing football in high school. It did nothing to detract from his appearance. If asked, Merilee would probably say it only enhanced it. "I know you already said it wouldn't, but are you sure this won't be too awkward for you?"

"I wouldn't have said yes if I thought it would be. We're all adults now. Heather and I aren't the same people we were, and all those feelings we had are long gone. She's moved on, and so have I. Old history. Besides, it's a little too late to change my mind now, isn't it?"

"True," Merilee said, allowing herself a secret smile as she snuggled into the mink stole. Even the traffic jam on Highway 400 that took forty minutes to get through didn't faze her. After ten minutes, she stopped looking at her watch, enjoying the sense of having no cares or responsibilities for at least another half hour. She turned to Wade again. "The maps look great—thanks so much for the frames and for hanging them."

"You're welcome. And they do look nice there, don't they?" He frowned, studying the line of cars at a standstill in front of him. "I can't believe I didn't know about that cemetery until now—either from her or my grandmother. Sugar swears that's not the reason she won't sell the property, though."

"I think I understand. She's the last holdout. I respect that. If I'd lived here all my life and seen all these changes, I wouldn't want anything else to change, either—especially if I could control it."

Wade drummed his fingers against the steering wheel. "I'm pretty sure that's part of it. Except . . ."

"Except what?" Merilee asked, but she thought she knew. Thought she could hear the sound of running feet in the dark woods and the scent of pine straw filling her nostrils. She didn't know how much Sugar had told Wade about her past, and it wasn't Merilee's place to tell him.

"Except there's more to it. There was an old farm with a family cemetery on it near the Forsyth County line that used to belong to the Prescotts. When it was developed, they kept the cemetery there on the little hill and planted trees around it to protect it. Even Sugar said it didn't look half bad, which, as you know, is a huge compliment. So she knows it can be done and done well.

"And it's not even about not putting up another neighborhood—although Sugar doesn't hide how much she hates the idea, which probably has more to do with her hatred of developers than with preserving her land. But when we used to discuss it, she would get an almost feral gleam in her eye, so I stopped bringing it up, just for self-preservation. It just left me with a feeling that . . . there's something else."

Merilee settled back in her seat without saying anything, thinking of all the bad memories Sugar might have of the woods—of Dixie. And Curtis. But wouldn't that make her want to see them razed?

The traffic eased up and Wade maneuvered his car into the fast lane, and soon they were barreling down the highway. Merilee closed her eyes, enjoying the hum of the engine and the steady rumble of the road, determined to enjoy the evening and forget the past, despite all the warning bells sounding in her head telling her otherwise.

Twenty-seven

When Wade and Merilee reached the neighborhood at Lake La-nier, the line of valeted cars started long before they were near enough to see the house. They were immediately met by a young man dressed like a nineteenth-century butler, wearing a white tie and tails, who greeted them and happily took the key to Wade's car.

Wade leaned toward Merilee and whispered, "I feel underdressed."

Merilee whispered back, "Me, too. I somehow don't think a corset and hoop skirt would be out of place."

The decorating committee—its plans tightly guarded—had out-done themselves, as evidenced by the golf cart disguised as a carriage that quickly appeared to take them up to the house. Merilee was pretty confident that Heather had probably tried to get real horses and car-riages so it would be more authentic, but the logistics would have been impossible, even for her.

The theme music from *Gone with the Wind* played loudly on hidden outdoor speakers as their golf cart / carriage approached the front door and the line of people waiting to go up the front stairs. "Are you sure we're in the right place?" Wade asked. "Because that looks like a re-ceiving line at a wedding."

"No, we're definitely at the right place, and that's definitely a receiving line, because that's Heather greeting all the guests. I bet Dan is probably hiding somewhere."

"Can't say I'd blame him," Wade said as he helped her from the golf cart and guided her toward the stairs and the growing line of people.

When Heather spotted them, a look of sheer relief passed over her face and she beckoned them to cut the line. Excusing themselves, they rushed to join Heather.

"Thank goodness you're here," Heather said, seeming genuinely surprised and relieved and pressing her hand with the giant diamond ring against her heart, as if she'd truly believed Merilee would skip the gala on which she'd been working more hours over the last two months than she'd dedicated to her actual paying job.

"Of course we're here. I meant to get here earlier, but there was an accident on 400. Is everything all right?"

Heather smiled brightly. "It is now." Her face seemed flushed, and Merilee assumed it was from the space heaters placed strategically along the steps and the threshold of the house. Or maybe it was just the excitement of the night. "You look lovely," Heather said, taking in Merilee's dress and then kissing her on each cheek. "Except for that hideous stole." She wrinkled her nose. "Is that mothballs I smell?"

"You look beautiful, Heather," Wade said, interrupting before Merilee had to think of an appropriate response.

"Thank you," she said, smiling deeply, so that a hidden dimple appeared in her right cheek.

And she did, Merilee admitted to herself. Of course, Heather Blackford always looked gorgeous, and especially tonight, with her hair piled on top of her head, hidden crystals sparkling from the intricate curls, and the amazing column dress that hugged her perfect figure, the side gathered in elegant waves and clasped with a giant diamond brooch at her tiny waist.

Still, there was something missing. Nothing obvious, but . . . something. Merilee wondered if it could be the color of Heather's gown, which was a pale yellow, definitely a color made for blending in instead of standing out. Merilee had assumed Heather's gown would be red or fire orange, or something that would make her a beacon in a crowd of sparkling beautiful people. If Heather had wanted to find a gown in a color that would make her blend in unnoticed, then she'd found the perfect one. She wondered if Heather had simply not wanted to compete with the elaborate theme decorations for the party. Lindi had already warned her that they were over-the-top and to prepare herself.

"Where's Daniel?" Merilee asked.

Heather shook her head. "I sent him down to the wine cellar to bring up a few special bottles for our table, but that was a while ago. He's probably hiding." She grabbed Wade's arm and brought him to stand next to her. Addressing Merilee, she said, "Would you mind checking the wine cellar for me to see if he's still there? And if he is, please tell him he's neglecting his duties as host. Just be careful on those steps—you should probably take off your shoes. I'll just borrow Wade to fill in until Daniel returns, if you don't mind."

Wade shot Merilee an amused glance.

"Of course not," she said. "I'll be right back."

"One more thing," Heather said, indicating that Merilee should step closer. She leaned in to whisper in her ear. "Can you please hold on to this for me? It's too big and I don't want to lose it, and I have no place to put it right now." Merilee felt Heather tug on her hand and then place something against her palm before closing her fist over it. Heather stepped back. "And please put that stole somewhere—anywhere. I'm quite sure that's mothballs I'm smelling."

Wade raised his eyebrows at Merilee as she smiled and backed out of the receiving line on her mission to find Dan. After escaping the crowd on the front steps, she paused in the foyer that opened up into the great room. It had been transformed into a banquet hall that closely resembled the Twelve Oaks barbecue in one of the opening scenes of *Gone with the Wind*.

Long dark green velvet drapes with gold trim now hung from the floor-to-ceiling windows that lined the back of the room. Perfect replicas of live oak tree limbs festooned the walls, one of them even sporting a wooden rope swing dangling from it. A large screen had been hung on the wall, and the actual movie was playing, the sound off, but the theme song clearly audible from the speakers outside. It was the scene with Scarlett in her white dress and green sash sitting down surrounded by her suitors. Merilee looked away. She'd always hated the movie, mostly because her mother had been nicknamed Scarlett when she was younger. So much more meaningful than "Tallie," she'd always been happy to point out to Merilee.

All the furniture in the room had been removed and the doors to the large patio opened to double the size of the already-huge room, tall heaters placed liberally around the patio to make sure nobody got chilled. Round tables, elegantly set with china, sterling, and crystal, had been set up both outdoors and indoors, table numbers written in gold gilt perched at the top of centerpieces made of fluffy cotton bolls and magnolia leaves spray-painted gold. Auction paddles were placed strategically above each place setting for the live-auction portion of the evening.

Pushed against the perimeter of the room were smaller tables with the silent auction items Merilee had worked so hard to procure, including the diamond tennis bracelet donated by her employer. She was happy to see several people already milling about, placing bids on the lined forms. As soon as she'd found Dan, she'd go check on the bids to see how they were progressing and determine if she needed to encourage the waitstaff to be more liberal with the wine and cocktails that were currently being hawked on silver trays by butlers clad in white tails and ties.

Outside in the backyard, a white tent—its front designed to resemble the columned antebellum Greek Revival mansion of the movie, Tara—had been set up to house the band and the dance floor for the postauction entertainment.

Merilee headed toward where she remembered the stairs leading down were, assuming that was her best bet to take her to the wine cellar, but stopped when she became aware again that she held something in her hand. Opening her palm carefully, she found herself looking at the gorgeous pearl ring Dan had purchased for Heather for their anniversary.

It was as beautiful as she remembered, so exquisite. She wondered if Heather had liked it. Merilee opened her evening purse, but it barely fit her large phone, lipstick, and keys, and she was afraid if she shoved in the ring she might scratch it or damage it in some way.

She remembered how well it had fit at the store and, after just a brief hesitation, placed it on her finger. She allowed herself a moment to admire it, to wiggle her fingers to catch the light from the chandelier above, then went to find Dan. As she neared the top of the staircase leading down, she noticed several women coming out of a pair of double doors through which she could see a large bed and coats strewn on top of it. Unclasping the hooks at her neck, Merilee took off the stole and headed through the doors, smiling at the women as she passed them, aware as she did of how they immediately stopped talking.

A waitress was walking by with a silver tray of champagne flutes, and Merilee quickly took one and drained it as she walked into the bedroom. She tossed the stole on the bench at the foot of the bed and turned around to leave, but stopped for a moment, noticing her surroundings.

It was undoubtedly the master bedroom, the size of it about the same size as the cottage she lived in with her two children. On an end table sat a framed wedding photo of Dan and Heather, looking like a toothpaste commercial. They were standing on what appeared to be the front steps of a large home, enormous fluted columns directly behind them, two massive mahogany-stained doors standing out from behind the happy couple, with an elaborate fan window adorning the top and matching sidelights along the sides.

Merilee stared at the photo, something about it vaguely familiar. Had they been married nearby? Because she was sure she recognized those doors and columns. It wouldn't surprise her if she drove by the house every day and didn't notice it. She was always so busy going over her to-do lists in her head that she sometimes ended up in the parking lot at work with no idea how she'd gotten there.

She peered through an archway to what looked to be a sitting room with a rounded wall of windows, a gas fireplace in the middle. Oil portraits of both girls, painted when they were around three or four, were hung above the mantel, a smaller photograph of the entire family sitting in a frame on a small table next to a chaise longue. The Blackfords were almost a cliché of the perfect family, of two beautiful people who fell in love and had two beautiful children and then started an empire.

Merilee was glad her mother didn't know Heather, or about this party or this house or any of it. Because then she'd be comparing Merilee's life with Heather's and finding her daughter's lacking. Deanne wouldn't notice how far Merilee had come since the divorce, or how she didn't cry herself to sleep anymore. Because none of that mattered to Deanne.

She backed out of the room and found another waitress with champagne flutes, and replaced hers with a full one before heading down the back stairs. The basement level was similar to the one in the Blackfords' Sweet Apple house, with a wrought-iron railing on the open stairs leading downward. But these were spiral and more narrow, and Merilee was wearing four-inch heels and a gown that reached just below her ankles, not to mention having already downed a glass of champagne. Recalling Heather's advice, she bent down and unbuckled her shoes before slipping them off and leaving them in a corner of the top step. Gripping the railing tightly with one hand and clutching her champagne flute in the other, she proceeded to walk down the stairs without incident.

A dark shape bounded toward her from down the long and wide corridor, startling her for a moment until she recognized the Blackfords' dog. "Puddles," she said, hoping he wouldn't jump on her dress or make her spill her champagne. Just in case, she quickly finished the glass and placed it on a step behind her. "Hey, boy," she said, leaning forward to scratch behind his ears. "Where's your daddy?"

"In here," called Dan from somewhere down the hallway.

She began walking, noticing the theater room on one side, a game room with pool table and bar on the other, an exercise room with sauna tucked in between, and then, finally, an opened glass door with the stale scent of old cigar smoke coming from it. She poked her head inside and spotted Dan, his tuxedo jacket hanging from the back of the wooden chair he sat in.

He half rose when he spotted her. "Have a seat," he said, indicating the chair across the small table. An opened bottle of Glenfiddich sat in the middle, a half-empty glass sitting in front of him. "I came down to grab a few more bottles of wine for Heather, and I got distracted." He grinned. "This was Heather's anniversary gift. A ten-thousand-dollar bottle of scotch. Only the best for our Heather." He raised the glass and took a long sip. "Want to try some?"

"I, uh, don't usually drink scotch."

"But this isn't an ordinary scotch, Merilee. This is a ten-thousand-dollar bottle of scotch. If I could think clearly, I'd calculate how much each sip is worth and then I bet you'd be impressed. Have a seat."

She hesitated, knowing Heather was expecting her to bring Dan back to the receiving line right away. But there was something so forlorn in his expression, so lost and lonely, and so in need of companionship, that she decided to sit, if only for a few moments.

He stood quickly and walked behind the bar to retrieve another glass. "On the rocks?" he asked, placing two cubes from a freezer behind the bar into the glass without waiting for her answer. Sliding back into his seat, he poured three fingers' worth into the glass and placed it in front of her.

"Slainte," he said, raising his glass.

"Slainte," she repeated, clinking her glass against his. She meant to take a small sip, but the ice cubes shifted and she swallowed more than she'd intended, making her cough.

He smiled at her. "Don't spit it out or I'll fine you."

She laughed and took another sip to make him feel better, even though she was pretty sure she could drink a glass of Drano and not be able to tell the difference. She shivered in the damp coolness of the room, missing her stole, mothball scent and all. Dan stood and placed his tuxedo jacket over her shoulders before reclaiming his seat.

He noticed the ring on her finger as she placed it around her glass. "Did Heather give it to you?"

"No, of course not. She said it was too big for her—which surprises me because Gayla at the store said she'd checked Heather's file for her ring size before she wrapped it—but Heather said she was afraid she'd lose it. So she gave it to me to hang on to until she had a moment to put it somewhere safe." She began sliding it off her finger. "Here, why don't you take it . . ."

Dan held up his hand. "No. You should hang on to it. If Heather asked you to do something, you'd better not disobey."

She looked at him, not sure if he was joking or not, then slid the ring back on.

"Did she love it?" she asked.

Half of his mouth lifted. "I'm not sure. Probably not. She never likes anything I pick out for her. I tried to tell her why I'd selected it, but she was too busy making sure the flowers in the tall pots on the dock were just right. I probably should have waited until tomorrow."

Dan stared into his glass, moving it from side to side to watch the colors change in the light, reminding Merilee of the fabric of her dress. "Did you know our chef used to work at the French Laundry in Napa? I can't tell you what Heather did to entice her to come work for us, but nothing would surprise me. One of the chef's jobs is to oversee the menu at Windwood—did you know that? I wonder how many schools have a French Laundry chef planning their menus."

His words were slurring and she wondered how much he'd had to drink. As if reading her thoughts, he said, "Heather gave this to me earlier this afternoon because she probably knew I'd be needing it. She said I should hide it in the wine cellar so I wouldn't be expected to share." He grinned his boyish grin, and Merilee felt younger, somehow. Like they'd both been swept back in time to when they were young and nothing mattered except winning the next football game and sitting with your best friends in the lunchroom. But then his face sobered and he sat up straighter, and the moment passed.

"It's not that I'm antisocial or that I dislike any of those people upstairs. It's just . . ." He stopped for a moment before continuing. "It's just that I work hard all week, and when I'm done with work, I want to spend my downtime with my wife and kids. And dog." He looked down at Puddles and scratched him behind two velvety black ears. The dog reciprocated the look of adoration as he tilted his face toward Dan. "I love quiet time with my family, playing cards or fishing. Or just . . . nothing. Enjoying each other's company. Yet every moment of down-time is scheduled to the hilt. I can barely catch my breath."

He pressed his forehead against the table. "I'm sorry. I'm really not complaining—I know I have a wonderful life. Surrounded by a terrific family and good friends. I'm just . . . tired. It's been a very long week." He looked up and smiled grimly at her. "I suppose I should go back upstairs."

"Yeah, we probably both should," Merilee agreed. She reached across the table and took his hand, trying to communicate that she understood his desperation probably better than most. "Whenever I'm faced with doing something I don't want to do, I always tell myself that I can survive anything for a couple of hours or however long it's supposed to take. Just think—this will all be over within a few hours, and your Glenfiddich will be waiting for you here, right where you left it."

He nodded, his lips pressed together in grim determination. "You're a very smart woman, Merilee. Just like Heather. Except . . ." He stopped, then looked guiltily at her.

"Except what?"

"Except you have a level of compassion. And sweetness. Heather used to have it, too, but she seems to have lost it along the way. It seems the more she has, the more she wants. And she won't be satisfied with less than perfect. That's a very hard ideal for a man to live up to. I sometimes find myself thinking that Heather wishes she'd married Wade after all." He leaned closer, and she could smell the scotch on his breath. "You'd be happy with all this, wouldn't you? You'd be happy with me."

Before Merilee could answer, he'd touched his lips to hers. There was no passion, no lust, nothing except loneliness and a shot in the dark, and it seemed to Merilee that they both realized it at the same time. They drew back simultaneously, each flushing and stammering out words that did nothing to erase the awkwardness or embarrassment of what had just happened.

"Daniel?"

They both turned toward the doorway at the sound of a woman's voice, while Puddles lay sleeping at Dan's feet and didn't even lift his head. Merilee had no idea how long she'd been standing there, but judging by the look on her face, probably long enough to have seen Dan kiss her. Merilee recognized the woman but couldn't recall her name, most probably because she was seeing her in an evening gown, with styled hair, not in a ponytail or tucked into a tennis visor. She was out of context here in the Blackfords' wine cellar, which was why Merilee couldn't come up with a name. But the woman had no problem recalling Merilee's.

"Hello, Daniel. Merilee," the brunette said, her gaze taking in the held hands and the two mostly empty glasses of scotch. "Heather sent me down here to look for Daniel. He's MIA, apparently. Looks like I hit pay dirt."

Liz. The woman's name was Liz and she'd been on the decorating committee and was Heather's tennis doubles partner. As if scripted, Daniel and Merilee unclasped their hands, belatedly realizing what it must look like to an outsider.

"Liz," Merilee said. "I love your dress." She hadn't even noticed the dress. She was just eager to start a casual conversation that had nothing to do with explanations that didn't really need to be made.

"Thanks. Yours is stunning. Heather's been talking about it for weeks now—saying she'd better watch out since you'd be irresistible in it." Her smile faltered as she glanced nervously at Dan. "You'd both better hurry. I think everyone's here and Heather's about to give her welcome speech." She turned to Merilee. "She'll probably want Merilee to do some whetting of appetites for some of those auction items."

"Of course," Merilee said, standing and handing Dan's jacket back to him, avoiding his eyes. "Time sort of got away from us, I'm afraid. My date must think I've deserted him." She bent to look under the table, then under her chair.

"Can I help you find something?" Dan asked.

"My shoes. I remember taking them off, but I don't remember exactly where I put them."

Liz raised an eyebrow but didn't say anything. Merilee didn't know her very well, but she could only imagine how this would play out in the retelling, especially in light of the Tybee Island incident. "I haven't seen them," she said. "But there's a tub of flip-flops out on the back patio for the dancing later on. You could put on a pair until your shoes show up."

Dan grabbed several bottles of wine from one of the racks on the wall, then followed the women out of the room and up the stairs, the sound of people talking growing louder and louder as they left the hushed and carpeted atmosphere of the basement. Merilee couldn't help but wonder if Dan felt the compelling pull to return to the peace and quiet as much as she did.

Merilee couldn't find her shoes. She thought she remembered putting them on the steps, but they weren't there when she climbed up from the basement to rejoin the party. Liz sent one of the waitresses to pull a pair of flip-flops from the barrel for Merilee to wear until she could locate her own shoes. Wade seemed relieved for the reprieve when she found him, Heather's hand on his arm as they stood speaking with a table full of partygoers. She seemed almost disappointed to relinquish Wade and slip her arm into Dan's.

Wade pulled Merilee away, back toward the long green drapes. "You look shorter," he said.

"I can't find my shoes." Merilee pulled back the hem of her skirt to show off her flip-flops. "I sure hope someone finds them—they cost more than my monthly rent." At his expression, she said, "Don't judge. I have never done that before nor will I ever do it again. I'll blame it on Heather's influence."

"Understood," he said, and then, without warning, leaned down and kissed her. It was brief, and soft, but the electricity generated could have powered a small house. And so completely different from what she'd felt when Dan had pressed his lips against hers.

"Wow. What was that for?"

He shrugged. "Because I've been wanting to do that for weeks now, and I thought you wouldn't mind."

She licked her lips, wanting to taste him again, and the light changed in his eyes. "Just so you know, I didn't mind. And I wouldn't mind you doing it again."

"Merilee?" They both turned to see Heather walking toward them. "It's time to get started. Wade, go ahead and sit at the first table. You're seated directly on my right. They're about to start serving the first course."

Wade sent Merilee a knowing smile as he moved away to sit down, and she felt warm despite the cool air blowing in from the open doors behind her.

The rest of the evening was fueled by more champagne and wine, a lively auction with dizzying amounts of money being exchanged for luxury items to benefit the school, and the anticipation of what might happen later. Merilee refused to think too much about it. Maybe that had been her problem all along—planning everything, worrying about each step she had to make as a single mother with all the responsibilities suddenly on her shoulders. It was freeing, and wonderful, and made her look forward to something for the first time in a very long while.

As she hit the gavel for the last time—after announcing the winner of a year's worth of tuition—she was feeling like finally all was right in her world. The dinner and auction had been a success, and she was eager to celebrate all the hard work she'd shared with these women. She passed Lindi and her husband on the way down to the backyard, where the band had already begun to play under the tent and several couples were twirling on the dance floor.

"Great job," said Lindi. "And awesome earrings, by the way. I was noticing them from the back of the room. You didn't even need my necklace."

"Yes, I did—and the purse, too. Lily made sure she put my lipstick inside so that I would have it available after every sip and bite I took tonight."

Lindi laughed, then gave Merilee an impulsive hug. "Sorry, I had to do that. You look so . . . happy. And relaxed. I don't think I've seen you look either in the three months since I met you."

"Thanks. I am happy. And relaxed." She beamed. "And I need to go find my date because I'm in the mood to dance, and I've been told that he's a very good dancer."

"Who told you that?"

"He did." They both burst out laughing and Merilee was still grinning when she found Wade and he took her out on the dance floor and confirmed that he was, indeed, a very good dancer.

The evening passed in a blur of smiling faces, of loud music and cool fall air carrying with it the smoke from bonfires lit around the yard, groups of tables and chairs set nearby for people to take a break from dancing or just to enjoy the stars in the clear violet sky.

Merilee kept searching for Heather, wishing her dress had been red or orange to make her easier to spot, wanting to get the final tally on the auction. And, Merilee forced herself to admit, to hear some word of recognition from Heather for all her hard work. But as the evening wore on, she couldn't spot Heather in the crowd. She hoped she was dancing and not holed up in her office punching numbers to confirm the gala's success.

She was dancing a two-step with Lindi's husband, Paul—also a great dancer—when Liz tapped her on her shoulder, making them pause in the middle of a step. "Heather wanted me to let you know that someone spotted your shoes on the dock." She pointed behind her to the dark lake and the dock, where the boats had all been raised out of the water for the season, thick dark shadows against the moon-lapped waves.

"On the dock? Are you sure? I can't imagine why they'd be there."

"I'm only the messenger and that's what Heather told me."

Merilee looked past Liz toward the house. "Have you seen Heather? I've been looking for her for a while and haven't seen her."

Liz shook her head. "I haven't either. She texted me to let you know about the shoes. She said she's been trying to text you to let you know, but your phone's turned off."

"What? It shouldn't be." She glanced over to one of the tables where she'd placed her purse. "Not that I've remembered to check it, anyway. I must have done it by accident or just forgot I'd turned it off. Wouldn't be the first time."

"Mom brain," said Liz. "Happens to me all the time. That's probably how your shoes got on the dock—either you put them there and forgot, or somebody else was wearing them thinking they were theirs." They both laughed as Liz waved good-bye, then headed off toward one of the bonfires. Merilee began walking toward the dock for her shoes but figured she wasn't done dancing yet and her feet would thank her for keeping the flip-flops for a little while longer. Merilee resumed dancing, keeping an eye out for Wade, hoping for one last dance with him. He'd been requisitioned earlier by Heather asking for his help in assisting some of the other men in taking down the tables and chairs and moving them outside to the waiting catering truck.

The song ended and the band began to pack up as dancers drifted from the dance floor to pick up purses and coats and say good-bye. Merilee heard a dog barking from the dock area and, after one last look for Wade, headed down to search for her shoes and say good-bye to Puddles.

The barking got louder as she approached, the tone different from what she'd heard before. It was insistent, angry, almost. "Puddles," she called, walking carefully down the sloping lawn, the grass slippery under her feet.

The dog bounded toward her from the dock, but instead of stopping and allowing her to pet him, he immediately began to run toward the dock again, pausing to look back as if wanting her to follow him. "What is it, boy?" she asked, silently praying it wasn't a water moccasin or some other critter that could bite, fly, or run faster than she could.

She wished that she'd brought her phone so she could turn on the flashlight to guide her way. There were no lights on the dock, probably to keep partygoers away from it, but the crescent moon shone brightly from the sky, casting everything in its milky glow.

Puddles ran back to her and nudged her hand, urging her to follow. With one last glance over her shoulder to where her purse and phone were, she began following the dog down the main dock until the dog took a turn around the corner of a smaller walkway stuck between two boat lifts. The wood creaked and swayed as she carefully lifted her hem and then slowly followed the dog until she reached the turn in the dock. It was darker there, the light hidden between the two lifted boats, but she could make out the shape of the black Lab waiting for her. As soon as he saw her, he resumed his frantic barking, his head facing the water.

"What is it, boy?" she asked again, moving just an inch forward, waiting for her eyes to adjust and hoping she wouldn't see something thick and coiled and shining in the moonlight. "What is it . . ." The word died in her throat.

The dock lifted on a gentle wave, allowing in a triangular slice of moonlight, illuminating something in the water. Something that appeared to be a mannequin stuck between two pilings of the dock and wearing a white shirt and dark trousers. Merilee blinked hard, suddenly feeling how very cold it was outside and wondering who'd put a mannequin in the water. She jerked back, almost stumbling backward off the dock. She heard an unearthly sound, a piercing scream that went on and on while the dog continued to bark. When she found she couldn't breathe any longer, she realized the screams were coming from her own throat.

Twenty-eight

SUGAR

Wade held open the door to his fancy foreign sports car, then waited for Sugar. She glanced into the backseat at a black-clad Merilee, who appeared to have not slept in the week since she'd discovered Daniel Blackford's body floating facedown in Lake Lanier.

"You look terrible," Sugar said as she carefully lowered herself into the seat, praying her knees could get her back up again. "Black is not your best color."

Merilee sniffed as she raised a wadded tissue to her nose, the white glaring against her black leather gloves. "Thank you, Sugar. I had no idea."

Wade closed the door as Sugar grimaced, glad to have forced something besides shock and sorrow from Merilee. There'd been a lot of both in the last week, and not just on Merilee's part. Sugar had taken the news about Daniel hard. How did an expert swimmer and sailor, someone dressed in a tux and not known to drink alcohol to excess, drown on his own property at a party to which he was playing host? The autopsy results hadn't been announced to the public yet, but Sugar hoped that he'd had an aneurysm or something to explain the unexplainable.

Because he shouldn't be dead. In a fair world, he wouldn't be. But, as she'd learned again and again over the last ninety-three years, life was never fair. Nor did it promise anyone that it would be. Maybe that was the point of life—that the water wasn't always supposed to be smooth. That all the little storms were supposed to teach you how to keep your head above water no matter how high the swells.

"Nice hat," Wade said in an attempt to break the silence that sat thick and heavy inside the car.

"It's older than you by about forty years, but it still looks good enough to wear. I've worn it to every single funeral I've ever been to."

"Good for you," Wade said, but his voice sounded distracted as he glanced again in the rearview mirror to see Merilee, who seemed focused on something outside her car window.

It had begun to rain, and a thin drizzle coated the windshield, the wipers automatically swishing the moisture away. The wipers on her old Lincoln had sounded like semiautomatic gunfire, according to Daniel, and suddenly she was feeling the pinpricks of tears behind her eyes. She blinked rapidly, unwilling to break her promise to herself this late in the game.

"We'll have to stop back at the house to get my casserole for Heather and the girls before the reception after the service."

"You made a casserole?" Merilee's voice sounded raw and scratchy.

"Of course. I made cheese straws, too. You can carry them inside so people will think you made them."

Merilee turned her head to look out the window again without comment.

"Have you spoken with Heather?" Wade asked Merilee, his gaze focused on the rearview mirror.

"No. I've called a few times, but someone else always answers. I can't imagine . . ." She stopped. "She hasn't called me back. I was hoping to have a chance to talk with her today—I have something I need to return to her."

Wade glanced again in the rearview mirror, but Merilee didn't say anything else.

"I've just never heard of a funeral without a visitation," Sugar said.

"It doesn't seem right. It's always a nice way to see a person for the last time and say your final good-byes. I just don't understand why Heather would skip all that."

Wade patted her clenched hands on her lap. "After the autopsy, he was cremated. They usually have the urn at the service, and you can say your good-byes then."

She pulled her hands away. "It's not the same." She shook her head, trying to think of the appropriate words to express her disappointment. "It's not the same," she said again.

The service was well attended, which was usually the case when someone young died. If she ever made it to heaven, she'd demand an explanation for this and all the other unexplainables she'd encountered over the last nine decades. Her determination to have life explained to her was probably why she'd been allowed to stay on this earth for so long—her come-to-Jesus meeting was bound to take some time and ruffle a feather or two.

As they walked down the aisle looking for room for three in a pew, Sugar became aware of how people seemed to look straight ahead as they approached, rooted like anchors in their spots despite plenty of room in the middle of the pew. On the pretext of adjusting her hat, she turned her head to direct her stink eye at one such couple, only to find an entire row of mourners looking at Merilee's back. One person pointed while whispering to the woman next to her. She continued to follow Wade and Merilee as a sick feeling began to grow in the pit of her stomach.

They'd reached the front of the main aisle without any luck and were returning down the outside aisle when Wade stopped at a pew where a man was quickly putting down coats in the empty spaces next to the aisle. As if unaware of what the man was doing, Wade slid the coats into a pile, then motioned for Sugar and Merilee to sit. With an exaggerated mouthed *thank you* toward the man with the coats, Wade joined them on the end of the pew, doing a fine imitation of those around him by staring ahead and ignoring everyone else.

The blond woman sitting directly in front turned around to see who'd just sat down. It was that Sharlene person who Merilee carpooled with who couldn't stay off Sugar's grass because she was always talking on the phone. The woman shouldn't be allowed to walk and talk on a cell phone, much less operate a moving vehicle with children riding as passengers.

Sugar saw Merilee's eyes widen in recognition and then saw her open her mouth to say something, but immediately shut it when Sharlene turned around again, pretending she hadn't seen them.

Merilee went absolutely still, focusing on the altar and the small table with the wooden urn on top, suddenly aware that everyone was looking at her while pretending she wasn't there. Wade, sitting next to her, took her hand, and Merilee squeezed it tightly.

Heather sat in the front row, her blond hair in stark contrast to a black suit that looked like she'd been poured into it. Her two daughters, little replicas of their mother, sat beside her, pressing wet faces onto the sleeves of Heather's jacket. There were no grandparents in attendance, but a man who looked startlingly enough like Dan for Sugar to assume it was his brother sat on the other side of Bailey, his long arm stretched along the back of the pew behind Heather's shoulders.

As if sensing someone watching her, Heather turned and met Sugar's gaze. Sugar held it until Heather turned away. Several times during the short service, Sugar allowed her eyes to stray to the front pew, catching Heather surreptitiously watching Merilee and Wade before refocusing her attention on the pastor and the urn carrying the ashes of her recently departed husband.

Following the service, Merilee walked quickly from the church, keeping her gaze on the ground in front of her, ignoring the clusters of people huddled under black umbrellas who looked right through her. Wade and Sugar followed her under their own umbrella, unable to convince Merilee that Wade was happy to get wet if she wanted shelter from the rain. As they reached the bottom of the steps, someone called Merilee's name, and she looked up with such an expression of relief that Sugar almost clapped.

"Lindi!" Merilee said, embracing her friend, then stepping under the offered umbrella. "I can't tell you how glad I am to see you."

Lindi said hello to Wade and Sugar, then hugged Merilee again. "I was a little late—Paul's at home with two sick children—so I was standing in back of the church and getting a pretty good view of everything. What was that all about?"

Merilee looked close to crying. "I don't know. Heather's not returning my calls, and nobody's talking to me. It's like because I found Dan in the water, they think I'm guilty of something."

Lindi stepped back, her eyes compassionate. "Please don't give any thought to what people are saying. Daniel's death is a shock to everybody, and they just want to find a reason, an explanation."

Merilee blinked at her. "What do you mean? What are people saying?"

Lindi looked sincerely baffled. "Look, you've been through a hell of a time. I don't think this is the time or the place . . ."

"What is it, Lindi? What's going on?"

"I'm sorry. I thought maybe you'd heard some of the rumors. I know they're all lies, so I didn't bother you with them. Why don't we meet for coffee this week and we can talk about it?"

"What rumors?" Merilee insisted. "Lindi—you might be my only friend. Whether they're true or not, you need to tell me."

Lindi looked as if she might cry. "I'm sorry. I really thought you knew. I heard it this week in the carpool line, but I figured it was just gossip. Something bored housewives made up to make what happened to Daniel even more tragic and awful—as if that's even possible."

"What rumor?" Merilee asked again, her voice higher pitched than usual.

Lindi seemed to consider her words. "People are saying that this isn't the first drowning you've been involved with."

Merilee clutched at her throat, pulling at the collar of her coat as if she suddenly couldn't breathe. "They're talking about my little brother?"

Lindi looked surprised and then a little sickly. She put her hand on Merilee's arm. "No. Someone else. They're saying you were married before Michael. And that your husband drowned under suspicious circumstances. I told them they were all lies. That you and I are friends and you hadn't said anything . . ."

Wade grabbed Merilee's elbow before her knees buckled, keeping her upright.

"Let me go get you something to drink," Lindi said, already turning back toward the church steps.

"No," Merilee managed. "I just want to go home."

Lindi looked at Wade. "You'll get her home and make sure she's all right?"

"Of course." He put his arm around Merilee and she leaned into him.

"I'll call you later," Lindi said, brushing hair out of Merilee's eyes and raising Sugar's opinion of lawyers up exactly one notch.

They made it to the car and drove in silence on the short ride home. Merilee stared out her window, her face the color of a bleached bedsheet. Wade parked in front of the cottage and had unbuckled his seat belt as if to get out, but Merilee put her hand on his shoulder. "Don't. Please. I need to be alone right now. Thank you for the ride." She opened her door and placed both feet on the ground.

Never having been one to listen, Wade followed her out of the car. "That's it? Thank you for the ride? You haven't said one thing to me about what happened that night. And now this. And all you can say is 'Thank you for the ride'?"

"I'm sorry." Merilee turned and ran up the porch steps, then let herself into the house without looking back.

Wade climbed back into the car and shut his door, then sat for a long moment without putting the car in drive. "What was that all about?"

"It's not my place to assume," Sugar said.

"If she was married and widowed before, don't you think she would have mentioned it?"

Sugar looked at Wade over the tops of her glasses to make sure she got her point across. "That's not what you should be concerned with. She'll tell you the truth if you ask her. For some reason, she's taken a shine to you. What worries me is who *did* know, and why they decided to let that particular cat out of the bag now."

The rain began to fall again, hard this time, splashing against the windshield as the wipers silently swished back and forth in a steady rhythm. Sugar looked through the rain toward the woods, her view obscured intermittently by the blades, the tops of the trees fuzzy in the rainy haze of late morning. But she didn't need to see the woods to know they were there. She knew where they were and what they looked like whether she could see them or not. Just like she knew that Merilee was hiding something, a secret she'd never wanted to reveal but that Sugar had known existed from the first moment she'd met her. Because, as Sugar had learned, everybody has at least one secret that could break a heart.

. . . .

THE PLAYING FIELDS BLOG

Observations of Suburban Life from Sweet Apple, Georgia
Written by: Your Neighbor

Installment #9: Death and Taxes

As Benjamin Franklin was fond of saying, there are only two guarantees in life: death and taxes. I've always found it reassuring not having to wonder if I'll get that tax bill or if one day I'll die. Because we all will. Someday. Sadly, it will happen to some of us sooner rather than later.

For those of you who aren't from around here, there are certain customs we here in the South adhere to when someone dies. First of all, bring a casserole to the deceased family's home. Or deviled eggs. There's very little (grief included) that cannot be made softer by either one of these. When in doubt, look in the back of your favorite cookbook under the "freezes beautifully" section to choose a variation of noodles, cheese, and bean dishes to bring to the bereaved family.

Second, go to the funeral. Even if you only knew the deceased from the post office line or from sitting on the same bleachers at your son's football games, here in the South you're expected to be in attendance. How else are they going to get rid of all those casseroles?

Lastly, a Southern funeral is not the place to wear your new red sundress. Think black or brown or blue, and definitely low heels. Nothing flashy or anything remotely sexy. Wearing red to a funeral is frowned on in the South just as much as wearing white to a wedding unless you're the bride.

Why, you may ask, am I bringing up such a somber topic? In case you are not aware, we have recently lost an important member of our Sweet Apple community. A husband, father, and local businessman was found dead at his home on Lake Lanier last week during a gala fund-raiser for a local private school. Nobody—including the police—seems to know exactly what happened, as the poor victim wasn't known to dabble in destructive behaviors and those who knew him well—including his beautiful widow—claim the circumstances of his death are simply beyond comprehension.

The death is being called an accident, but nasty rumors are churning up like a cyclone over warm waters. And if we get enough hot air blowing, we're going to create us a hurricane. Sadly, all the rumors and innuendos seem pointed at the poor woman who happened to discover the body. I don't claim to be an insider, but then, I don't have to be one. Just listening to the crowd at the local coffee shop, I'm going to assume that they all must be insiders because they all had more fuel to add to the fire. Everybody had an opinion they were sure was based on fact, supporting all sorts of allegations about that poor woman. And because I don't support gossip, rumors, or innuendos, I'm not going to repeat any of them here. Just know that nobody's been arrested (according to one account), and I'm quite sure there was no conspiracy or mob involvement. This is Sweet Apple, after all. Not Chicago.

Now, I don't know how many of you are familiar with the Bible, but I'd wager that most of you know the story about stoning the sinner and how only the person without sin was supposed to cast the first stone. There's been a lot of talk about certain people having secrets from their past, and how secrets are a lot like chickens: They always come back home to roost. Show me one neighbor who doesn't have a secret and I'll show you a liar. Remember that when you pick up a stone with the intent to throw it.

Which brings me to today's Southern saying: "You're driving your chickens to the wrong market." That's what I'd like to say to all those people in the coffee shop trading rumors like they were at the New York Stock Exchange. And if you need me to define that one for you, then I'd just say that you won't hurt your back totin' your brains. Bless your heart.

Twenty-nine

MERILEE

Colin looked up at his mother where she stood on a ladder, hammering a hook into the side of a tree to hang the ancient bird feeder she'd found in the back of the hall closet. She'd remembered Sugar telling her how Lamar had hung bird feeders around the house and how she'd kept them stocked with seeds in an effort to make good karma when Tom went to fight in the war. Not that it had worked out, but it had set a precedent for Merilee and given her a project to keep her busy while hiding out from the rest of her life.

"It's crooked," Colin pointed out as she hung the wooden feeder on the hook, the ubiquitous field glasses pressed to his eyes as if he needed them to judge the less-than-expert hanging job his mother was attempting.

"Thanks," she said, wiping her hands on her jeans as she climbed down the short ladder and looked up to admire her handiwork. Or lack thereof. The bird feeder definitely hung at an odd angle, but perfection wasn't what she'd been going for. "I don't think the birds are too picky this time of year—they're just wanting food. And if they don't like it, they can move on."

He smiled broadly and she hugged him just because. Colin was the only one who still approached his life totally unaffected by the fact that his mother was a pariah. His sister walked around like a black cloud hovered over her head.

"When can we go back to school?" he asked, his head tilted back to examine the birdhouse again. "We're supposed to be starting an art project with Popsicle sticks this week and I was going to build a super-cool birdhouse mansion."

Merilee regarded her son, trying to remember not to frown. She'd taken a brief leave of absence from her job and had pulled the kids out of school for a few days of personal leave. Not that the school offered that, but the administration seemed almost overly helpful when she'd come to ask if such a thing was possible. Lily had seemed relieved, mostly due to the fact that only Jenna Matthews would sit next to her in any of their classes, and none of the other cheerleaders were speaking to her.

"I was thinking tomorrow would be a good day to start back. But I'll drive you and Lily. Mrs. Cavanaugh stopped by yesterday to let me know that the carpooling situation wasn't working out for her the way she'd hoped, so it'll be just the two of you and me, buddy." She forced a smile she didn't feel. Mostly because Sharlene Cavanaugh had stopped by to snoop, to ask questions about Dan that Merilee had no idea how to answer, and had allowed her eyes to roam over every surface and through every door crack in Merilee's house.

The front door was thrust open as Lily ran through it, sobbing as she collapsed into Merilee's side. Lily had been extra emotional, even for her, ever since she'd heard the news about Dan. She'd always been an empathetic child, feeling others' hurts sometimes more than she'd feel her own, and her heart had broken for her friend. It might have been easier for her if Bailey had answered her phone so Lily could tell her how sorry she was that her daddy had died.

Merilee ran her fingers through Lily's hair, feeling its baby-fine softness, reminding her of how young Lily still was and how it was too early to have to deal with real life at this age. Merilee had always assumed that David's death might mean she'd paid her dues already, and if that wasn't enough to protect her from life's seemingly insurmountable hurdles, then maybe her own kids would get a hall pass. At least in that one respect, she and Sugar were very adept at lying to themselves to get through another day. Or another decade. Surely Sugar realized that by now. But it was one thing to realize it and another thing to accept it. Self-denial was a wonderful substitute for reality.

"What is it, pumpkin?"

Lily kept her face buried in Merilee's sweater, muffling her voice and making it hard to understand her. Merilee placed her finger under Lily's pixie-like chin and raised her teary face to look at her. "Say that again, please."

"Bailey finally answered her phone and she said she can't come over this weekend to spend the night and that she can't come over ever or speak to me again."

"What?" Merilee held on to enough reason to know her anger was out of proportion to the crime. But she had tried to reach out to Heather for more than a week, with no response at all, and her nerves were frayed. She needed to talk with Heather, needed to know whether Liz had told her she'd seen Dan kissing her. Needed to explain to Heather that it had meant nothing and that Dan had loved his wife until the day he died. Surely Heather knew all this, though, without Merilee's telling her. They were friends, after all. "But that's ridiculous! Did she say why?"

Lily pressed her face into Merilee's sweater again and nodded. Turning her face so she could be understood, she said, "Mrs. Blackford told her not to. And when I asked her why, she hung up on me." This was followed by a loud hiccup and then hard sobbing, with Lily's head pressed against Merilee's hip bone so hard, she imagined it leaving a bruise.

Merilee knelt on the ground, the coldness of the earth seeping through her jeans. "Sweetheart, the Blackfords have suffered a horrible loss, one that we can't comprehend. They are grieving in their own way, and we need to give them space now to allow them to do it. You've called and left messages to let Bailey know you're thinking about her, so she knows how you feel. Maybe her mother just doesn't think that Bailey's ready to spend the night away from home yet. The ball's in her court now. Give her some time, and I know she'll call you."

Merilee wasn't sure how much of that she believed. She'd reached out to Heather in every way possible—including through Patricia and Claire and every person she knew on the gala committee. From the people who'd actually answered her phone calls, she'd received the same response—that Heather was grieving and couldn't talk about it yet. But Merilee was supposed to have been Heather's friend and had even considered Dan to be her friend, too. She'd found Dan's lifeless body floating in the lake—maybe she just needed to hear from Heather herself that she didn't blame Merilee for not getting there sooner to save Dan.

Or didn't Merilee count because she was too new to what Lindi referred to as Heather's "posse"? She'd done everything she could think of to reach out to Heather except showing up on her front step, not wanting to intrude on what she imagined to be Heather's desire for a very private grief. But knocking on their front door was exactly what would happen if Merilee still hadn't heard from Heather by the end of the week. She'd even bring a casserole. She would have smiled at the thought if her own heart hadn't been weighed down by the heaviness of her grief for Dan and for his family, and for her own daughter's misery.

"Wade's here!" Colin shouted, running toward the drive.

"That's Mr. Kimball to you, young man," she said, trying to think of what she was supposed to say to Wade.

"Mr. Kimball's here!" Colin shouted again, the binoculars bouncing against his skinny chest as he ran to greet their visitor.

Lily wiped her nose on her long sleeve and seemed to perk up at the mention of Wade's name. Sticking her hand in Merilee's—something she hadn't done in a while—she walked with her mom to where Wade was climbing out of his truck.

"Hello, strangers," he said, but his eyes were on Merilee. "Thought you might have fallen off the edge of the earth because I hadn't heard from you since the funeral. And either you've changed your number or you keep forgetting to return my texts and phone calls."

"I'm sorry," Merilee said, feeling chagrined. She'd treated Wade the same way Heather had been treating her, but with a lot less reason. Unless being caught in a lie of omission counted. "It's . . . complicated."

"I'm sure it is," he said. "Want to talk?" He jerked his head in the direction of the porch swing.

"Ugh. Adults talking." Colin pressed his palms against the sides of his face like a vise. "I'm going inside to watch TV," he said as he marched up the porch steps. Merilee knew that he'd already watched his amount of TV for the day, just like he was aware that his mother wouldn't argue if he watched a little more right now.

Merilee regarded her daughter. "Didn't Jenna bring you homework from Mrs. Adler? You might as well get it done, because you have no idea what she might bring home for you today."

"I guess." She stubbed the toe of her sneaker into the dirt. "And I suppose that I'm still not allowed to read the blog?"

"Absolutely. There's nothing in it that you need to know about. As soon as everything calms down again, we'll reevaluate. Until then, the blog is off-limits."

"Yes, ma'am." With a heavy frown, Lily let herself into the house, her feet dragging as if she'd just been condemned to seven years of hard labor.

Merilee felt the same way as she headed to the porch and sat down on the swing, bracing herself for Wade's weight as he sat next to her, keeping a hand's width distance between them.

"So . . . ," he began, giving her the chance to explain herself. When she didn't say anything, he continued. "Whatever we have between us, whatever you want to call it, doesn't matter right now. At the very least I thought we were friends. I told you about my rather painful past with Heather, yet you didn't think you should reciprocate about your own past. Specifically, that you'd been married before Michael."

"I didn't think it mattered."

"So it's true? You were married? And widowed?"

She couldn't look in his face, her shame like bile in the back of her throat. "Yes. I was married right out of college."

He continued to look at her, making it clear that he was expecting her to say more. "What could be so bad about your first marriage that you didn't think you could tell me?"

She took a deep breath, not sure how much she could tell him. "He drowned. On our honeymoon."

Wade sat back, digesting this bit of information. "I'm sorry, Merilee. I really am. That must have been horrible for you."

She focused on pushing the swing with her feet, looking at everything except his face. "Oh, it was."

He waited for her to say more, but she wasn't ready. Couldn't even imagine finding the words she hadn't spoken in more than a decade. Because she couldn't take the look of recrimination and doubt in his eyes if he knew the rest of the story.

Unaware of her inner turmoil, he said, "There's one thing I keep thinking about. Who knew about your first marriage? And why would they choose now to talk about it?"

She looked at him with surprise, wondering why the thought hadn't occurred to her. "I have no idea. No one here knows. Even Michael." She caught his sidelong glance. "My only excuse is that I was young and stupid and I wanted to put that horrible time behind me. When I met Michael, I simply pretended it hadn't happened. All I wanted to do was move forward."

He was silent for a moment. "Heather's called me a couple of times. She wanted me to know that you're not the person I think I know. That I should be careful."

Merilee slid from the swing to face him. "What?"

"I don't know what she's talking about, and I don't care. I hung up each time she mentioned you. I want to say it's because she's out of her mind with grief, and she's looking to blame anyone for her sadness. But I've known her for a long time, and I think there's something more." He looked up at the hooks holding the ropes of the swing, as if hoping they'd hold the weight of his words. "I don't think she's your friend, Merilee. And I don't think it's because of Dan's death."

Merilee started to protest, but he held up his hand to stop her.

"Let me finish. She wasn't your friend before, and I know she isn't now. You haven't been in a position to hear this, but maybe you are now. When you first met Heather you were vulnerable—newly divorced, knew no one at the school—and she latched onto that. She's always been really good at seeing the weak spots in people, and yours was your loneliness. I haven't yet figured out why, because she's always looking for something in return for anyone she ropes into her circle. But you're too nice. You don't really buy into all that brand-name-and-appearances game that Heather and most of her friends like to play. And you don't play tennis."

He'd tried for a lighter note, but Merilee was too upset and too angry to go along. Jabbing her finger into his shoulder, she said, "She is my friend, Wade. I know she broke your heart, which is why you have this grudge against her, but I've seen her many kindnesses toward me and my kids. Her husband just died and she must be out of her mind with grief and not thinking clearly. There has been some horrible misunderstanding, and if I haven't heard from her by Friday, I'm going to go to her house and knock on the door and talk to her face-to-face."

He held her gaze. "You do that. And when she closes the door in your face, just remember that there's more to friendship than giving people stuff and having your minions do things. It's about showing your vulnerabilities. You wear yours on your sleeve, so it was easy for her. But did she ever show you hers?"

Merilee couldn't remember the last time she'd been so angry. And it wasn't just his insistence that Heather wasn't her friend. Because in a small corner of her brain, she had the niggling suspicion that there might be some truth to his words, which would make her the biggest fool out there. Heather had never seemed vulnerable, not even at the moment when she'd come to see why Merilee was screaming outside on the dock. She'd taken Merilee aside and tried to comfort her as all the remaining guests gathered around them.

"We've got company." Wade stood, too, and put his arm around her shoulders right at the moment Merilee realized who it must be. A dark four-door sedan with a man wearing a jacket and tie in the front seat. She'd seen it before, after all.

"Oh, no," she said, hearing the sob in her voice. "No, no, no." The backs of her knees hit the edge of the swing, but Wade kept her standing. She had a brief flashback from fourteen years before, another front porch, another dark sedan. Another man found floating in the water.

"Are you okay?" Wade asked.

She couldn't answer. Because as she watched the man get out of the car and approach them, she suddenly knew that nothing would ever be okay again.

The man showed her a badge that she didn't look at. "I'm Detective Richard Kobylt from the Gainesville Police Department. Are you Merilee Dunlap?" He stopped at the bottom of the porch steps.

"Yes, that's me. Is there something I can help you with?"

"I was hoping you could come down to the station and answer a few questions about the evening of October twenty-ninth." He gave her a friendly smile. "Just down to the Sweet Apple police station—no need to go all the way up to Gainesville."

Breathe. Breathe. She'd been through this before, but it didn't make it any easier. "But I've already told the police everything I know. I heard the dog barking and I followed him—"

"These are just routine questions, ma'am, filling in some blanks in the report, that sort of thing."

"Right now?" she asked. "I have my children—"

"Sugar and I will watch them," Wade said calmly. "It's better to get this over with now. We'll all be here when you get back."

"Can I drive myself?" she asked, remembering the humiliation of being driven through her hometown in the back of a cruiser.

"That won't be a problem. You can follow me if you're not sure where the station is. Is that your minivan?" When she nodded, he said, "I'll go ahead and move my car in front of yours."

She nodded. "I just need to grab my purse and keys and let my kids know what's going on." Without looking in Wade's direction, she went inside. Her hands shook as she picked up her purse and kissed each child on the forehead. A river of ice had taken over her bloodstream, and she wondered whether she'd ever feel warm again. After slipping on her wool peacoat, she stepped outside. She'd told Lily and Colin to stay inside, but she knew they'd be pressed up against the front window, Colin's binoculars held up to his eyes.

"Thank you for watching the children," she said to Wade as she walked past him.

He grabbed her arm. "What aren't you telling me?"

She tried to find her anger again, but it had been buried under the ice-cold blast of fear that rattled her bones inside her coat. "A lot of people think I was responsible for my husband's death. If the police know about that . . ." She stopped, unwilling and unable to think beyond that.

"Were you?" he asked, his eyes boring into hers. But all she could see was her mother's face, telling a television news reporter how ashamed she was, because she'd raised her daughter better.

She broke away, then ran down the steps to her car, starting it and driving away without looking back, her hand already reaching for her phone and hitting one of the numbers she kept on her favorites list but rarely used. There'd been a time, after her grandfather had died, when her father had tried his best to be the kind of parent she needed. The kind she could turn to in trouble. That had ended with John's death, when all faith in her had vanished.

Her mother answered on the sixth ring. Merilee almost hung up or asked for her father. But she clung to the memory of how much they'd once loved her. And how much she'd once loved them.

"Mama? I'm in trouble again. Somebody died, and I was there, and the police are asking questions." She was crying now, tears of fear and desperation, carrying with them the last shred of hope that her parents would realize after all this time that she was still their daughter.

"No, Merilee. Not again. I will not have you do this to me again. We had to move to another town last time because of you. I will not have you shame us again. Please don't call back until you've sorted all this out on your own. We cannot help you."

The phone clicked and there was nothing to listen to but air. Merilee dropped the phone to clutch the steering wheel, trying to stop her hands from shaking. She suddenly thought of her grandfather and of the maps they'd begun collecting together as proof that everything you loved changed no matter how much you wanted it to stay the same. She thought of Sugar, too, holding on to her woods as if she could keep her past intact, oblivious to the world spinning inexorably and utterly out of control.

Were you? It wasn't until she was parking her car in front of the police station that she remembered Wade's question as they'd stood on the porch, and how she'd left him without an answer.

Thirty

SUGAR

Sugar carefully applied her lipstick before picking up the silver tray full of chocolate chip cookies. They were Colin and Lily's favorite and she was glad she'd had a fresh batch right out of the oven when Wade called to tell her about Merilee being asked to go down to the police station. Nothing like a healthy dose of something sweet to soften the blow of your mother being questioned by the police. Or the death of a friend who had died way too young.

Sugar made her way slowly to the cottage, where Colin sat on the porch steps, watching her approach with his binoculars facing the wrong way. "Hello, Miss Sugar," he called out as she stopped directly in front of him. "Have you ever noticed how tiny everything is when you look through the other side?"

"No, I don't believe I have. Although my brother Jimmy used to ask me the same thing. Now, if you don't want me to spill these cookies all over the porch, may I suggest you take the tray and offer me your elbow?"

"Yes, ma'am," he said as he stood and took the tray, then helped her up the steps.

Wade looked surprised to see her when she entered the kitchen, where he sat at the table with Lily, her schoolbooks and papers stacked in neat piles around her. "Did you sprint? I just hung up the phone with you a couple of minutes ago."

"More like lumbered quickly, like a turtle with its shell on fire, I expect, but I wanted to get here as fast as I could. We've got work to do."

He raised his eyebrows as she set about putting several cookies on individual plates and pouring two glasses of milk. "Why don't you children go take your snack into the living room and watch a video?"

"What's a video?" Colin asked.

They all turned to Wade. "She means a DVD. I'm sure you've got something to watch. Sugar and I need to talk."

"I'll pick the movie!" Colin called out, sprint-walking toward the living room while balancing his milk and cookies.

Lily stayed behind, a deep furrow between her brows. "It's about my mom, isn't it? Is she going to jail?"

"Of course not," Sugar said. "The police just needed to ask her some more questions. Sadly, she was there when Dr. Blackford died, so they have lots of questions." She met Wade's gaze for a moment. "You can ask your mother more when she gets back. But for now, go take a break. And if you need anything, just let us know. Unless it has something to do with how to watch your movie; then just ask Mr. Kimball because I have no earthly idea how those things work."

Lily's lips lifted in a little half smile as she picked up her own plate and glass and followed her brother into the other room.

"I'm worried," Wade said as she joined him at the table. "I asked Merilee about the rumors. She was married before Michael. Her husband drowned on their honeymoon, which is probably what has fueled the gossip train here in Sweet Apple. Two men drowning while Merilee was present is almost too much of a coincidence to be believed."

Sugar stayed silent, knowing there was more and that he was debating whether to tell her. "And?"

"And Merilee told me that when her first husband died, a lot of people thought she was responsible."

"Oh. My." She'd known there was something. Had known it since back when she'd first met Merilee. But she'd had no idea it was something as big as this. "Did you ask her if she had anything to do with it?"

Their eyes met. "She didn't answer."

Sugar stayed silent. She wouldn't judge, or jump to conclusions, even after all the facts were placed in front of her. Because she knew they rarely told the whole story. "What do you think?" she asked instead.

"I have no idea what to think. The Merilee I know couldn't possibly be responsible for someone's death. But I'm not a good judge of character, am I? I once thought I wanted to spend the rest of my life with Heather."

Sugar leaned forward. "Does Merilee have any idea who started the rumors? It had to be someone she told."

He shook his head. "Nobody knew—not even Michael. It's like somebody is intentionally stirring up trouble for Merilee and using Dan's death as an excuse. But if she hasn't told anybody, including her ex-husband, then who would know about it?" He picked up a cookie, then proceeded to crumble it between his fingers onto the table. Sugar frowned at him, but he didn't seem to notice.

He looked up. "I bet that's how Bill and I recognized her—from the newspaper stories around the time of her first husband's death. Especially if there was some doubt about how he died. That kind of tragedy always makes the news. Her picture would have been all over the place, I'm sure. She said she was married right out of college, and he died on their honeymoon. Assuming she married Michael shortly afterward, and was married to him for eleven years, that would have been about the time I was living nearby, in Augusta. I probably saw it on the local news.

"I Googled her, you know—that means searched the Internet—that first time I saw her and thought she looked familiar. She just didn't show up because I was using her maiden name, Talbot. Or maybe it did show up but I ignored it if it had her married name, too, and I had no idea she'd been married before Michael."

Sugar closed her eyes for a moment, trying to recall something important. Something that had to do with Merilee and her first husband. She supposed she should be glad that her long-term memory was still so intact. Her short-term memory sometimes decided to become another vexation to her spirit.

"What is it?" Wade asked.

She closed her eyes tighter, trying to see a face. Nothing. Her eyes popped open and she was surprised to see Wade staring at her with a worried expression.

"I want to say that I met her first husband, that I know what he looks like, but that can't be right, can it? Because I'm sure I didn't know Merilee back then. But I could swear on a stack of Bibles that I know him . . ."

Lily came back into the room. "Can we have more cookies? Colin ate his so fast and then ate mine, so I only got one."

Wade stood to get more from the tray on the counter while Sugar stared at Lily thoughtfully. Lily had been with her. Yes, that was right. She'd been with her . . . when? When they met . . . "The yearbook!" she said with more excitement than was probably necessary. It was always such a happy surprise when her memory worked. "His picture was in Merilee's yearbook—at least I think it might have been him." She smiled warmly at the little girl. "Lily, would you mind getting your mother's yearbook—the one you and I were looking at—and bringing it here? We're trying to help your mother, so I don't think she'd mind if we took a look at it."

"Sure." Lily ran toward her mother's bedroom and returned quickly with the book.

"Thank you, dear. Don't forget the cookies."

"Yes, ma'am," Lily said, taking the plate and hesitating just in case the adults asked her to stay, then walked slowly back to the front room.

Wade placed the book before Sugar and opened the cover, revealing signatures sprawled across the two pages. "She had a lot of friends."

"Yes, she did," Sugar said, remembering what Merilee had told her about her high school years and about the girl named Daisy. With fingers that didn't move as nimbly as they once had, she flipped through pages until she reached the sports team section, past the cheerleading photos and then to the football team. "I'm thinking this must have been her first husband. She told me he died, but not that they were married at the time. I'm assuming there can't be more than one."

Wade turned the yearbook to face him. "Nothing would surprise me at this point." He focused on the photo of the football captain with the heart drawn around his face. "John D. Cottswold," he said out loud. "You think this is him?"

"Oh, yes. That's the only photo of him in that entire book that doesn't have his handwriting beneath the picture asking 'Tallie' to marry him."

"Tallie?"

"Yes. Lily and I think that was her nickname in high school—a shorter name for Talbot. Although I can't imagine why they thought they needed to abbreviate a two-syllable word with another two-syllable word. I've never understood teenagers. Even when I was one."

Wade looked like he might say something but refrained. He picked up the laptop near where Lily had been sitting and carried it to the doorway. "Lily—would you mind if we used your laptop to look something up?" Facing Sugar, he said, "I need a bigger phone. I can hardly read this tiny screen anymore."

"Welcome to my world, young man."

Lily called out, "It's not mine—it's my mom's. But I don't think she'd mind. The password is eight ones. She wanted just four, but they needed eight."

"Naturally," Wade said as he settled himself back at the table, opened the laptop, and began to type. After only a few moments, he said, "Bingo." He was silent for a long while, his eyes moving from side to side as he read from the screen, then returned to the top and read it again.

"Are you going to allow me to read it?" Sugar asked, growing impatient.

"I don't know if I can make the font big enough. I could read it to you, or sum it up. Either way, it's pretty awful."

"I don't know if I can focus that long without needing to powder my nose or take a nap, so just sum it up, please." She was surprised to find she wasn't nervous, although she'd thought she would be. If only because she was very, very sure that Merilee Dunlap hadn't done any-thing that Sugar couldn't understand or justify.

Wade studied the screen for a moment before speaking. "Merilee and her husband, John, went scuba diving on their honeymoon in Ha-waii. They were both experienced divers, having been certified while in high school and then continued to take dive trips through their col-lege years at UGA. According to police reports, during a dive John lost consciousness and sank to the bottom, about a hundred feet below the water's surface. While trying to reach him, Merilee claimed she knocked off her mask and had to return to the surface. When she dove back down to try to reach him, the strong current had taken him away. They re-covered the body the next day. Cause of death was drowning, although there were questions about a mechanical failure in his breathing appa-ratus, which may or may not have been tampered with."

Their eyes met. "She must have been heartbroken." Sugar stared back unblinking, as if daring him to say what they both were thinking.

"His family pushed to have her arrested for murder. They were well-off and fairly prominent in their hometown. Pretty influential, which is probably why their suspicions gained traction. It never went to trial—the case against her was dismissed." He sat back in his chair, his brow furrowed. "It's an odd coincidence, don't you think? Her little brother, then her husband. And now Daniel Blackford."

"I suppose so," said Sugar, her voice not as firm as she'd have liked it to be. "Or Merilee is just very unlucky. Because I don't believe for one moment that she was responsible for any of those horrible accidents. I have always prided myself on being a good judge of character. Re-member how I disliked and distrusted Heather from the moment you introduced her? And I was right in my original assessment, which is why I never changed my opinion."

He was still looking at her, but not really listening. "Either Merilee is very unlucky, or . . ."

"Or . . . ?" Sugar prompted.

"Or somebody knew about her first marriage, and about the drown-ings, and was just waiting for the right time to talk about it."

"Like a convenient drowning?" Sugar's eyes widened.

"Something like that." He stood. "What's Merilee's friend's name— the one who told her about the rumors at the funeral?"

Sugar blinked several times. "Do I know the answer to that? If I do, I'm afraid I don't remember."

"It's Lindi Matthews. Her daughter is my friend Jenna," Lily called from the next room. "I can get her phone number if you want."

"That would be great—thank you," Wade called out. He shook his head. "So much for protecting the children from all of this."

They heard Lily's feet thundering down the back hall before she appeared with a school directory. "Here. It has Mrs. Matthews's work number and cell number, too." Lily looked up, her expression one of such worry and agony, Sugar was afraid she'd look like one of those wrinkly dogs when she was older. "Why are you calling Mrs. Matthews? Does Mom need a lawyer?"

Wade squatted down and smiled at the little girl. "Actually, I wasn't even aware that Mrs. Matthews was a lawyer. I want to call her because I think your mom needs a friend right now."

Sugar pressed her lips together and gave Wade her serious look. Standing, she took Lily by her shoulders. "What do you say we have pizza delivered for lunch? You talk with your brother and decide what you want, and then Mr. Kimball will order it and pay for it, too. All right?"

Lily looked slightly less upset as she returned to the front room to talk with Colin.

Turning to Wade, Sugar said, "Why do you want to talk with Lindi?"

"Because I want to find out who started the rumors. I'm sure someone told the police, which is why they have more questions for Merilee." He sat and began drumming his fingers against the table. "There's something not right about any of this. Not right at all."

While Wade took his cell phone from his pocket and began dialing, Sugar removed her glasses to clean them, wondering how they always managed to get so dirty when she was doing absolutely nothing. After resettling them on her nose, she turned her head to look out of the window at the woods, testing her vision, wondering if the blurriness was because of the distance or a spot she'd missed on the lens.

She recalled a few words of wisdom her father had told her long ago, something she was sure she'd repeated to Wade. Something about digging where you're not wanted. Because most people have secrets. And most of them should be allowed to stay hidden. No good had ever come from poking a stick down a hole. Because sometimes you got a garter snake, but sometimes you got a rattler.

She thought she could see Dixie hovering at the edge of the woods, facing the house. Sugar blinked twice and the dog was gone. She turned around and placed her hand on Wade's arm as he held the phone, speaking to another person on the other end.

"Let it go," she said, her voice quiet. "Let it go," she said again, thinking about another time, another death.

He took her hand as if she hadn't said anything at all, and continued to talk into the phone.

MERILEE

Merilee took the cup of coffee from the detective and sipped it without blowing on it, unaware that she was burning her tongue until she'd swallowed.

"Careful—it's hot," Detective Kobylt said. She'd been escorted to the interview room and introduced to Detective Scott Harrell of the Sweet Apple Police Department, who would be assisting with the investigation. They'd explained that the two detectives would be working the case together, since Lake Lanier was in a different jurisdiction from Sweet Apple, where everybody involved lived. And where the Blackfords knew everyone, including the chief of police and the mayor, according to Sugar.

Detective Harrell sat casually on the table behind where they'd placed Merilee, the other detective leaning against the wall. She was the only one drinking coffee, and she wondered if that was supposed to mean anything.

"Thanks for coming in, Ms. Dunlap."

She smiled at the detective, trying to move her frozen cheeks before they cracked. "You're welcome. Although I'm not quite sure why I'm here. I already told the police everything I know about . . . that night. I've thought about it and thought about it and I haven't come up with anything new that I could add. If I had I would have called."

The two detectives exchanged a look, and then Detective Harrell spoke, his voice kind and his Georgia accent oddly reassuring. Like she was among friends. And she couldn't help but wonder if this was intentional. "Ms. Dunlap—can you think of any reason why someone might want to harm Dr. Blackford?"

"Harm him? No. He was the nicest man. Everybody liked him, as far as I knew. I never heard a bad word said about him."

"So you'd never heard anybody threaten him or argue with him?"

"Never. Like I said, he was very well liked. A big contributor to the community and to the school. I considered him my friend."

The detective clasped his hands over his knee, which was bent over the edge of the desk in a studiously casual pose. "Ms. Dunlap, have you ever been arrested?"

She wondered if the hot, icy feeling rippling through her chest was a sign of a panic attack. Or a heart attack. She almost asked them how they knew that, but she didn't. They were detectives. It was their job to dig. But why would they have focused on her? Because she was the one who'd found Dan's body? Something nudged the inertia in her brain, something telling her that an important piece was missing from this puzzle, and she seemed to be the only one who didn't know what it was. Or where it might fit.

"Yes," she said. "But, as I'm sure you've already discovered, it was an accident. A horrible accident."

"But charges were brought against you?"

A spark of anger elbowed aside a large slice of her fear. "Yes. And then dismissed. I'm sorry, but what does this have to do with Dr. Blackford's death?"

The detective leaned nearer to her. "Your first husband drowned when you were the only person present. It just seems odd that a second man would drown in similar circumstances. And we understand your younger brother also drowned when you were a teenager."

She put down the coffee. "They were all accidents. Horrible, awful accidents."

The detective studied her for a long, silent moment. "The coroner's final report has been kept out of the news, so it's not common knowledge yet, but Dr. Blackford's death does not appear to have been the accident that was originally assumed. Which is why we need to ask more questions of you, and other people at the party who might have witnessed events."

"What 'events' are you talking about?" She was almost relieved at this point, because whatever else they had discovered could have nothing to do with her. She'd heard the dog barking and gone down to investigate and had found Dan. There was nothing more to her story.

Detective Kobylt pushed away from the wall and walked toward her. "Ms. Dunlap, were you and Dr. Blackford having an affair?"

"What?" She almost tipped her chair back as she attempted, and failed, to stand. "Excuse me? No. Of course not. We were friends. Why would you ask that?"

Again the two men exchanged looks. Detective Kobylt pulled out a chair and sat across the table from Merilee. "Didn't you spend a weekend with Dr. Blackford at his family's home on Tybee?"

Oh, God. "No. I mean, I was supposed to be there for the weekend, but he didn't realize I was there . . ." She stopped, knowing there was no way she could go over what had actually happened that wouldn't sound like one huge lie. "Heather—Mrs. Blackford—can explain all that. She's the one who invited me to stay at the house."

Without comment, Detective Kobylt slid a manila folder on the table toward himself and opened it, flipping through papers for at least a minute. Merilee wondered if it was a tactic to unnerve her, the sound of papers rustling in the dead silence of the room meant to shatter whatever sense of calm she might still have claimed.

Finally, he spoke. "You were on the gala committee, correct?"

"Yes. I was in charge of the auction items."

He met her eyes. "And on the night of August eighteenth, you were late for the committee-head meeting because you were at the Blackfords' house, where only Dr. Blackford was present. We understand that you claimed you thought the meeting was at the Blackfords' house, even though all the other committee heads knew to go to the clubhouse."

She took two deep breaths, remembering the calming technique shared with her by her old therapist. "Yes. I had it on my calendar that it was at Heather's house. I must have misunderstood."

"I see," he said, nodding. "And when Dr. Blackford came to your place of work and kissed you, and when you received private phone calls from him while at your daughter's cheerleading practice, those were just misunderstandings, too? Not to mention dozens of private texts to Dr. Blackford made from your phone."

Merilee grasped the edge of the table. "I have no idea about the texts. I have no recollection of *ever* texting or receiving a text from Dan. For anything. And as for the other incidents, there's nothing to misunderstand. Those were perfectly innocent. Dan came to my place of work to ask for my help in buying an anniversary gift for his wife. The kiss was a friendly kiss—on my cheek. Again, if you'll just ask Heather, she can clear up all this."

Detective Kobylt studied her closely, watching every move on her face as he asked his next question. "I understand that Dr. Blackford paid for a ball gown for you. From a shop called Fruition. I'd never heard of it, so I had to do a little research. Apparently, you can't buy anything in there for less than a thousand dollars."

Merilee wondered if someone had turned up the heat, because all of a sudden she found herself sweating. "Oh, no. That was Heather. She must have used Dan's credit card—he'd left his wallet in her purse."

"So Mrs. Blackford purchased the gown for you?"

"Yes," Merilee said, sitting back in her chair, knowing exactly how that sounded, just as she knew that any explanation would only sound like a lie.

Neither of the men said anything, and after trying to sit still and not make a sound, Merilee adjusted herself in her seat, bringing both their gazes to her. Detective Harrell stood and walked to the corner of the room, where a corrugated box sat on top of a row of filing cabinets. He brought it over to the table and opened the loosely sealed top before pulling out a plastic baggie and placing it in front of her.

"Do you recognize this?"

She peered through the clear plastic at the tube of lipstick. "It looks like the Revlon lipstick I usually use."

"The color is Silhouette," he said without looking at it. "Is that the shade you wear?"

She nodded. "Yes. And I think that might be the tube I let Heather borrow. I bought another one—I have it in my purse right now if you want to . . ."

"We found this in Dr. Blackford's jacket pocket. And you're saying Mrs. Blackford borrowed it from you?"

"Yes. If you would just ask her, it would save you a lot of trouble."

The detective nodded. "We've already interviewed Mrs. Blackford, Ms. Dunlap. Her recollections are quite a bit different from yours. I'm sure we'll get this all straightened out—we've just got a few more questions."

Without looking up from the folder, Detective Kobylt said, "Were you aware that Dr. Blackford was drinking more than usual the night of the gala?"

She took another deep breath, trying to get her heart to slow down. "To be honest, I don't really know how much he would usually drink. Heather made sure our server kept our wineglasses topped off all through dinner, but I didn't notice how much he was drinking."

"Dr. Blackford's blood-alcohol level was almost two and a half times the legal limit when he died. Surely you noticed that he was intoxicated?"

"To be honest, we all were a bit drunk—except for my date, because he was my designated driver. I didn't notice Dan specifically, although he certainly wasn't acting normally. He sat at the dinner table without really contributing to the conversation, which wasn't like him at all. Maybe that's how alcohol affected him. I don't know. I did know he'd started drinking early—way before the party started. His wife had given him a bottle of expensive scotch earlier in the day that he'd already been enjoying when I saw him in the cellar."

"Where you were holding hands and kissing," the detective said, reading from the folder again.

She sat very still, afraid to move. "He was my friend. I've told you that. He was talking about how all he wanted to do was spend quiet time with his family. The whole party scene wasn't really . . . him. He preferred fishing, or watching a movie with his kids. That sort of thing. He was kind of sad when we spoke, so I reached for his hand as a friend would. And the kiss . . . it was just a misunderstanding." She winced at the word, at the way she sounded. As if she were guilty of everything they were assuming. Except she wasn't.

Detective Kobylt studied her without comment, his silent perusal interrupted by the other detective. "Why were you down in the cellar?"

"Heather asked me to go find Dan. She'd sent him down there for wine and he'd been gone longer than expected. She didn't want to leave the receiving line, so she asked me to go get him."

"Why didn't she call or text him?" the detective asked, his neutral voice probably meant to be soothing, but it filled Merilee with terror.

"I have no idea. I don't remember seeing her purse, so maybe she didn't have her phone. You should ask her."

Detective Harrell smiled gently but it did nothing to erase the pit of fear that grew in her stomach. "Ms. Dunlap, why were you at the dock? According to witnesses, you were on the dance floor and then left when the band started packing up and walked toward the dock—even though everybody else was heading up toward the house."

"I was looking for my shoes—Heather had told someone that my shoes had been spotted on the dock—although I have no idea how they might have gotten there. So I headed that way, and that's when I heard the dog barking. Look, I already said all this to the Gainesville police . . ."

"We know. And we appreciate your patience. But there are still a few things that need clarifying." He reached into the corrugated box again and pulled out a larger clear plastic bag and placed it on the table directly in front of Merilee.

"Is this yours?"

Sitting on the table in front of her, nestled inside the bag, was one of the outrageously expensive evening shoes she'd worn the night of the gala. "Yes. It's mine. Do you have the other one, too? I thought I'd lost them both at the party."

"How did you think you lost them?" Detective Kobylt asked, his expression somehow making it clear that he thought she was stringing together lie after lie.

"Because I took them off before heading down to the cellar. The steps were steep and circular, so I took them off so I wouldn't trip. They're pretty high, as you can see."

"And where did you leave them?"

She was confused for a moment, wondering if they were trying to make her stumble on her own words. "On the top step. That's where I took them off. But somebody must have moved them, because when I climbed back up the steps, they were gone."

"They were just gone?"

Merilee felt the anger again and was glad. It gave her something besides fear to latch onto. "Yes. At the time, I thought maybe someone thought they were a hazard and stuck them in a closet to get them out of the way—I had no idea. I just knew they were gone. Where were my shoes found?"

The detectives looked at each other for a long moment in a silent understanding, making Merilee want to squirm. But she sat perfectly still.

It was Detective Harrell's turn to talk. "This one was found on the dock, near where Dr. Blackford's body was found in the water."

"And the other one?" It barely sounded like her voice.

"Missing. We haven't been able to locate it."

"Do you think it might have fallen in the water?"

"Anything's possible. We're sending in a team of divers to see if we can locate it."

They were both studying her a moment before Detective Harrell turned to her again, his voice still gentle but his words like bullets. "It's important we find it. Although the official cause of death is drowning, it appears that Dr. Blackford was helped into the water with a blow to the back of his head. According to the coroner's report, the injury to his head is consistent with the shape of a stiletto heel."

For a moment she thought she might throw up and could tell that the detectives were thinking the same thing, as they both took a step back. *Breathe. Breathe.* She never thought she'd be thankful for her previous experience with law enforcement, but she was now. She stood slowly, leaning on the table. "This interview is over. If you'd like to talk with me again, you'll need to go through my attorney."

Since all three of them knew that she was free to go, she walked out of the interview room, Detective Harrell holding the door open for her—this was Georgia, after all—and almost made it to her minivan before she threw up.

Thirty-one

MERILEE

Lily and Jenna practiced their cartwheels at the public park while Colin climbed on the jungle gym with another boy around his age he'd met on the swings. It was warm for early November, and both boys had discarded their sweaters, hanging them over the pretty picket fence that divided the play area from the grassy one. But Merilee shivered inside her own sweater. Ever since the interview with the police detectives, she'd felt exposed. Laid bare. She was all too familiar with the feeling and remembered how long it had taken to recover the first time. She wasn't sure if she had the energy to survive it again.

Lindi had met her at home when she'd returned from the police station, and Merilee was too numb to be angry with Wade for calling her. Too upset with herself for calling her parents, which had done nothing except magnify Merilee's helplessness. Her aloneness. She was on the brink of another depression, like the horrible darkness that had descended after John's death and her arrest. She'd even considered calling her old therapist but had been unable to break through the inertia to even look for her contact number. She'd thought she'd recovered from John's death and the aftermath, had moved on, with fading scars.

But the wounds she'd sustained were like driftwood from a wreck, resurfacing again and again no matter how much she tried to push them away.

Despite Merilee's protests, Lindi forced her into an outing to the park, saying the fresh air would help clear her mind as they figured out what to do next. It hadn't occurred to Merilee until she was parking her minivan at the park that Lindi had included herself in the planning.

Lindi sat next to her on the bench, scribbling in a small notebook everything Merilee told her about the police interview, her handwriting as neat and precise as she was. As if to test Lindi's limits of friendship, Merilee had told her about John and his death and the accusations that had led to her arrest. But Lindi had just taken notes and nodded when Merilee told her all the charges had been dropped.

"Why are you doing this, Lindi? Your life would be a lot easier if you didn't associate with me."

Lindi looked up from her notepad. "Who said I wanted an easy life? People with easy lives are boring. They haven't had any reason to build their character. And it's good for Jenna to see me stand up for something I believe in. And to see what real friends are."

Merilee felt her lips tighten, reminding her of Sugar when things were getting to the point where she might have to show emotion. "Stop or you're going to make me cry. You don't even know me, Lindi. Not really."

"I know you enough. I also know Sugar Prescott and I trust her judgment. She doesn't like many people, as you know. And the fact that she does like you is enough for me. Not to mention I like you. It's not every woman who can deal with what you've had to face in the last year or so and not be a crumbling mess."

"Who said I'm not a crumbling mess?"

Lindi's face was serious. "You're a lot stronger and braver than you give yourself credit for."

"I said the same thing to Sugar. After she'd told me a story from her past. It nearly broke my heart to hear it."

"Yes, well, you and Sugar have a lot in common—not that I'd ever let her hear me say that out loud. There's a resiliency about you two that I hope I can teach to my daughter. Although I will say you're sniveling a little bit now—but I'm sure it's temporary."

Merilee tried to look stern but ended up laughing instead. "I hope you're right about this being temporary. Sugar's going to wear out her lips the way she presses them together in disapproval every time she sees me."

"Yes, well, she has a point." She reached down and slid something out of the outside pocket of her computer bag. "Before I forget, here's the business card of my friend I was telling you about, Cynthia Turlington. She's a criminal defense attorney. She's very nice, but very, very good at what she does. You need to call her today." She tapped her pencil against the notebook. "I don't like any of this. It's all circumstantial, but Daniel was a very prominent man. I know they must be itching for an arrest to be made."

Merilee took the card and stared at it without really seeing it. "I feel so stupid, allowing myself to be interviewed by the police without an attorney. I knew better—I've been through this before with John. I had no idea where their questioning was headed—I thought I was just one of the many partygoers who were being interviewed. Just following procedures. Besides, wouldn't asking for an attorney at that point have made me look guilty?"

"No. It would have made you look smart."

Merilee sighed. "Okay. I'll call her. But first I want to head over to Heather's house and speak with her face-to-face. If I just talk with her, ask her to tell the police everything to clarify all these . . . misunderstandings—"

"No," Lindi said, cutting her off. "Absolutely not. I'm not your lawyer, so you can do anything you want. But I am your friend, and I think that's the stupidest idea I've heard since my husband—and father of our young children, I might add—said he'd like to try skydiving. You told me that the police had already questioned her and that her side of things didn't exactly mesh with yours. I want to give her the benefit of the doubt right now, seeing as how her husband was just found murdered, but I've known her too long to believe that she doesn't know exactly what she's saying and doing at all times. Even in the throes of grief. You need to be very careful around her is all I'm saying."

Maybe that was the thought that had been bothering Merilee. The fact that the police had already talked to Heather, and yet her story was different from Merilee's. There had to be a reason. Weren't guilt and anger two parts of the grieving process? Maybe Heather was going through those stages now. Still, it shouldn't be affecting Heather's memory, especially when what she wasn't remembering correctly skewed the truth of actual events that involved Merilee.

Lindi bounced the eraser end of her pencil on the notebook. "Oh, one more thing." She reached down into her large bag, and pulled out a small laptop. "You should shut down all your social media accounts until all this has blown over. Even in family law, I advise my clients to do this. Warring parties usually end up taking the ugly accusations and barbs online for the world to see, and that doesn't help anybody's case. Rest assured the detectives in charge of your case are checking out your social media to see what's there and what people are saying."

"Oh, well, that should be easy. The only thing I have is a Facebook account, and I haven't put anything on it except for a profile picture of the kids."

"I know—I saw that when I friended you. Cute pic. Anyway, we should still shut it down. Trust me—people think Facebook is like picking your nose while driving in your car. You might think you're alone and anonymous, but you're not. We can still see you. It's really amazing what people think is okay to post on someone's Facebook page."

She opened up the laptop and typed something onto the keyboard, then waited a moment. She squinted as a page popped up, then moved back. "Are you sure you only have one Facebook account?"

"Yes. I barely use one, so I certainly don't need more than that."

"Wellll," Lindi said slowly, "it appears you have what's called a 'fan page,' too. There's a link to it right on your personal page. It's a public page, so anybody can view your photos and posts without you knowing they were there."

"Are you sure it's me?"

"Oh, yeah. It's you." She placed the laptop on Merilee's lap and tilted the lid to give Merilee a better view. Merilee stared at the page for a long moment, trying to remember when she'd taken these photos. And when she might have posted them. *But she hadn't.*

There were dozens of photos of her at the beginning of the school party at Heather's lake house, at various school functions, assemblies, and class trips, and at the gala party—all of them with Dan. The last one was of them dancing, her hand on his shoulder and his at her waist, their foreheads almost touching as they talked and smiled, close so they could hear each other on the crowded dance floor. At least that's what she remembered. But the angles of these photos were much more . . . intimate. It embarrassed her to look at them, to know them for the lie they were, but she was still unable to glance away. There were photos, too, at the Pilates group class. She remembered several people taking photos with the disposable cameras Heather had handed out at the beginning of the year. But she didn't remember any of these being taken—especially the one of her on her back where she was doing some horrendous ab exercise. The photo was cropped to concentrate on her pained expression. Merilee wondered for a moment why this one had been posted, then realized to her horror it appeared she was in the throes of passion. There were more of her in the carpool line wearing a private smile that looked more like a smirk, and on the school trip to the dairy farm, where Dan had also been a chaperone. A photo of the two of them looking under a cow at each other. She'd remembered that, recalled that Dan had said something funny about nice calves, and she'd laughed. But in the photo, it appeared to be two people flirting.

"Dear Lord," she said, pushing the laptop toward Lindi, unable to look at any more. "Who would have done this?"

"I'd like to say some random person hacked into your account, but I think it's clear it's someone who knows you. Who knows you well. Do you remember someone snapping pictures of you?"

Merilee shook her head, still stunned. "Heather gave all of us moms disposable cameras at the beginning of the year, remember? We were supposed to take pictures at every event and then give her the cameras so she would have the photos for the end-of-year albums she makes for the children and the teachers. I think my first camera is still in the car because I always forgot to use it. It's enough I remember my purse and my phone and don't leave a child in the car. But everybody was always snapping pictures. I just never noticed anybody taking pictures of . . . me."

Lindi was studying her closely. "Who else knew your Facebook password?"

"No one. I mean, I had no reason to give it out—I barely remembered that I had an account. Except . . ." The thought was so bizarre that she held back.

"Except what?"

Merilee focused on the girls, now practicing backbends and walk-overs, and tried to clear her mind. To clarify if what she was about to say was the truth.

"Heather. Heather knows my account password because she's the one who set up my page. She told me I should change my password to keep it private, but I didn't. I hate passwords because I never remember them."

"Heather knew that, too, I bet."

Merilee jerked her attention back to Lindi. "What are you getting at?"

"Don't you find all of this a little too . . . coincidental? I mean, think about it. Heather knew your Facebook password. If you didn't post these photos, then who else?" She glanced back down at her notebook. "And these texts that you don't remember sending or receiving—did Heather ever have access to your phone? Would she have known that password, too?"

Merilee thought she might be suffocating. She was breathing in but no air seemed to be going into her lungs.

"And of course she had access to Dan's phone, too," Lindi added.

Merilee remembered giving Heather her phone to hold when she was trying on gowns for the gala. And all the other times—at committee meetings and coffee meetings at Cups where she'd left her purse and phone in plain view. Even at the Pilates class. It never occurred to her that she should have kept them both more secure.

"But anybody could have taken my phone without me knowing."

"But does anybody else know your password?" Lindi said steadily.

"I don't understand. My phone never showed me receiving any texts from Dan. Surely I would notice if I had a number next to my 'message' button on my screen."

Lindi picked up her phone, used her thumbprint to unlock it, and then showed Merilee her screen. Clicking on the "message" button, she pulled up a message, then swiped her thumb to the left, and then hit the big "delete" button. "Pretty easy, huh? And if she had Dan's phone, she could do the same."

"But that's crazy. Why on earth would she—or anyone, for that matter—do that? What could they possibly hope to gain? Especially Heather. There is nothing that I have that she could possibly want. Nothing."

Lindi studied Merilee carefully. "Don't sell yourself so short. I don't think any of us really know Heather or what it is she really wants. Or thinks she wants." She thumped her pencil against the pad again. "What about Michael and his girlfriend? Was it an amicable divorce? Are you fighting for custody and he wants to discredit you?"

"As much as I'd like to paint Michael as the villain, he wouldn't do that. He's done a lot of crappy things to me, but he'd never do something like this. We had a pretty civil divorce and we split custody—very amicably. Besides, his brain appears to be located below his belt. If that's not what's guiding him, then I see no connection to any of this."

"Did he have one of Heather's cameras?" Lindi asked.

Merilee thought for a moment, remembered Lily bringing home two cameras and saying she was giving one to Michael. "Yes, but . . ."

Lindi raised her eyebrows. "Being in the business I am, I've seen seemingly normal people do out-of-character and outrageous things for the pettiest of reasons. Nothing would surprise me." She was silent for a moment, her pencil tapping out a regular rhythm on the notepad. "Is there anything since you met Heather at the beginning of the school year that sticks out as something she might be upset about?"

Merilee shook her head.

"All right. Then is there any chance you might have met Heather in the past? Maybe said something to her that she might have taken offense to?"

"No," Merilee answered quickly, sure of her answer. "I'd remember Heather. She'd be pretty hard to forget, don't you think?"

"True," Lindi said slowly, tapping the pencil in a furious motion. Merilee reached out and placed her hand on the pencil to get her to stop. "Sorry," Lindi said. "It helps me think. Not now, apparently, because it looks like we have lots of roads on the map, but none of them seem to intersect." She paused and met Merilee's gaze. "Were you having an affair with Dan Blackford?"

Merilee pulled back. "Absolutely not. I could never do that—you know my feelings about infidelity. Do you think Heather thinks I was? And that's why she's not talking to me?" She put her head in her hands. "Is that what everyone's saying?"

"Don't get ahead of yourself," Lindi said, her voice soothing. "Let's just look at the facts. You weren't having an affair with Dan; we know that for a fact. The rest is just coincidental." Lindi scribbled something in her notebook. "You need to understand something, though. If the police are calling this a homicide, they're going to be looking for suspects with a motive. And if they believe that you were having an affair with Dan, that could be something they'll pay special attention to."

Merilee started shaking, and Lindi took her hand. "There's no hard evidence that indicates an affair or your involvement in Dan's death because there isn't any. Keep reminding yourself of that, okay?" Lindi squeezed her hand. "I've got your back."

Merilee nodded as Lindi let go of her hand and sat back. "If you don't mind, I'd like to come with you when you meet with Cynthia. We've known each other since law school and she was always telling me I should be in criminal law because I like solving puzzles and figuring out who's really telling the truth. Not that I don't get enough practice with that in family law, but you know what I mean. Anyway, I'd like to share my thoughts with her, along with all of my notes. And then I promise to leave her to what she does best, and that's to be your legal counsel." She thumped her pencil against the notebook a couple more times before abruptly stopping. "Sorry. I just want to help. Call Cynthia today, all right?"

"You're making me nervous, Lindi."

"I'm sorry. That's not my intention. I'm just trying to make you prepared for a worst-case scenario."

"Now I actually *am* nervous."

"Please, don't be. You've done nothing wrong. And you're not alone in this. I know it's not been your experience to open yourself up to others—and I understand why. Your trust has been shaken by your parents and your husband, the people who should have protected you. I know it's asking a lot, but I want you to trust me. As your friend. Not because you might need my help as someone who knows the law. But as someone who can maybe lighten your load a bit. Here." She pressed her palm against her heart. "My mother used to say that to me. And maybe you need a little mothering right now."

Merilee glanced away, embarrassed to have Lindi see the tears forming in her eyes. "I wouldn't know what that's like."

Lindi squeezed her hand. "Then maybe it's time you find out."

"Thanks," Merilee said, squeezing back. A cold wind struck them from the side, making Merilee shiver. "I can't understand this weather. It's November, and we're getting alternating seasons all in the same day, it seems."

Lindi looked up at the sky, a mixture of cobalt blue and odd streaks of grayish clouds. "I agree—something's up, I think. Hurricane season doesn't officially end until November thirtieth, you know. Maybe there's a storm brewing somewhere."

"It's fixin' to come up a bad cloud," Merilee said.

Lindi laughed. "From that blog, right?" She shook her head slowly. "As much as I hate to admit it, there are a lot of pearls of wisdom that can be found in it."

Lindi packed up her notebook and laptop and called over to the girls, while Merilee went to extricate Colin and gather all of his shoes and clothes—he'd discarded everything except for his pants—from the playground. His binoculars had been carefully stored in Merilee's purse. At least there was one thing in his life he could keep track of.

As they walked toward the parking lot, Merilee thanked Lindi again and gave her an impromptu hug. "Thanks. I do feel better and not so alone anymore."

"You never were, Merilee. Sugar's got your back. And so does Wade. It's not a sin to trust people, all right? You just need to make sure you know which ones."

"Thanks again. I'll let you know when my appointment with Cynthia is."

Lindi gave her a thumbs-up as she helped Jenna into their Prius, then slid behind the steering wheel. Merilee waved good-bye as they drove away, waiting for Lily and Colin to haul themselves into the backseat of the minivan.

As Merilee drove home, she occupied her mind with thoughts of how she'd finagle a midday bath for a very reluctant Colin, weighing the merits of cleaning up dirty footprints and clods of mud all day as she followed him around, or just figuring out a way for a surprise attack so that he was immersed in the tub before he knew what was happening.

"Mom?" Lily said from the backseat.

Merilee met her daughter's eyes in the rearview mirror, dark circles under her eyes accentuating the perpetual frown of worry. "Yes, sweetie?"

"Are you going to jail?"

The minivan jerked as her foot accidentally hit the brake. "No, honey. I've done nothing wrong, and they don't put innocent people in jail." She hoped lightning wouldn't strike her, because anybody who read the news or watched the hundreds of crime shows on TV knew this to be an absolute lie. But she had to believe it. Just as much as Lily needed to.

Apparently mollified, Lily sat back in her seat, complaining that Colin was sitting too close and Colin complaining that she was breathing on him. Merilee couldn't bear to scold them, so relieved to be experiencing something normal.

Merilee parked the minivan in front of the house and waited as they got out, still arguing. She paused for a moment, looking up again at the sky, which mimicked her conflicted emotions: calm yet cloudy, a balmy temperature with cold winds behind it. She set her feet on the ground as a strong wind blew the last leaves from a hickory tree on the side of the house. "It's fixin' to come up a bad cloud," she said to no one as she shut the minivan door and headed up the steps.

Thirty-two

SUGAR

Sugar sat on the porch swing next to Wade and watched the police cruiser and unmarked sedan head back down the driveway. They'd barely turned onto the road before Merilee's minivan pulled in from the opposite direction, making Sugar believe that the timing had been planned.

"I just need to know one thing, Wade," Sugar said.

"Oh, no. Ever since I was a little kid, those words always got me in trouble. What do you need to know?"

"Are your intentions toward Merilee honorable?"

He looked relieved. "What do you mean by 'honorable'? Do you mean do I intend to marry her? I have no idea—we're too early in our relationship. Assuming what we have might actually be called a relationship. Do you mean will I respect her and stand beside her right now? Then yes. I think she needs a friend now more than she needs a lover."

She patted his leg. "Good boy. Although I suspect your definition of 'lover' isn't the same as mine, but let's not split hairs."

He sent her a sidelong glance as he stood to greet Merilee and the kids, knowing she'd seen the police vehicles. She'd been back to work for less than a week, and he was fairly sure the police had known this, too, which was why they'd planned to be at her house when she wasn't.

The minivan screeched to a stop as the rear door slid open and Lily and Colin ran toward the porch. "Did you see the police car?" Lily asked.

"Did you bring cookies, Miss Sugar?" Colin asked simultaneously, racing up the steps on his sister's heels.

Before anyone could answer, Merilee slammed her car door and stood in front of it, trying—and failing—not to look worried. "Why were the police here?"

Wade held up a copy of the paper the policeman had given him. "They had a warrant to search the premises."

The two children squeezed onto the swing on either side of Sugar as Merilee put her foot on the first step and stopped like she was too tired to continue. "What on earth could they have been searching for?"

Before Wade could answer, Sugar patted the children's knees. "I brought cookies. Why don't you two run inside and watch some TV before you start your homework?"

"Cookies!" Colin shouted as he slid from the swing and raced inside, letting the screen door slam and leaving the front door wide open.

Lily sat calmly, her frown lines deeper than Sugar remembered. "I know you're trying to get rid of us for an adult conversation."

Sugar patted her back. "That's correct, young lady. Be glad you're a child, and try to stay that way as long as you can. You'll be an adult for the rest of your life, so you might as well enjoy it now."

Lily's frown deepened, but she slid off the swing and entered the house more sedately than her brother, closing both doors quietly behind her.

Wade waited a few moments to give Lily time to move away from the door. "I'm not sure what they were looking for, but I think they might have found it. They didn't leave empty-handed."

Sugar patted the seat next to her, but Merilee shook her head. "I'm sorry, dear. They asked me if I was the landlord and if I had a key, so I let them in. Otherwise they'd just come back later, and I didn't think you would want the children here for that. I gave them my own key, even though it would have been easier to use the key you keep under the mat." She sent Merilee a reproachful look.

"What did they take?" she asked.

"A couple of things," Wade said. "The detective said he'd leave an inventory sheet on the kitchen table. I didn't want to intrude, but if you want me to go get it now, I will." He put his hands gently on Merilee's shoulders and moved her toward the swing. "Sit down. You look like a strong wind could blow you over."

Merilee did as she was told, surprising Sugar. Or maybe she shouldn't have been surprised. There were many times in her own life when she'd needed a moment between crashing waves to catch her breath.

"Thanks, Wade," Merilee said. "I might as well know. It's not like the whole town won't know what they took after this week's edition of the paper comes out."

When Wade returned, he handed her a white piece of paper, the words SWEET APPLE POLICE DEPARTMENT clearly printed at the top. Merilee took a moment before glancing at the top item. "Heather's ring. They took Heather's ring."

"One of the officers said it was stolen," Sugar said. At Wade's questioning look, she said, "People assume I'm hard of hearing, which is correct, but I have a very good hearing aid."

"But it wasn't stolen," Merilee insisted. "I sold it to Dan at the store. It was an anniversary present for Heather. At the party, Heather told me to hold it for her because it was too big, and she didn't have a place to put it. So I wore it all night and didn't have a chance to give it to her after . . . after . . ." She stopped. "I thought I'd hold on to it for safe-keeping for now and return it later. But I haven't had a chance because she won't answer my phone calls."

Wade cleared his throat. "I noticed it on your finger, so I'm guessing a lot of other people saw it, too."

Merilee stared unblinking at Wade. "But why would Heather think I stole it? She handed it to me—at the top of the stairs, remember? You were standing right next to me, and she'd just grabbed you to fill in at the receiving line until I could find Dan."

"I remember standing there, and her leaning into you, but I don't remember her giving you the ring. I just remember seeing you wearing it."

"Oh, God," she said, sinking back in the swing. "Couldn't they have just asked me for it?"

"That's exactly what I asked," Sugar said. "Sounds a lot more polite than going into somebody's house and taking it. That nice detective said that if he'd done that, you might have hidden it."

"But why would I . . . ?"

"Because they were told it was stolen," Wade said gently.

"But it wasn't," Merilee said again, her voice rising. "And Heather knew that. Do you think she forgot with all the stress over Dan's death?"

Wade met Sugar's gaze. "Merilee . . ."

She waved her hand at him. "I know, I know. I'm just trying to pretend that everything is normal and that I haven't walked into this alternate universe where nothing is making sense." She closed her eyes tightly, then opened them again quickly, reading the rest of the list. Sugar watched as what little color on Merilee's face disappeared. "No. No. This isn't right . . ."

With shaking fingers, she handed the paper to Sugar, who could read the header without her magnifying glass but little else. She immediately gave it to Wade.

He read out loud. "One high-heeled purple Christian Louboutin— I have no idea how to pronounce that—woman's evening shoe." He frowned. "Sounds like the ones you wore to the gala. But I thought you lost your shoes at the party."

"I did." Her chest rose and fell like she was trying to suck in enough air to keep her alive. "The police found one of them on the dock, near where Daniel went into the water. The other one was missing. The detective told me that Daniel was hit on the back of the head with what looked like a stiletto heel and that's what knocked him into the water. And he was too drunk . . ." She stopped. "But I wasn't wearing those shoes when I came home. I know I wasn't. Am I going crazy? I know I didn't have that shoe." Merilee was shaking so badly that Sugar felt the vibration through the swing.

"But the police would have to have had a reason to search for these things . . ." She stopped, her eyes widening with realization. "Sharlene Cavanaugh. When she came to tell me she couldn't carpool with me anymore. She could have called, but now I'm thinking Heather must have sent her. To see if she could come up with a reason for the police to search my house. She must have seen the ring. I had it in the box on the hall table to remind me it needed to be returned to Heather."

"And the shoe?" Wade asked.

"Whether she saw it or not, I didn't put it in my house. I know that for sure."

Sugar felt a tightening in her chest, a strange feeling that had come on suddenly a few days before and then decided to stay. Maybe it was her grief over Daniel, or rather her bottling up of her grief. Or maybe it was her heart breaking, having finally reached its capacity for loss. She took Merilee's hand and held on.

Wade grabbed on to the swing's rope to steady it, then squatted in front of Merilee. "You were wearing flip-flops when I brought you home that night—or early morning, I should say. And you had that tiny black purse that wouldn't fit a shoe. I'll go to the police and let them know that there's a kink in their story. That should help. Or at least let them see that there's something wrong about this whole thing. I'm sure they're planning on interviewing me again, but I'll beat them to it."

Sugar pressed her lips together. "As Detective Olivia Benson would say on *Law & Order: SVU*, Merilee, you're being set up."

Merilee jerked her hand away. "That's ridiculous. I'm sorry, Sugar, but seriously. This is real life. That kind of thing doesn't happen in real life. And especially not in Sweet Apple."

"You're right," Sugar agreed. "Detective Harrell said that the most common crime he deals with nowadays in Sweet Apple is identity theft. Maybe I should try that, see what it's like to be a twenty-year-old again. Of course, I'd have to live through the years in between all over again, and I don't think I have the stomach for it."

Merilee sent her an angry look, making Sugar glad. Because anything was better than the helpless-victim persona Merilee appeared to be adjusting to a little too well. "But who would have put that shoe in my house? And why would Heather tell the police that I stole a ring when she knows that I didn't?"

Both Sugar and Wade looked at her, waiting for her to answer her own question.

Merilee sat against the back of the swing, deflated. "Heather knew that I kept the key under the mat. She also knew all my passwords." She put her head in her hands. "Oh, my gosh. She's the one who told me to take off my shoes so I wouldn't trip down the basement stairs." She shook her head. "It's like I made everything so easy for her. Practically helped her set up every single piece of evidence the police have to make me look like I had something to do with Dan's death." She jerked her head back. "Including a motive. Those pictures on Facebook." Her eyes widened. "The whole Tybee house incident—all things Heather orchestrated to make the police think I was having an affair with Dan. Like I would ever do that to his family—or mine. Like my kids and I haven't already gone through all the trauma of Michael's infidelity."

Wade rubbed her back, and Sugar watched as she tensed, imagining Merilee resisting the desire to lean on someone. She'd made that mistake before, and Sugar doubted she was eager to repeat it. Sugar wanted to let her know she understood but that sometimes you needed a friend to trust. Just as much as she knew that Merilee would have to figure that out on her own.

"She killed him, didn't she?" Merilee said, her hands limp on her lap. "She killed Dan, that poor, sweet man. And now she's trying to set me up to make me look like I did it. I'm so stupid. So incredibly stupid."

"There has to be a reason, Merilee," Wade said softly. "This is so out-of-this-world crazy that I can barely wrap my brain around it. Is there anything, *anything* you can think of why Heather would want to hurt you like this? Because if we can figure out her motive, we might have enough ammunition to point the finger of blame at the right person."

She shrugged away from his touch and he dropped his hand. "I told you, I don't know." She sat back, her face miserable. "And why would Heather want to hurt Dan?"

Sugar snorted. "Money, plain and simple. In addition to the houses and business, I bet there's a very hefty insurance policy, too. She married him for his money; I know that for sure. Remember how she used to call you after she was married, Wade? Even on her honeymoon."

Merilee sent Wade an accusing look. Apparently they hadn't yet reached the full-disclosure phase of their courtship.

"And I'm betting Merilee wasn't randomly selected to take the fall," Sugar continued. "I could call Heather all sorts of names, but stupid wouldn't be one of them. My guess would be she somehow found out about that whole business with Merilee's first husband and, being the horrible person she is, decided to use it."

Merilee sucked in her breath, as if ice had just been poured down her back.

"I'm sorry, Merilee," Wade said softly. "We can't tiptoe around the sad facts of this case. There's too much at stake."

Sugar turned to Wade. "Who are Heather's people? I know she's from Georgia, but where was she raised? We never met her family during all those wedding parties, and I can't seem to recall why."

"She was born in Augusta. Her parents were in their late forties when she was born—she was an only child, but not the kind whose sudden appearance at their age was welcomed by her parents, according to Heather. They were killed in a car accident when she was in middle school, and she went to live with her aunt and uncle nearby. They were dirt poor, from what Heather implied, and I don't think they welcomed another mouth to feed. I never met them—even after our engagement. They weren't close, and I don't think Heather had any contact with them after she graduated from high school and went on to Georgia State. I remember her telling me that she spent the school holidays with friends. Then she moved to Buckhead to associate with the types of people she thought worthy—her exact words—and worked for an interior design store until she married Dan."

Merilee was slowly shaking her head, staring down at her hands. "None of that intersects with my own life. None of it. I have no idea how she might have found out about John." She turned her hands over, palms up, as if she were begging. "I need to talk with Heather, confront her. Because she's the only one who has the answers."

Sugar actually wagged her finger at Merilee, something she'd been wanting to do for a long time. "That woman wouldn't help you any more than a hawk would help a rabbit cross the road. You stay away from her or you'll end up jumping from the frying pan and into the fire."

"Think about it," Wade said. "Heather killed Dan—I think we all know that's true. She's the only one who would benefit from his death—and let's not forget she was at the party and was involved in every piece of circumstantial evidence the police are using to build their case against you. And now she's trying to get away with murder and set you up."

Merilee lifted her gaze from Sugar's finger to meet her eyes. "I just wish I knew why. What if it was something I said or did that made her target me?"

Sugar gave her the sternest look she could muster. "This is not your fault. Heather is crazy, and you can't reason with crazy. So stop wallowing in what-ifs. Unless you killed someone, none of this is justified. You need to get more angry and less sad. And then go do something about it."

Merilee pulled back as if she'd been struck. "I didn't kill anyone. Contrary to popular belief that I'm a serial killer, I'm a nice, normal person. Or at least I used to be." She stood, jolting the swing. "I have to call my lawyer now and tell her about the search, and find out what the hell I'm supposed to do next. And hopefully it involves hanging Heather with her own rope."

Sugar sat back, trying not to look smug, while Wade took Merilee's hand as she moved to the door. "Do you want me to stay?"

Without looking at him, she shook her head. "I'm not good company right now."

He let her go and she entered the house, closing the door softly behind her.

Sugar moved the swing with her foot, her memories thick around her, as they always were when she was at the cottage. The wind seemed to blow at them from different angles, as if confused as to its purpose, scuttling dry leaves along the steps and walkway. She'd have to remember to bring Merilee a broom.

"What are you thinking?" Wade asked. "Whenever you put your jaw like that, it always warns me that you're up to something."

"Of course I am—and so are you. This whole business with Merilee is worrisome. It's a circumstantial case, and the police know it, but my friend in the mayor's office says Heather is pushing for an arrest. She's promising to bring down all sorts of hellfire and fury on the chief of police if an arrest isn't made soon. They're all feeling the pressure to find something incriminating. Like a shoe that they find hidden in plain sight."

Wade lifted a brow. "How do you know all this?"

She pressed her lips together. "I'm an old lady, which means I'm harmless. Whenever I ask a question, I always get an answer. I expect they think I'll forget it before I can repeat it." She allowed her lips to lift just a little.

"I'm going to the police station now, to speak with that Detective Harrell. Let him know I remember the flip-flops," Wade said. "And thank God that I do."

"Why?" Sugar asked. "Do you need the evidence to convince yourself that Merilee is innocent?"

He shook his head. "No. I don't need evidence. I just need to sound sane when I speak to somebody else. Nobody believes in blind faith anymore."

She stood carefully, pausing a moment for all her blood circulation to know that she was now upright.

"Where are you going?" Wade asked.

"To make a good dinner for Merilee and those children before she orders pizza again. That delivery boy is here so much I'm going to start charging him rent."

Wade took her arm and helped her down the steps but knew better than to ask if she wanted a lift back to her house. At the bottom of the steps, she turned to face him. "I'll tell you one thing. I don't know what's going on, but I know for sure that Heather Blackford is responsible for all of this. And that woman doesn't know who she's messing with. Karma or not, she's got it coming to her, and I want to be there when it arrives."

• •

THE PLAYING FIELDS BLOG

Observations of Suburban Life from Sweet Apple, Georgia
Written by: Your Neighbor

Installment #10: Truth and Lies

I'm not going to pretend that we aren't all talking about the news item that not only has been splashed on the covers of three local-area newspapers including our own *Sweet Apple Herald* but, owing to the prominence of the victim, has been reported in the *Atlanta Journal-Constitution*. If I start seeing national news media trucks, I'm packing it in and calling it a day. Because this is the sort of tragedy that is best left to be grieved in the privacy of our own homes and not broadcast into strangers' lives when people are eating their dinners or putting on makeup and need background noise. Because, neighbors, this is a story about a human tragedy that has no business being relegated to the background.

This murder—yes, we've all been made aware that his death was not an accident—is a tragedy. The victim was a loving father of two little girls who adored him and who miss him now, and who will miss him when he's not there to walk them down the aisle at their weddings. It's as heartbreaking as it is cruel, and the gossiping I'm hearing in the nail salon, coffee shop, and grocery store is not only vulgar but demeaning. And hurtful for those left behind. Well, for most of those left behind.

There's a lot of talk and innuendo about what happened or didn't happen. About who's involved and whose name hasn't been mentioned. To all parties concerned, remember one thing: Truth, like oil, will always rise to the surface. I know there're at least two of you who are worrying something fierce about the truth—one because she's afraid it will remain hidden. And the other afraid that it won't. I'd like to say that worrying makes big shadows of small things. But there's nothing small here. A man has been killed, and despite a lot of finger-pointing, only one person—two if you can count a dead man—knows the truth.

Now, enough of all this ugliness—it's almost Thanksgiving, and I'd like to turn our focus onto happier topics. So on to a lighter note. As we approach the holidays, I want to remind everyone that they're all about family and not about the perfect turkey or the prettiest table settings. Good food and a beautiful home are wonderful to have and to share with loved ones, but not at the expense of enjoying your company.

I have it on very good authority that the prebaked turkeys and honey-baked hams at Costco are divine and probably better than you can make in your own kitchen. Their sides of mashed potatoes, green bean casserole, and macaroni and cheese will rival your own. They come in these convenient foil baking tins with the instructions right on the lid. When they're done baking, and your house is smelling like home cooking, you just put them into your own china serving pieces and nobody's the wiser. It's a win-win: delicious food that everybody enjoys, and a hostess who's not passed out from exhaustion at the head of the table.

I know there are a lot of diehards out there who will insist it won't be as good as what they could bring to their table or what grandma makes. I understand. It's hard to switch parties mid-election (and that is the first and last political comment you will see on this blog). But the Wright brothers didn't invent the airplane by saying their bikes worked just fine.

After the sad news in our community, this Thanksgiving let's not forget to give thanks for family, good friends, and neighbors. They are truly life's blessings, and we shouldn't forget to be grateful for them. Sadly, every garden has some weeds. The hardest thing sometimes is in determining the good people in your life from the rotten ones, because unlike apples, you can't tell a good one from looking at their skin.

That brings me to this edition's Southernism: "One day you're the peacock, and the next you're the feather duster." It's natural to have a turn of fortune—people change jobs, move towns, lose at poker. It happens to everybody. We've all been the peacock or the feather duster at different points in our lives. The good thing about bad times is that's when you're able to tell who the good people in your life are. Those are the people who will stick by your side even when you lose your looks or your bank account dips into the red.

Which is why our recent tragedy made me think of this particular Southernism. Because I would bet my last dollar that I know who's responsible. And to that person, let me say this: Right now you're the peacock, strutting about allowing people to admire you in all your perfection. You think you're untouchable, but you're not. Your days as a feather duster are coming, and there's no avoiding it, and I don't think you're going to have any friends left who will be willing to stick by your side, because they'll be afraid that whatever it is you've got is catching. You think you've covered your tracks, allowed someone else to take the blame. You think you've gotten away with murder. But you haven't.

And you and I both know who you are.

Thirty-three

MERILEE

Merilee kept her eyes focused on Bob Van Dillen and the HLN weather report on her television set, watching the rotating hurricane symbol in the Atlantic as it approached the southeast coast. As of two days before, the Category 4 storm was supposed to head north toward New England before veering east and dissipating out over the ocean. Except it hadn't. In typical hurricane fashion, it had made landfall in the coastal Carolinas the previous evening and was slowly traveling inland, creating havoc through rain, sleet, hail, and the occasional tornado.

She never watched morning television, and definitely not the weather, but Sugar had insisted that she do both while Sugar made breakfast. The scent of frying bacon and fresh biscuits came from the kitchen, saturating the house, reminding Merilee of what a home should smell like. Sugar had opened the freezer door the previous evening to store leftovers and had seen the boxes of frozen waffles Merilee usually fed Lily and Colin for breakfast on school mornings. Merilee shouldn't have been surprised to find Sugar on her doorstep the next day with supplies for a home-cooked meal.

Merilee had been too distracted to protest. Ever since the police search and the discovery of the shoe, she'd been unable to focus. She couldn't remember the last time she'd eaten, and even the smells from the kitchen weren't enough to convince her to make herself a plate of food. She'd managed to dress for work but wasn't sure if she should even bother. She hated the way people watched her and how the conversations in the break room seemed to stop as soon as she walked in. Merilee especially hated the smug look on Gayla Adamson's face whenever Merilee saw her at the store. This couldn't possibly be her life. Not the independent life she'd worked so hard at and carefully cultivated for herself and her children. A life to be proud of. Not the train wreck it had become.

She became aware of her children laughing as Sugar came into the room and placed a heaping plate of eggs, bacon, and two biscuits on the coffee table in front of her. "You'd better eat something, Merilee. You're nothing but skin and bones."

Merilee managed a smile. "Some people would think that's a compliment."

Sugar didn't reciprocate and kept her lips in a firm, straight line. "It's not. And I'm going to stand right here and watch you take a bite before I go back to the kitchen and make sure your children aren't fighting with sharp knives over the last biscuit."

From the look in the old woman's eyes, Merilee wasn't sure if she was joking. She picked up the fork and stabbed it into the eggs, then stopped as she heard more laughter from the kitchen. "What are they doing in there?"

"Take a bite and I'll tell you."

Merilee did as she was told, hardly tasting the food in her mouth.

"They're looking at your yearbook. I'm afraid it was left on the kitchen table and nobody thought to put it away." Sugar didn't even look sheepish at her admission, even though they both knew that it had been Sugar and Wade who'd looked at it last when digging into the rumors about Merilee's past. When Merilee had seen it, she'd been angry at the intrusion. At least until Lily had pointed out that they'd been trying to help her.

She swallowed. "What are they finding so funny?"

"The hairdos and fashion choices, mostly. But some of the people have funny things written beneath their pictures, apparently. I don't have my reading glasses on, so I can't tell you which ones. They found one especially funny because they thought it looked like someone they know."

Merilee put down her fork at the approach of a car in the drive and stood. "That's Michael. Please go tell the children their dad is here to take them to school."

Sugar pressed her lips together even more tightly, leaving Merilee to wonder what she was more disappointed about—the fact that Merilee had barely eaten two bites or the fact that Merilee had chickened out completely and refused to show her face at the school and had asked Michael to take over the morning school drive at least until Christmas break. After which she had no idea what would happen.

He was walking toward the porch when she stepped out to join him. "How are you, Meri?"

"I've been better. Thanks for driving the kids this morning and picking them up this afternoon. Their after-school activities have been canceled because of the weather, so if you could just bring them straight home, that would be great." Friday was a teacher workday, and although technically Michael was supposed to have them only for the weekend, he'd happily agreed to take them Friday, too. She needed time and space to figure out what she was supposed to do next.

As if on cue, a few fat drops of rain plopped down in the dirt in front of them, followed by a rapid-fire pattern of splats. "Come on up to the porch," she said, stepping back into the shelter of the slanted roof just as the leaden skies opened up to a deluge. "I'd invite you in, but Sugar's here."

He nodded in understanding. "Are you going to be all right?" She'd called him the night before to tell him about John before he heard the rumors, assuming he hadn't already. There had been no recrimination or pointing fingers, just an understanding that he knew what it was like to make mistakes. It was an odd thing to be grateful for, but she was.

She looked in his face and for the first time didn't feel the hurt of his betrayal. She saw instead the face of the friend he'd been for so much of their marriage, the friend she wished she still had. She shook her head. "Not really."

"You have someone to stay with you over the weekend? You shouldn't be alone, for many reasons, but especially with this storm coming. It looks like we're in for a bad one."

"I'll be fine here—I have a cellar and it's stocked with flashlights, batteries, and water. And Wade got me a weather emergency radio."

"Good. Don't forget to keep your phone charged, just in case you lose power." He smiled softly. "For the record, I like Wade. I like that he thought to get you an emergency radio."

She smiled awkwardly, not sure how to respond. "You have a basement in your new house?"

"Yeah. We have a safe place for all of us—and I've stocked it with survival supplies, so don't worry about Lily and Colin."

"Thanks—I will probably still worry, but I'll at least know that I don't need to."

The children burst out of the house wearing their dark blue school uniform rain jackets and carrying their backpacks and anything they needed for the weekend.

"I can't find my rain boots," said Lily with a frown. "I know I didn't leave them at school, but they're not in the closet."

"I'll look for them—they didn't walk away on their own, so they must be here somewhere. Maybe by the time I find them, you'll have grown two sizes and can fit into them." They'd been another ill-fitting gift from Merilee's parents, and if they were lost forever she'd be okay with that. Merilee knelt on the porch and opened her arms. "Come give me a hug—I won't see you until Sunday."

Lily hugged her first, as usual—because she was the oldest—then gave her mother a big kiss on the cheek and then a second hug. "What was that for?" Merilee asked.

"Just because. Jenna said that I need to be extra nice because you're having a hard time."

"And I already feel better because I got two of the greatest hugs from my best girl."

Lily smiled, then pulled her favorite pen from her pocket. It wrote in four different colors, and when you pushed a button on the side, it lit up in rainbow colors. "In case you get scared at night in the storm and we're not there to make you feel better."

"Thanks, Lily. I'll put it by my bed."

Lily ran from the porch toward the car, her head low as the rain poured down in sheets. Merilee felt something being placed over her head and looked in surprise at Colin, who was adjusting his binoculars over her chest. "In case you need company," he said, which didn't make any sense but made Merilee smile anyway as she hugged her son.

"Are you sure?"

"I'm sure. It's supposed to rain all weekend. And Dad lives in a neighborhood with lots of houses so there aren't a lot of birds and stuff. I'll just wait until I get back. Take really good care of them or Sugar will be mad."

"Will do," she said, standing.

He ran to the top step, then ran back to give her another hug, holding on as he looked up at her. "If the lights go out, don't be scared. Everything's the same in the dark—if you close your eyes, you'll remember what it looks like when the lights are on."

"Thanks, sweetie," she said, bending down to kiss the top of his head before he turned and sprinted to his dad's car and shut the door.

Michael paused for a minute. "Call me if you need anything, all right? Anything."

She nodded as he turned up the collar of his jacket and dashed to his car.

"Colin says those binoculars have magic powers, you know. And that he sees the white dog all the time."

She turned, surprised to see Sugar standing in the doorway, her apron still tied around her waist. "Does he, now?"

"He's got a bright imagination. You've raised two fine children, Merilee."

She turned back around to face the empty drive, which was quickly turning into puddles. "By some miracle, I think you're right."

"It's not an accident," Sugar continued. "I think we become good parents by either copying what our parents did or doing the opposite. The trick is in deciding which way you want to go."

Merilee stared out toward the car disappearing down the drive, the wind spritzing water over her face. "I'm scared. I'm really scared."

"Good," Sugar said, not unkindly. "Remember that feeling, because you're going to need it."

Merilee's cell phone rang and she quickly looked at the screen. It was her attorney, Cynthia Turlington. She pictured the woman, with her no-nonsense haircut and crisp suit, imagined her walking in the rain and not getting wet, as if even water were afraid to touch her. Merilee let it ring a few more times before answering it, fairly confident that whatever Cynthia had to tell her wasn't going to be something she wanted to hear.

Cynthia sounded out of breath. "Good, I'm glad I caught you. Either what they found at your house when they searched it was what they needed, or somebody's putting a lot of pressure for an arrest to be made. Either way, there's a warrant out for your arrest."

Merilee stepped closer to the edge of the porch, welcoming the cold blast of rain as it hit her skin. "They're going to arrest me?" She was amazed at how calm her voice sounded.

"Don't panic, all right? Are you at home?"

"Yes. The kids just left for school, and I've decided I'm not going in to work today."

"Good. I'm on my way to pick you up and take you to the police station so you can turn yourself in."

"Turn myself in? But I haven't done anything. Won't that make me look guilty?"

"Actually, it should do the opposite—make you look more like you're willing to talk with the police, and it will look good to the judge setting your bail. I'll be with you the entire time. They're not allowed to talk to you without me."

She glanced back at Sugar, remembering what she'd said about being scared. "All right," she said, her voice sounding like it belonged to someone else.

"You're at home?" Cynthia asked again, as if Merilee might have already started running.

"Yes. I'm here."

"Okay. Stay put. I'll be there in about twenty minutes—maybe a little more with this weather."

Merilee clicked the "end" button without saying good-bye, noticing the binoculars hung around her neck. She touched them, hoping she could feel the magic powers Colin was convinced they had, but felt only cold, damp metal instead.

She wasn't scared. She was petrified. Petrified of being sent to jail and never seeing her children again. *Remember that feeling, because you're going to need it.*

She turned around to find Sugar watching her closely. "Are you all right?"

She shook her head slowly. "My attorney is on her way to take me to the police station to turn myself in."

Sugar raised what was left of her eyebrows. "And is that what you're going to do?"

Merilee met Sugar's gaze, feeling the weight of the binoculars around her neck. "I don't know. I'm pretty much out of options, but before I go anywhere I need to talk with Heather first. I'm going to ask her point-blank why she killed Dan. And why she's trying to pin it on me. I don't really expect her to answer, but I've got to try."

"Will you be armed?"

"Of course not. I have no idea how to use a gun anyway."

"That's a shame. Because I have a .380 that's small and easy to shoot and pretty accurate if you're not too far away."

Merilee would have laughed if Sugar hadn't looked so serious. And if Merilee thought she could remember how. "I know this is a bad idea, but please don't try to stop me. I can't really see that I have anything left to lose."

Sugar frowned. "Does your attorney know you're doing this?"

"No, and I'm pretty sure she wouldn't approve."

"Probably not," Sugar said. "And I agree that this is probably a bad idea, but at least you're doing something. Too many people sit around with an open mouth waiting for a roasted chicken to fly in. I never thought you were one of those people."

Merilee frowned, then headed inside to grab her purse and her rain-coat, carefully placing Lily's pen on her nightstand before returning to Sugar. "I could drive you home if you'd like. It's raining pretty hard."

As if to punctuate her words, a loud rumble of thunder shook the sky.

"I'll stay here and listen to Bob Van Dillen as I clean up the break-fast dishes and wait for your attorney to tell her where you've gone. How long do you want me to delay her? Just don't make it too long in case Heather does something else."

Merilee gave her a grudging smile. "As long as you can. I've got a lot to say to Heather. And please don't worry. She's got staff, and I doubt she'll do anything to me where there are witnesses."

The guard at the gate of Heather's neighborhood smiled in vague rec-ognition, realizing he should know her yet too embarrassed to ask her for her name, and let her through with a wave. Merilee had prepared for several scenarios to get her through the gate, including begging, so she was pleasantly surprised it had been that easy.

She remembered the first time she'd driven to the Blackfords' house in the rain, the night she'd thought the meeting was there and not at the clubhouse. Dan had been there, and she'd seen his aloneness and, in retrospect, she realized, his unhappiness. She wished she could go back in time and tell him to leave then. To pack up and go somewhere, anywhere away from Heather. Maybe then he'd still be alive. Except this was real life, and there weren't any do-overs. A lot of people lived their lives as if there were, but Merilee had never been one of them. And neither had Dan.

She parked the car and turned off the engine, stopping her wind-shield wipers so that her view of the front door was quickly obscured with the heavy sheets of rain. This was a pointless exercise and she knew it. It was ill-advised and not likely to help her case. She'd simply run out of options.

Without bothering to put her rain hood over her head, she left the car and walked calmly to the front door. It was only as she rang the doorbell that she realized she was still wearing Colin's binoculars. They gave her courage somehow. Maybe they reminded her of Jimmy, or even of the magical properties Colin had given them. Either way, they gave her the strength to remain where she was instead of bolting back to her car.

She heard the barking of the dog before footsteps on the marble. Glancing through the wavy lead glass, she saw Puddles bounding toward her, scratching at the glass. The sting of tears pricked the back of her eyes as she remembered the frightened barking from the night Dan died, the panicked look Puddles had given her as he'd led the way to his owner's inert form in the water. She hadn't been raised with dogs, but she'd seen his devotion and knew he grieved.

Claire must not have recognized her at first because she opened the door, and when she tried to push it closed again, Puddles had already leaped out and had his front paws on Merilee's chest in an attempt to lick her face. He was yelping ecstatically, greeting an old friend.

She scratched the dog behind the ears and kissed him on the top of his head before turning to a worried-looking Claire. "I'm here to see Heather."

"You shouldn't be here," the young woman said. "Mrs. Blackford will be upset if she knows you came."

Instead of feeling afraid or intimidated, Merilee felt oddly free. Maybe it came from believing there was nothing left to lose. "I don't care. Please let her know that I'm here and I'm not going anywhere until I speak with her." Using the dog as her collateral, she latched onto his collar and moved forward into the foyer, not caring if she got rain on the black-and-white marble floors.

Puddles continued to bark and cry and nuzzle her, as if he'd been starved for attention since Dan's death, and it empowered Merilee further to feel the anger push away some of her sadness.

"Is there a problem, Claire?" Heather appeared from the rear hallway, looking as if she'd just come back from a vacation on the coast of France rather than from three weeks of grieving a murdered husband. Despite its being November, her skin gleamed with a golden tan. Her hair and makeup were immaculate, and she was sporting a new, shorter hairstyle that flattered her face. She wore a dusty pink Chanel suit with matching pumps and was fastening a large pearl earring to her ear, making it obvious that she was on her way out. Puddles moved behind Merilee, as if seeking protection, and Merilee wished she could tell him that she felt the same way.

Heather stopped when she saw Merilee and smiled. "What are you doing here?"

"I want to find out why you're trying to ruin my life."

She tossed back her head and laughed, and Merilee felt herself grinding her teeth again. *Where had she heard that laugh before?* "So dramatic, Merilee." She turned to Claire. "Would you mind leaving us alone, please? I'd like you to call the police now, and tell them we have an intruder. And take that dog with you. He's scratching my floors."

Claire gave Merilee a quick glance, then called for the dog. "Come on, boy. Let's go back to the kitchen and get you a treat."

The dog's ears perked up at this last word, and even though he glanced back at Merilee twice, the promise of a treat won out. He bounded toward Claire, steering clear of Heather as she faced Merilee.

"I thought you'd already be in jail. Why are you here?" Heather asked, her face a perfect mask of righteous indignation.

"You and I both know that I had nothing to do with Dan's death, but you're clearly trying to frame me for it. And I want to know why."

"You're delusional, Merilee. You were having an affair with my husband and then you killed him when he made it clear he would never leave me for someone like you."

As hard as it was, Merilee kept her chin raised. "Dan was devoted to you, although I can't see why. And you killed him. Even if you get away with murder, I just need to know: why me?" She took a deep breath, trying to still the panic she felt bubbling up her throat. "Please, Heather. We're both mothers. Can you please think about my children? About what this would do to them?"

"What about my children?" Heather screamed at her. "What about my two fatherless girls? Did you think about them before you murdered their father?"

Either Heather truly believed what she was saying or she was insane.

Which made Merilee suddenly very, very afraid. The sound of cars pulling up outside made Heather relax. With a satisfied look she said, "Good. Looks like the police are here to take you to where you belong."

Merilee understood then that everything was truly hopeless and she was no closer to an answer than when she'd driven up the steep driveway. But she wasn't done trying. "Why, Heather? I just want to know why."

She turned around and opened the door right as Detective Kobylt and two uniformed police officers reached the top step. "Ms. Dunlap?" he said. "You are under arrest for the murder of Daniel Blackford. You'll need to come with us now to the station." One of the uniformed officers began to read her her rights as he handcuffed her and escorted her to his patrol car. Another car pulled up and she recognized her attorney, Cynthia Turlington, who rushed over. "Don't say a word, Merilee, until I get there."

Merilee nodded, feeling only numbness. The officer put his hand on Merilee's head as he helped her into the backseat. She was soaking wet and shivering but felt neither the rain nor the cold. Just . . . nothing.

They drove in silence down familiar streets as Merilee stared out the side window at the soaking, gray landscape, the stripped trees mourning the warmth of summer. She felt an affinity for them, understanding what it was like to be laid bare.

She replayed the scene in Heather's foyer over and over in her head, hearing that odd, grating laugh and knowing it meant something. But the pouring rain clouded her vision, her panic muddling her thoughts, so all she could do was hear that laugh over and over, and wonder why.

Thirty-four

SUGAR

As Sugar bustled about the kitchen, cleaning dishes and pans and wiping counters, she kept glancing at the phone, its long spiral cord hanging limply against the wall. She hoped Merilee would call her to let her know that everything was all right and that Heather hadn't done something awful. Although it was hard to imagine that woman doing anything more awful than she already had. Sugar's one consolation was that it was daylight and Heather's staff would be there to prevent any violence from either one of them.

The phone rang and she let herself sigh with relief as she dried her hands and lifted the receiver.

"Sugar Prescott? This is Cynthia Turlington, Merilee's attorney. I just saw you at her house a few hours ago trying to delay me, so thought I'd try there first."

Sugar decided it was better not to say anything, so she just murmured a greeting.

Cynthia continued. "Merilee wanted me to let you know that she has been arrested and is being held until her arraignment. I'm trying to make that happen no later than tomorrow, since it's Friday, and if it goes beyond that they can hold her over the weekend."

"That's unacceptable," Sugar said.

"I know, and I agree. I'm going to do all I can to make sure she's home tomorrow. Even one day in jail is too much, but I'm afraid it can't be helped. She would like for you to call Wade Kimball and let him know."

"I'll call him as soon as we hang up. Does she need bail money?" Sugar asked.

"She's asked me to contact her ex-husband. He apparently has ready cash, and Merilee believes he won't say no."

"I would hope not," Sugar said, her opinion of Michael rising slightly above that of a boll weevil, but still less than most human beings of her acquaintance. "I can bring her anything she needs from home."

"She said you'd think of that, but she doesn't want you driving in this weather. She mentioned something about your newly returned Lincoln not being reliable in wet weather. Anyway, she said she'll manage."

Sugar pressed her lips together.

"I'll keep you posted on any new developments. And please don't worry. The case against her isn't very strong, and she's in good hands."

They said good-bye and Sugar immediately dialed Wade's cell number. It went straight to voice mail, as did his office number. She left messages in both places, letting him know that it was an emergency and to call her back. Not that she would ever admit it to anybody, and not that she'd ever put an answering machine in her own home, but being able to leave a voice message was the best thing since sliced bread. So was indoor plumbing, but she wasn't going to advertise that, either.

With her thoughts somewhat more at ease after hearing the attorney's reassurances, Sugar decided to vacuum and dust the whole house before returning to tidying the kitchen. Housecleaning always had a calming effect on her, and besides, Merilee would appreciate a clean house when she returned.

Sugar popped back into the front room a few times to check on the weather. Carolina coastlines were underwater as the hurricane continued to churn. Although now downgraded to a Category 3, its power was still evident in the harsh weather it was dumping across three states. She checked her hearing aids, making sure the batteries were still strong, knowing without them she wouldn't be able to hear a tornado siren even if it was going off right beside her bed.

Sugar continued tidying the kitchen, wiping the crumbs from the table. The children had left the yearbook opened on the corner of the table, and not wanting to get any water on it, she picked it up. She was about to close it and move it to the clean counter when something caught her eye. Three letters spelling out "Moo" were big enough for her to see without her reading glasses, but everything else on the page was a blur. This had apparently been the page the children were giggling over.

She put the book faceup on the counter, telling herself she'd get to it later, but found she kept looking over at it, curious as to what they'd found so funny. Finally, she put the sponge on the sink and dried her hands, then pulled her reading glasses from her pocketbook. Settling down in the chair with the yearbook opened on the kitchen table, Sugar studied the page.

Printed in bold letters across the top of the page was the word SE-NIORS. She remembered flipping through these pages before with Lily. They were different from those dedicated to the underclassmen. Each student was given a third of the page for their photo, a quote, and a little saying about where they expected to be in ten years.

Sugar only glanced at the photos on the page, barely pausing to read the silly aspirations of eighteen-year-olds—as if they had any idea about life at that age. Her attention was drawn to the bottom third of the right-hand page, the one with the word "Moo" written on the photo that Lily and Colin had been laughing at earlier because they said the person reminded them of someone they knew.

The girl's first name had been scratched out with black marker, making it indecipherable. Written in large letters underneath the picture was the single word "Daisy." What must have been meant to be cow ears had been drawn on the sides of her head, and a cartoon bubble coming from the girl's mouth had the word "Moo" written inside it.

She stared at the face, past the brown hair, limp and dirty as it hung over the girl's forehead. Her face was round, the hint of a second chin already appearing below a face covered with splotches of mild acne. But looking at the face, she could see exactly what it was that Lily and Colin had seen. The smile, the shape of the nose. The pretty blue of the eyes. Sugar's gaze traveled to the section beside the picture, where the girl's quote and aspiration were. The aspiration had been scratched out and something else written beneath it in black ink. "In ten years I will weigh six hundred pounds and be in the *Guinness Book of World Records*. And even then John Cottswold won't know or care that I exist."

There were two short quotes and they'd been left alone. Sugar read them twice, the second time out loud.

Revenge is sweet and not fattening.
Alfred Hitchcock

Revenge is a dish that tastes best when it is cold.
Don Corleone, *The Godfather*

Sugar sat back, feeling the tightness in her chest again, and wondered if her nausea was related to that or was simply from looking at the yearbook page. When she felt she could breathe normally again, she sat up and looked at the girl's last name: Waters.

With shaking fingers, she flipped to the index and went directly to the "W's." There was a long column of last names starting with "W," but only one female, who had just two page numbers next to her name—one being her defaced senior page, which Sugar had already seen. She turned to the second page listed, surprised to find herself on the cheerleading team page.

Leaning in closely, Sugar spotted the girl's unmarked photo on the bottom right, the caption reading only *Cheerleading Trainer*. Sugar only knew what that was from what Lily had told her—how one of her teammate's younger sisters was their trainer but complained when she had to refill their water bottles or touch dirty towels. There was a whole lot of difference between a cheerleader and a trainer, then. And looking at the plump, unsmiling girl in the photo holding a limp pom-

pom, Sugar understood all too clearly the quotes she'd chosen for her yearbook page. Not just the irony that they were both about food, but that they were both about revenge.

Holding on to the edge of the table, Sugar stood, waiting a moment for her equilibrium to return. She wished Wade would call her back so she could share what she'd just learned. She'd call the attorney, Cynthia, and let her know just in case. But first she had another phone call to make.

The school directory Lily had given Wade and Sugar to look up Lindi's phone number was still on the kitchen counter. She opened it and, after adjusting her reading glasses, began turning the pages until she'd reached the right letter of the alphabet. A low rumble of thunder rolled through the sky, the rain continuing to fall in heavy sheets as Sugar moved toward the phone and picked up the receiver. She carefully dialed each number, checking each time to make sure she had it right, then waited for someone to answer. The voice on the recorded message was as familiar as it was hateful, and Sugar enjoyed leaving her message probably more than she should have.

"Hello, *Daisy*. We know who you are. It might not be enough to put you behind bars where you belong, but it's certainly a good start. Revenge might be best served cold, but karma has its own icy boot, and you're about to feel it up your backside."

With shaking fingers, Sugar hung the receiver in the cradle and sat back down in the chair to regain her strength. When she could breathe again, she picked up the phone to dial the attorney's number, written carefully on the notepad by the phone, but heard only empty space. She hit the receiver twice before acknowledging that the phone was dead, a pole most likely taken down by the storm. For the first time in her life, she wished she had a cell phone.

After putting on her raincoat and grabbing her pocketbook and car keys, she headed out into the storm and carefully made her way to the carport on the side of her house, where Wade had parked her Lincoln. He'd reluctantly returned that foreign car and given back her own— not promising that it would crank in wet or cold weather. There was only so much that duct tape and glue could accomplish, he'd said, and she wasn't sure if he'd been entirely joking.

She turned the key in the ignition and listened with satisfaction as it hummed to life, the engine not as smooth as it could be but humming nonetheless. She pulled out of the carport and had made it to the front of her house before the car jerked, coughing and spluttering, and then the engine died completely. She tried turning the key again, hearing only the dry chugs of breath of a dying old man before she couldn't get even that when she turned the key over and over.

Pursing her lips, she stared out the windshield, going through her options again and again before deciding that at least until the rain let up and she could walk to the main road, all she could do was wait.

MERILEE

Even though it was only around five o'clock in the afternoon, the storm howling outside and the time of year gave the skies outside a smudge of charcoal, the light barely hanging on to the day. She was beyond exhausted after the night in jail, her arraignment, and the whole ordeal of having to plead not guilty one more time for a crime she hadn't committed.

Cynthia had had the foresight to bring Merilee's minivan from Heather's driveway to the police station, so at least she didn't have to ask for another favor from Michael, who'd paid her bail without question, reminding her of why she'd married him in the first place.

As she made the slow drive home through the rain, she kept reaching for her phone to call Sugar, remembering each time that the police had kept it, having obtained a warrant to search it.

She knew calling Wade would have been pointless whether or not she had access to her phone. Wade, unable to reach Sugar, had called Cynthia to let her know that there'd been a construction accident on one of his sites and that his cell phone was buried in about ten feet of mud. He would come to Merilee's house as quickly as he could, but it wouldn't be anytime soon.

The Lincoln was parked outside Sugar's house, and the front porch lights as well as the lamps in the front parlor were on. She considered stopping and letting Sugar know she was home but decided she'd call her once she'd had a chance to change her clothes and eat something. She was just so danged tired. Cynthia had told her she had everything under control and to trust her to do her job. All she wanted Merilee to do was to get a good night's sleep and call her in the morning so they could discuss their game plan. Even with all that was going on in her head, Merilee knew a sleepless night spent in jail and the mental exhaustion of the last weeks would knock her out better than any sleeping pill.

The rain was still coming down in sheets, pooling in thick puddles on the drive, making it nearly impassable by car or foot and causing Merilee to consider it a near miracle that she didn't get stuck. As she climbed the porch steps to her house in the quickly diminishing light, she noticed Lily's rain boots tucked into the far corner of the porch. She almost brought them inside but left them there to show Lily that when looking for missing items, she should actually open her eyes.

Merilee let herself into the house, using the key under the mat and then bringing the key inside. Tonight was the beginning of not being so stupid and naïve ever again. If Wade was already on his way and didn't have his phone, he wouldn't be able to call her—she wasn't even sure he had the landline number—he'd just have to bang loudly on the door if she'd already gone to bed.

The house sat in nearly complete darkness, so she quickly walked through it, turning on all the lights, leaving the binoculars—thankfully given back to her with her purse at the police station—on the kitchen table where Colin could find them when he returned home. She'd always found a dark house sad, reminding her too much of the days after David had died, when her mother hadn't risen from her bed and the house had remained dark long after the sun had set.

Merilee spotted the yearbook neatly closed on the counter next to the phone and thought that Sugar must have put it there while cleaning the kitchen. She took a step toward it, wanting to put it away, but stopped. She'd take care of it tomorrow, when she wasn't so danged tired.

She flipped on the TV, putting on the Weather Channel more for background noise than for anything else, but paused as she read the crawl at the bottom of the screen. Fulton County was listed in the red zone, alerting residents that a tornado had been spotted. She muted the television for a moment, listening for sirens, but all she could hear was the steady thrum of the rain against the roof and windows.

Next she checked the answering machine, where there were zero messages—no surprise there. Nobody called her landline anymore—except for Sugar—because everybody knew her cell number. She reached for her cell phone for about the tenth time since she'd been told the police were hanging on to it, then headed toward the bathroom to draw a bath.

She wasn't usually a bath person, preferring the ease and speed of a shower in the morning before work. But she felt as if she needed soothing tonight and thought she might use the lavender bubble bath the children had bought for her for Mother's Day. She'd not linger too long, knowing that bathing during a storm wasn't the best idea. But after the twenty-four hours from hell she'd just had, Merilee desperately needed to relax.

After putting a stopper into the porcelain claw-foot tub, she turned on the faucets, then dumped a generous amount of bubble powder into the weak stream of water. So much for bubbles. At least the old plumbing still worked. While waiting for the tub to fill, she stripped off her clothes, tossing everything into the laundry basket. She wanted no smells to remind her of the jail or of her time spent there. After grabbing one of Lily's large barrettes off the sink, she wound her long hair up into a messy bun and clipped the barrette in place.

A violent fork of lightning lit the sky, brightening the small space with its tiny black-and-white hexagonal tiles and chipped white porcelain pedestal sink, giving everything a gothic glow. A crack of thunder shook the house just a moment later, the lights flickering in tandem with another flash of lightning.

She turned off the taps, and even though she heard no sirens, she wasn't going to get in the tub now. With every muscle in her body protesting, she pulled out the stopper, watching sadly as the two inches of water drained. At least the power was still on. She would turn on the television and find a nice relaxing movie to watch.

She glanced up at the small toiletries shelf above the tub, staring at an empty space, taking a moment until she realized what was missing. It was the small marble carriage clock she'd placed there to keep the children on track in the mornings. It wasn't there. Nor was it on the floor, behind the toilet, or under the sink. It was heavy, which was why when she'd found it in the back of her bedroom closet, she knew it would stay put if she placed it there on the shelf. Except it hadn't.

A cool chill pricked at her skin. She grabbed the plush blue chenille robe behind the bathroom door, knotting the tie around her waist. It had been Michael's last birthday gift to her, and many times she'd thought about giving it away, but she couldn't because she loved it too much. It was her favorite shade of blue, and so incredibly soft that on cold nights she even slept in it.

She placed a strip of toothpaste on her toothbrush, using Lily's tube of paste. Her daughter was methodical about squeezing from the bottom to keep an even flow of paste until the last drop. Colin's tube looked like a tangled, warped mess from a midair explosion. It had been such an exercise in manipulation to get the toothpaste out that Merilee had finally given in and bought separate tubes of the same brand just to save her sanity.

Merilee studied her face in the mirror as she brushed, looking for any new lines that the stress of the last twenty-four hours might have caused, listening to the sounds from the television set and the slap of rain against the window. She started to feel relaxed. Or, if not relaxed, then more calm.

A movement from the open doorway, reflected in the mirror behind her, caught her attention. She stopped, listening, her eyes focused on the mirror's reflection. Had she forgotten to lock the door? "Wade?" she called out through a mouthful of toothpaste. She waited for a moment before spitting into the sink. She rinsed her mouth quickly, then called out again. "Wade?"

She paused in the doorway, hearing the television and the relentless force of the rain against the house. Maybe the lights had flickered again, casting a quick shadow as they dimmed and then regained their brightness.

Pulling together the lapels of her robe, Merilee peered into the empty front room, then padded down the hall toward her bedroom. She was almost halfway into the room before she realized something was wrong. She stopped, trying to figure out what it was. Turning slowly to face the bed, she saw it.

On the corner of the white quilted bedspread lay her high school yearbook, opened to display a layout of senior photos. Her gaze drifted to the right-hand side; she knew which page she was looking at before she saw the photo in the bottom corner.

The yearbook hadn't been there when she'd taken off her clothes. She knew it hadn't. Because it had been on the kitchen counter. Closed. She remembered seeing it there, even though she should have put it away. But she hadn't picked it up, had she?

The splash of water hitting the porcelain of the tub in the bathroom startled her, sucking the air out of her lungs.

Trying to avoid the creaks in the wood floors, she stepped carefully to the doorway and peered out into the hall. The sound of water filling the tub was louder here, the scent of lavender overwhelming, as if someone had just poured the entire box of bubble powder under the spout. Her blood thickened in her veins, rolling in viscous waves as it pumped its slow way through the chambers of her heart.

"Wade?" she called again, her voice barely above a whisper.

A figure stepped out of the bathroom, and Merilee screamed.

Thirty-five

SUGAR

"Damn."

Sugar rarely cussed, and definitely never in public. But she was in her own living room, watching an exciting repeat episode of *Murder, She Wrote*, and just as they were about to reveal the murderer, the power had gone out.

She was prepared and had a flashlight and an extra set of batteries on her coffee table—both gifts from Wade. The flashlight was a tiny one, light and plastic so she could hold it and carry it without taxing her hands too much. She didn't want to admit that she was grateful, having lived through all kinds of storms and tornado warnings and having never needed more than a candle and a match. At least this way she didn't have to worry about setting the whole house on fire because of her shaking hands.

Using the little flashlight to guide her, she made her way to the kitchen to make sure it wasn't just her house without power. Merilee's house was in complete darkness, too, so it had to be the danged storm. She frowned. This outage was very inconvenient. It was still too early to go to bed, but she couldn't watch television or read a book without proper lighting.

Sugar stared through the window again, deciding what to do. Merilee was home—Sugar had seen all the lights turned on, the house blazing like a bonfire—meaning they could probably see the house from Mars. Even though Sugar didn't pay the electricity bill, it still irked her.

She needed to talk with Merilee, to tell her what she'd discovered in the yearbook, let her know that she'd already told Daisy—she couldn't think of her by any other name now. If Sugar had known that Merilee would actually spend a night in jail, she would have waited another day. No sense in giving Daisy a head start.

She glanced over at the wall phone. Why hadn't Merilee stopped at Sugar's house first? Maybe she'd tried to call and found out that the lines were down. Feeling desperate, Sugar had even put on her raincoat and taken it off twice already, planning on heading out in the storm to walk back to Merilee's house, but had allowed good reason to intercede. She wouldn't be of any use to anybody if she fell in the mud and couldn't get back up. Her teeth began to hurt, so she forcibly relaxed her jaw. She should try the phone again.

Sugar pointed her way with the flashlight, then picked up the phone, listening for the dial tone. Dead silence. She pushed down the receiver several times, but the phone stayed quiet.

"Damn," she said for the second time in less than an hour. She'd have to ask in the next Bible study if there was something in the Bible against swearing. She was sure she knew the answer, but she couldn't think right now. Too much going on these days, what with Merilee going to jail and those poor children needing someone to cook for them. It was a wonder she remembered to put on her dress in the morning.

She looked out the window, having already decided she'd just go to bed early and go over to Merilee's first thing, when something small and white ran past her back door outside. Pressing her glasses up her nose, she peered out again, wishing for about the hundredth time that she could see at night. It was horribly inconvenient, and, if anyone asked her, she'd say that it was rude of the good Lord to add night blindness to her growing list of things about getting older that were downright hateful.

She blinked, trying to get her eyes to try a little harder, staring at the spot where she was sure she'd seen Colin's dog. It wasn't his dog, of course, but she'd taken to calling it that because he said he saw it so much. Sugar pressed her nose against the cold glass of the window, as if that would work, and instead knocked her glasses off her face.

Leaning down, she used the flashlight to find them, then took a while straightening before putting them back on her nose and looking out the window. There. There it was again. It was hard to tell exactly because of the dark and the rain, but she was sure that white smudge outside in the grass was the little dog Colin claimed to have seen.

The thunder rumbled overhead, the lightning casting a bluish white glow over the porch and the boxwood hedges and the grassy area behind the house. It was the dog. She was sure of it now. And it was sitting and staring back at her.

As quickly as she could move, she went to the back door and opened it, hoping the dog wouldn't be too scared to come to her. It shouldn't be out in the storm, wet and without shelter. It would be cold and probably hungry.

"Come," she called, not knowing what people said these days to call their dogs. "Come here, little doggie. Let's get you inside from the rain." She was speaking to the dark now, waiting for the next flash of lightning. As if answering her prayer, a bolt of lightning streaked across the sky as thunder cracked above, showing her the dog at the moment it turned and ran in the direction of Merilee's house.

She closed the door against the cold and wind, deciding what she should do. Only a fool would go out in this weather. But that little dog was alone and must be scared. Maybe if it hadn't looked so much like Dixie, she might have let her good sense prevail over any sentimentality. But it couldn't be helped. Besides, she needed to talk to Merilee.

Her mind made up, Sugar moved cautiously through her dark house, the small but powerful beam of the flashlight guiding her way. She made her way to the front hall closet, which opened with just a push. Wade had changed out the door just for her when her arthritis started getting bad in her right hand.

She found her raincoat again and carefully placed the flashlight on the hall table, knocking over one of the pictures in the process because she couldn't see. The coat buttons were beyond her abilities, but she could still tie a decent knot with the thick belt ties to keep the coat closed. She stuck her hand in one of the side pockets and found a plastic rain hat. She'd once had dozens of them, but over the years they'd deteriorated or had been torn in too many places to be useful. Nobody seemed to use them anymore; they were as out of style now as permanent waves.

After placing it on her head, she did her best to tuck in her hair and knot the ties under her chin before retrieving her flashlight. She'd made it to the door when thunder crackled above her, and the sky lit up with an odd green hue as lightning split the night and the storm sirens began to wail.

MERILEE

Merilee pressed herself against the hallway wall and stared at Heather Blackford in the bathroom doorway. She held the marble clock in one gloved hand, the steam from the faucet filling the room behind her. She was in head-to-toe black, in one of her designer workout outfits with a matching hoodie. She wore only socks on her feet, and Merilee found herself staring at them, as if the socks might explain something.

Heather followed her gaze. "I didn't want to track mud into the house, and there was a lot of mud on my boots—or Lily's boots, I should say—because I parked my car about a mile away and had to walk."

Lily's boots. The ones she'd seen on the porch. She was having problems putting this together, understanding what Heather was trying to tell her. "Why are you here?" Merilee asked, some sense of preservation making her inch her way past the bathroom, toward the front room, where a weather alert was currently blaring from the television.

Heather stepped in front of her, blocking her exit, and laughed, the sound grating. And memorable. And there it was, like a cold slap to her face; Merilee finally knew *why.* "Daisy," Merilee said quietly, as much in awe as in terror.

"Don't call me that," Heather shouted. "That was *never* my name."

Merilee shook her head in confusion, trying to get all the pieces to fit together. Wondering if this was the karma Sugar was always talking about. "But why are you here?" Merilee asked, not because she didn't know, but because she couldn't think of anything else to say.

"Sugar called me and left a message. Apparently she saw your yearbook. Happily, your night in jail gave me the time I needed to think and plan. Because if Sugar figured it out, I knew it was just a matter of time before you did, too. Although in high school you were pretty stupid. I was always so much smarter than you, remember?" She clutched the marble clock in front of her for a moment. "I've found that it's the girls who are born beautiful who are always the most clueless. They figure out pretty early on how to get by on looks and charm, so there's no need to work on brains or anything practical. It's the ugly girls who have to cultivate their cunning and brains." She took a step closer to Merilee. "Don't you think?"

"High school was a long time ago, Heather. None of that stuff matters anymore."

"None of that matters?" Heather sneered, her face twisted into somebody Merilee couldn't recognize. "You ruined my life. Do you have any idea of what it's like to be one of the Daisies of the world? The kind of person people despise even though they have no idea who that person really is?" She laughed again, and Merilee cringed, wondering how she'd forgotten that sound. "Of course not. And if you'd just gone to jail like I'd planned, you'd know. But now our plans have to change."

A sharp snap of thunder followed by a brilliant flash of light charged the atmosphere, the stench of burnt ions floating in the air.

Heather smiled her beautiful Barbie smile. "It's the perfect night for a suicide, don't you think?" She held up the heavy clock. "Or an accident. I haven't decided yet. This clock gave me the idea. People slip and hit their heads all the time, especially in the bathroom. And a drowning would be just perfect under the circumstances. Suicide or accident; it won't matter. As long as you're gone, and the last thing you see is my face. My new face. Not the one you tormented in high school."

Icy-cold fear shot through Merilee's body, as if she'd been electrocuted. *Think*. "Heather, you're right. You are smart. So think about it. My yearbook gives away your motive for setting me up for Dan's death. Killing me won't change any of that."

Heather pretended to think for a moment. "True. But you'll be dead, and that's something I've been dreaming about for years. Ever since you killed John. I loved him, you know. You didn't deserve him. You got away with murder then, so it seems right that you get punished eventually—even for a crime you may or may not have committed." She smiled pleasantly; she was like a cat playing with her prey. "I just wanted to torture you for a little bit, keep you guessing. Like you did to me in high school, pretending to be my friend when no one was looking."

Heather stepped closer as Merilee pressed herself into the wall at her back. "But why did you kill Dan? I can understand why you'd hate me, but why Dan?"

She chewed on her lower lip. "Well, that's the thing. He wanted to make changes to our lives—our perfect lives. He wanted to sell the Tybee house, and maybe even the Lake Lanier house. Downsize our house here in Sweet Apple. I mean, can you imagine? The very life I've worked for, and he wants to downsize it?" She paused as if really expecting Merilee to agree with her. Instead, Merilee said nothing, looking for an opportunity to escape.

Taking Merilee's silence as agreement, Heather continued. "Besides, I was already tired of him. I only married him for his money, you know. If I'd any idea that Wade would become as successful as he has, I would have stuck with him. Then I would have had everything I wanted. And now, with Dan out of the way, I've got my second chance for the truly perfect life."

Heather smiled, and it was as if tiny icicles had invaded Merilee's bloodstream. "I ran into Wade over the summer, and I remember thinking that exact thought, but I had no idea how I was going to get rid of Dan. Divorce is so messy, and so expensive, that I couldn't figure out what to do. And when you moved here, and I recognized you without your having any idea who I was, it was like all my dreams had come true. I finally had an answer to everything that ailed me."

"Heather, come on. Think about your children. You need help—let me call the police now and they'll make sure you get the help you need—"

Heather yanked on the tie to Merilee's robe, keeping her close, jerking her into the bathroom, their feet splashing in water. Merilee fought to pull away, but Heather raised her other hand, the one holding the marble clock, a good enough threat to keep Merilee under control. The water poured over the sides of the tub now, the black-and-white tiles around it already submerged in lavender-scented suds. Heather was taller than Merilee, and stronger from all the hours she spent with her personal trainer. Merilee would lose any physical fight. Her only chance would be reason. And staying calm despite what her brain and body were telling her.

"When the police know our connection, they'll focus on you. I know you see that."

"True. Maybe they will; maybe they won't. But you'll still be dead. And I'll have the best lawyers money can buy. Even if I have to spend a few years in the loony bin, it will be worth it to know you suffered even one tiny percentage of what you made me go through."

Spittle hit Merilee's cheek, flying from the mouth of a woman she no longer recognized. She pulled back, frightened of the hate and rage distorting Heather's beautiful face. Knowing she could neither understand it nor reason with it. Merilee's feet slipped in the water as Heather continued to push her backward until the backs of her legs bumped into the side of the tub.

She thought of Lily and Colin and knew she had to keep trying. "Heather, I'm sorry! I'm so sorry for what I did to you. I hate myself for it; I do. I still beat myself up about it, because you didn't deserve it. None of it. Because I liked you. You were funny and smart—you always got better grades than me, remember?—but those were two things my mother said I could never be. And that made you an easy target for me, and for that I'm so, so sorry."

Heather's face contorted, her skin a florid red in the heat of the bathroom. "You're sorry? It's a little too late for that, don't you think?" She raised her arm with the clock, prepared to strike at Merilee's head just as an earsplitting crash of thunder vibrated through the house and a brilliant flash of lightning sent an eerie surge of electricity pushing through the walls. Merilee had one last look at Heather's enraged face as the lights pulsed brighter for a brief moment and then went out.

Merilee ducked and shoved as hard as she could, catching Heather off-balance, making her lose her grip on the robe's belt. Heather fell backward with a grunt, colliding with the toilet; what sounded like the tank lid smashing onto the tile floor followed.

Stumbling forward in the dark, Merilee headed for the doorway, knocking her head against the doorframe before finding herself in the hallway. Something whizzed by her head and crashed into the wall behind her. It might have been the clock, but Merilee didn't stick around to find out. She scrambled toward the front room in a blind panic, hitting a wall and then pounding her knee into a piece of furniture. She heard Heather close behind her, heard her breathing hard.

A flash of lightning illuminated Heather holding up a triangle of broken porcelain, its edges as sharp as a razor's. She lunged forward with it as the house descended into darkness again. Merilee threw herself over the back of the sofa she'd discovered she was standing against during the brief flash of light. Heather followed, crashing first into the console table behind it, the phone and answering machine hitting the wood floor with an oddly flat bell ring.

"You bitch!" Heather screamed, right behind Merilee now, so close Merilee could smell her sweat.

Merilee tripped over something low, twisting her ankle, the fall momentarily stunning her. Heather raced toward her, stumbling into immovable objects and sending more fragile things crashing to the floor.

A sharp and searing pain shot up Merilee's arm as she crouched on the floor next to the ottoman, realizing that Heather had cut her with a blind stab of the jagged piece of porcelain. Ignoring the pain in her arm and ankle, Merilee sprinted forward in what she thought was the direction of the kitchen.

Heather stumbled again, and Merilee used that brief second to catch her breath, to try to gain her bearings. Somewhere in the deep recesses of her brain, she heard Colin's voice. *Everything's the same in the dark—if you close your eyes, you'll remember what it looks like when the lights are on.*

Merilee closed her eyes and saw the front room—the armchair, the console, the cedar chest. The ottoman she'd just flipped over. She pictured the path from it to the kitchen doorway, knew she'd pass the shelves Wade had made for her, then a right to the kitchen and the back door.

A crash of glass shattering jolted her eyes open and she dashed forward, holding out her hands to feel what she passed as she moved. *Ottoman. Shelves. Sharp right, kitchen doorway.*

Her feet felt the change from wood floors to linoleum. She could hear Heather gaining on her, bumping into walls and furniture but not slowing down. Another flash of lightning poured through all the windows, illuminating everything, pinpointing Merilee's location and showing Heather charging toward her.

Merilee ran blindly in the direction of the door. *A knife.* She'd barely had the thought before she dismissed it. She knew she could reach the door in time. Probably not a knife.

She hit the door hard, sticky blood from her arm dripping onto her hand and the doorknob. She jerked it to the right, sliding open the dead bolt at the same time with her other hand, then ran out into the sodden night.

She made the mistake of pausing, just for a moment, wondering where she should go next. And then the lightning flashed and Heather was in front of her, slashing at her with the piece of porcelain gripped in her hand like a knife.

Merilee dodged and ran blindly. She'd made it around the corner of the house when something sharp sliced down the middle of her back. She jerked to the side, trying to throw Heather off-balance. Heather's sock-clad feet slipped on the saturated grass and she went down with a loud grunt, then lay perfectly still. Merilee began to run again, knowing exactly where she should go.

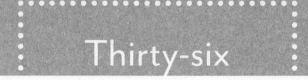

Thirty-six

SUGAR

She wasn't afraid. It would take a lot more than a storm siren to scare her at her age. She'd been through too many in her lifetime to warrant much notice. Besides, there was so much more in life to be afraid of. Like making sure you and your family had enough food to eat to survive, or sending a husband and brothers off to war. Or trusting a friend with a secret.

The rain struck her in the face as the wind threatened to remove her plastic cap. She'd be annoyed if it blew off and her hair got soaked. She'd just had it done at the beauty parlor and she'd paid a small ransom for the pleasure. Keeping the flashlight trained in front of her just in case she spotted the dog, she kept to the grassy side of the dirt driveway, not wanting to get stuck in the mud, following it slowly up to Merilee's house, questioning her sanity more than once.

She couldn't make out any flashlight beam from inside, which worried her. What if Merilee was asleep? Because Sugar was quite sure if Merilee had heard the sirens, she'd be on her way to get Sugar right at this moment. But there was no sign of the young woman and no flicker of light from inside.

Her knees and hips were screaming at her now, and as she studied the front steps, she wasn't sure if she could climb them by herself. She put her hand on the porch railing as wind and rain and leaves swirled at her feet. What was she doing? If she broke a hip, she and Willa Faye would be roommates before she knew it.

There were fewer steps at the back porch because of the elevation, and they were wider and less steep. She'd have a better chance of climbing those without getting hurt.

The wind was at her back as she rounded the house, focusing on the circle of light from her flashlight to guide her. She reached the corner just as the sky roared above her, three lightning flashes following in quick succession, granting the world a few seconds of broad daylight. Sugar stared at the back porch and the door swinging in the wind, the empty kitchen beyond.

Cupping her hand to her mouth, she tried calling Merilee's name, but the word was thrown away by the wind. Holding her breath as if that might somehow contain the pain, she climbed the steps one at a time, clutching tightly to the railing, then pausing for a long moment to recover when she reached the top.

Following the beam of her flashlight, she entered the kitchen. "Merilee! Are you here? Merilee, it's Sugar! We need to get to the cellar." No answer. Her flashlight traveled from the floor to the doorway, illuminating the kitchen table. Jimmy's binoculars sat on the edge as if he'd just put them there and left the room. She picked them up by the strap. If there was a tornado tonight, it wasn't taking Jimmy's binoculars.

Gritting her teeth against the pain in her joints, she walked to the doorway of the kitchen and stopped. Furniture and broken glass lay everywhere, as if the tornado had already struck, but only on the inside of the house.

"Merilee? Are you here?" Being careful not to trip on anything, she used the flashlight to guide her down the hallway, the heavy scent of lavender filling the air outside the bathroom. Her feet sloshed through water and she moved the flashlight down to her feet, amazed to find standing water. Her first thought was a roof leak, until she became aware of the sound of running water.

Aiming her flashlight into the bathroom, she saw the faucets running, a waterfall spilling over the sides and onto the floor tiles she remembered selecting with Tom. She couldn't stand to see such wastefulness, and despite everything else going on around her, she was compelled to trudge forward and turn off the faucets. The sirens seemed louder now, the wind more frantic as she backed out of the bathroom and made her way as quickly as she could to the back bedroom.

The bed was still made, the familiar yearbook lying on its back in the corner of it, but Sugar didn't stop to figure out why. She made her way back to the kitchen as fast as she could manage, peering into the other two bedrooms to make sure they were empty, a growing pit of worry consuming her as she continued to call Merilee's name.

She stood on the back porch, clutching the flashlight and the strap of the binoculars, feeling an odd change to the wind as it seemed to pick another direction. She could only hope the dog had found its own refuge from the storm. She was exhausted, and storm sirens or not, she found herself wishing that she'd just gone to bed when she'd had the chance.

Her plastic bonnet flew off, but she barely noticed as a piercing scream carried by the wind reached her, causing every hair on her head to stand up. Refusing to feel the pain and stiffness in her knees and hips, she headed down the steps as fast as she could just as another scream whipped the air around her.

MERILEE

The fall must have winded Heather, because she lay still long enough for Merilee to make it to the cellar. Wade had made her practice opening the doors—not that it made them lighter, but she now knew how much force she needed to put behind the effort. She also knew that they were unlocked. Since nothing inside was valuable, she'd seen no need to lock them. In a life overly burdened with bad luck, this was the first time in a very long while that Merilee found herself catching a break.

She'd flipped up the latch and managed to open a single door when she heard screaming. Unbroken lightning lit the sky like daylight as hail began to fall, stinging her skin as she turned to see Heather running toward her at an awkward gait, rage contorting her beautiful face.

She's hurt. Merilee reached down and grasped the handle of the open door to close it behind her before Heather reached her. Her fingers, slick with blood and rain, slipped, and she fell back but managed to keep her ground, reaching for the handle again as Heather lunged at her. Heather's movements were slower, almost lethargic, and Merilee was able to dodge out of the way, losing her footing and jumping onto the top cellar step to keep herself from falling.

No! Merilee was trapped. Heather grinned as she realized it, too. She took a step forward, raising her porcelain weapon. Merilee raised her own arms, instinctive self-preservation erasing the futility of it.

She opened her mouth to scream, but it wasn't her voice she heard. It was Sugar's, and just before she closed her eyes to block out Heather, she imagined she saw Sugar slamming Jimmy's binoculars into the side of Heather's head.

Instead of feeling a sharp sting from the broken porcelain, Merilee was aware of something heavy hitting the closed cellar door. She opened her eyes to see Heather lying facedown, half-off the door, hail viciously striking her blond head. And Sugar was there, still holding the binoculars, pressing the heel of her hand against her chest.

The hail intensified as the sky behind Sugar lit up again with steady forks of lightning, the color of the sky shifting from ash gray to a deep green. Heather groaned and dug an elbow into the ground as if she were trying to rise again. Merilee shouted, "Sugar—hurry!"

Sugar stared at her, swaying, not seeming to understand what Merilee was saying. Heather groaned again as an ominous sound rumbled through the skies, vibrating in Merilee's chest. With warning protests from her ankle, Merilee dashed toward Sugar, put her arms around her, and then half dragged and half carried her down into the cellar, unceremoniously dumping her on the final steps so she could yank the cellar door shut and pull the latch. Her last sight before she closed the door was of a sky the color of okra, and of Heather, blood mixing with hail and rain dripping down the side of her face, on her hands and knees crawling toward the piece of porcelain that had embedded itself in the grass.

Merilee ducked into the cellar, pulling the door closed behind her, taking two tries to slide the latch because of her shaking fingers. A sound like a roaring freight train passing through and then the thick scent of cut pine enveloped them in the small space beneath the old house. Merilee grabbed a camping light—thanks to Wade—and flicked it on, finding Sugar at the bottom of the steps with her eyes closed.

"Sugar!" she screamed, racing down the steps to gently move the old woman to a more comfortable position. She reached for Sugar's wrist, feeling a feeble yet steady pulse.

"Stop doing that. I'm just resting my eyes," Sugar murmured.

Merilee sat back with relief. She knew Sugar wasn't well, but at least she was alive and alert.

"I'm thirsty," Sugar said. "I hope you have some water. But if you've got only your sweet tea, I'm desperate enough right now to drink some."

And then Merilee began to laugh, absurdly and uproariously, at the circumstances that had brought her and this woman here, to this exact spot, to talk about sweet tea and marvel at the strange power of those who called themselves survivors.

Thirty-seven

SUGAR

Sugar pursed her lips as she studied the hospital gown in an unflattering shade of green that she'd been forced to wear, as well as the needles and IV tubes that were stuck to her skin with tape that would hurt when it was yanked off. Her arm hurt from where they'd had to open up an artery and stick in a wire to put in a stent. That would definitely leave a scar.

She felt unsettled and at loose ends, annoyed at something she couldn't name. She frowned at her visitor. "Nothing new from the blog? I'm already tired of listening to the news about the storm and Heather Blackford."

Merilee shook her head. "Not a word—which surprises me. I'm sure the blogger has a lot to say about what's happened. I'm actually looking forward to it." She smiled at Sugar. "You're lucky, you know." Merilee sat on the side of the bed with the latest edition of the *Sweet Apple Herald* under the bandaged arm resting on her lap, her crutches leaning on the bed. "If it hadn't been for the tornado, we might not have known about that blockage in your heart."

"You mean if you hadn't thrown me down the stairs, they wouldn't have needed to take me to the hospital and run all those tests."

"I didn't . . ." Merilee stopped, then smiled. "You're right. So you're welcome."

Sugar grunted. "So, what's the final damage to the house?"

"Just roof shingles blown off both houses, and a few bricks from the chimney in the farmhouse, water damage to the tile floor in the cottage bathroom, but that's about all. The tornado touched down in the woods, then took off the roof of Sweet Apple High School before skipping into the new subdivision behind your property. Toppled a few street signs, but happily no one was seriously hurt. Wade said he'll have everything fixed at both houses before you get home."

"Ha. He wants it all fixed up to sell. He thinks if I were in that place with Willa Faye, they would have been able to tell I had a problem with my heart."

Merilee shook her head. "No. But he does worry about you living on your own. I agree that you'll need home health care while you recover from your surgery, but as far as any permanent plans, no decision can be made without you, okay? You've been making your own decisions about your life for a long time, and nobody's going to mess with that now. Especially not me. I've seen what you can do when you're angry enough."

Despite herself, Sugar let out a bark of laughter. "How is Heather Blackford?"

"Hurting, I hope. She has a concussion, and we both broke our ankles. I have no idea how we managed that and continued to run on them. That whole night is such a blur."

Sugar thought for a moment. "I lost my last plastic bonnet. I have no idea how I'll replace it."

Merilee looked back at her, unblinking. "That is a tragedy. But at least the binoculars aren't hurt. Not even a dent. They certainly don't make things like they used to."

"No, they certainly don't." Sugar looked at her arm, so pasty against the sheets, her veins a pale blue swimming beneath the skin's surface. "I'm not going to pretend that I'm sorry Heather's not dead. A lifetime in prison is a good substitute."

"They're charging her with attempted murder for what she tried to do to me. I don't think it will be too hard to pin Dan's murder on her, too. They've dropped the charges against me, so at least they're on the right track."

"Good. But poor Dan. He was a good man. One of the best." Sugar blinked away a tear that insisted on clouding her vision.

"He was," Merilee agreed. "And so is Wade. Stupid man. When he couldn't get through on the phone to either you or me, he drove through the storm to get to us. I still can't believe he did that, but I'm glad he was there to tell us the coast was clear and to help us out of the cellar. Thank goodness he thought to borrow a cell phone so he could call an ambulance. Still, it was stupid."

"And you carried me down the steps with a broken ankle," Sugar pointed out.

"You mean I threw you."

Sugar tried not to smile.

Merilee leaned over and took her hand. "And you saved my life." Tears formed in her eyes, and she let them slip down her cheeks.

Sugar looked down at the sheets. "Well, Heather wouldn't have been there if I hadn't called her and left that message."

Merilee squeezed her hand. "You saved my life," she said again. "And that's all that matters."

"At least it gave me the chance to give Heather a sharp blow to her head. She had it coming to her."

Merilee smiled. "The things we do for those we love," she said.

Sugar pressed her lips together.

"We don't have to say anything more about it, and we can go back to pretending you don't have a heart. But I know the truth. And I suspect Wade does, too." She let go of Sugar's hand and sat back in her chair. "You haven't asked me about the damage to your woods."

Sugar stared back blankly. "I shouldn't have to. If there's something to say about them, I would think you would have told me already. You seem to like talking."

Merilee's face remained expressionless. "The tornado cut them in half. You can smell freshly cut pine for miles around your property."

Sugar didn't say anything, focusing instead on smoothing the blankets over her lap.

"It didn't touch the cemetery."

"That's good."

"Wade said the flowers you placed on several of the graves the last time you visited were still there. Untouched. It's amazing, isn't it? How a tornado that can knock down trees with such force can leave something as delicate as a flower completely untouched."

"Amazing," Sugar agreed, wondering why she felt so tired all of a sudden, when she should be more alert than ever before. But she was tired. It was exhausting to hold on to a secret for so long.

Merilee continued. "But when Wade went in to make sure the cemetery was okay, he did find something interesting not too far from there."

"He did?" Even to her own ears, she didn't sound convincing.

"He found what he's pretty sure is an unmarked grave. Well, not exactly unmarked. It's a small mound with two large rocks marking the top and the bottom, but nothing was written on them. It was protected by a pine bough that was partially covering it, but it looked good as new when Wade lifted the branch off. He said it appeared to have been there for a long time, but somebody has been keeping it clear of weeds. But no flowers. They could have been blown away in the tornado, but probably not if the ones in the cemetery weren't. You can't see one from the other, according to Wade, but they're close enough so that when the tornado picked a place to draw a line, the cemetery and the one lone grave were on the same side."

Sugar met Merilee's gaze. "Where's Wade now?"

"I sent him to your house to pick up a few things I thought you'd need while you're in the hospital. So you'd be more comfortable while you're away from home. Like your nightgown. And lipstick."

Again, the annoying prickle behind her eyes. "Thank you," Sugar said. Her gaze slid involuntarily to the door, then quickly back to Merilee's face. "Tell him not to go in my daddy's library downstairs with the closed door. It's a mess in there, and I don't want him to see it."

Merilee pulled out her phone and began typing. "I'll text him now."

She lifted her gaze from the screen. "So you'd have time to tell me the rest of your story, if you'd like."

Sugar studied Merilee, recognizing a part of her younger self. They had both left their girlhoods long behind them, probably before they'd been ready. But they'd survived the transition, bruises and all. Maybe it had been the holding back of a secret that had kept them alive, kept them breathing. Kept them moving forward. Yet Merilee had no more secrets to tell, her life now an open road allowing her to choose where to turn. Or not turn at all. Sugar straightened her shoulders, marveling at how rounded they'd become over the years. Maybe that's what the burden of a secret kept for nearly seven decades did to a person.

"The army trunk in the cellar . . . ," Sugar began.

Merilee leaned forward. "Yes?"

"I didn't put it there." She paused, her fingers plucking at the fabric of the blanket. "But I know who did."

SUGAR
1943

I lay in bed, unable to sleep. I was in my old bed in the farmhouse, where I'd returned shortly after Tom had gone overseas. My daddy was back at Camp Gordon negotiating for more POWs for manpower on the farm. His crop production was twice what it had been before the war but operating with about half the manpower needed because of all the men heading out to fight.

I'd preferred to stay in my new house, which still smelled of fresh pine and reminded me so much of Tom, and sleep in the bed we'd shared for such a short time. But Mama was scared now to be by herself, and since I knew why, I thought it best that I stay with her on the nights Daddy had to be away.

An owl hooted outside my window from the old hickory tree. The bird hadn't been there before Jimmy died, but almost every night it kept me company as my belly grew. Most people couldn't tell I was pregnant yet, even at four months, and I was happy to let them guess.

I didn't care if it was a girl or boy, but I prayed that it would be born healthy but small, on account of people knowing how to count nine months from a wedding date.

I grabbed Jimmy's binoculars from the nightstand before sliding out of bed and moving the curtains away from the window. An enormous harvest moon lit up the autumn sky and the entire room through the glass. Very cautiously, I slid the window sash up, going slowly over the sticky parts that liked to cling together and make noise. Mama slept lightly, every bump and crack enough to awaken her.

I put the binoculars to my eyes and trained them on the branches of the hickory, trying to spot my feathered friend. I tried for a good five minutes without any luck. *Hoot. Hoot.* The bird was still there, then. I moved the binoculars' aim very slowly through the branches, up and down and then from side to side. *Hoot. Hoot.* In my frustration, I jerked my gaze toward the bottom of the tree and froze. A figure stood in the shadows of the branches, staring at the back porch.

I suddenly remembered the smoke from the chimney in the old deserted house, remembered the feeling of unease as Tom and I had driven past it. I now knew with certainty who had been in that house. And I knew who was leaning down now to pick up a rock and walk toward the back door, with its small windows big enough to fit an arm and a hand.

I stepped back, holding my breath as if he could hear it. I kept backing up, light-headed from fear, until my legs hit my bed, jolting me. *Mama.* I had to get to my mother. She was downstairs and all alone.

I ran out into the moonlight-flooded upstairs hallway, everything awash in a milky glow that blurred all the edges and made it difficult to run without tripping. I made it to the top of the stairs and had my hand on the banister before stopping at the sight of the figure outlined like a shadow at the bottom of the steps.

I hadn't heard the window break, but I'd been in the opposite corner of the house. I could only hope that my mother had heard it and locked her door or at least thought to hide.

"Well, hey there, Sugar." Curtis Brown stood at the bottom of the steps looking up at me like he'd been invited to tea and I was expecting him. "It's so nice of you to greet me. I was a little disappointed you weren't at the other house, but this is fine, too."

I didn't say anything and remained where I was, wondering how bad I'd get hurt if I jumped from my bedroom window since the sash was already open. But I couldn't leave Mama. She was downstairs, and Curtis was between us.

"I brought my trunk, figured I'd stay awhile. See, once I decided the army wasn't cut out for me, I've been at loose ends. I hear your daddy's travelin' again. Isn't that convenient? And with that retard brother of yours dead and his nigger friend diggin' trenches somewhere across the ocean, it looks like it's just you and me and your idiot mother. So I thought you could use some company." He smiled, and in the moonlight it looked like a snarl, his teeth pockmarked with black shadows.

I couldn't speak or shout or move. It was as if I'd become suddenly paralyzed, my feet glued to the floor. Curtis had been climbing the stairs as he spoke and had reached the halfway point before I'd decided what I was going to do. What I had to do. I still had the binoculars around my neck, and they were heavy enough to do damage with enough force behind them. I clutched them with one hand, feeling how heavy they were. How solid.

"Curtis Brown." I almost didn't recognize my mama's voice, since those were the first words I'd heard her speak in a very long time.

He kept moving up the stairs toward me like he hadn't heard anything, my grip on the binoculars tightening. The loud click of a gun's hammer being pulled back made him stop. I knew it was Daddy's gun, the one he now kept in his bedside table because of several burglaries on neighboring farms that had been happening over the last couple of months. But I had no idea that Mama knew where it was. Or how to use it.

"Curtis Brown," she said again, her voice low and scratchy from disuse, but it was definitely hers.

He turned around. "Now, Miz Prescott. You shouldn't be carrying a gun. You might hurt yourself, and we wouldn't want that, would we?"

He began walking slowly back down the stairs, casually, like he wasn't in any hurry. "Why don't you just give me the gun, and then you can go back to sleep while I finish up some business I have with your daughter?"

He took another step before Mama lifted the gun and aimed it at him. "Get out, or I'll shoot," she said, her weak voice making a joke out of her words.

He threw back his head and laughed, then took one more step so he was close enough to reach out and grab the gun. "Let me have the gun, Miz Prescott, and we can all go back to what we was doing."

She took one step back, allowing him enough room to turn toward the front door. He looked in that direction, and for a brief moment I thought he would leave, that he'd disappear out in the darkness and we'd never see him again.

Except he didn't. He took a step toward Mama and the night exploded with a burst of fire and gunpowder. Curtis dropped like a puppet with cut strings, a dark puddle slowly seeping onto the pine floors.

The gun fell from Mama's hand and landed near Curtis's head. She was so still, and she wouldn't stop looking at him. I knew I needed to turn on a light to make sure he was dead, but I couldn't do that with her still there. I thought of Tom, and his love for me, and that gave me the strength I needed to think and to do what had to be done.

I put my mother back to bed and gave her some of the sleeping medicine Dr. Mackenzie had given her. Then I returned to the foyer and turned on the light. Curtis was wearing his khaki uniform top and pants, but all insignia had been removed. It was like when he'd decided not to return to the army, he'd excised them from his life but had been too practical to return clothing he could wear.

The bullet had hit its mark in the middle of his chest, just like a bull's-eye, and although it had done the job quickly, I felt oddly disappointed. Like he should have suffered more for what he'd done to me and my family. His eyes were open, caught in the moment of surprise, blood pouring out from under his back and crawling its way to the entranceway rug.

Forgetting modesty, I pulled my nightgown over my head and shoved it under him, hating the feel of him beneath my fingers. I needed to alert the sheriff. Needed to tell him my mother had shot Curtis Brown. It was clear he'd broken into the house. That we were two lone women trying to protect ourselves.

But then I thought of my mother shooting him to protect me. Of doing something nobody would have thought her capable of—least of all herself. Even though she'd saved my life, the person she'd once been and perhaps still was would die a thousand deaths if people knew what she'd done. Knew she'd killed a man in cold blood whether he deserved it or not. Maybe the sheriff would press charges—I had no way of knowing what circumstances would allow my mother to escape formal charges. But to her, even in her addled mind, the court of human opinion was all that mattered.

With a calm resolve, I went back upstairs and put on a dress and shoes without stockings. Then I threw on a coat and ran all the way to Willa Faye's house and rapped on her bedroom window. She must have seen that I was in shock and took over. It's what I loved about Willa Faye. Because she was silly and pretty, nobody gave her credit for her brains or her ability to figure things out and know exactly what needed to be done.

She picked the spot in the woods for Curtis's grave and we spent most of the night digging the hole and burying him. I felt nothing when I dumped the first clod of dirt on his face, watching until we couldn't see the moonlight reflect against his skin anymore. It was Willa Faye's idea to bury him without his uniform so that if the body was ever found it would be harder to identify. We still had his trunk to deal with, so we figured we'd put the uniform in there. We were going to throw rocks in the trunk and sink everything in the lake—including my nightgown and the rags we'd used to clean up the blood—but Willa Faye said we should hold on to something in case there was ever a reckoning for what had happened that night. Mama was a religious person, and I knew Willa Faye was right. But I knew I'd never speak of it to anyone while Mama was still alive.

So we got a sheet from the house and wrapped most of what was in the trunk and all the bloody rags and my nightgown with a bunch of rocks and sank it all in the lake. Willa Faye said she'd put the trunk someplace where it would be forgotten. I didn't ask where and we never talked about it. Willa Faye was small, so I knew she couldn't have moved it very far, but it didn't matter. Nobody would be asking after Curtis Brown.

I've kept the weeds off Curtis's grave all these years because I think Mama would have wanted me to. But that's all, because he doesn't deserve any more than that. And I keep the secret still in honor of Mama's memory.

We never spoke of that night again. Even Mama. She retreated back into her world and didn't speak another word until she died. But Willa Faye and me, not a word about it between us. It bonded us. Branded us as best friends. Because I will always remember that when I told her I needed help burying a body, the first thing she said was, "Let me go get my shovel."

Thirty-eight

MERILEE

"Mom! Come here!" Colin shouted from the front porch. Merilee quickly put down the pine boughs with red and green ribbons she'd been using to decorate the mantel—following specific directions from Sugar—grabbed her crutches, and moved as quickly as she could out onto Sugar's front porch, expecting to see their arriving visitors. It was early, but if Sugar was involved, Merilee was prepared to see them get there up to an hour earlier than expected.

She nearly collided with Lily, who was jumping up and down with excitement. "Hurry, Mom," she said, helping Merilee down the steps and then around the side of the house. The ground was hard with the first frost, making it easier to hobble across the grass with crutches. She wondered if all the excitement was about Sugar's sheep wearing the bright red bows that Wade had been threatening to dress them in for more than a week.

Trying to catch her breath, she paused at the corner of the house and looked at the woods. She still wasn't used to seeing the swath of red earth where trees had been just a month before, the scent of pine still thick. Sugar had given Wade permission to clear the felled trees, but that was all. At least for now. Lindi and a law school friend were helping her establish a trust that would forever preserve her woods and family cemetery and the farmhouse, barn, and cottage in perpetuity. To remind future Sweet Appletonians of what it had once been like long before roundabouts, SUVs, and coffee shops had taken over the landscape.

Sugar seemed almost happy now, knowing it would all be taken care of after she was gone. Merilee wondered if the unburdening of her secret might have also been the cause of Sugar's lighter spirits. Merilee felt happier, too. Maybe it was the mutual unburdening that had brought them closer together, but she suddenly felt full of possibilities. Like happiness was possible and even within her reach.

"Mom, look!" Lily said, pointing to where Colin—without shoes or socks despite the December cold—sat in the grass with something white and fluffy on his lap, the ubiquitous binoculars around his neck.

Merilee blinked. "Is that . . . ?"

"It's the white dog I kept seeing! See? I told you it was real! She just came out of the woods and ran right to me. Does this mean I can keep her?"

Merilee came closer and saw that the furry white bundle in her son's lap was indeed a dog. "Does she have a collar?" she asked hopefully.

He shook his head. "Nope. So we can keep her?"

"Well, we'll have to put missing-dog posters up, and take her to a vet to see if she has a microchip . . ."

"And if she doesn't belong to anybody, can we keep her?"

Merilee smelled the pine and thought of what Sugar had told her about her beloved dog, Dixie, and about a little white dog that had led her to Merilee the night of the storm. She thought of all the little bread crumbs in both of their lives that had led them down paths they hadn't planned but had managed to navigate anyway.

Merilee smiled. "Yes. We can keep her—as long as she doesn't belong to anybody else, we can keep her." Both children whooped with joy, and the little dog looked at her with round, dark eyes behind very dirty and matted fur, and Merilee was pretty sure the dog belonged to them now.

"Mom?" Lily looked up with bright eyes, her brow smooth for the first time in a long while. "Can I invite Jenna over to see the dog?"

Jenna was Lily's new BFF, according to Lily. Merilee approved, knowing how important it was for her daughter to have someone like Jenna to share her secrets with. And to share something as lovely as the joy of welcoming a new dog.

"Sure. Tell her she can spend the night, too. She can help finish decorating the tree with us, if she wants."

The sound of a car pulling up brought them back to the front of the house. Wade was helping Sugar out of the backseat before heading to the front passenger seat to assist his grandmother. He'd taken them both out to lunch, something he did frequently, since Willa Faye didn't drive and Sugar hated spending the money.

Willa Faye was tiny, about Lily's size, with flaming red hair and dancing green eyes. She could see where Wade got a lot of his personality, just by looking in the face of this old woman.

"Merilee," Wade said, "I'd like you to meet . . ."

Willa Faye held out her arms to Merilee. "She knows who I am, and, darlin', I'm so happy to finally meet you. You're just as pretty as Sugar said you were."

Sugar grunted as Merilee laughed and allowed herself to be embraced. "And you're exactly as I pictured you."

"Like a Hollywood movie star, right?" She winked at Merilee, then allowed Wade to help her up the steps while Colin escorted Sugar, having reluctantly relinquished his hold on the dog to Lily.

They settled themselves in the front parlor while Merilee gave Lily instructions to bring out the Christmas cookies they'd made—using Sugar's memorized recipes—and Wade excused himself to help bring in the teapot and cups.

"Colin—please get a water bowl for the dog, and put some of the leftover chicken in another bowl to see if she's hungry. And then give her a bath. Who knows what's in that fur."

"Yes, ma'am," Colin said seriously. "You won't ever have to ask me again to feed Dixie or fill her water bowl or bathe her. I just hope she doesn't like to chase birds, because then that'll be a problem."

"Dixie? Where'd you come up with that name?" Merilee asked, startled.

He shrugged. "I don't know. It just kinda fits."

Merilee met Sugar's gaze for a brief moment. "Yeah. I guess it does."

The two old women sat together on the sofa, and Merilee had a glimpse of them in their youth, of their smooth skin and shiny hair. Their unlined hands cupped over delicate ears as they whispered secrets.

Wade and Lily came in with trays of tea and cookies and set out everything on the coffee table. As Lily handed Merilee a plate, Wade said to her, "Did Sugar tell you that the DNA results came back from the lab? There's no familial connection between Sugar and the person whose blood was on the shirt in the cellar. I guess we'll never know the story behind it."

"I guess not," Sugar said as she accepted a plate of cookies from Lily.

He smiled as he handed his grandmother a cup and began to pour another for Sugar.

"I understand you're stepping out with my grandson," Willa Faye said.

Merilee choked on her cookie. "Stepping out?"

"She means dating," Wade said as he sat down next to her and took a cookie from the tray. "I told her we were dating."

"We are?"

He nodded. "It's not just anybody I will agree to cart around while their leg is in a cast. Or put up their Christmas tree and decorate their house."

"I guess we're dating, then."

"Ew," Lily said as she took another bite of her cookie, but Merilee knew she was happy about it. Michael and Tammy were getting married in a month, and Lily would be the flower girl, which was also good news. As had been the news that after the Christmas holidays, Lily and Colin would be returning to their old school and their old friends. It had ultimately been the children's choice, since Merilee couldn't decide whether the stigma of your mother being arrested and then exonerated for murder or your father impregnating your math teacher was worse.

Wherever they went would be a challenge, but she knew Lily and Colin would eventually find their social group in school. The trick was in determining who your real friends were. Heather Blackford had taught her that lesson the hard way. But as Merilee watched Sugar and Willa Faye, she knew a person needed only one really good friend to get through all the hard stuff. And to help bury any bodies along the way.

The things we do for those we love. Like protecting a secret. Or driving through a tornado. Or allowing your son to keep a dog. It was something she thought about frequently now, remembering how Sugar had saved her life and how Lindi had never doubted Merilee's innocence. Her parents' desertion had somehow lost its sting in recent months as Merilee had discovered these new and unexpected friendships and the love they contained.

"So," Wade said, sitting back on the sofa, his arm around Merilee's shoulders. "I've had a question burning my tongue. When Sugar was in the hospital and Merilee sent me here to pick up a few things, I got a text from Merilee asking me not to go into the office on the first floor."

Willa Faye turned to her old friend. "You didn't. He *is* my grandson, you know. That's like a red flag to a bull."

Sugar pursed her lips. "I was under heavy pain medication, or else I would have thought twice about it."

"Anyway, I went inside the room, and you'll never believe what I saw."

"A state-of-the-art computer and Internet router," Merilee said.

He sent Merilee a questioning look. "You knew?"

She nodded. "Right after the third or fourth blog post, I believe, I was at your house with the children, learning how to make fried chicken and gravy. Apparently Sugar doesn't believe I can survive as a woman in Georgia without knowing how to do that or fold a fitted sheet. I needed to use the powder room and opened the wrong door. I saw the computer and printer and a copy of one of the blog posts sitting on top. I remembered her saying that she once had a newspaper column a while back in the *Atlanta Journal*. She kept that Smith-Corona typewriter on the dining room table for show, which is exactly something Sugar would do. That's when I figured out that Sugar was our anonymous blogger."

"And you never said anything." Sugar sounded almost disappointed. Merilee grinned and took a sip of her tea. "I guess I can keep a secret, too."

• •

THE PLAYING FIELDS BLOG

Observations of Suburban Life from Sweet Apple, Georgia
Written by: Your Neighbor

Installment #11: Life Goes On and Other Myths

As I'm sure you're all aware, this has been a consternating month for us here in Sweet Apple. What with a murder, an attempted murder, and a tornado, it's like the Tower of Terror, Times Square, and Armageddon all rolled into one. I know some of us are thinking that life will never be the same in our corner of the world.

But it will be—mostly. That's a good thing. Life shouldn't be an unbroken road of wonderful. It's the curves in the road that build character and show us our mettle. Every path has its puddles, but that doesn't mean we can't or shouldn't travel them. We just need to remember to wear our boots and bring along our friends and those who love us. They can lift us over some of the puddles, or pull us out when we fall in. And we can do the same for them. Life's journey doesn't mean much without friends who love you to come along for the ride.

We're very lucky to have emerged relatively unscathed from the tornado, unless you're one of the pine trees that got put through the sawmill of that particular storm. It was nice seeing neighbors helping neighbors, and our Sweet Apple police and fire departments working extra hours to make sure we were all safe. It's why I live in a small town, and even though I feel the outer limits of the city of Atlanta pressing on us like a bruise, I hope we never lose what's special about living here.

Before I move off the topic of our recent tragedy, allow me to share a few words of wisdom that I gleaned from all these